I0655421

DESTINY

Published by Kaleidoscope Productions
1467 Siskiyou Blvd. #299; Ashland, OR 97520

ISBN 978-0-938001-43-0

Cover design by Angel Love
Book layout and Editing by Sumara Elan Love

Copyright © 2015 by Embrosewyn Tazkuvel

All rights reserved
This book including the cover illustration, may not be
copied except for personal use by the original purchaser.
The book may not be reproduced or retransmitted by any
means in whole or part, or repackaged, resold, or given
away for free as a download, in whole or part, in any form.

Distribution
Only legally available to be purchased as a paperback book
through retail or online bookstores, or in eBook format
through major online retailers and their affiliates.

PLEASE DO NOT PARTICIPATE IN PIRACY.

BY EMBROSEWYN TAZKUVEL

Secret Earth Series
INCEPTION *(BOOK 1)*

DESTINY *(BOOK 2)*

Psychic Awakening Series
AURAS

How to See, Feel and Know

SOUL MATE AURAS

How Find Your Soul Mate & "Happily Ever After"

UNLEASH YOUR PSYCHIC POWERS

PSYCHIC SELF DEFENSE

CLAIRVOYANCE

TELEKINESIS

DREAMS

Celestine Light Magick Series
ANGELS OF MIRACLES AND MANIFESTATION

144 Names, Sigils and Stewardships to Call the Magickal
Angels of Celestine Light

WORDS OF POWER AND TRANSFORMATION

101+ Magickal Words and Sigils of Celestine Light to
Manifest Your Desires

**CELESTINE LIGHT MAGICKAL SIGILS OF HEAVEN
& EARTH**

Higher Light Series
ORACLES OF CELESTINE LIGHT

Complete Trilogy of Genesis, Nexus & Vivus

LOST SERMONS OF YESHUA OF NAZARETH

22 STEPS TO THE LIGHT OF YOUR SOUL

LOVE YOURSELF
Secret Key To Transforming Your Life

88 REASONS TO LOVE YOURSELF

NOURISHING YOUR SOUL

DEMON HUNTER

11 SIMPLE STEPS TO CHANGE THE WORLD

AWAKENINGS

Secret Earth Series
BOOK 2

DESTINY

Embrosewyn
Tazkuvel

TABLE OF CONTENTS

Chapter 1
VOICE HEARD AROUND
THE WORLD

Gads, what a trip! My first inkling of the long life I was going to experience came shortly after I returned with everyone from the other-dimensional world of Ferrtho. We came back through the spiral blue-light portal to the same place in the courtyard at my family's house in Bethany from which we had departed. With our return, I had the opportunity to experience the time distortion from the perspective of one of the Timewalkers.

To my great disappointment, I was left behind when Yeshua, my sister Miriam, Salome, and his apostles made an earlier journey to Itodon, a world in another dimension. I had been both sad and somewhat offended when Yeshua explained he didn't feel I would be up to the challenge of the strangeness they would experience on that strange world. It seemed a very weak argument at the time to leave me in Bethany while they all went out and had great adventures. After all, my sister Miriam went with them, and even her companion Salome was included.

At the time I was almost insulted that Salome was deemed capable of enduring whatever they would encounter on the other world, but I was not! Up to that point I considered Salome's sole talents to be singing, dancing, and looking beautiful. As I found out on our joint visit to Ferrtho, she possessed far more potent abilities, ones I would count myself lucky ever to master.

I thought they were all joking with me and rubbing salt into my wounded pride when they returned from Itodon a few hours later and claimed they had been gone for days in that mysterious place. Now I was the one returning after having been away for almost fourteen days and nights, as I had counted time while on Ferrtho. But to my wife Hannah, my children, and everyone else who had been aware of our departure, it seemed as if we had been gone less than a day. Though I had now lived this experience from both sides, it was still a difficult concept to wrap my head around.

Everyone in our traveling group stayed at my house in Bethany overnight and rested after our event-filled trip. The following day Yeshua said he had an important talk he wanted to give to all the Children of Light. Despite everything I had personally experienced, including dying, visiting the afterlife in the Celestine Kingdom, being resurrected, and most recently traveling through time and space to a world in a different dimension,

I still thought too small when it came to Yeshua. I soon came to realize I needed to expand my concept of possibilities whenever he was involved.

When he said he wanted to talk to all the Children of Light, I assumed he meant those of us who could easily gather in Bethany. As he soon explained to us, what he actually intended to do was speak to every single Child of Light in the entire world at the same time, telepathically! And not just those who knew of him, but every man, woman, and child in the world who lived a life worthy of being called a Child of Light, regardless of their current religious beliefs or social standing. Slaves and kings alike would hear his words if they were worthy.

And so we did, and the experience was marvelous beyond description. As he was nearing the end of his sermon, Yeshua uttered the fateful words that spoke of my own millennium-spanning destiny, though I did not know it at the time. Speaking to us all, he gave a prophecy and a promise: *"When you are no more upon the Earth, the fullness of Celestine Light shall be taken from it for two thousand years, save for those who remain as Earth Stewards, and the people of the world shall wander in the darkness they created."* I had no idea what he was referring to at the moment he said it, but all was soon to be made clear to me.

DESTINY

Chapter 2
PRELUDE OF AN ANGEL

Yeshua lingered on the Earth in a physical form for almost six weeks after his resurrection. The sermon heard by Children of Light around the world proved to be the last he would give before his final ascension to the Celestine realm, which unexpectedly happened shortly after his telepathic sermon.

Concerning the sacred ceremonies that occurred during Yeshua's ascension, including the amazing Circle of Power I was honored to participate in, I will not speak of the historic events in detail in this book, as I already gave an in-depth accounting of them in Inception.

In revealing the story of my life from this point on, I am focusing more on the heretofore hidden secular and otherworldly episodes that changed the history of Earth and saved it from destruction on more than one occasion, while mankind continued blissfully on, unaware of how different their fate would have been without the intervention of the Guardians.

Nevertheless, I cannot completely ignore the spiritual aspects of my life and the events that have swirled around it, for it is in the Celestine Light that all is rooted. That was especially true during these early years when I was at the very beginning of my amazing journey.

And the spiritual aspects certainly cannot be glossed over with regard to my sister Miriam, a woman whose mysterious true nature I was still incapable of grasping at this early juncture of my life, despite all the inexplicable, miraculous things I had seen her do and heard others speak of in awed voices.

In truth, despite mounting evidence to the contrary, it was still very difficult to erase from my mind that she was just my sister, the little girl I had grown up watching over and protecting. To accept that she was now someone much more, not solely because she was the wife of Yeshua, the Lord of Light, but because she was a force to be reckoned with in her own right, was a ponderous challenge, one that became increasingly difficult to ignore in the coming days, despite my best efforts.

I was in such a euphoric state after the events of Yeshua's final departure from Earth that I don't even remember how we ended up back in the courtyard of my house in Bethany. But so we all did, albeit each and every one of us still under the magic of those moments and wandering about somewhat in a dreamy daze for a while.

The next day, after an incredibly sound sleep, I awoke wonderfully refreshed and enthusiastic about getting back to the routine of my life. For many people, the routine of life is boring at best and often drudgery resigned to being endured at worst. But for me, though I sometimes loathed the travel and forced time away from my wife and children, I loved the diverse and continually interesting challenges my life as a trader afforded me, especially living in Israel, which sometimes seemed like the crossroads of the world.

I thoroughly enjoyed my interactions with all of my family and employees, as well as people from all walks of life: from the nomads of the desert, to Roman officers, to Pharisees, Samaritans, Greeks, Persians, and Egyptians, and just common folk of many religious persuasions. I thanked God several times every day that Yeshua had resurrected me and given me the opportunity to be immersed again in a fulfilling life. I was soon about to discover that my current immersion in exciting and fulfilling events was no more than a toe stuck in a vast lake, compared to the dunking that was coming.

For about a month after Yeshua had ascended, I was happily engaged in my accustomed life. The world seemed almost idyllic. Profits were up in business, my children were happy and being taught well in both the ways of Celestine Light as well as knowledge of the world they would need to navigate. Hannah and I were like two young lovers again, and our affections for each other seemed to have amplified since I had returned from the dead.

Miriam, Salome, and the apostles all left at various times during the two days following Yeshua's ascension. The apostles returned to their families, most of whom lived in one of the four Celestine communities at the north end of Lake Gennesaret.

Miriam and Salome, on the other hand, seldom told anyone where they were going or when they would be returning. This caused not inconsiderable worry and, in my opinion, unnecessary annoyance with some of us, mostly me.

The third week of the month, I journeyed to Galilee, as I did each month, to meet with my buyer and the local fishermen at Tiberias to discuss the quantity of fish we needed for our retail outlets in the bazaars of Jerusalem and Bethany the following month and to leave a payment with the local moneychanger.

My fish buyer had no facilities or guards to safely keep gold, which was our sole method of payment to the fishermen. Like most businessmen, I contracted with a moneychanger at Tiberias to make payments on my behalf to the fishermen, as my buyer directed, and to pay any other merchants from whom I or my agents had made purchases. The moneychangers kept gold for many businesses in a stout, stone-walled, underground facility, heavily guarded by former soldiers. I suppose they were the world's first banks.

Using the services of a moneychanger was a common practice in the days when trust among people in business was implicit and sealed with nothing more than a promise to abide by the verbal agreement. It was a fidelity and trust I never saw or even heard of being broken by anyone.

Contrarily, one thing I have noticed over the millennia is that the less trusting people became, the longer their written contracts extended. In the modern world, even something as simple as renting a house may require a ten-page agreement, but only after you have been credit qualified by the twenty-page authorization for a credit company to snoop into every aspect of your private life!

The longer, more detailed, and convoluted the legal documents have expanded, the more insidious and ubiquitous the legal wrangling, suits, and countersuits have become. Ah, I digress. But I do miss the days when lawyers were about as rare as polar bears in Israel.

I was met in Tiberias by the apostles Cephas and Yohhanan. They knew the day I would be arriving and arranged to be there to meet me. Cephas was an old business associate. My family had been buying fish off of his family's boats from before both of us were born. His father was killed when Cephas was only sixteen by a drunken Roman soldier, when his father refused to give the soldier fresh fish for free when his boat was unloading.

As the eldest son, Cephas inherited the business after his father's death and proved to be a good fisherman and an astute businessman. He rapidly grew the family business from two boats to six.

Yeshua was wise when he called Cephas to be chief among his apostles. He understood business and people. Along with his knack for making allowances and adjustments for circumstances, he had many qualities of an effective leader. Despite his considerable abilities, he was humble and did not hesitate to call upon others when he knew they had a skill or knowledge he lacked, or encourage them toward leadership when he felt they had capacity for more than they had done before.

Seeing Cephas and Yohhanan approaching, I assumed they were there to discuss fishing. But the subject never even came up. After warm hugs of greeting, Cephas bluntly asked me, "Do you know what is going on with the brothers and sisters in the community that say they are meeting Miriam at your house in Bethany in five days? They refuse to tell us, the apostles, anything at all. And Miriam and Salome have not been seen since we all last departed Bethany. Do you know where she is or anything about this strangeness?"

I was startled in my ignorance! "No, Cephas. I have not the faintest inkling of what you are speaking about. I have not seen or heard from Miriam either. I have no idea what she has been up to. Though all are always welcome, nobody in my household is preparing for any visitors. How many brothers and sisters are you talking about?" I queried in curiosity.

"They are all married couples," Yohhanan interjected. "It was just happenstance that we even discovered they were making the journey to Bethany in five days. Kira, the wife of Aaron, let it slip when she was with my wife and three other sisters, when they were meeting about what actions to take regarding the fungus beginning to grow on the grapes in the Capernaum vineyard. She mentioned that she and Aaron were going to your house in Bethany, but when my wife Lanana asked her the reason for their trip, she evaded answering."

Cephas picked up the account. "Later that day, after we made personal inquiries, we discovered a total of six couples we know of from our communities that are planning on meeting Miriam at your house in five days. And none of them will tell us why."

Yohhanan chided him, "Perhaps they really do not know why."

Cephas huffed in doubt at Yohhanan's remark. Looking to me, he explained, "They each say they are merely faithfully following a summons from Miriam and do not know anything about the reason for their meeting in Bethany. They say she asked them not to speak of their trip, as it was only for them and she did not want other members of the community to attend. That is the part that does not set well with us and is very suspicious. From the apostles, there should be no secrets, and Miriam has not even contacted us, let alone explained what is going on. And what could be only for them and not for all the brothers and sisters?"

"Oh men of little faith!" The startled look on the faces of Cephas and Yohhanan confirmed that, like me, they were suddenly hearing Miriam speaking in their heads!

"Meet me at the villa in Magdala at mid-afternoon," she directed, "and I will explain all."

"Wait, Miriam! Where have you been?" I shouted in my mind. Miriam did not answer. I heard Cephas and Yohhanan also ask her questions as well, but all we heard in reply was, "Mid-afternoon at the villa."

"What do you think this is all about?" Yohhanan asked as we began to walk toward the villa, as it was already past noon.

"I haven't a clue," Cephas retorted. "And I am sorely displeased that Miriam is going around doing things that involve brothers and sisters of our community without telling us."

"It is an often irritating habit she has had all of her life," I explained with some exasperation. "She thinks about doing something and she just does it. She is very quick to make decisions and act upon them, often without first seeking advice from others. Which would be fine if she were always correct, or if the actions she took did not also affect others. But it is not that infrequent that she is mistaken in her choices and that others also pay the price."

Cephas and Yohhanan nodded their heads in understanding. They looked at each other obviously in common thought and, in unison, said, "The River Qishon."

"What about the River Qishon?" I asked curiously.

"You do not know what happened on the Qishon?" Yohhanan asked, incredulous.

I shook my head negatively. "Not anything of substance," I admitted. "I recall hearing that the wives of the apostles who were on the trip were threatened by a few drunk men when they were bathing in the river. As all of you came back in one piece and no one ever talked about the incident, I assumed the twelve men, including all of you apostles plus Yeshua, were more than enough of a show of force to frighten the drunkards away."

Yohhanan looked over to Cephas. "Can I tell him?"

Cephas shrugged his shoulders. "I am surprised he does not already know, as Miriam is his sister and Yeshua his brother-in-law."

"Alright then," Yohhanan agreed. He looked at me and stammered a bit before he spoke. It seemed as if he was afraid of hurting my feelings. "Miriam killed some men," he blurted out suddenly.

"What!" I exclaimed in shocked disbelief. "How could Miriam kill a man? And where were the apostles of Celestine Light that she would ever need to be in a position to defend herself?"

"Wait a moment!" I staggered as a thought hit me. "Did you say Miriam killed men, as in more than one?"

Yohhanan nodded. "She killed two for certain. She also blinded two others, but Yeshua gave them back their sight. There were more that didn't get killed, but they were pretty broken up and may have died later. Certainly there were many parts of their bodies that were never going to work the same again."

I stared at Yohhanan in utter disbelief. "What you are saying is preposterous. Miriam, my sister Miriam, my sister Miriam, a woman, killed two men, maybe more, blinded two others, and severely broke body parts of some more?"

Yohhanan and Cephas looked at each other a bit perplexed, as if they could not understand why I found Yohhanan's story ridiculous. "Yes, that is what happened," Cephas agreed matter-of-factly, nodding his shaggy head affirmatively.

He looked at me with disapproval. "Lazarus, you are a very hard-headed man. When are you going to accept that Miriam is more than you remember; more than your younger sister? It is certain that the Miriam you recall from your childhood memories and the Miriam we know from nearly a decade of shared experiences are not very similar. We have watched Miriam grow in her power and personality as an apostle, learning to use her gifts of power in the Celestine Light. Yeshua taught all of us how to recognize and use our gifts, but Miriam was his best student. And now she is an angel of Elohim as well."

"If this is true," I said, doubting both the story of Miriam killing somebody and still unable to comprehend how she could be an angel, "why am I just hearing about it now?"

"You have been made aware of the changes in Miriam for years, I think," Cephas cajoled. "You have just been too happy continuing in your role as the protective big brother and unwilling to accept the new reality."

"Nor can I see how you could possibly doubt it any longer," Yohhanan added. "Yeshua was very specific in the great Circle of Celestine Light when he ascended, that Miriam is an angel of Elohim, with all the powers of that office vested in her."

"There is that," I admitted somewhat reluctantly. "But her being an angel is still nebulous to me. In any case, that just occurred, and you are speaking of an event on the River Qishon that happened years ago.

"I don't know why you would want to blame Miriam for any men that died upon the river. I cannot conceive of any way she could have had anything to do with such a deed. The very fact that there has been a conspiracy of silence these many years leads me to suspect there is much more to the story."

"Truly there is much more to the tale," Cephas agreed, "but it is almost all about Miriam—the sister you thought you knew, but you did not.

"After the event, Yeshua asked everyone that had witnessed it to say nothing about it to anyone. As you said, this happened some years ago, and since then the little bit you heard about the women being accosted by drunk men has leaked out. But that is only a tiny part of the whole story."

"As we are going now to Magdala to meet Miriam, I would appreciate if you told me the complete account," I appealed.

"Yeshua said my sister is an angel. If you tell me more about her as you have known her, perhaps I will be able to see her more fully in the light she deserves, instead of through the eyes of a brother who still has trouble seeing her as more than a meddlesome sister."

Cephas and Yohhanan both nodded their heads in agreement. "This was years before she was called to be the Angel of the Covenant," Cephas explained. "All of us were just beginning to understand that we could wield special gifts of Celestine Light that would allow us to control unseen forces. None of us could actually do anything yet. We just learned the principles and techniques.

"Yeshua told us on many occasions that anything he did we could also do, but no one had really had any success yet at manifesting the miraculous powers of Celestine Light except for Miriam."

Cephas looked over to Yohhanan. "You talk for a while," he encouraged.

Yohhanan nodded silently in agreement. "Your sister could do a few things, especially with minor levitation, but of course she had been with Yeshua as his wife for many years before he called us as apostles and began our training. But she had never manifested anything major, such as healing a leper or defying the laws of nature, as Yeshua did on almost a daily basis.

"Not long before, we had departed from the towns of Gabae and Besara. We were traveling on the Roman road that followed the River Qishon and terminated at the Great Sea.

"The day was quite hot. At a spot where the road was elevated a good distance above the river we spied an inviting pool of clear water down below. The women giggled in excitement and asked to go down to bathe in the pool. Besides Miriam and Salome, there were eight other women who were wives of the apostles who were accompanying us on the trip, including my wife and the wife of Cephas.

"The women scampered down the embankment and waded out into the water with all of their clothes on. They were frolicking and laughing and seemed to be having a wonderful time. All of us men stayed up on the road so we would not impose on their modesty while they were in the water.

"We were just talking about this and that when suddenly we heard a shout from Salome. 'Yeshua,

Cephas! Come now to us, for we are attacked.'

"We quickly ran over to the edge of the embankment and were horrified to see seven men wading across from the far side of the river and heading straight for our wives! Immediately, we made to launch ourselves down to the river to defend our loved ones.

"But Yeshua held up his arms and asked us to remain where we were. *'It is in times of greatest challenge that the true person of light and power can emerge from within the shell in which they are usually held by everyday life,'* he said.

"*'Let us watch for a moment to see if Miriam discovers who she really is.'*

"It was very, very difficult to stand there and watch the scene unfolding below," Yohhanan lamented. "I confess that I had a moment of doubt and even anger that Yeshua was restraining us. I was thinking, *what could Miriam possibly do?*

"Up until that fateful day I never really thought of Miriam as being any different than any of the other apostles, other than she was a woman and Yeshua's wife. Yeshua obviously knew a lot more about her potential than we did. If he was confident enough in Miriam to not intervene in the situation below on the river, then I realized I needed to have faith in him and calm my doubting anxieties.

"Standing on the raised road, we were not that far away from the river. We could see the men and hear them as they were yelling demeaning slurs at our wives. They were obviously very drunk. Miriam told us later that she thought their behavior was so demented that they must be possessed by devils. We saw her lift her hand up toward them and heard her say forcefully, 'In the name of Elohim, I command the devils within you to depart!'

"But her words of banishment to the devils had no effect. The men just laughed and kept coming across the river. Miriam was standing near the middle of the river. Our wives had already scurried to the shallows or onto the shore.

"Salome was quickly moving through the water toward the beach, thinking Miriam was right behind her. But when she heard Miriam command the devils to depart, she realized she was still standing in the river, and she turned back to go and be with her.

"Now it was Miriam, who had her back to our shore and was facing the men coming from the far shore, who did not perceive that Salome was returning from behind and to her right to be by her side.

"Some of the men were almost to Miriam, but she seemed to be in a daze. She told us later it was true, and that she was almost no longer cognizant of the men as she was trying to understand why she had been unable to banish the devils.

"Miriam's disconnect from the moment was shattered when she heard Salome scream just a short distance to her right, as two of the men approaching from that direction grabbed her and made to drag her back across the river. Then a very scary thing happened."

Cephas nodded in agreement. "Until that moment, all we had ever seen from Yeshua were miracles of Celestine Light that were peaceful and healing. We actually did not know there was any other kind of Celestine power. I am not overstating or exaggerating to say that except for Yeshua we were all stunned by what happened next."

Cephas rolled his hand at Yohhanan, indicating he should continue telling the story.

"We saw Miriam turn quickly to face the men who were molesting her beloved Salome. She did not speak a word, but thrust her right hand forward very forcefully. Her fingers were spread wide and turned up. Immediately the men holding Salome let go of her arms as if they were burning logs. They slapped both hands upon their eyes and screamed in agony as they fell into the water."

"As strange as it sounds, we could physically feel Miriam's fury," Cephas interjected. "It was a palpable energy that touched our auras. I felt a cold shiver of primal fear pass through me."

"I too felt it," Yohhanan added. "If we who were her brethren felt the fear, think of the terror those men must have felt."

Yohhanan continued his account. "Without giving the men wallowing in agony in the water another thought, Miriam swirled around in her raging fury to engage the other five assailants. She thrust her arms forward forcefully one after the other, with her fingers turned up and spread wide as she had with the two men she blinded. With every thrust of her arm, one of the men lifted out of the water and flew backward through the air.

"Not fell backward, but flew backward! Right thrust, left thrust, right again, until all five men were hurled violently to the other side of the river. They landed with bone-crushing impact on the rocks and in the trees on the far side."

"If you could have seen us up on the road, it would have been quite a sight," Cephas said, chuckling in recollection. "I am sure all of our mouths were agape and hanging down as far as they could go. What we had just witnessed Miriam do was completely beyond our comprehension of what was possible."

"I looked down at our wives on the river bank," Yohhanan added. "They were huddled together, holding on to each other closely, staring wide-eyed at Miriam. They should have been grateful that she had saved them, but they were obviously still in shock and fear, not about the men, but about Miriam!"

"What happened next?" I asked, encouraging them to continue revealing the details of this heretofore secret encounter that was still shocking me to my core.

"Salome and Miriam met in the river and

held each other in a tight embrace," Yohhanan elaborated. "All of us men went down to the river. Those of us with wives present comforted them. By the time Yeshua approached Miriam and Salome, they were still hugging each other tightly.

"He passed the two men Miriam had blinded, who were still thrashing about in the shallow water, screaming and sobbing in pain. They were not far from me, and what Miriam had done to them was quite gruesome. Where their eyes had been was just burned flesh. It was as if the skin from their faces had just melted over their eyes.

"Miriam was not sobbing, but she had tears in her eyes. From the look on her face it was obvious she was horrified and remorseful about what she had done.

"Yeshua came up to her and Salome and wrapped his arms around them. He touched Miriam on her cheek tenderly and told her, 'All is well, my love. You are not as other women, and you have always known that. We will speak more in a moment, but know that I love you. Be not afraid or ashamed of what you have done here today. All things were as they needed to be.'

"Yeshua went over to one of the blind men who was sitting still now in the shallow river. He lifted him up by the man's right arm, then put his right palm over the man's eyes. In a loud voice he commanded, 'Evil spirit, you are cast beyond outer darkness.'

"The man let out one more loud scream, then collapsed into Yeshua's arms. We marveled when we saw his eyes, for they had been restored to wholeness except for a little scarring around the edges. Yeshua passed the man off to Philip, who guided him over to the river bank.

"Then Yeshua went over to the other man and performed the same miracle, restoring his sight except for some scarring that remained around the edges of the man's eyes. Yeshua motioned to me, and I came over and helped the man to the river bank, setting him down next to his companion. They both continued to sit there in a daze.

"Some of our brother apostles waded across the river to the far side to see what they could do to help the other marauders Miriam had flung through the air like they were rag dolls. Toma was standing over a man bent over a large rock on his back. His arms were hanging down limply, and Toma yelled over to us that the man was dead. That was the first we knew that Miriam had actually killed one of the men, and it was very sobering to realize and to consider what the implications and consequences might be.

"Yudas Iscariot found another man with his posterior up in the air and his head wedged down in some rocks. He shouted to us that this man was also dead. Two dead men! We were in such a state of shock. Just a few minutes before, the women had been gaily frolicking in the water, and now we were dealing with death and uncertainty.

"Three other attackers were pulled down from where they had become entangled in the trees lining the far bank. All of them had broken bones, arms, legs, and ribs mostly, but at least they were all alive."

Seeing the human destruction she had wrought, Miriam was inconsolable. She put her head on Yeshua's shoulder and was weeping openly. 'What have I done, my Lord?' she grieved.

'I did not mean to kill them or even to hurt them, merely to push them away and keep them at bay until you arrived with the men. Why could I not cast out their devils? What is this darkness that has come upon me?'

"Yeshua held her closely, nestling her head beneath his chin, while Salome embraced her from behind.

He comforted her, 'Miriam, weep not; your motives were only from the purest love to protect Salome and your sisters whom you love. Though the power you manifested wreaked havoc reminiscent of darkness, in you, that power came only from the purest Celestine Light of your soul.

'In time, you will learn to find a place of calm inside of you which cannot be shaken by any storm; then the Celestine Light of your soul will come forth as you desire, in greatness or subtlety. But on this day, the storm shook you, and the light rushed forth barely contained like a whirlwind, acting in might before your head had time to calm your heart.

'But do not lament the fate of these men. Because of their drunkenness, they received evil spirits and would have done terrible things, even murder, to you and your sisters had you fallen into their hands. Darkness such as this, driven into sudden violence and maim, is only countered by a power of greater force to subdue it.

'In most things, love and light will rule the day, and few can fight against it. But know too that there are times and situations when even the hand of Elohim goes forth with a mighty sickle to hew down the wicked. It is only that type of power that they fear, and only that which can bring them to a place where they can feel and understand the love and the light that can follow.'"

"Yeshua took Miriam's hand, and they waded together over to the other side of the river. Salome held Miriam's other hand and followed. The river was chest-deep for Yeshua at its deepest and up to the necks of Miriam and Salome, but it flowed slowly, and they did not seem to mind.

"They went right over to the injured men who had been laid out on the beach. All three of them were either unconscious or semi-conscious. Yeshua first cast evil spirits out of each man, then healed them of their injuries.

"But there was something very strange about the healing Yeshua did," Cephas interrupted. "He did not heal the men completely. It was the same as the two who had been blinded. Though he restored their sight, he left scars around their eyes. With these men, he healed broken bones but not well. He left legs and arms a bit crooked. I could not imagine why he healed them only partially and asked him about it."

"'Even without devils these men do not live even a shadow of the light,' Yeshua explained. 'They do not have repentance in their hearts for the evil they have wrought. Let them therefore carry a crippling memory of this day, that perhaps in the future, having considered for many days the cause of their pain, they might yet repent and seek the light.'"

"I do not know if it was because Miriam and Salome had been attacked, or if it was simply a more than just reward for evil deeds, but I never saw Yeshua only heal people partially before or after that day," Cephas reflected.

"And his actions were confusing to some of the other apostles as well," he added. "Yuda the son of Cleophas overheard his explanation to me and asked him if, knowing their true natures, thoughts, and feelings, even while they were unconscious, their fate would have been the same if their hearts were full of repentance."

"Yeshua told him it would have made a difference. He spoke so we all could hear: 'If they had had a place in their hearts for remorse for what they had done and all their other wickedness; if they had desired to make a full and honest restitution for their evil acts; they would have been made whole on that day.'"

"Then there was the inconvenient detail of two dead bodies," Cephas lamented. "Yeshua's brother Yakov of Nazareth asked what we should do about them. Yeshua's answer was surprising. But then that was a day full of many surprises, so what was one more?"

"Yeshua directed, 'Let them lie where they are for their friends to attend.'"

Cephas looked at me wryly. "Though your resurrection was yet to come some years in the future, Yeshua had already resurrected two men that I knew of before our trip along the River Qishon. Considering this, I asked him why he would not heal the dead men and call their spirits back into their bodies. He went on to explain aspects of those blessings that I was not aware of."

"'To return a life is a great gift, one that requires a passion to see them live again and a willingness to part with much of your own life essence for a time, that the dead may be revitalized,'" Yeshua explained.

"'These were evil men before they ever drank or had a devil. They died with rape and murder upon their minds and have paid the price for their folly and foolish choices. I love the men they could have been, but have no passion to see the men they would still be return to life, hurting others. Nor am

I willing to part with my essence for such as these.'"

He turned to begin crossing back to the other side of the river, but Miriam held onto his arm and restrained him. "My Lord, I have a passion to see these men live again," she pleaded. "And I am willing to part with some of my essence for a time that it might be so. Is it possible that I might be a bridge between Heaven and Earth to bring the aeon of Elohim so that these men might live again?"

Yeshua held Miriam's gaze for a long moment, then answered her, "Yes, Miriam, it is possible. All that you have seen me do, any Child of Light may also do with knowledge, none more so than you, if you have faith, love, and passion, and do all things as you must. But knowing the evil hearts of these men, why would you desire them to return to a life of further evil, where they will continue to do evil to others, likely even rape and murder, even as they tried to do to you and your sisters? For they are unrepentant in their hearts."

Miriam spoke softly in reply, "I grieve for having been the cause of their death, even though they might have been the cause of mine and my sisters' had I not acted. Nevertheless, I know that they must also have wives and children who will miss them if they never return. Please tell me what I must do that they might live again."

This was high drama for all of us. Each man and woman present stopped everything they were doing and waited with curious interest to hear how

Yeshua would reply.

He ended up telling my sister something she could not abide. He said, "You must love them with as great a love as you have for me, or for Salome, or for Martha, or for our children. You must have faith in yourself and your ability to do this, and in my word telling you that you can, and in the power of Elohim through the Celestine Light, by which the river of life flows. You must have a passion to see them live again, a passion as strong as you would manifest were one of our children to die before their time. Lastly, you must merge your aeon with theirs, which even in death still resides with them for a time. You must join your aura to the parts of them that are broken, and from those parts in your own body, you must let flow as much of your own life essence as is necessary for them to be healed on the inside and the outside and be made whole."

Miriam was crestfallen at his words. "O my Lord, your words hurt my heart," she anguished. "For though I desire these men to live again, I know I do not have within me all that you say I must. I cannot love them like I love you, or Salome, or Martha, or our children. Though I would gladly give them a portion of my life essence and have faith in all that you said I must, I cannot find within me a passion as great as I have for our own children."

She started crying again, and both Salome and Yeshua comforted her with embraces and kisses on her cheeks and forehead. Yeshua told her, "Miriam, sweet Miriam, as I said before, be not afraid or ashamed of what you have done here today. All things were as they needed to be. Sometimes the lessons of mortality are painful, even for you, even for me. But the future will be brighter, and you will become more glorious because of the lessons you have learned here today."

Cephas stopped speaking and Yohhanan did not start. The story was too fascinating to have ended there. "What happened next?" I asked in anticipation.

"Then we departed the River Qishon and continued walking until we got to the beach of the Great Sea," Yohhanan said simply.

"That cannot be the end of the story," I exhaled loudly in disappointment.

"Well, it is the end of the account of the events at the River Qishon," Cephas concluded. "It would take a journey of many days to relate to you all of the peculiar and wondrous things we could tell you about your sister Miriam. But look, we have arrived at the villa!" he announced, sweeping his arm up so that we lifted our eyes and saw we had in fact arrived. The story they had shared was so fascinating that I had lost complete track of time. In my mind, it seemed as if we had just departed Tiberius a minute before.

Because of my family's fish-procuring business, we maintained this small villa in Magdala for family members and friends to stay in when they were visiting Tiberius or other areas in Galilee. The villa was located south of the hamlet of Magdala on a small hill above the road overlooking the lakeshore, less than a half-hour walk north from the city of Tiberius. It was quite spartan and nondescript, but Miriam had been so enchanted with it that she spent a lot of her young adulthood staying there, most often accompanied by Yasmissa, a longtime trusted employee who acted as her chaperone. After Miriam and Yeshua were married, it became their retreat from the world, the place they would go when they needed a day or two of solitude together.

Sometimes I get melancholy when I remember events like this that occurred almost two thousand years ago in my life, and all the wonderful people I have known and been associated with who are no longer living the physical life on Earth with me. It is not always easy being the last surviving immortal. But the sadness is most often completely replaced by smiles of joy as I recall all the good times and cherished relationships that came about because of my long and fruitful life.

Remembering Miriam's fondness for the villa caused me to reflect on how the public perception of her has evolved during the last two millennia. As I recounted earlier, in much of Judea and Galilee she was considered a witch by most people who had seen or heard of her. Many had never seen her do any of the wonders of which she was capable, but they heard rumors of her feats, which only grew larger with each telling. That became especially true in the eleven years she remained on the Earth after Yeshua had ascended.

The Children of Light, certainly all the leaders among us, came to know her as the Angel of the Covenant during those eleven years. From a witch to an angel, what a transition of perception! Later, after she too had departed from the physical life and all the original apostles had passed away, many divergent groups emerged other than the original Children of Light from the Lake Gennesaret communities. They were collectively called "Christians," or followers of the "Christ." But this was not a title ever claimed by Yeshua while he was on the Earth, or used by any of the Children of Light.

These sects worshiped in various and diverse ways, often based heavily upon their prior beliefs before embracing their limited version of Yeshua's teachings. There was quite the war for the hearts of believers among the sects. The group that grew up based in Rome became the predominant sect once the Roman government gave them official sanction. Then the persecution of the other sects became deadly.

The "heretic sects," as they were labeled, were hounded into oblivion. Their scriptural scrolls, churches, and shrines were burned. Their members were often killed if they refused to convert to the "true faith" as defined by Rome.

People today are all aghast at radical Muslims beheading other Muslims who do not adhere to their extreme or particular nuanced beliefs. The historical reality is that similar atrocities were executed upon Christians identified as heretics by other Christians during the first few centuries after Yeshua's ascension, especially in the times after the third century.

The five main heretic sects were, in various degrees and in some aspects, closer to the true teachings of Yeshua in their beliefs than the large sect at Rome. Many of them still enshrined Miriam as one of Yeshua's apostles, some as the apostle to the apostles. And some, still with Children of Light among them, understood her special nature as an angel. But by the third century after Yeshua's departure, very few Children of Light still holding to the fullness of his true teachings could be found on the Earth, for they were persecuted most of all.

It was after this time that the public perception of Miriam made a devolution. The persecuted sects retained the knowledge of the importance and power of women. But as was common among most religions and governments of the day, the church at Rome was strictly patriarchal. Women were not allowed to be in authority over men and were taught to be subservient and obedient to men, particularly those in ecclesiastical authority.

This was such an important foundation of their beliefs that it became the primary reason to extinguish the heretic sects which valued and elevated women to places of leadership and honor, particularly Miriam. From her lofty throne as an angel of Elohim, she was dashed down to earth in the annals of men and religions, scorned and falsely labeled a prostitute by the men of power in the world.

If Miriam had cared to challenge those pompous early church leaders who set the tone of disrespect for women for generations to come, how they would have trembled in their boots and pissed themselves in fear.

Centuries later, the church at Rome reassessed her, admitting she was not a prostitute and likely had a special place among Yeshua's followers. That she did. Later, she was further elevated to sainthood, though the slander of her being a prostitute is still a common misperception. Witch, wife of Yeshua, apostle, angel, prostitute, special follower, to saint. Has any one person ever had such convoluted perceptions among the people of the world as my sister Miriam?

Today the world calls her Mary Magdalene, which in itself is an evolution of the name we knew her by, Miriam of Magdala, even as the name Jesus has evolved from Yeshua. Though our family was from Bethany, she adopted her identifying town as Magdala because of her affinity for the quaint little villa and her long hours of reflection, prayer, and personal growth, as she looked out upon the gleaming lake expanse from her vantage at the villa.

Though it wasn't yet mid-afternoon, shortly after we arrived at the villa we saw Miriam and Salome walking up the trail on the road coming to Magdala from the north. As her brother, I greeted Miriam with a warm hug. But Cephas and Yohhanan both greeted her in the way the Children of Light did in those days, touching or almost touching palm to palm and saying, "Namaste," followed by her name, a form of greeting Yeshua had adopted in his youth after being visited by Anish of Bharat. All three of us also greeted Salome in this manner.

After the greetings, Cephas got right down to business. "Miriam, why are you approaching certain members of the communities and asking them to meet you in Bethany some days hence? And why have you not spoken with me or any of the apostles about the mysterious purpose of this meeting?"

Miriam looked at Cephas for a long moment as if she were contemplating how to answer him. She had a slight crease on her forehead at the spot on her brow above her nose. That telltale would be imperceptible to most people, but having grown up with her, I knew it was an indicator that she was a bit upset.

I was expecting a sharp reply but saw her countenance soften, and so was her answer. "Cephas, forgive me. I should have contacted you and the other apostles first. I was given a most momentous charge from Elohim regarding the people I spoke to. It only affects them. In my haste to ensure they would all arrive on the necessary day, I spoke to them without first alerting you to my mission. Again, please forgive me."

Cephas was completely disarmed by Miriam's contriteness. "All is well, Miriam. We are all still learning and growing in our callings. Tell me now, what is your mission, and why are you calling upon some of our brothers and sisters but not others to meet with you in Bethany?"

"I can only answer you in part, Cephas," Miriam offered. "I was given a charge by Elohim to give a special blessing and calling to twelve couples."

She looked over at me. "You and Hannah are among the twelve, Lazarus." I raised my eyebrows in surprise, certainly anxious to learn more.

"I cannot tell you what their calling or blessing will be," she explained. "In order for their responsibility to be fulfilled, no person living now upon the Earth can know of it; even among the Children of Light, and even among you, the apostles."

"Wait a moment," Yohhanan interjected somewhat indignantly. "You are saying that twelve couples are to receive some high and holy blessing, and that not only are we not allowed to know the specifics, but none of the apostles are numbered among those to receive this special blessing and calling?"

Miriam nodded her head in assent. "I'm sorry if that offends you, Yohhanan. But it is true. Yeshua specifically told me that none of the apostles should be in the group. Please do not take offense. You each are exceedingly worthy, but you also have already been called to high and holy callings as apostles. That is your life's work. You are even now so busy you barely keep up with the responsibilities that are currently being carried upon your shoulders. You have no more time or strength to carry more."

Both Cephas and Yohhanan mumbled and grumbled under their breath for a moment, but they knew Miriam had spoken true.

"The calling of the twelve couples will put a responsibility upon them that will not be initiated or fulfilled for most until many years after they have left Israel," she elaborated. "All the time that you will know them here will be as it has always been. There is no need for you to even think about this anymore, as it will have no effect upon your life or theirs for as long as the Communities of Light exist in Israel."

"I know that still leaves you unfulfilled. But I ask you to please think of it no more." She looked at them with a mischievous smile. "Don't make me have to put a spell of forgetfulness upon you!"

After a little nervous laughter at her hopefully jesting comment, we all spoke about it no more. Before parting, we did the Lanaka, an exercise to bond energy together on the hill overlooking the lake that was glittering like stars upon the water with the bright afternoon sun shining upon it. Cephas and Yohhanan then bid us goodbye and headed north to rejoin their families and fellow apostles at the Communities of Light.

Once the apostles were gone, I hurried over excitedly to Miriam. "Tell me, dear sister, what is this great mystery calling?"

Miriam looked at me with raised eyebrows and a slight, humorous grin upon her face. "You will have to wait until the appointed time, Lazarus, and hear it with everyone else. You know how I dislike repeating myself."

"Seriously, Miriam?" I complained with more than a little frustration. "I am your brother. Certainly that must merit some extra privileges."

She nodded in understanding. "In days past that was true, Lazarus, but now my calling is greater. All the men of the Children of Light are my brothers and all the women are my sisters. In my calling, I can no longer have favorites or give special privileges to one that are not given to all. I love you, Lazarus. You will always have a special place in my heart full of cherished memories. But you must accept that I am more than your sister Miriam."

"I have been told that a lot lately," I admitted ruefully.

That was the moment in time when it first hit me deep in my heart, mind, and soul; the moment I had been resisting admitting for some time. Finally

I began to accept the truth, albeit still with some reluctance, but overwhelmed by the love in my heart and my mind's weakening ability to continue denying the facts. The radiant woman standing before me truly was no longer just my sister Miriam of Magdala. She was, she is — the Angel of the Covenant. I had no conception of the enormity of that, or the impact it was going to have on my life. But I was soon going to find out!

Chapter 3
THE GATHERING

It was a long two-day walk back to Bethany from Tiberias. Usually I would make the trip in four or five days, stopping for business at numerous places along the way, but this return trip I needed to make as rapidly as possible to ensure Hannah and I were present for the meeting with the other couples Miriam had called for the secret meeting.

After Cephas and Yohhanan departed, I invited Miriam and Salome to accompany me on the journey to Bethany in the south. But after parting goodbyes they demurred and headed back on the trail north to Magdala. That was confounding to me as it was the wrong direction.

Mumbling under my breath in confusion, I thought to myself, "If Miriam expects to be present at her own meeting she best start walking in the right direction."

Then again, I had to remind myself that she was an angel now, and likely had more rapid means of transportation available to her. As I had been told that she was now part of both the physical and spirit world, perhaps she could fly as I did after my first death when I was a spirit. However, if Miriam flew on angel's wings, I couldn't fathom how Salome would travel with her. But perhaps she could come along for the ride. Who can understand the way of angels? Surely not me.

I was somewhat haggard and dirty when I arrived home in Bethany after my rapid trip from Tiberias along the dusty roads. Despite my appearance, Hannah greeted me with a long, passionate kiss and a tight embrace, which was invigorating to my mood and a reminder of one of the great reasons I loved to come home from trips.

I noticed five goat-hair tents pitched out behind the house when I returned and, as I assumed, Hannah said they were couples from the communities that had all shown up in the last day, heeding a summons from Miriam to meet at the house in Bethany. Another couple that did not have a tent she put up in the guest bedroom. I wondered where the remaining absent couples were. They had best make haste as tomorrow was the big day.

Hannah said the visitors knew nothing more than that they should meet Miriam here and asked me if I knew what it was all about. I told her the little additional information that Miriam had shared when I was at the villa with her.

"The good news..." I told her enthusiastically, "is we are one of the twelve couples. It must be a very important blessing as Miriam said she was acting under the direction of the Elohim."

"I am glad it is something we can share together, whatever it is," Hannah said as she softly caressed my cheek with her hand and kissed me tenderly again.

Two other people straggled to our house over an hour after darkness had set that night, but they were not a married couple and did not arrive together. One was Elissa, the former High Priestess of the pagan temple at Tyre. The other was the giant warrior Kudar-Iluna from the lost tribe of Amorites.

Though they were not married and were not even acquainted with one another to my knowledge, perhaps unbeknownst to them they were about to be introduced and married tomorrow by Miriam.

Elissa had been accompanied by two armed escorts whom she dismissed after she arrived, so I assumed they had just been paid to bring her to Bethany. She wouldn't have to worry about protection while traveling anymore if she was married to the Amorite warrior.

Kudar-Iluna was perfectly content to sleep outside under the stars. The impossibly tall, massively strong warrior and former brigand was used to the spartan life.

Elissa, with her lustrous, long hair partially arranged in a beguiling braided coiffure that topped her head like a crown, and her flawless radiant skin rivaled Salome for beauty and sophistication. But she seemed quite happy when we offered her a space on the floor of our front room to sleep for the night.

Assuming Kudar-Iluna and Elissa were soon to be a couple, there were still five pairs that had not shown up. And of Miriam and Salome, there was no sign or word by the time Hannah and I retired for the night.

The following morning dawned bright and clear. There was a definite excitement and anticipation in the air as we gathered to prepare and share breakfast together with all the visitors in the courtyard. As was our custom when we had guests, we deferred the normal work of the day and made breakfast an extra-long affair so we could socialize; not a two-minute dash on the run often seen in modern times, as people gulp their morning meal or skip it altogether in their haste to make their interminable commute to work on time.

A few of the wives had arisen well before sunrise to prepare and bake fresh bread in the outdoor wood-fired ovens. They made a hearty, savory bread, filled with spices and small chunks of vegetables that we dipped in olive oil. It could be a meal in itself and was a staple throughout the day whenever anyone was hungry.

Well before the bread, we ate a variety of fruit and let it settle for a good hour before partaking of the bread. Both men and women roamed about the property after the sun rose, picking a nice assortment of ripe fruit, some from domesticated plants and others from wild ones that grew near our home. When we all sat down for the first course of the morning meal there were clay plates piled with grapes, carob, dates, figs, pomegranates, and mulberries.

Of course the conversation on everyone's tongue was about the mystery of our gathering in Bethany. I seemed to know the most and shared with everyone the tidbits Miriam had given me at the villa, but none of us even came close in our guessing games to the true and fateful purpose of our meeting.

Everyone was familiar with Kudar-Iluna and couldn't help but take notice of him. But none who were at my home that day had actually ever been this close to him, except for me. Kudar-Iluna was a head taller than the tallest man and extremely well-muscled. He also wore his long blond hair in a conical topknot, apparently a style of his tribe. It just added to the perception of his extreme height. Both he and Elissa seemed out of place. To my surprise, it didn't seem like they were warming up to one another much as they sat as far apart in our courtyard grouping of tables as you could sit.

Where Kudar-Iluna was the embodiment of raw physical power, Elissa exemplified the pure feminine of the highest class. Her smooth, white skin and piercing blue eyes implied that she was originally from a northern race, and it was the one thing she had in common with Kudar-Iluna, although her hair was as black as a raven. She was adorned with intricate jewelry including gold arm wraps, a golden tiara, and a spectacular gem-encrusted necklace that attached to her neck, draped her shoulders, and spread out like a fan across her upper chest, terminating in a brilliant jeweled pendant that seemed to almost glow in the early morning sun. I had seen Miriam wear something similar, but only on two very special occasions.

Elissa's clothes were clean and fashioned from the finest materials with a classic Greek-style cut. They radiated with a spectacular color blend of white and the rare Tyrian purple. She actually looked quite out of place among us. Then again, she would have looked out of place anywhere in Israel, even at the king's court. It was somewhat of a mystery to me how she could be so expensively adorned and stylishly dressed, as I knew she had escaped from Tyre with nothing but the clothes on her back.

Though she was now numbered among us and lived our lifestyle as far as diet, I had heard that she had not integrated well with the brothers and sisters in the community. She faithfully did her part to labor with the other sisters, but she was an unmarried woman in her late twenties who lived alone and dressed like a rich Greek princess. Other women in the community dressed much less ostentatiously and only adorned themselves in their finest jewels for weddings and other very special occasions. Elissa, on the other hand, wore her wealth every day and traveled everywhere with burly bodyguards. Considering she was a walking invitation to brigands and thieves, having bodyguards seemed prudent.

Shortly after her arrival among the Children of Light, she asked some brothers to build a small stone home for her up on a hill above Chorazin. She soon began offering her services there as an Oracle. Seeing the way she was dressed and adorned, her predictions of people's futures must have been accurate and profitable. I know her home had continued to expand in size, and that wasn't from the free labor of the brothers.

Miriam spoke very highly of her when they returned with her from Tyre. She said Elissa had a natural affinity for the powers of Celestine Light and had been the only person in the temple who had been able to see through Yeshua's illusion of snakes, which even fooled the apostles. The very fact that she was numbered among us this day testified that there was a spiritual depth to her of substance and promise that perhaps wasn't obvious just looking at her.

Thinking of Kudar-Iluna and Elissa got me pondering Miriam's choices for the other members of our clandestine mystery group that had thus far arrived. Some I had met, others I knew of, and some were total strangers to me. They included:

Gimiel of Capharsalama and his wife Sanah. He had been in a mob that had sought to kill Ephres, the man who loved men instead of women. Yeshua had stopped the gang and his words of sanity and wisdom led to the conversion of Gimiel and his family. Shortly thereafter they moved to the Communities of Light.

Teoma, whose father Dryhus Yeshua had saved from a life of abandonment and despair years ago on the road from Gimron, and his wife Rachel;

Daksha, the son of Anish of Bharat who had taught Yeshua the ways of the East in his youth, and his wife Vidya, a couple that had only come three months earlier to the Communities of Light;

Gaweson and his wife Fatima, who were the first Nubians to become members of the communities. Their families had joined the Children of Light before Hannah and I were even married, having become devoted followers of Yeshua from his time among them when he and Miriam and their young children were in Egypt;

Bai and his wife Ting, a couple I had never seen or heard of, also appeared at our house in Bethany. The only word they could speak that anyone understood was Miriam. I had seen a few people of their black-haired, yellow-tinged skin race once when I was on a caravan in Persia. My understanding was they were from a country even further east than Bharat.

Dionysodoros, or Dion as we called him because of his tongue-twister name, and his wife Xenia were converts from Hippos, a uniquely Greek city on the eastern shore of Lake Gennesaret. They had been friends of the Greeks Adronicus and Yunia who had welcomed Yeshua, Miriam, Salome, and the visiting apostles on their one and only trip to the city. Shortly after meeting Yeshua, Yunia and Adronicus relocated to the Communities of Light, but they returned to their hometown multiple times, and there were over two dozen Greek converts who had immigrated to the Communities of Light because of their proselytizing. Dion and Xenia were two of them.

There was also a young couple from Bethsaida, one of the four Celestine communities at the north end of Lake Gennesaret. I had never met or even heard of them before, but my wife Hannah had met them the previous year when she and some of the other sisters from Bethany had taken their children to the hot springs of Tiberias and stayed overnight at our villa near the lake. She told me their names were Aaron and Kira and that he was a weaver by trade.

While I was reflecting upon my fellow passengers on the mystery boat, a couple walked through the gate that completely surprised me, although it should not have as he was present at Yeshua's ascension, so must have had a very pure heart. It was a moment before I recognized the man, dressed in quality but ordinary clothes, as Valerius, the Roman Centurion from Jerusalem.

He met Yeshua one day on the road while he was traveling with the apostles and pleaded for him to come to his home and heal his favored servant who had taken quite ill. Yeshua was so impressed with the faith he had in his ability to heal his servant that he did so at that very moment.

I heard that Valerius had returned home to find his servant completely restored to health, but I had never heard about him again and certainly would never have expected to see him here if he hadn't appeared at the ascension.

Valerius walked over to our tables and introduced himself and his wife Laelia. We cordially invited them to join us for breakfast, and room was made at the table for them as they squeezed onto one of the benches next to Bai and Ting. "My apologies for coming late," Valerius pleaded. "I really do not know any of you, and it is somewhat awkward for us to be here."

"I know of you, Valerius. A good and honorable man by all accounts," I assured him. "I am Lazarus and this is my wife Hannah," I said, putting my arm around her.

"You are the man that Yeshua brought back from the dead?" he asked. "I remember seeing you at the ascension."

"I am that man," I admitted. "My one claim to fame."

"You were really dead?" he asked with sincere curiosity.

"For five days so I am told," I quipped with a wry smile.

He raised his eyebrows. "That must have been some experience," he conjectured, nodding his head as he contemplated it.

"More than you can imagine," I reflected with a little chuckle. "Perhaps if we can find a few moments together I will share more about it with you and your wife, but now let us have all the others introduce themselves so we can begin our mutual friendships."

Valerius nodded and each of the others at the table went around and introduced themselves, except for Bai and Ting, who just mimed a greeting and smiled broad, friendly smiles.

After everyone had introduced themselves, Valerius told a little more about himself. "These are not my normal clothes," he explained. "I am a Roman Centurion and usually wear my military garb." There was an audible gasp from multiple people at the table. Romans were the enemies and hated occupiers of our land to many of us. To find a Roman officer in our midst was fearfully shocking to some.

Valerius could see his announcement did not sit well. "Do not worry, my friends," he pleaded. "I stand with the Children of Light. If I were given a direct order to do you harm, I would rather take my own life."

You could hear several slow exhales at his words, as unconscious holdings of breath were released with relief.

"I came here today, dressed as one of you and on the prescribed morning and not earlier, so I could arrive most inconspicuously and not draw Roman attention to our gathering."

His explanation was a balm of calm. Several people thanked him, and everyone welcomed him and Laelia once more.

After the introduction of Valerius, we began the fresh baked bread and olive oil course for our morning meal. It was so fulfilling and delicious! I haven't had bread that scrumptious for many centuries. Nobody makes bread like that anymore, nor would it be healthy to make it a daily meal as we did in ignorance most days in Bethany.

Yet even after all these years I still fondly remember the enchanting aroma of the herb-filled bread and its divine texture of being crunchy on the outside and sensually soft and fulfilling on the inside. I do miss it, at least as an occasional treat. I've tried making it myself from my wife's exact recipe, but it never comes out nearly as satisfying as the way my Hannah used to make it.

After breakfast, while we were just sitting around getting to know each other better and trying to communicate with Bai and Ting with hand signals and facial expressions, three other people walked in the gate.

One, who came with his wife, I knew. He was Nicodemus. For me at least, he was an even bigger surprise than Valerius. But like Valerius, I shouldn't have been surprised, as he was another that had been drawn to be present at the ascension because of his clear harmony and resonance with the Celestine Light.

But Nicodemus was a high-ranking Pharisee, a religious group that had been actively opposed to Yeshua and his teachings. It took a conscious mental effort not to automatically be cautious because of that affiliation. I knew he had come one night in secret to see Yeshua and ask him theological questions. According to the account I was given by Miriam, he had a sincere interest in knowing the truth. But that was quite some time ago, and I had not really heard much about him since, until seeing him at Yeshua's ascension.

Although I wasn't certain, I thought he might also be a member of the Sanhedrin, the ruling religious body of the tribes of Israel. It was the Sanhedrin that had actively sought the death of Yeshua and their machinations that convinced the Roman governor Pontius Pilate to have Yeshua crucified. Even the turmoil that arose at Yeshua's tomb from Miriam appearing and toppling the guardian stone would never have taken place if the Sanhedrin had not talked Pilate into posting guards at the tomb.

Nicodemus disarmed my worries immediately

with his peaceful spirit. He walked over to me forthwith with a warm smile and eyes alive with love. With his staff and long white beard, he seemed like a vision of an ancient prophet.

"Lazarus, dear Lazarus," he said, embracing me as soon as I stood up to greet him. "It is so good to see you alive! I knew who you were long before you died and came back to the world. But it is such an honor now to meet you in person, especially as we never had a moment to speak together at the ascension of Yeshua as we were all so awed and enthralled by the moment."

I still was not used to my macabre claim to fame and never was very good at handling accolades, especially concerning my resurrection. After all, it wasn't anything I did! It was something that was done to me by the Lord of Light. Yet for some reason people still insisted upon congratulating me as if I had won the gold coin after a hard-fought race.

Nicodemus took his wife's hand and brought her to stand before me. Like him, she was an elderly lady with gray hair, a welcoming smile, and a most gentle and loving countenance. "May I introduce the love of my life, my dear wife of forty-two years and six children, Avital."

I made a little bow with my head and put my two hands up. "What's this?" Avital asked.

"This is the way we greet Children of Light," I explained as I shifted a bit to face Nicodemus, realizing proper custom in the land was to not touch a woman, even her fingers, unless first given permission by her husband. We didn't keep such customs among the Children of Light, but Nicodemus was a Pharisee, so I hastily thought it best to follow the proper protocol.

He held up his hands to meet mine. "Namaste, Nicodemus," I greeted him. His eyes smiled back at me along with his lips. I love meeting people who have eyes that smile. It is such a sure sign of unrestrained joy in their heart.

Nicodemus lightly touched his palms to mine. "Namaste, Lazarus. Now what does it mean?"

"It is a saying from Bharat that was given to Yeshua in his youth by the father of Daksha, who sits across the table there," I explained, pointing to Daksha as he waved at Nicodemus.

"It means the god that is inside of me honors the god that is inside of you." That description seemed to delight everyone and, unbidden, all at the table turned to those next to them and touched palms and greeted one another by name with Namaste. Hannah was quickly standing next to me and was the first to greet Avital in the Celestine way.

Next, Nicodemus went over and greeted Valerius with Namaste. They obviously knew each other as they both lived and worked in Jerusalem.

"Valerius, it is so good to see you here. I was very surprised to notice you at the ascension, so now prepared, I am less surprised to see you here today, but still curious. When did you become a follower of Yeshua?"

"I don't think I officially am yet," Valerius told him, "but I want to be, and my wife Laelia as well. But in truth, I must keep it a secret for the moment. It would not be accepted in the Legion to be a follower of the teachings of a conquered people."

"I understand," Nicodemus assured him. "It is not much different for me. Although there are several among the Pharisees that are leaning toward the teachings of Yeshua, and though it is not forbidden, it is frowned upon, as it puts our knowledge of the sacred scrolls into question."

"You of course did not mention the day of ascension to any of your colleagues?" Valerius inquired with caution in his voice.

"I am wiser than that, Valerius," Nicodemus affirmed. "Not that anyone would actually believe me if I related the events. In my own mind, I keep needing to continually convince myself that it was not some massively vivid, imaginative dream. It is a breath of fresh air to hear you speak of that glorious moment. If you too remember experiencing it, that helps convince me that it really happened."

"Likewise," Valerius assured him. He waved his arm around, encompassing everyone at the table. "I do not know any of the people here, and most were not at the ascension. I really have not had much to do yet with the Children of Light, so I am here knowing it is the place I need to be, but still feeling like quite an outsider."

"Miriam of Magdala came to you?" Nicodemus asked.

"Yes," Valerius affirmed. "Knocked on my door after we had already retired for the evening, of all things. At first, when I saw it was her, instinctively I almost called for the guard. As you know, she is a reputed witch of not inconsiderable power. At least those are the rumors in the lower ranks. But I had met her before and knew her to be the beloved of Yeshua. All my memories of her were benign.

"But the purpose of her visit, to invite me and my wife to this meeting with a promise of a life-changing event of great joy, certainly sparked my curiosity. What of you? How did you come to be here, Nicodemus?"

"Much the same as you," Nicodemus related. "I was in meditation in the privacy of my inner courtyard at my home. The gate was bolted from the inside, yet suddenly Miriam was standing by my side. I didn't even hear her approach or know she was there until I felt her hand upon my shoulder. I was so startled I practically jumped out of my skin!

"In truth, I have been a follower of Yeshua in my heart since the night I first spoke to him in private. I simply did not know how to act upon my desire. Even after the ascension, the event was so unbelievable that I was confused as to what I should do next. I knew my life could never be the same, but I was unsure of how it should change.

Miriam came and showed me the way."

With all the activity among those of us at the tables, I had forgotten for a moment the person that had come in the gate with Nicodemus and Avital. He was still standing near the gate and had made no attempt to come over to join our group. I tugged lightly on the sleeve of Nicodemus' tunic. "Who is the man that accompanied you and why does he stand off alone and not join us?"

Nicodemus glanced over at the man standing by the gate. "That is just one of my servants who accompanied us here to attend to our needs while we traveled. I should not have brought him, as this is a private gathering, and in truth he was not needed for the half-hour walk from my house to yours."

Nicodemus started to walk over to his servant. "I will tell him he is no longer needed and send him back to my house."

I grabbed his sleeve once more and gently restrained him. "Hold, friend. I suspect it may not be by casual circumstance that he is present. Let us wait until Miriam arrives. Perhaps it was her intention for him to be here."

"Don't be ridiculous. He is a servant and a Samaritan," Nicodemus scoffed.

"You are right, Nicodemus," I said soothingly. "Perhaps that is all he is. But Yeshua, on more than one occasion, said that the lowest will be the highest and the highest the lowest. Nothing is lost by waiting just a bit to see if Miriam attaches any importance to him."

Somewhat grudgingly, Nicodemus agreed.

Chapter 4
THE CALLING

About a half hour later, breakfast finally wound down. Shortly thereafter, Miriam came through the gate with Salome. She stopped for a moment before she came over to our gathering and spoke for a minute to Nicodemus' servant who had remained standing near the gate. When she and Salome approached our table, the servant accompanied them.

"Hello, cherished Children of Light," Miriam greeted as she stood at an open place at the end of the group of tables where we sat. "You are blessed for heeding my call to join me here on this day."

She turned and pointed to the servant. "This is Joshua. He shall be joining us as an equal member of our group and not as a servant," she explained.

Miriam looked intently at Nicodemus. "If that is all right with you, Nicodemus."

Nicodemus was flustered at the question and Miriam's focus upon him, but nodded his head in assent. "Of course, Miriam. As you wish. This is the home of your family and the meeting which you have called. I acquiesce to your desires in how you will conduct it."

Miriam gave him a warm smile. "Thank you, Nicodemus. I think you will find that you will gain more than lose if you continue what has begun here today."

Miriam leaned over and whispered to Joshua. He quickly went and grabbed a single stool by the well and brought it over to sit upon at the spot where Miriam had been standing by the table.

While he was gathering the stool, Salome came and squeezed onto the bench next to Hannah, and Miriam began to slowly walk in a circle around the grouping of tables so we needed to keep turning our heads to follow her.

As she walked, Miriam spoke. "Some of you, like my brother Lazarus, have known me all or much of my life. Some of you, such as Elissa and Gimiel, I have shared great adventures with at sundry times and places. Others, like Nicodemus and Valerius, have met me only briefly until recently. Bai and Ting have spoken with me only once before. And Joshua knows me not at all. But the Celestine Light of Yeshua has entered all of your hearts. It unites you as Children of Light, regardless of your race, your sex, your nationality, or your social class."

"How well you know me matters not, because this moment in your lives is not about me. It is about you, and the potential of your faithfulness as

Children of Light."

"Pardon me, Miriam," Nicodemus interjected. "You are esteemed, of course, as the widow of Yeshua and are known to be one of his twelve apostles, but where are the other apostles? It would seem no meeting of importance should occur without their authority and governance. If this is as momentous of an occasion as you have implied, why are you the only one here?"

Miriam looked with scrutiny at Nicodemus. He fidgeted a little nervously, involuntarily twitching his shoulders once. "Allow me to finish my introduction to this gathering, Nicodemus, and I assure you that you will have no doubt as to its validity and to why I am the only representative of the apostles present."

"I know rules and procedures are of great importance to the Pharisees," she reflected, "but the only laws the Elohim have asked us to follow are the Twelve Commandments of Sinai and the Great Commandment to be stewards of the Earth. Please make strides to disengage your habits of the Pharisees and strive to embrace the ways of the Children of Light. For a Child of Light you are, more than you realize. And that is why you are numbered among us today."

Nicodemus nodded his head in silent affirmation and acknowledgment.

Despite what she told Nicodemus, Miriam soon spoke to establish her authority. "Most of you know that Yeshua is my husband and that I have been numbered as one of his twelve apostles. I am an apostle no more."

No one jumped out of their seats in consternation at her words, but there was surprise and concern written on many faces.

Miriam continued. "I am very humbled by what I shall tell you next. I wish I would have no need to speak of myself, for I am not boastful, nor do I seek to be elevated above you, my brothers and sisters, but Elohim has called me to a high and holy calling, and I must fulfill it.

"I will tell you who I am and how I came to be as I am, but so you may know these are not merely fanciful words that I speak, you must know that I truly speak as an emissary from Elohim and not as Miriam of Magdala."

She looked over to the two former residents of Hippos. "Dion and Xenia, what language am I speaking aloud to this group?"

They looked at each other with big smiles and Dion answered, "In Greek, of course. I cannot tell you what a pleasant treat that has been and what a surprise to know that everyone here understands Greek."

Well, I understood Greek, but I wasn't sure anyone else present did. I had listened to every word Miriam had spoken thus far, and I was pretty sure it was all in Aramaic and that there was not one Greek word in the bunch. I hoped this didn't mean the Greek couple was a bit daft.

Miriam next turned to the Roman centurion. "Valerius and Laelia, can you tell me in what language I have spoken to the group?"

Laelia looked over at Dion and Xenia skeptically. "I am unsure of why our two esteemed colleagues from Hippos think you have been speaking Greek. I am fluent in that language, and I have not heard a word of Greek thus far."

"Contrarily, I have been so happy to hear you speaking Latin, Miriam!" Laelia chimed. "Thank you for this."

I nodded my head in astonishment as understanding dawned in my mind. The Greeks thought she was speaking Greek and the Romans thought she was speaking Latin. She asked the same question in what sounded like perfect Aramaic to me, to both the Nubian couple and the couple from the land east of Bharat. They both apparently answered in their native tongues. They too thought Miriam was speaking to everyone in the language of their home country.

"Now you see the power of Elohim manifested through me. I am a humble messenger from Elohim, our heavenly Father and Mother. By their power each of you hears my voice in the language that is your native tongue. Nor could anything such as this be an illusion or a feat of magic that could be duplicated by men. Therefore, you may know that it is of Elohim. For by no other means could this miracle be accomplished."

Valerius looked over to Dion and asked him in Greek, "She was speaking to you in the language of your fathers?"

Dion nodded his head affirmatively. "And to you in Latin?" he asked.

"Yes," Valerius affirmed.

There was a quick discussion, including improved pantomime among those of us gathered, confirming that everyone had been hearing Miriam speak only in their native tongue. It made a mighty big impression on everyone.

"One more demonstration I will give you before I explain who and what I am," Miriam expounded. She pointed to a date palm planted off by itself in a corner of the courtyard. It was an old tree and no longer very healthy or productive.

"Lazarus, you have been talking about getting rid of that tree for years and planting another, haven't you?"

"Yes, that's true," I agreed.

Miriam looked out over the gathering, lingering for a moment upon each person's eyes as she spoke. "In jest I have heard people challenge my brethren the apostles, saying, 'If you are true representatives of Elohim, call down a lightning bolt from the sky and prove it.' Of course this was never manifested. That was not a gift of power given to apostles. And even if it were, it would not be demonstrated simply to assuage the faithless desires of men.

"But you are a special group of Children of Light, called through me, but not by me. Elohim asks for you to fulfill a responsibility that will take your entire life: a life longer than you can begin to imagine; one where you will have the opportunity to manifest the great purposes of Elohim.

"This calling will be a mighty challenge for you. Weaker men and women would tremble and fail because of the many horrors they would have to see and the many heartbreaks of parting they would have to endure. Therefore, that you may be girded up in resolution, you must have no doubt. You must know that I am a true emissary from Elohim, and that they have given me all the authority and power to act in their name to fulfill their desires."

Miriam looked up toward the clear blue sky above. She raised her right arm straight up with her index finger pointing skyward. In a rapid movement, she suddenly swept her outstretched arm down. The moment her extended finger was pointing at the old date palm in the courtyard, there was a frighteningly loud clap of thunder and a sizzling sound of lightning just above our heads. In the same blink of an eye, a bolt of lightning crackled from the clear sky and struck the date palm, splitting it in two. The two halves fell away on opposite sides to the ground, hitting with thuds and smoldering with smoke.

Miriam calmly turned to look at us, a group of wide-eyed, very attentive people. "I hope between this little demonstration and the fact that each of you hears my words in your own language, a space will be opened in your hearts now to hear the fullness of my words and be receptive to the account of my own transformation and why that is important to you."

We all silently and eagerly nodded our heads in affirmation.

"All of you know that I am Yeshua's wife and until recently one of his apostles," she began. "What most of you do not know is why I am no longer an apostle."

She hesitated a moment, perhaps to collect her thoughts. "I have been with Yeshua through every important event of his life since we were married when we were both eighteen. Yeshua wanted me to be present for everything he said or did: from marvelous miracles to simple conversations. In this, I became a personal witness to all he taught and did. He knew that after he left this world, many would come and for their own glory or purposes, say falsely that 'Yeshua taught this,' or 'Yeshua did that.' I was called to be the true testifier of his life and teachings, the one that could not be refuted.

"I thought that was all there was to my calling, for that already was a great responsibility. But each day I traveled with Yeshua, he also taught me more of the Celestine Light. He taught me how to call up, control, and use for good many of the powers of that light.

"As he began to call apostles, he asked me to become one and to help teach the others, to show them how to use the light for good and call out their gifts of power as he had shown me. Then I thought once more that this was my calling, and a truly humbling and important responsibility it was.

"But then there came another calling and a greater responsibility still. This one involves all of the Children of Light, and it involves you. Over the years, as I have experienced the burdens and joys of fulfilling the responsibilities I have been called to, I realized that it is all part of our progression through eternity. There is no point when we are ever done, when we know everything, when we can stop and just retire and take endless rest. There will always be new challenges and with them new opportunities for personal growth and expansion. It is true for me, it is true for you, especially on this day. And it is true for every Child of Light wherever they might be.

"I am grateful for so much. I am grateful to you for being here and listening to the inner guidance of the Celestine Light in your mind and the true desire of the light in your heart.

"If you will bear with me a few more minutes, it will be helpful for you to know how it is I have come to speak before you now, at the direction and in the name of Elohim. This is necessary because if you choose to accept your calling, you must also accept me for who and what I am, as I will be your teacher during the next eleven years while I remain upon the Earth.

"The last day we had with Yeshua before he was taken to be crucified was when he gathered with me, Salome, and all of the apostles in the Garden of Gethsemane on the Mount of Olives. We found a secluded spot in the garden where there were no other people and knelt together in a circle to pray to our Father and Mother in heaven. Yeshua prayed first, then me, then Cephas, then Salome, then all of the apostles.

"When the last had finished praying, Yeshua took my hand and stepped with me into the center of the circle. He spoke to me in my mind in a gentle, soothing voice and asked me if I was prepared to fulfill the calling I was foreordained to before the world was. He had already told me that this was my destiny on three earlier occasions. I knew that this day was simply the one in which it would occur. I smiled at him and told him I was ready.

"Together we looked up into the sky. It was filled with large billowy, white clouds with much sunshine and blue sky showing as well. Yeshua spoke no words, but he called in the powers of heaven upon us. A dense, rapidly spinning pillar of impenetrable cloud formed and descended from the sky and enveloped us. Though Salome and the apostles were encircling us very closely, we could not see them, nor could they see us."

"I remember this moment so clearly," Salome

interrupted. "When the cloud touched down and came over Miriam and Yeshua, the wind was so strong all of us in the circle were thrown to the ground. But then, as suddenly as it descended from the clouds above, it retreated back up into the sky. It took Miriam and Yeshua with it, for they were no longer among us after the cloud departed."

"Thank you for your eyewitness testimony, Salome," Miriam commended.

"As the spinning cloud rose back into the sky and we with it, the feeling of weightlessness was exhilarating. When we stopped, we were high above the ground. I could not even see Salome and the apostles below me. Amazingly, we were able to walk on the top of the clouds as if we were on solid ground.

"I heard the sound of many trumpets blaring from a distance, but getting closer with every breath. Suddenly we were surrounded by heavenly beings dressed in robes of many splendid colors, and I asked Yeshua who they were. He told me they were angels that had come to witness the occasion when I would be numbered among them.

"I was in awe of the moment, scarcely able to comprehend where I was and what was about to take place, especially considering the ordeal I knew Yeshua was going to be going through beginning that very day when we returned to Gethsemane.

"Then a man, an angel, walked over to us. He had long, wavy brown hair and a flowing beard. He was wearing a beautiful robe with a myriad of thin multicolored and golden threads running through it in all directions, and he wore a wide purple sash around his waist.

"Yeshua put his hand on the man's shoulder and introduced him. 'This is Halakata,' he said. 'He is currently the Angel of the Covenant and will remain so in fullness and be your guide while you learn the secrets of your calling.'

"I greeted Halakata and asked him how long he had been the Angel of the Covenant. His reply made me smile. 'I have no idea,' he said.

"He told me he knew exactly when he was supposed to be any place in the Celestine Realms or upon any Earth in the heavens, but did not know how that related to the time as we keep it here.

"Yeshua patted him on his shoulder and told me that Halakata had served faithfully and well for a very long time, on this and on many Earths. He explained that Halakata had progressed in the expansion of his Celestine Light beyond the office of the Angel of the Covenant and had been called to something greater. Yeshua also assured me that Halakata would remain in his office for the full eleven years I would remain on the Earth, to help train me to use the special powers of the Angel of the Covenant with prudence and wisdom.

"Lastly, he asked if I accepted my holy calling to become the next Angel of the Covenant. I told him with conviction that I did.

"Then he spoke with great authority. He said, 'In the name and by the power of Elohim—so let it be!' And so it was.

"Suddenly, I was filled with a blinding white light. It came from within me and rapidly radiated out, filling the entire sky in every direction. Just as suddenly, the white light rushed back to me and filled my body completely with its essence.

"I had closed my eyes at the last moment, and when I opened them I felt so different inside. Every part of me was different. On the outside, it seemed like I still appeared the same for the most part, like the Miriam of Magdala that everyone had known. But on the inside, my heart beat with a different beat, my mind raced and was filled with knowledge I had never learned.

"All of the angels, including Halakata, had vanished in the blink of an eye. Only Yeshua still remained with me. As I looked at him, I was overwhelmed with love, and the testimony in my soul of who he was: the Lord of Light and the Son of Elohim, the first Son of our Father and Mother in the Celestine Realms.

"With that knowledge came a clear understanding about the duties of my calling as the Angel of the Covenant. My responsibility was to be a faithful emissary of Elohim by assisting Children of Light to keep their covenants to Elohim and to expand into their greatness by understanding and living divine principles of happiness, health, and longevity. As a special addition to my calling, for the next eleven years I am to be a teacher and protector of the Children of Light upon this Earth, and particularly to each of you."

Miriam stopped speaking and there was total silence as we continued to all look at her in awe. She broke the silence tugging on her long hair with a bit of levity. "The one weakness I needed to overcome when we returned to be with Salome and the apostles was the realization that all the white light remained in my hair. As you can see, though I am just a few years past thirty, my hair has been as blindingly white as the color can be ever since that day. In my initial vanity, I wanted to dye it back to black, but Yeshua told me to leave it as it was for the greatest power in my office."

Miriam laughed a little laugh. "Salome was quite curious about how and why my hair had turned white."

"It is true," Salome agreed with a soft laugh, "but I quickly got used to it and love her still."

"After Yeshua and I returned to the earth, the apostles knew what had occurred. They knew that one of the reasons we had come to the Mount of Olives was for my ordination as the Angel of the Covenant. Cephas came up and asked me, 'So it is done then? Are you now the angel that Yeshua spoke of?' "

"Yeshua told him that I was."

"I do not wish to speak any more about me,"

Miriam concluded. "As I said earlier, this day is about you. I just wanted to share these events in my life with you so you can know with certainty, when confirmed by your prayers, that the calling I will reveal to you next is a sacred calling from the Elohim. I am merely the messenger and the bridge between you and Elohim that will allow the transformation of your calling to take place."

Aaron raised his hand to draw Miriam's attention. She acknowledged him and he asked, "I am confused; angels are real people? I thought angels were special creations of the Elohim. You referred to them as 'offices' and seemed to say that different people such as you and Halakata were both the same angel. It is very confusing to me."

Yeshua had explained angels in great detail to those of us that were at his ascension. Most of those present that day in Bethany had not been a part of that transcendental experience, and they all nodded after Aaron's question, indicating they were as confused as he was in regards to the nature of angels.

"Angels are people as real as you, Aaron," Miriam began explaining. "They birthed out of their mother's womb and lived a life just like any other person. At some point, which may have been while they were still living their physical life or after they had passed from this life to the next, Elohim called and ordained them to be an angel.

"When they receive their calling, they are

changed by Elohim to be able to exist in any realm. Only angels can stand in the presence of Elohim on high, and also among men on the Earth below, and on every world of spirit or physical reality in between.

"In every place, they are beings of both physical substance and spiritual essence. They are blessed by Elohim to be able to withstand any environment and be unaffected by any poison or mortal blow. For even in their tangible physical nature, they are immortal.

"Nor can they be contained or restrained by any man, device, or prison. They can vanish as they wish and reappear where they will.

"There are three classes in the hierarchy of angels. They have powers and responsibilities commensurate with their level.

"The first two levels of named angels are not individuals but angelic offices filled by a progression of individuals over time called to that stewardship. Each serves only for a limited time. When they have grown in their calling as much as they can, they are released and another individual is called, set apart, and ordained to fill the office that bears the name of that angel.

"Nor are the offices specific to male or female, despite what the name might imply. The original Angel Gabriel was male. Subsequent angels holding that office might be male or female, and more have been female than male. They would still go by the title of the Angel Gabriel and perform the same duties of the office as the previous Angel Gabriel.

"Though I have been given the full powers of the office, I am actually just the apprentice Angel of the Covenant. Halakata will remain and still carry most of the responsibilities while he tutors me during the next eleven years, and I remain mostly here on this Earth. This is necessary to gain experience. Many things can only be learned by experience, as each of you will soon discover in what will be asked of you."

Avital raised her hand with a question, and Miriam nodded for her to ask it. "Are you perfect now?" she wondered.

Miriam stifled a little laugh in response. "I am not, and never will be," she attested. "Nor will any of us. Yeshua admonished all of us to always be striving toward perfection, making efforts each day to be better, more Celestine than we were the day before.

"The path of eternal life is also a path of eternal progression, even for the Elohim. Perfection is never reached. There is always more to know and better ways to be in our character.

"The perfectionist will never find happiness in life because they will always be finding fault in themselves and others, perpetuating a negative and sour energy hovering over their lives.

"As the template of the world and all existence is imperfection continually improving itself and evolving into more perfect forms, anyone who seeks unalterable perfection will always be doomed to disappointment and unending frustration. Better to do the best you can every day and be happy with what you did, not unhappy with what you did not.

"With that understanding, angels still have shortcomings. As my brother Lazarus will attest, I am often too quick to anger. I have also been known to make decisions too quickly without sufficiently listening to both my heart and my mind.

"However, you should know that whenever I, or any other angels, are on missions for the Elohim, we will fulfill them to perfection. There are many other angels that watch over us when we are performing our duties to ensure that they are completed in full as the Elohim directed.

"Yet know that I still have my imperfections of character, so please do not expect me to be perfect in every way. This is something I will never be, nor will you.

"As Yeshua taught, no matter how much you know, how sweet your disposition and wise your judgment, there will always be more to know and self-improvements to make, even for the Elohim. That principle is the very cornerstone of existence and eternal life."

Miriam took a deep breath, which she slowly exhaled, and then continued. "I must speak now for quite some time. There is a great deal I must share with you. I ask that though my talk may be long, that you do not interrupt me. I know you will have questions. Some will be answered along the path of my words. Kindly hold your other queries until after I have shared with you all that I must. Then I will be happy to answer the questions of those who have been patient."

Everyone nodded their assent, and Miriam began her momentous talk. "Because of your faith in Elohim; because of your thoughtfulness and kindness and comfort to your fellow men and women of this Earth; because of your openness to the unknown and willingness to walk paths few have ever walked before you; and because each of the couples here are Soul Mates, united in all abodes of energy, Elohim has called and set you apart to receive a high and holy calling. If you accept this calling, the template of your body will be changed in the twinkling of an eye. You will become nearly immortal in your body for the next two thousand years."

I think my mouth gaped open big enough to swallow a small saucer, and my eyes probably looked as if they were going to pop out of my head, so great was my shock at what Miriam had just said. Looking around at all the others, they were all in similar states of dumbfounded awe and incredulity.

Miriam smiled a slight smile as she saw the look on our faces. "Before you get too excited about the prospect of living for millenniums while still on this Earth, let me explain some important nuances and limitations, and later, why this gift is being granted to you."

Never has a speaker had a more attentive audience. Not a whisper of breath or shuffling movement of hand or foot could be heard as we awaited her next words.

"Everyone here, including you, Salome," she said, looking directly at her beloved companion, "can only be granted the blessing of this calling as a bonded couple. Four of you are currently single. If you wish to have your body template changed from mortal to immortal, you must first become married to one as worthy as you are for this sacred calling."

"As two of the singles here are women and two men, you might find your eternal companion standing near you even at this time. But if you do not have a resonance of love, one that connects you as Soul Mates, not just in your heart but in all of your abodes of energy, then do not feel an obligation. You should not marry anyone just for the convenience, no matter how sweet and worthy they might be for the task.

"For those of you here that are already bonded couples, if you accept this calling, in the name and by the power of Elohim, I will change your template today as I ordain you to your calling. You walked in the gate mortal. You will walk out of it nearly immortal, but with very important limitations which I shall speak of in a moment.

"For the four that are single, the calling is given

to you on this day, but you will not have your template changed into millennial longevity unless you appear before me with your bonded Soul Mate before I depart this physical life in eleven years.

"Now let me explain the limitations. Your body will continue to remain exactly as it is on this day, including the age you now are, as long as you do not poison it by the food you eat, the liquids you drink, or the lifestyle you lead.

"However, if you are older and wish to rejuvenate into a more youthful state, it is possible with the correct herbs and lifestyle choices, but youthening is not a part of this blessing. If you choose to do it, you must discover the secrets on your own.

"Even if you faithfully live as healthy as you should, you can still be injured or killed by weapons, or die by any violent means that would kill anyone else such as drowning, fire, poison, being felled by an attacker, or even an inattentive accident. You can still be afflicted by any sickness or disease and suffer the painful or fatal consequences, just like any other person.

"Of course, if you live a Celestine lifestyle and follow a Celestine diet, you will be naturally resistant or immune to most of the sicknesses and diseases that afflict the people of the world.

"Your blessing is simply to have a body that will continue to live in vitality without an end to years, as long as you don't allow anything to happen to it that would degrade or kill it. Life beyond that is up to you.

"There are also pains to this blessing. You will bury all of your children. Every mortal friend you make in your life's journey will also pass from your life while you continue living. You will never be able to remain living in one location too long, as your unreasonable and even impossible age will soon draw unwanted attention that could lead to either your execution as a witch or imprisonment and torture by the military or government trying to discover your secret.

"It is for these reasons that this calling is only for couples. As everyone else you know beyond this group will pass from this life, it is important that each of you has an eternal companion that will always be there to comfort you and share your life joys and happiness."

Miriam paused for a moment, took a deep breath, and continued. "Yet the reality is that many, if not most of you, will perish before your calling is ended in about two thousand years. Some of you are unlikely to survive for even five hundred years.

"Though your deaths may occur because of your own neglect or bad choices of diet, it also may not. You may do everything you should and still perish from the Earth, as the world is simply a very dangerous place, with many ways to die and soldiers and brigands at every bend, only too happy to slit your throat for a coin or a perceived grievance.

"If you live, helping this Eden world created with great love by the Elohim to not be destroyed by the foolishness of its inhabitants is one of your purposes.

"The reality that some of you will die before your calling is completed also means that some of you will be left alone without your Soul Mate companion. But in this I have good news.

"If anyone of you passes from the physical life before your companion, the one that passes, as long as they remain worthy, will be made a Charion angel by Elohim. Not an angel with an office and special responsibilities, such as I am, but the third level of angels. They are angels at large, if you will—an angel ready to carry out the will of Elohim if directed, but free to do good however they wish when they are not fulfilling a specific responsibility."

"Angels are the only beings blessed to be able to be in both a physical body and a spiritual body, to be able to walk physically upon the Earth and also to live in a glorified spiritual body in the Celestine Realms.

"But an angel's time in the physical is limited by the restrictions imposed by Elohim. If your loved one passes from the physical before you, they will be ordained an angel and able to come and physically be with you for one to two hours weekly. But more than this they cannot do.

"It was not always so. In days of old, after the twelve brothers and twelve sisters left the Garden of Eden, in the days coming up to Noah, male angels from the Celestine Realms, who had no life companions, lusted after the daughters of men on the Earth. Refusing to fulfill their responsibilities as angels, but retaining their special attributes, which at that time had not been limited by Elohim, they came down to the Earth and lived upon it and took the daughters of men as wives. In their wicked ways they introduced sundry diversions from the teachings of Elohim that caused a great regression in the progression of man.

"To ensure such calamity and perversion of the powers of angels could never again occur, Elohim changed the templates of most angels so they could only remain in a physical form for a couple of hours every seven days. This will still be a comforting solace to any of you who remain alone upon the Earth. If your Soul Mate passes before you, they will be able to return each week and touch you and hold you, talk with you and counsel you, until your time on the physical Earth is also done.

"There is still one more restriction upon your life as an immortal that you must be aware of and agree to abide. Once all of your currently living friends and family have passed from this life, you are forbidden from having contact with the mortal Children of Light other than in anonymous passing, unless specifically directed to do so by an angelic messenger from Elohim, which would most likely be me.

"You may not live among them, befriend them, or attend any of their meetings or activities other than as an anonymous one-time visitor passing through, never to be seen again.

"Similarly, you will never reveal that I am an angel to any of the other Children of Light currently living, including your own children and family. Most importantly, you must never reveal the nature of your calling to anyone, including your closest family.

"Neglect of this dictate, depending upon the severity of the transgression, will also be a cause to revoke your calling and return you to a template of mortality and a quick death if you are beyond the years you would have otherwise died."

Miriam's unexpected announcement on the need to remain anonymous and the consequences of missteps was creating clamoring consternation, pretty much among everyone.

She held up both of her hands to draw everyone's attention. "Hear me, most blessed Children of Light." Everyone quieted down—not quiet, but from a din to a murmur—as they looked to hear a greater explanation from Miriam.

"Though this seems like a most onerous requirement, fulfilling it is vital, both to keep you humble and on your task, and to ensure the maximum potential growth for all the Children of Light that you might come in contact with.

"Though you will be blessed with extended

longevity, you will still be filled with all the character flaws and foibles of man, against which you must be ever vigilant, especially as you will be given greater abilities and will develop more potent powers than those who are mortals, due to your extended number of years to learn and train.

"It is by overcoming your weaknesses that you become greater than you were. But the weaknesses will always be there in dormancy, even when you think you have conquered them. Given the right opportunity and circumstances, they can reemerge again to torment you, retard your personal growth and expansion, and, most dangerously, hurt others.

"One of the most likely causes of your demise as a near immortal is to be revered as a special holy man or woman because you are imbued with powers greater than mortals, or even, in the extreme, worshiped as a god. This would put you in situations where the evil character traits of pride and puffed-up vanity of self-importance you thought you had buried would have an opportunity to resurrect.

"Because of your accumulated knowledge from centuries of observation and learning, and your potent gifts of paranormal powers from a very long lifetime of practice, you would be put in situations where you thought you knew best, where you felt it no longer important or necessary to consider the knowledge or opinions of others, who would probably already be revering and deferring to you.

"Despots of mortality are insignificant next to the damage that could be done by a ruler with powers greater than all the people, who demands obedience and never dies. You would become no better than the fallen angels I spoke of, who became so wicked that they nearly destroyed the people of the Earth and ultimately Elohim cast them into outer darkness because of their evil."

"In addition to the active damage you could inflict upon the Children of Light if you were to associate with them, there is also a tremendous amount of harm you could do to them indirectly. People of all religious beliefs continually pray to Elohim, in the guise of the god of their understanding, for everything from good weather for crops, good luck in games of chance, safe births, and victory in battles.

"Most would be dismayed and confused, even to the point of the loss of their faith, to learn that the Elohim very rarely intervene in the affairs of men, even when the consequences of not intervening might be the death and destruction of good people, even Children of Light. This is by divine design to ensure all men and women have a full opportunity in this physical life to grow and expand by facing and overcoming challenges, and to find the inner strength to not be overcome by their failures and disappointments.

"Were one or more of you to be known in their midst, they would turn to you to solve their problems. They would never learn to find the greatness inside themselves by overcoming their challenges. They would never have personal miracles and experiences causing their faith to grow, which is a great power in itself that must be cultivated.

"If you were there to solve their individual and societal problems, they would never learn the give and take necessary to find mutually beneficial paths, even with those seeking different outcomes. Nor would they learn to be strong in their hearts and remain Celestine in their essence when life gives them disappointment and tragedy.

"One of the primary reasons men and women take a physical form and live a physical life in the first place is so they can learn and grow from their experiences. If you were living among them, your very presence would cause them to ask you to do for them instead of doing for themselves. Your presence, instead of benefiting them, would stunt their growth and block one of the primary reasons they came down to Earth in a physical body.

"I hope this explanation is a balm to your disquiet," Miriam said comfortingly. "If it is not, and if you think this is too much for you to faithfully bear, please get up now and depart from us in love and peace. Once you have departed, I will put a veil of forgetfulness upon you and you will remember the events of this day not at all."

Would you be surprised if I told you that not

one person got up to leave or even made a murmur of dissent? As Miriam explained the reasons for the dictate, it made perfect sense. No one was willing to walk out on such an amazing opportunity simply because some parts would be slightly challenging to live with.

"There is still one more limitation you should be aware of before you accept this calling," Miriam revealed. "If you fall away from the light and no longer are worthy to fulfill your responsibilities, your template will be changed back to mortality. If you are past the years you would normally have died, your body will age very rapidly. Within one to three days, you will shrivel and degenerate until you are nothing but old dust blowing away in the wind."

Whoa... that gave me pause, and a few others as well, I think. I was getting light-headed from everything Miriam was revealing. It was really quite a lot to take in all at once. But as I soon discovered, the bigger stretch of the mind was still yet to come—not so much for me, as I had some experience on other worlds. But for everyone else there... they were about to get walloped with something that would strain their credulity and capacity to imagine.

Seeing her audience still raptly attentive, Miriam continued unveiling the intricacies of our calling. "You must wonder what could possibly be so important that the Elohim would change your template to allow you, and only you, to live for another two thousand years in a physical body.

"There are multiple purposes and responsibilities with this calling. All of your lives, most of you have lived in the land of your birth. You know there is a bigger world out there beyond your homeland, but it has never seemed larger than you can imagine. The reality, my brothers and sisters, is it is far more immense than you can possibly dream.

"At night you see the stars in the sky, so numerous you cannot count them. Imagine that each star was a grain of sand, and that you could hold all the stars you can see at night in your hand as grains of sand. The Earth we live on is only one of the grains of sand in your hand. Now remember the longest beach you have ever seen, one where the beach goes on and on out of sight, and where the sand is so deep you can never dig to the bottom.

"All the stars you hold in your hand as grains of sand are infinitesimally insignificant compared to the uncountable grains of sand that are on the beach."

Miriam paused to ensure the momentousness of her next words was felt to the core of our beings. "Though this world and the small familiar part that you live in is all that you know, please understand that for every grain of sand on the endless beach of great depth, there is another Earth out among the stars filled with people like you. Upon most of those Earths are other creatures and beings such as you never imagined. Truly, there are uncountable Earths and other worlds teeming with life that exist out among the endless stars, far more than the one grain of sand that we live upon."

I expected everyone to gasp at her description, but to my surprise they all seemed simply intent on listening. Elohim had chosen well when he had chosen these good brothers and sisters. Then again, perhaps it was all just so incomprehensible to most and they listened without understanding.

Miriam continued enthralling us and stretching our imaginations. "Besides all of the worlds that exist among the stars of the sky that you can see, there are innumerable other worlds that exist in a different layer of the same place that cannot be seen from this world. They too are filled with beings and creatures that are unlike any you have ever encountered or heard of. Your calling also involves these shadow worlds.

"It is the custom of our land that two witnesses establish the truth of a testimony. I give you my testimony that these worlds exist and call upon Salome and Lazarus to bear witness of the truth."

She looked at me. "Lazarus?"

I stood up a little nervously, surprised to be called on without warning. But I knew what she wanted me to say. In as short a time as possible I related what had occurred when I traveled to the other dimensional shadow world of Ferrtho not long ago with Yeshua, Miriam, Salome, and the apostles. I was somewhat self-conscious that people would think me the greatest liar when I started talking about the tiny Hebs and their silent, silver floating airships, and their colorful, translucent city that stretched up into the clouds.

But to my relief no one laughed or got up and walked away. Contrarily, everyone seemed open, interested, and attentive. I left out the part where Miriam stuck my feet to the ground and made me mute, as that wasn't really pertinent to the description of the alien world or beings.

Next Salome got up and related her experiences on other worlds far more bizarre than the one I visited. She had been to multiple worlds with Miriam, Yeshua, and the apostles and described their travel through the portals and the lands and strange creatures they encountered very well. To my surprise, she too was received without heckling or scoffing and instead with keen and sincere attention.

Looking at Bai and Ting and the others who did not speak Aramaic, it seemed from their attentiveness that they must have been hearing Salome and me in their native languages, just as they heard Miriam when she spoke.

I even saw looks of fascination and curiosity on most faces—something I did not expect. In the modern world, there are science fiction movies and television shows that are not that far off the mark from reality in some instances. To a modern human, the things we talked about might be thought to just be fantasy, but at least it would be a fantasy that books, movies, and TV shows had prepared people to grasp.

Not so for even one person sitting at the table besides me and Salome. To the others, we were describing places and people incomprehensibly different in every way from their world, or any place, people, or creature on their world they had ever heard spoken of, to use as a reference.

I expected them to be looking around at each other in abject bewilderment, mocking us because they were incapable of even beginning to fathom the descriptions. But they were open, curious, and accepting, even of that which they could not begin to grasp until they personally experienced it.

I suppose it is not different from how we of faith accept the Elohim, the Father and Mother in the Celestine Realms. Even me, who traveled there, never saw them or heard the Father and Mother speak; yet I know they are real. The truth reverberates in my heart and mind.

My brothers and sisters of light who were present with me that day in our courtyard with Miriam had even more faith than me. They had not died and traveled to the Celestine Realms to know it is a real and tangible place as I had. None of them had seen the multitude of miracles from Yeshua that it had been my privilege to witness. None of them had been resurrected from the dead.

Yet their faith was as strong or stronger than mine, in a reality they had not seen, had not heard, and had not experienced.

I realized that is why they could sit there, hearing of strange worlds and creatures, and be completely receptive to the unknown. What they knew—their love for Yeshua, their conviction in Miriam—allowed them to have faith and trust in that which they did not know. A lesson I learned that day that has benefited me all my long life whenever I have had my own unknown bridges to cross: from the steadfast foundation of what you know with conviction is true, you can leap chasms of uncertainty with full trust in the success of your leap of faith.

"Let us get now to the central reason Elohim is willing to change the template of your physical life into virtual agelessness," Miriam continued. "The distances between the worlds of the stars are far beyond the means of the fastest ship to ever reach in a lifetime of sailing, even if they could sail among the stars.

"And the worlds that are found not in the stars, but in different layers could never be reached by a ship even if it were to sail eternally because they are not in the same time or space as this world and the worlds of the stars that you can see.

"But our Earth, and all other worlds, both those among the stars and those hidden in different layers, are all connected energetically and physically.

Herein lies both the benefit and the challenge, and a primary reason for your calling and blessing of longevity.

"You know if a room is closed up with no openings for air and the door always shut tight, it becomes dank and musty, the air stale and unhealthy, caked with accumulated dust and difficult to breathe. Each of the innumerable worlds is like a room in a house that has no ending or beginning. Each room is connected via a passageway to many other rooms. As long as the doors are open, fresh air circulates from one room to another, and rejuvenating energy from one world to another.

"This was the creative design of Elohim when all the worlds were brought into existence: that they might never grow stale and stagnate, but always be enlivened with new and diverse energy from other worlds; that all might maintain vitality for the health and well-being of their inhabitants.

"As these worlds are very different, so too are their energies disparate and often quite discordant with the energies of our Earth. This is actually necessary to ensure there is a good mix of dissimilar energies to foster an enlivened and vibrant state on all the worlds that exchange dynamism with one another.

"If only energy was exchanged between worlds there would be less need for your calling, but in order for the creations of Elohim to have the opportunity to grow from challenges of their wits and wills, when the gateways are fully open, in addition to the flow of energy, any creature or being can pass through the gateway from one world to another.

"Most that enter from other worlds are fairly benign and cannot venture far from the portal as their resonance for their home world is like a lodestone pulling them back into the passageway. The farther they venture from the gateway, the greater is the force pulling them back to their world.

"However, if they can push with all of their strength through the point of greatest resistance, they can break away from the lodestone-like pull and be free to live their lives on this Earth if the environment of air, water, and temperature will support them. That is normally the outcome, as the more intelligent ones would not try to remain here in the first place if it was not a hospitable environment.

"Many of the strangest animals that you see in this world, the ones that are simply bizarre compared to the normal templates of animals, are likely creatures whose ancestors escaped from other worlds to inhabit this one. But it is not these mostly benign creatures that inhabit this Earth that are of concern or need the attention of your calling.

"The Elohim are watchers, not kindly overseers enmeshed in the lives of their subjects. They are the architects of creation. They laid the foundation. They created and put in place the template and environment by which all things can live, reproduce, grow, expand, and in some instances even evolve and change from the form they were created into something different.

"Understanding the eternal nature of all things, except in extreme circumstances, the Elohim do not interfere or intervene in the lives of their creations. Instead, they give each person complete freedom to rise or fall, expand or shrink, depending upon their own wise or foolish choices and actions. This is true even when imprudent actions and choices result in death and misery. In the context of eternity, pains are not long, and even death is not an end, merely a bump on eternity's road."

"As this is so, you might wonder why bother to pray to the Elohim, if there is little likelihood that they will answer your prayers. Though your prayer may be personalized and addressed to the Elohim, please understand that they are merely the essential focus to initiate the actions you seek by your prayer. Though your prayer does not motivate them to act directly on your behalf, it does tap you into a direct connection to the source of all power and creation.

"When you pray to them, you are actually coalescing your own power and calling upon the many other energies of the universe that can aid you. If you pray together with others for a common cause, the power of the prayer is magnified many times more than your numbers.

"Nevertheless, the Elohim do take action through their chosen stalwarts when the grand design they put in motion is threatened to be altered in ways that would thwart, impede, or reverse the eternal progression of their creations toward greater light. Such as it was when the fallen angels perverted the world. Such as it is now and will continue to increasingly be in the future with undesirable visitors coming through the gateways. You are the defenders they have chosen to turn the tide and hold back the flood upon this world.

"And know that you are not alone. There are others just like you, on many of the worlds of the stars: worthy and valiant Children of Light that stand as guardians of their worlds even as you will for yours.

"Recently on some worlds, and for a longer time on other Earths, various dangerous and lethal creatures from other star worlds and the shadow layers worlds of different times and spaces, have begun entering through the portals, in numbers high enough to cause serious disruption, danger and even eventual extermination of the native people and animals to the worlds to which they are escaping.

"Unlike most unwanted visitors that are quickly pulled back to the resonance of their home world in the shadow spaces, these creatures are not. They are either strong enough or sufficiently intelligent that they break through the resonance barrier. A few types are intelligent enough that they have learned to consciously use the portals to spread to other worlds and make an organized effort to do so.

"Some of the creatures, such as Zartus bugs, are already a scourge on many worlds, creating such havoc that entire nations are dispersing and civilization is reverting to more primitive states. These are the types of consequences that you are called to counter as they radically alter the Elohim's template of creation and eternal progression.

"Many of the uninvited intruders that have come here and to other Earths have acute sentience and intelligence. When you encounter them do not underestimate their threat simply because they do not look like you or any creatures of your world. Though they may appear like bugs, strange animals, or even a form of human, some will be more intelligent and cunning than most people you meet; some will be far more. Many are also physically stronger than you and have deadly means of attack and self-protection that are unlike the people and animals of this world with which you are familiar.

"On this Earth there are one hundred and forty-four permanent portals that lead to the same number of star worlds or shadow worlds in the layers. Each of those in turn have gateways that lead to still other star worlds and shadow worlds. Each couple will be responsible to be guardians of twelve of the permanent gateways.

"Once you have increased your own talents and become Adepts of the Celestine Light, you will be capable of opening your own gateways at any location that will take you to any world among the stars or in the layers that you wish to visit. Lazarus and Salome already have some experience with this ability as they described to you.

"You will be given two tools and a new sense to aid you in your calling. If you choose to accept this responsibility, at the time of your ordination, you will be imbued with an inner knowing that will allow you to feel the presence of any creature that is alien to this Earth if they are within a few minutes' walk from your location. The closer you approach them, the more intense the feeling will become. And the more experienced you are, the further away you will be able to sense dangers."

Miriam held up a clear quartz crystal on a chain. "You will also be given this tool of Celestine Light. It has been specially forged by the Elohim. In order to create and maintain a bond with the crystal, you must continually wear it on a chain around your neck or in some other permanent way that keeps it in contact with your bare skin.

"It will only work for you if you have a personal bond with it. If any creature that would be a serious threat to this Earth or its inhabitants comes through one of the portals which is under your stewardship, the crystal laying against your skin will alert you by becoming quite hot.

"Once alerted, hold it in your left hand with the tip pointing outward and slowly rotate in a circle. It will have an attraction and undeniable pull in the direction of the gate to which you need to make haste."

She held up another small object, but I could not quite make out what it was. "Oftentimes, when you receive a warning from your sentinel crystal that something dangerous has come through a portal, it will be too distant for you to arrive there traveling by foot before the intruder has established resonance with this Earth and departed from the gate vicinity.

"Though it also looks like nothing more than another pretty quartz crystal, this unique device was fashioned by the Savasi. It will allow you to travel instantly to any portal under your guardianship, and you shall each receive one. Keep it on your person, even on the same chain as the other if you like. But be sure any chain is not easily broken or able to slip off your neck and be lost.

"The proximity to your aura will affect a bonding that will only allow the tools to function for you and no other person, unless you are deceased. In that case, another Adept could bond with it over time. No two look alike. Once you have received yours and are bonded with it, there will be no mistaking it for another.

"As I already mentioned, some of you, perhaps even most of you, for various reasons, will not remain upon this Earth for the full duration of your two-thousand-year calling. It will be the responsibility of the mate of anyone who vacates their calling early, through either death or unworthiness, to continue alone in the protective stewardship of the gateways.

"If both the husband and the wife of a guardian couple are no longer upon the Earth or fulfilling their stewardship, it becomes the responsibility of one of the remaining couples to assume stewardship of their portals.

"In this case it may take up to a year of wearing the other person's guardian crystals for a bonding to form that will enable them to work for you. This includes the crystal that can transport you to the portal in an instant. During this transition time, you will need to personally visit each gateway on a regular basis until you have bonded with the new crystals.

"There are also reasons this is a two-thousand-year calling and why it is likely to be only a two-thousand-year calling. In addition to greater knowledge and expertise gained from experiences, your own power and abilities will grow over time.

"During your first hundred years as a Guardian, you may be able to sense alien dangers that are within a five- to ten-minute walk. By your five-hundredth year, you should be able to sense dangerous creatures from worlds of the spaces at least a day's walk from your location. By your thousandth year you will be able to sense the dangerous interlopers several days' walk away. If you make it to your two-thousandth year, you should be able to sense danger to the Earth or its inhabitants from anywhere on this world.

"As the threats will likely increase over the centuries, especially from the foolish leaders of this world as they gain more and more destructive power in their weapons, so will your knowledge and ability to counter them.

"Most of your efforts will be to fight against threats from other worlds against which this Earth has no natural defenses. But there will be occasions when you will need to turn your attention to the foolish leaders of this world and use your powers to prevent their idiocy from destroying the Eden Elohim has created.

"Prior to about two hundred years ago, there was not a need for Guardians on this Earth. Dangers from other star worlds and shadow worlds had not yet presented much of a threat, and the destructive weapons of the Caesars of this world, while violent and rending, could affect nothing other than on a very small scale. However, as time passes the destructive capabilities of the weapons of men will grow, even to the point that all of the world could be destroyed if the Guardians of the Earth do not prevent it. This is a fate that has already occurred on other worlds.

"By the time you have reached your two-thousandth year, you will personally have grown and expanded in this holy calling as great as you have need. It will be time for you to reunite with your loved ones that passed lifetimes before and to move onward to a new and greater calling, invigorated by different challenges that you might continue to become more than you have been.

"Normally, the Elohim would not ask you to remain in a calling like this for so long. But because of the vanity of men and the desire of a few to have dominion over the many, the Celestine Light will become very weak in this world for many hundreds of years, even more than a millennium. There will not be many Children of Light upon it who are worthy and capable of replacing you as Guardians.

"The Elohim foretell a return and expansion of the Celestine Light upon the Earth as you near your two-thousandth year. There will be Children of Light capable of fulfilling your stewardship as Guardians. Worthy Children of Light born in those days will be called and ordained as you will be today to be the Guardians of Earth. You will then be freed from this stewardship to pursue an even greater one.

"The small number of invasive creatures from other worlds that have traversed the portals up until now have either been no threat or were removed by the angels of Elohim. But the numbers of the dangerous ones have increased and will continue to do so. The responsibility of protecting your Earth must be given to those of you who call it home, not continue to fall upon the angels of Elohim. It is only by doing for yourself, even in the face of adversity, that you grow into your potential.

"When you are called to do your duty and protect your world when it is threatened by dangerous intruders from other worlds, you will have three options. Any person or creature other than the highest-level Adept of the Celestine Light cannot pass through a portal without being held within the lodestone pull of its resonance for at least an hour and often much longer. This is true for any and all creatures you will be called to defend against. It is during this time, while they are confined to a small geographical area, that they are most vulnerable and easiest to confront. You would be wise to act during that window of opportunity if at all possible.

"If you have enough time and means to subdue the intruder into unconsciousness without injuring or killing it, you can put a forget spell upon it, which I will teach you, and carry it back through the portal to its home world. Once there, put a revulsion spell upon it for the portal, then return to your world. When the creature awakens it will have no memories of its travels through the gateway. Instead, it will have an intense revulsion, even fear of the portal, and will never make attempt to transit it again.

"The second method you can use to abate a threat is to put an energy net across the entrance to the portal. This is trickier than it sounds. It cannot be a permanent net as it would interfere too long with the needed energy flow between worlds to keep both vitalized. Also, because the gateways are not static, but expand and contract on a regular basis as they breathe, energy nets can be stressed and deteriorate until they simply fall apart. But a net is a good choice at times, especially when you are faced with a great number of harmful creatures coming through and you simply need to quickly plug the outlet.

"The last option is to take the life of the invading creature. This should be a last resort as all life is precious, but you are justified in taking a life in self-defense, or in defense of your family or world. Do not hesitate to take this extreme measure if neither of the other options is viable. Remember, every malevolent creature you do not neutralize in one way or the other is a threat to the life of the people and animals of your Earth. It is your Earth you will be guardians and stewards over. It is your Earth that you must protect."

Miriam stopped speaking and just looked at us in silence with the beginnings of a smile upturning the corners of her lips. I wasn't sure if she was finished inundating us with knowledge or was pausing to see if anyone had questions. But she did not speak and neither did anyone else. For our part, I think most, if not all of us that had been listening to her, were still too numbed by the enormity of it all for our brains to activate our mouths to articulate words.

"It is time now for those of you who are willing to assume the calling I have explained, to be ordained and set apart to fulfill it," Miriam announced. "Any who are not prepared at this time in their heart and mind, in their faith and conviction, need to depart now in love. You will have no memory of this meeting and no shame in going about your life as you always have. As this is a calling for couples, if one of you is uncertain about taking on this stewardship, you both must depart from us now in love."

I looked at Hannah and she at me. "I am ready and excited," I whispered to her.

"As am I, Lazarus," she agreed quietly with a big smile. "I am humbled and thrilled to have such a blessing. Our lives are never dull in the Celestine Light, are they?"

Looking around the tables, I noticed all the other couples having similar whispered conversations. The four that were singles just looked back and forth from one to another with no words and inscrutable silent messages writ upon their faces. Salome seemed to be trying to avoid eye contact with anyone other than Miriam. But she got no solace from her, as Miriam just held her index finger to her lips to ask Salome to remain quiet and not question her at the moment.

"I sense that all of you remain committed to this stewardship. You were chosen well," Miriam affirmed. "Your many questions about specifics: the how, when, and why, will all be answered in the coming days as I begin your training. But now it is my privilege and blessing to represent Elohim and ordain you to this high and holy calling. Remain where you are seated. I shall walk around behind each of you to lay my hands upon your head to call and set you apart with this stewardship and invest you with the sixth sense Elohim has promised you."

She looked at me. "And I shall begin with my brother Lazarus and his beloved Hannah."

Miriam took off her sandals and walked barefoot over to where I was sitting on a bench at the table with Hannah. She came up and laid both of her hands upon my head, connecting the Alpha/Omega energy gateways in her hands to the ones on the top of my head.

"Remove your sandals, Lazarus," she directed, "and clasp your hands together in the prayer position." I did as she asked. My silent curiosity in my own mind, as to why, was quickly answered.

Miriam looked to the others. "As I have asked Lazarus, so I ask all of you. Prepare yourselves by removing your footwear and resting your bare feet upon the bare ground. Hold your hands in the prayer position once I come to you. This connects the three pairs of energy gateways in your body in a most powerful loop. Through your feet comes the grounded energy of our Earth, our home, and with it a connection to all life upon it. The energy flowing from my hands into the gateways at the top of your head imbues you directly with the essence of the Elohim to whom I am linked. With your hands together in the prayer position you seal off the possibility of any outside energy interfering. You are for this moment the truest, most pure connection between heaven and Earth."

She looked off to the side and down at me. "Are you ready, Lazarus?"

"I am," I nodded affirmatively.

"Lazarus of Bethany," she began, "at the direction of the Elohim and by their authority, I ordain you to the calling of Earth Guardian. You are set apart to be a defender of all life upon the Earth; to protect the living people and creatures of Earth from any dangers, be they native or invaders from other worlds, against which they would have no defense or that would irreparably harm the balance and abundance of life on the Earth."

"As long as you remain worthy, the template of your physical body is changed at this moment from mortality to immortality, provided you care for it and nurture it, are prudent, and do not allow it to be felled by sickness, accident, or an enemy's blow.

"You are also endowed from this very moment with a new sense, a sixth sense, that will alert you to any dangers from any living creature, being, or threat of any kind that has entered this world from another, or is native to this Earth and threatens destruction to the template of life laid down by

Elohim.

"May you be blessed to fulfill your calling as a worthy son of Elohim. In the name of Yeshua, the Lord of Light, so be it."

Tears flowed freely down my cheeks, and a feeling of utter euphoria filled me as Miriam spoke, and each and every person around the tables gave their confirmation of my ordination with a hearty, "So be it!"

One by one, beginning next with my wife Hannah, Miriam circled the tables, standing behind each person and ordaining them to the same blessed calling as Earth Guardian. One by one, we all endorsed them in their new stewardship with firm affirmations of, "So be it!"

With each of the four who were not yet couples, she ordained them to their calling but did not yet give them the sixth sense or change their physical template into near immortality.

When the last of us had been ordained, Miriam finally sat down. I could see her take a deep breath and slowly exhale as she relaxed and embraced Salome. I realized her talk and our ordinations were probably the first big responsibility in her new calling as the Angel of the Covenant, and she must be relieved that it had all gone well.

Of course, we were all so enthralled and curious about our new stewardship that we never left the table for the remainder of the day. We stayed, asking questions of Miriam and reveling in and being astounded by her answers until the night had descended and it was too dark to continue. All of us were affected in different ways and had varying life situations that would need to be worked through. But we each knew with the deepest conviction that our lives would never be the same again.

Chapter 5
PORTALS

Miriam asked us to all meet again at my house in Bethany exactly one week later to begin our training as Earth Guardians. Needless to say, with everyone anxious to begin, nobody was late! She requested that all employees be given the day off so only those she had invited were at my house. Even all the children were taken over to cousins on the other side of town.

It seemed like déjà vu as once again we were all seated at the tables in the courtyard as Miriam addressed us. "Good day, stalwarts of the Earth. Today you begin your training as Earth Guardians. A word of caution. It is not too early in your immortality, even while you are still within your normal human lifetime, to lose your life from foolishness. You will be exposed to many dangers in your training with unfamiliar creatures and environments. See that you follow my instructions implicitly, else you end your journey before it has actually begun."

That was a sobering way to begin, I thought. It

pretty much drained all the excitement that had been building during the last week of anticipation. But I did not have long to reflect before Miriam called upon me.

"Lazarus, please come and stand next to me."

I got up slowly and came to stand next to my sister, still somewhat glum about being reminded that we were mortal immortals as the first words out of her mouth.

Standing to Miriam's right, she placed her hand upon my shoulder. "As you know, Lazarus has already traveled to other worlds, as has Salome," she added, glancing over and smiling at her long-time companion sitting next to my wife Hannah.

"Today you will have the opportunity to visit several worlds very briefly so you can experience the different environments and become accustomed to some of the creatures that inhabit them.

"Some of you will travel to shadow worlds inhabited by beings of lesser light than any of the people or creatures of this Earth. Most of those creatures will hurt you if they can.

"Others will visit star worlds that are as vibrant, beautiful, and full of higher life as this one that we call home. Some of you will travel to places that have Alamars like you but more primitive in their lifestyle. Others will have Alamars and similar races but far more advanced in their civilization than those you have known.

"Do not be lulled into complacency by the

beauty of the worlds or the similarities of the inhabitants to you. Just like the world we live in, you will be considered an enemy by many you might encounter simply because you are a stranger and different. I would advise you to have no interaction with the local creatures or inhabitants. Try to limit your visits to simple, safe observational excursions.

"Some of you will encounter more bizarre places where the inhabitants may be less or more advanced than you, but they will not be Alamars like you or in any way resemble Alamars. How will you react if you encounter a creature that for all appearances seems to be a giant bug but is more intelligent than you and more advanced in its civilization than the cities you have known?

"Or perhaps you will encounter an enormous mosquito as large as you that would like nothing better than to drain every drop of blood from your body.

"There will be dangers on any world you end up visiting, but you must come to know these worlds that connect to yours and the malevolent creatures that may someday come through portals where you will be the only defense to protect your world.

"To help you grow into this stewardship, it should be a goal of yours every day of your life to always be learning more, always gaining new knowledge about everything in existence.

"Knowledge is power. I exhort you to be knowledge sponges. Sometimes, standing alone, it is a greater power than your most potent Celestine gifts. But used in conjunction with abilities you have honed, knowledge allows you to better utilize your natural and blessed power. It ensures a greater chance of success in any endeavor in direct proportion to the knowledge you have available to aid you."

Taking a couple of steps away from me, Miriam held her hands in the prayer position over her chest for a moment, bowed her head, then quickly looked up and thrust her palms, still pressed together, skyward. At their highest point she separated her hands and lowered her extended arms sideways while forcefully saying, "Extavaz."

Immediately we were encircled by numerous opaque, electric blue tunnels, with translucent spinning entrances a little wider than the height of a man, leading outward from the courtyard and passing through anything they encountered, from a wall to my house!

I quickly looked around and counted twelve in total. It was very weird looking at those that passed through my house. It was as if the rooms of my house, including my bedchamber, suddenly had large semi-translucent pipes running right through the middle of them.

As the tunnels appeared, everyone sitting at the tables stood up in shock, wonder, and perhaps some fear of the unknown. There were quite a number of different looks on people's faces.

Miriam encouraged everyone to walk around the courtyard and peer through the entrance of the various tunnels to see what they could perceive at the other end. There were soon many exclamations of amazement as everyone did as she bid and saw glimpses of the many worlds at the other end of the tunnels.

"These tunnels are all passageways to other worlds," Miriam explained as she walked among us while we peered through one tunnel entrance after another.

"Many are shadow worlds that occupy the same space as this Earth and the worlds of these heavens. However, these places cannot be seen by looking at the stars in the sky. Though they occupy the same space, they are on a different level of energy. As such, they are usually imperceptible. In most cases it is not an energy disharmonious to the energy of this world; it is merely different.

"Other portals lead to star worlds, which are places on the same physical plane as the Earth we live upon. If you had a ship that sailed the stars and could traverse the great distance between star worlds, you could travel on that ship and someday reach your destination. But star worlds can be reached in a much shorter time simply by traveling through a gateway tunnel similar to one of these you now see in the courtyard."

Pretty much everyone seemed very confused by Miriam's explanation of the shadow worlds and the star worlds, so she tried to explain it further.

"Think about a bucket filled with twelve layers of different materials. The bucket holds the endless expanse of life that Elohim has created."

Everyone was kind of paying attention to what she was saying but also somewhat distracted by the fascination of looking at what was beyond the far end of the various tunnels. Seeing she wasn't holding everyone's attention as well as she would have liked, Miriam asked me to bring a large bowl and a thin clay pipe. She asked Hannah to bring her some swaths of fabric about a foot in size.

Hannah and I quickly returned with the items she requested, and everyone gathered around as she explained further. She reached down to the hard-packed courtyard ground. Where her hand came to rest suddenly turned into loose sand like at the ocean beach.

She reached into the sand and scooped some into her hand, then poured it into the bowl. Though the sand she picked up was light in color, as it came out of her hand it was very blue. Gathering a few more handfuls, she emptied them into the bowl. Soon a layer of blue sand covered the bottom. But she had somehow increased its quantity because the bottom was covered at least two inches thick, which was far more sand than she had dropped into the bowl.

"Imagine if you will that the blue sand represents every speck of your Earth: all the land, the oceans, the animals, the plants, and all the people exist in the blue sand."

Miriam placed one of the swaths of fabric over the blue sand. She grabbed another handful of sand and emptied it into the bowl. This one came out bright red in color as it dropped from her hand into the bowl. After the red layer had completely covered the blue layer, Miriam asked us to, "imagine the red sand is another Earth. The people, plants, animals, and everything about it are different than your Earth.

"A very important part of understanding is that though both the blue and the red occupy the same bowl, there is a barrier between them. Even though each touches the other along their entire plane, because of their differing energies and the barrier, they cannot perceive one another under normal circumstances. The people of the blue world only know about the blue world, and the people of the red world only know about the red."

Miriam continued scooping up sand and added a third layer of yellow, then another of purple, and another of green, each separated by a layer of fabric. "In this bowl there are only five layers," she explained. "But in the immensity of what the Elohim created, there are innumerable layers, innumerable worlds, both the kind you can gaze toward when you look at the stars and the shadow worlds that you cannot see no matter where you look with eyes of man."

Miriam reached down and lifted up the finger-thick clay pipe I had brought her. She held it on each end and stared at it for a moment, and it suddenly turned into the clearest glass. Everyone looked at it in wonder, not just at Miriam's miraculous transformation but at the glass pipe, a marvel never before seen. We had glass vessels and glass blowers in Israel, but none who could make a clear straw of glass such as we saw Miriam create from the clay pipe.

Miriam smiled, seeing the attentive look on everyone's face, and continued her explanation. "The shadow worlds exist in the same space, the same bowl, but on a different energy level separated by a barrier."

She poked the clear tube into the top layer of green sand. "But the barrier can be pierced."

Even as she spoke we saw the glass tube descending down further than the top layer of green sand. When it stopped it was clearly resting on the bottom of the bowl.

Miriam invited each of us to come and stare down the glass tube, which we all did one by one. The tube had, through some Miriam magic, passed through each of the fabric barriers and we could dimly make out the various layers of colored sand, as it was midday and the sun was directly overhead, somewhat illuminating inside the tube.

"The glass tube passing through the barriers and various layers of colored sand is like the twelve passageways you see around you," Miriam explained.

"In both cases, the tunnels created allow passage between worlds that are normally unseen and unperceived.

"But when a portal is open, any creature, including you or any other person, can pass through from one world to another with as few as a dozen steps."

Miriam lifted out the glass tube. It was filled with the five colored sands all mixed up together and not separated into distinct layers as you would expect from the cloth separation barriers.

She held the tube up for us to look at as she blocked each end with a finger. "Just as you see all of these sands intermingled, so the energies from all of the shadow worlds have the opportunity to pass through the gateways and intermingle with the energy of your Earth and the innumerable other Earths that exist among the stars of the sky.

"However, not just benign energies pass through from one world to another. Any person or creature near a portal can also pass through it into another world. Most of these creatures have no resonance for the new world. Like iron to a lodestone, they are soon pulled back to their own world. The further they move away from the portal, the stronger the attraction pulling them back becomes.

"Nonetheless, there is a point they can break through the attraction pulling them back and be free to roam the new world. Most of them will not live more than a few days to a few weeks on other worlds because the new worlds, in many cases, do not contain the food many creatures need to sustain their lives, or the environments are too hot or too cold, too light or too dark, or the air is toxic to them.

"Humans can survive eating a wide variety of foods, but that is not the case for many other creatures, both from this world and others. Many have highly specialized diets and do not have the physical capacity to digest other types of food, so they soon die of starvation when they transit to an alien world.

"The problems that arise from creatures coming from other worlds are of two varieties. The creatures that soon perish can often still inflict pain, suffering, and death upon the people and animals of this world before they die themselves.

"Then there are those that pass through the retraction barrier, become free to roam your Earth, and have the ability to survive upon it and in some cases thrive and reproduce on it. As your Earth has no exposure to creatures such as these, they can wreak havoc and considerable death and destruction upon its defenseless people and animals. One of your primary responsibilities as Guardians will be to prevent these types of creatures from escaping onto this Earth."

Miriam swung her arm around, pointing to the

portals surrounding us. "Each of these portals leads to a world with particularly deadly creatures. Some are on shadow worlds and others on star worlds. As couples, choose one of the twelve portals and pass through it to the other side.

"I will surround your bodies with a thin translucent shield of limited protection. You will be able to walk freely about, observing the creatures and the vegetation, but neither plant nor animal will be able to penetrate the shield with a bite, claws, poison, or a sting, or even crushing strength. But be cautious where you walk, as there are limits to this protective skin. If a giant rock falls on your head, or you fall a great distance off a cliff, or into a pool of water and cannot swim, you may perish.

"Regardless of which portal you choose and which world you visit, time will not pass there in the same manner it does here. Try to keep track in your mind of the passing of time as you count it on this world.

"Though this is intended to just be a quick look at a different world, the dangers you may encounter will be very real. If you remember to follow my instructions and admonitions, I'm sure all will be well. If not, and you manage to remain alive, please return to the courtyard after a few hours."

Chapter 6
THE OTHER SIDE OF THE
BEDCHAMBER

Not surprisingly, after Miriam's announcement ending in, "if you manage to remain alive, please return to the courtyard after a few hours," it did not motivate anyone to move very rapidly toward the portals. We all continued to just mill about. Miriam didn't have much patience with our timidity.

"Scoot!" she commanded. "Your lesson for the day is on the other side of the gateway, not standing around in a courtyard in Bethany."

With some remaining hesitancy, we all moved off toward the entrance to a portal. Hannah and I chose the one passing through our bedchamber. It was our sacred space, and it almost felt defiled knowing there was a way alien creatures could be traipsing through it. I wanted to see for myself who those bodacious interlopers might be.

I was curious to see who the single people would pair up with. Right away it was obvious that both Salome and Elissa wanted to go with Kudar-Iluna. Both completely ignored the Samaritan servant

Joshua as if he did not even exist. I expected such would be the case and wasn't surprised. Kudar-Iluna was an enormous man, formidable in every way, and somewhat good-looking in a rugged sort of way. He was certainly the person anyone would trust to defend them from physical danger or get them out of any predicament requiring physical strength. He was also a Celestine and long-time member of our communities of light.

Joshua, on the other hand, was just an average man physically. But he was also a Samaritan, a people scorned by Israelites because of their perversion of traditional Hebrew teachings. Nor could it be overlooked that he was a lowly servant. Not at all someone either Salome, the daughter of a king, or Elissa, the former High Priestess of the main pagan temple in Tyre and a wealthy, highly esteemed independent woman, would naturally pair up with.

Hannah was ready to enter the portal, but holding her hand, I gave it a gentle tug backward and pointed toward Salome and Elissa. I wanted to see how their mutual desire to go with Kudar-Iluna would end up. While we were waiting and watching, all of the other couples disappeared down the portals they had chosen.

"I have known Kudar-Iluna. He is not a stranger to me," Salome asserted.

"He stood by me during Yeshua's ascension, and he should stand by me now!" she insisted.

"Poof!" Elissa exhaled dismissively. "From what I remember, it was you who stood by him, not the other way around."

Kudar-Iluna had a broad smile on his face as he watched the women wrangling over who would accompany him. I don't know if it was because he found the situation humorous or liked the idea of two women fighting over the pleasure of his company.

"You are a Tyrian, and Joshua is a Samaritan. You two foreigners would be best together," Salome insisted.

"Thank you for such excellent logic," Elissa complimented. "By that reasoning, Kudar-Iluna should accompany me, as he is an Amorite who is also a foreigner in this Hebrew land."

"Not true!" Salome refuted. "He comes from an ancient people who were here before the Hebrews. He is a son of this land, even as I am a daughter. You need to go with the other foreigner," she insisted, pointing to Joshua. The poor guy just stood off all alone, obviously sad that neither of the women wanted to have him accompany them.

Before the disagreement between the ladies could progress any further, Miriam walked over to them. "Sisters, sisters with high and holy callings. Are you holding yourselves to the high standards of Celestines in your thoughts and actions?" Both women held their heads down meekly in silent reply.

"It would seem the two of you need to get to know one another better, that you might become dear friends. It is a long journey you embark upon to be immortal for two thousand years. Your only true friends will be other immortals. It would be wise to begin cultivating your friendships even from this moment.

"Therefore, I want the two of you to travel together through a portal. Kudar-Iluna will go with Joshua."

Looking around at everyone's faces after this pronouncement, it didn't appear as if either of the men or women were happy with this arrangement. But as Miriam had declared it, nobody was going to object.

Hannah and I watched both of the other pairs disappear into portals. We were the last remaining and waved to Miriam in parting as she stood alone in the courtyard and we entered the gateway.

"Is this going to be similar to the world of Ferrtho you traveled to with Yeshua?" Hannah wondered as we transited the short, opaque, white-walled tunnel.

The walls were dimly translucent, and we could make out our bedroom furniture as we passed through the room. The portal tunnel simply cut a circular passageway through anything in its path. But the objects, be they furniture or walls, still remained, albeit with a large hole in them. I wondered what would happen if an animal or person was standing in the way of a portal passage when it opened. Would they end up with big holes in them as well?

"I do not know," I answered honestly. "Ferrtho is the only world I have been to. From what Miriam said and remarks I have heard from others that have traveled to shadow worlds, there can be great differences between them."

We didn't have long to ponder. After just a few steps we were at the other end of the portal. It was actually quite a pleasant-looking world we saw before us. We came out upon a ridge overlooking a verdant valley. The air temperature was a bit hot and humid but not too uncomfortable. A bright yellow sun shone overhead in the blue sky, very similar to the sun of our Earth, just a bit larger. Everywhere we looked was densely forested with tropical, frond, and palm-like plants which were astoundingly green in many shades of the color.

"Oh my! Look at that huge waterfall in the distance," Hannah exclaimed, pointing across the valley at the far perimeter wall of mountains.

It was truly a sight to behold. Even in the distance, it was easy to discern that it was taller by far not only than any waterfall I had ever seen, but greater in height than even the loftiest of the great cedars in the mountains of Lebanon.

"An hour is not much time," I noted. "We could walk for a half hour and then return to the portal, or just sit here by the entrance and observe what comes by. Which would you prefer?" I asked Hannah.

"I want to go explore!" she said enthusiastically. "Think about it. This is an entirely new world. We are the first humans from our Earth to ever come here. The very, very first people. No other human eyes have ever gazed upon the beauty we see. And it is more lush and beautiful than any land I have ever imagined! Surely even the Celestine kingdom could be no more delightful than this."

"It is comparable to the Celestine realms in its splendor," I agreed.

"And we are protected from anything physically hurting us," Hannah added. "As long as we watch our step and do not fall off a cliff, I cannot imagine a more exciting way to begin our training to be guardians."

"Alright then, let's be off!" I said, grabbing Hannah by the hand and heading down the hillside toward what appeared, by the meandering dark line at the bottom of the valley, to be a stream or river hidden beneath the dense foliage.

We did not get very far. We had been walking down the slope about five minutes when suddenly a dark shadow came over us, blotting out the sun. I was still holding Hannah's hand as we were walking. Together we looked up to see what could be causing a shadow in the cloudless sky.

We didn't have more than a horrified moment of discernment before the talons of a gigantic bird seized us in its monstrously large feet. Each of the scaly five digits on the foot was as big as one of my legs. And the sharp talons on the tip of each toe were as long as the large swords of the desert nomads of Sinai.

Up, up high into the sky the great bird carried us, firmly grasping me in one foot and Hannah in the other. In moments we were a long distance from the portal, and I seriously doubted we would be able to return to the courtyard within a few hours as Miriam had requested.

It was a very strange sensation to be in the grip of mighty talons but, because of our protective body shields, to not feel the bone-crushing clamp in the slightest. I had no doubt the monster was trying to squeeze the life out of us as it flew. It was sure going to be unpleasantly surprised when we arrived at wherever it was taking us to find that we were still alive!

Hannah got her wish to see the great waterfall. After what seemed only like a couple of minutes, the mighty bird beat its massive wings with extra effort and carried us up the face of the waterfall to a cliff on a mountain overlooking the falls. Into a massive cavern it flew and lightly dropped us upon the bare rock floor just inside the entrance.

A riotous cacophony of screeching sounds greeted our arrival, and two of the scariest-looking creatures you could ever imagine came charging out of the dark abyss of the cave. Gaping mouths with pink interiors and serpent-like long tongues opened wide to devour us! Though they were featherless and quite ugly, I had to conclude that these were baby versions of the giant bird that had effortlessly plucked us off the hillside by the portal.

I was at a complete loss as to how to react. I quickly put both arms around Hannah to try and shield her from the ravenous baby monsters, but could think of no way to proactively defend us from the two frightening monsters. There were no sticks or loose rocks or anything I could throw at the little demons. And their gigantic mother was guarding the cavern entrance, preventing any escape. Of course, I had left my short sword back in Bethany, remembering Yeshua's admonition when we traveled to Ferrtho to not bring it, as it wouldn't be of any use. Well, it certainly would have been of some use in this false paradise!

In a matter of seconds, it was too late to do anything anyway. I was just reaching for the short little dagger I always carried in my belt. Not that it would be more than a pinprick to these enormous baby birds. But before I could even pull it out, one baby hellion grabbed me in its beak and the other grabbed Hannah. A violent shake by each bird ripped us out of each other's grasp. Before I could even react, the bird turned me upside down above it and, with rapid head bobbing, began swallowing me whole! It took just a moment for me to pass through its mouth. I took a deep breath of air just before my head entered the suffocating confines of the bird's throat as my body headed downward into the darkness toward its putrid stomach.

They say memories of your life pass before you in a second as you are about to die. I had no such memories, which I took as a good sign. But my mind suddenly was working at a speed I never imagined possible. In the single second after my head first entered the darkness of the creature's throat, I thought of Hannah suffering the same fate as me. But ere that thought entered my head, it was replaced with a rapid calculation of how I could escape and free Hannah too before we both suffocated from lack of air to breathe inside the bellies of the baby monsters.

For me it was easy. I freed my dagger and started poking the bird as fast and as many times as I could wherever I could reach. It took less than a dozen stabbings with the dagger on the soft, vulnerable inner tissues before the little demon squeezed its stomach muscles and violently ejected me back out of its mouth onto the cave floor.

The baby that had swallowed me was still having dry heaves and was out of the fray. The other baby looked at me in disbelief, as I'm sure they had never seen a prey that had popped back out after it had been swallowed.

A quick glance toward the mother bird showed only her legs at the cavern entrance, so apparently she had not seen me expunged and had not yet realized something was amiss. Before she could become aware, I rushed toward the other baby, which was about the size of an Asian elephant. Before it could react, I leaped up upon its back, straddling its neck right where it met its body. I was just about ready to drive my dagger into its neck, then slit its throat to free Hannah when I heard a voice in my head screaming in Aramaic.

My first thought was it must be Hannah. Who else would be speaking Aramaic in my head? But the next words I heard banished that foolish thought!

"Hurt not my baby, bug who has a brain!" It was the mother bird speaking to me in my mind, in Aramaic. How, oh how, could that be possible, let alone be possible on some strange and distant world?

I hesitated but a moment, as I knew a moment was all Hannah had before she would suffocate in the gullet of the bird. The sharp edge of my Damascus dagger was against the bird's exposed throat as I held on to a mass of its neck feathers with my other hand in case it tried to throw me off.

"My wife will live!" I screamed aloud, looking at the enormous dark brown feathered head and gigantic angry yellow eyeball of the mother bird peering into the cave.

"If your young one does not expel my wife before I take two more breaths, I will slit its throat."

The young bird must have understood my threat.

No sooner did I speak than the baby monster heaved a few times while bobbing its head, and Hannah was quickly spit out upon the cavern floor as I had been. She was greatly disheveled and dazed, but praise Elohim, I could see she was still breathing, taking in deep lungfuls of air as she sought to revitalize her lungs from the claustrophobic suffocation she had been enduring. I leapt off the baby monster and quickly was at my wife's side.

The mother bird entered the cavern with her head leaning forward, looking at me very threateningly. She eyed me in menacing silence for a couple of long minutes while Hannah and I cradled each other with our backs against one of the cavern walls for the tiny amount of protection we imagined it afforded us.

"I thought I heard you talking when I was carrying you to the nest," I heard the mother monster speak in my mind, once again in Aramaic, my native language.

"But I concluded it was just the wind, as everyone knows bugs, other than Nart Bugs, can do naught but mumble gibberish because they have such tiny little brains."

If I could hear her, I assumed she could also hear me. So I answered her in my mind, hoping we had a two-way telepathic connection. "I can speak. I can think, and I can feel in my heart," I asserted.

My reply prompted stoic silence from the giant bird, so I continued talking to her in my mind. "I can see you too have a heart that loves your babies. My wife and I also have children that we love and wish to return to. We did not come here to harm you or your young ones."

"I am still thinking I will let my babies eat you," the mother monster grumbled. "Your apparent intelligence is surprising, but not enough to deny my babies a meal. Answer some of my questions and perhaps I will let one of you go free."

I did not have anything to barter a better deal. Though I had no intention of being eaten again, or allowing Hannah to be, I decided to play along with the mother to see if some means of escape would present itself.

"Ask your questions, bird. Perhaps my answers will delight you enough that you will let both of us go free."

"Unlikely," the mother said. "Was that an attempt at humor? You are a most curious bug."

"I, we, are not bugs," I protested.

"You are small, nearly defenseless, and have no purpose in life other than to be food. You are a bug. But it is most curious that you can speak Taglag in your mind. How did you learn our language, and do other bugs like you have the ability to speak in your minds?"

I shook my head negatively. "It is you that are speaking my native language of Aramaic. I was startled beyond belief to hear it. Perhaps it is that we speak in our native tongue and the other hears the words in the language they comprehend."

"It would seem to be so," the mother bird agreed, "but I have never encountered this before. All the intelligent beings upon this large world communicate in their minds except the Nart bugs, but none are fluent in the languages of other species unless they have studied them for many circuits around the sun."

"What is your name?" I asked, hoping to establish a bit more of a rapport.

"I am Latalizq," she responded. "I have never imagined a bug to have a name or a need for one, but as you asked me for mine, it can only mean that you also have one. What is it?"

"I am Lazarus," I said, putting a finger on my chest.

I gently touched Hannah's face. "And this is my beloved wife, Hannah."

"Wife? What is a wife?" Latalizq asked.

The bird had babies. How could she not know what a wife was, I wondered?

"My mate, the mother of my children, my eternal companion and best friend," I explained.

"You remain always with the same bug to produce children?" Latalizq asked with some incredulity. "That is certainly evidence of your primitive brain. There is no surer way than continually reproducing with the same sex partner to guarantee the genesis of a weak and sickly posterity."

"I noticed you did not have a male partner

around," I said. "I thought perhaps he was just out on important big bird business."

"I cannot even comprehend the thought of having to endure a boorish male day in and day out," she replied. "What purpose could a male possibly serve other than a few minutes of pleasurable sex to ensure fertility?"

"Well, they could help get food for the babies or guard them from predators while you are away getting food," I explained, thinking about the ways of birds on my Earth. Although I gulped a bit afterward, realizing it was probably not a good idea to be bringing up the subject of food again as Hannah and I were still on the menu.

Latalizq rolled her big yellow eyes upward. "As if any male would ever have the slightest interest in spending time caring for young ones. You bugs have very strange ways. It is no wonder you are far down on the food chain.

"On another subject, bug, where are you from? I have never encountered bugs like you before. You look like Narts, but you can talk in your mind and are not riding a Nagasa. It is amazingly curious that you can speak telepathically like an intelligent creature, but obviously are a reject of nature as you have no defensive capabilities except your tiny hand tooth."

"Lazarus," is all I said in response. I wanted to know what a Nart and Nagasa were, but held my question to make the more important point that I had a name and was not an item of food.

Latalizq eyed me menacingly again. "Answer me, bug."

"Stop calling me 'bug' and use my name, and I will answer your questions."

"Just because I wanted to know your name does not mean I will stoop to speak it," she objected. "One does not call the food they eat by a personal name. It is quandary enough that I am speaking to you."

I crossed my arms over my chest and glared right back at her. I knew this was a crucial moment. I had seen many people back home who, once they had named one of their chickens, goats, or sheep, became attached to it in a way that they always spared it from the dinner table. I was hoping such a trick would spare our lives as well.

"Lazarus is my name. Call me by my name and I will answer all of your questions," I promised.

"Very well, bug Lazarus. Where are you from?"

I sighed in a bit of exasperation. I suppose "bug Lazarus" was some forward progress in our situation.

"Why do you wish to know, big bird Latalizq?" I asked, throwing some of her own disrespect back at her.

Latalizq gave me that evil eye look again and, crouching down, fully entered the cavern, sticking her massive head close enough to us that we could feel and smell her fetid breath as she exhaled.

"Answer me, little bug Lazarus, or you will regret your temerity," she threatened.

In response, I held Hannah protectively closer with an arm over her shoulder and held my dagger pointing out. Though I felt I was making progress establishing a rapport in my conversation with Latalizq, I wouldn't have hesitated to stab her in the eye if she tried to grab us in her massive, sharp-edged beak.

Then, before my mind could comprehend or my muscles react, without the slightest warning and with a blurring speed I wouldn't have thought possible, Latalizq snapped her massive head forward and, before I could even blink, deftly ripped the dagger right out of my hand. She backed out of the cavern, spit the dagger over the side of the cliff, and returned to once more tower over us, blocking most of the light coming in through the cavern entrance with her huge, feathered body.

"As you might have surmised, little bug Lazarus, I have become bored with our conversation. Now that your ridiculous hand tooth is gone, I have decided to let my babies eat you, for they are very hungry. But rather than have you slowly suffocate inside their bellies, I will give you a fast death by quickly tearing off your heads if you first tell me where you are from."

I knew I had to keep talking. Every second we were talking was a moment we were still alive. "Why do you want to know where we are from?"

I asked.

She cocked her head back and forth each direction as she contemplated her answer for a moment. "I will be honest with you, little bug Lazarus. I have never found a prey so defenseless and easy to catch. I want to find more of your kind that I might raise more chicks with a plentiful food source."

"Why would I give you such information?" I asked with incredulous disbelief.

"You think my wife and I are so enamored of a few more minutes of life that we would betray our entire race to a similar fate? You are very wrong and are an unbelievably stupid bird, far less intelligent than I had given you credit for!" I spat defiantly.

If these were to be my last moments of life, I wanted to go out boldly, not whimpering and cowering in fear.

And it seemed that my last moments were coming as Latalizq took two more steps to be upon us and opened her horrendous beak to grab us. I said a quick prayer to Elohim for deliverance just before she was going to engulf me and Hannah in one bite.

I was just about to tell Hannah that I loved her and would forever when she thankfully spoiled the moment and remembered something important that I had forgotten, being so caught up in the drama of the moment.

"Stop!" Hannah yelled with a voice louder than

I knew she was capable of. Though she yelled out loud, I also heard her in my mind. It was a weird sensation.

Latalizq stopped in mid-bite and stepped back a single step. "The female speaks too?" Latalizq marveled.

"It will not help you, female bug. I have already made my decision."

Once again she stepped forward, and once again Hannah yelled out at her. "If you feed us to your babies, we will die, but so will they!" Well, I didn't see how that was true. But it did once again stop Latalizq from grabbing us to feed her babies.

"I am listening, female bug."

Hannah stepped away from me and moved toward the enormous monster in front of us. "You want to know where we are from, Latalizq? We are from another world, one you cannot see. We came through a portal that connects our worlds. We can pass through it, but you cannot. Besides being too large to fit through the opening between worlds, the gateway only opens when we command it for our passage."

Latalizq laughed at Hannah—a very spooky, hollow laugh. "A comedian bug! So imaginative in your tale! Perhaps I will spare your life, female bug, and just feed the male to my babies. Perhaps you can live as entertainment."

She looked over at her babies for a moment and changed her mind. "No, you both need to die now, as I have two babies to feed, not just one."

Before she could move, Hannah once again held her hand up, shouting, "Stop!" I was pretty amazed at the boldness and bravery of my wife. Who was this woman I had never seen before?

"I was not jesting or telling a tale," Hannah asserted. "If your babies eat us, they will soon die. Though you cannot see it, we are covered in a thin protective bubble. Though it is true that we can be suffocated, there is nothing you can do to physically hurt us, including chewing off our heads.

"You could feed us to your babies and they could swallow us, as has already happened once. But you are very fortunate that the last time your babies quickly regurgitated us. Had we remained inside them for even another few breaths, the poison in our protective bubble would have killed them. So it would be for any creature that ate us or any of our kind."

Wow! I had no idea my sweet little wife could tell such whoppers! A poisonous protective bubble? I never got that memo, but she was keeping us alive, so I wasn't going to do anything to interfere with her unorthodox method.

"It is certainly an imaginative story, female bug," Latalizq said, "but I do not believe you."

"I can prove it!" Hannah yelled out loud and telepathically. "You would be wise to let me do so before you make the fatal mistake of feeding us to your babies."

Oh no, now Hannah had gone too far. There was no way for her to prove the lie she had told. I was pretty certain we were not coated in poison.

"I will call you on your bluff, female bug," Latalizq glared ominously.

"If you prove it, I will let you and the male bug Lazarus live. If you are wasting my time while my babies grow hungrier, I will not behead you quickly, but rip open your bodies with my talons, giving you slow deaths so my babies can have the pleasure of drinking your warm blood and picking at your bodies for tasty morsels while you are still alive."

Oh boy. This was not sounding like Hannah was making our situation better. I raised my hand and took a step forward, intending to interject. I didn't have a particular interjection in mind, just a fleeting hope of preservation, or at least forestalling an agonizing death.

However, before I could land my step or think of a thought, Hannah spoke again. "Surely you thought it strange that we were not crushed by the death grip of your talons while you flew with us through the air bringing us here," Hannah pointed out.

"That was odd," Latalizq agreed.

Hannah boldly stepped forward until she was standing right next to one of the bird's massive legs and foot of terrible talons. Gads! Then she reached out and touched the naked part of the foot by a toe with a protruding, razor-sharp talon.

"Go ahead and grab me, Latalizq. Do your worst. Crunch my bones. Tear me limb from limb if you can."

Hannah lifted up both her arms, spread wide like a human sacrifice, and looked up at the giant bird. In a blinding movement, Latalizq grabbed my dear wife in her mighty foot, encircling her with five long talons, then grabbed her beautiful head with her other foot and made furious efforts to rip it off.

Hannah did not scream or make a sound, and I prayed mightily every moment that Miriam was 100% correct about us not being able to be physically harmed.

Latalizq's efforts to rend Hannah asunder became so vicious and violent that it almost seemed she was fighting with herself. Her babies backed up into the further recesses of the cavern, and I retreated until my back was once again against the stone wall. I watched, both horrified and hopeful, as Latalizq became a whirling demon of frenzy. Her own feathers were flying off her body as she tumbled on her side, then on her back, pulling and ripping at Hannah, caught between her two fearsome feet extended above her.

After what seemed like several minutes, Latalizq gently released Hannah and stood clothed in disheveled feathers, gulping in huge breaths of air, exhausted from her own efforts of destruction. Hannah calmly walked back to be with me as if we were on a pleasant outing in the springtime.

I, on the other hand, was quivering like a leaf inside, not in fear for my life but in worry about my precious Hannah. I never in my wildest dreams could have imagined she would do what she did, or that our shield skins would be able to protect us from such violent thrashings. Even after she held my hand, I couldn't stop shaking inside for a moment.

"Don't tell me the man who came back from the dead has lost faith in the promises of the Elohim and their angels?" Hannah asked.

"No," I assured her in a faltering voice, "but perhaps my faith in our protection was not as great as yours," I admitted.

"That was only part one," she confided.

She gave me a chaste kiss on the cheek. "Let us hope Latalizq is accepting of part two," she whispered as she let go of my hand and stepped back to face the monster bird.

"Latalizq, is there honor among your kind?" Hannah asked.

"What do you mean?" Latalizq queried in reply.

That did not bode well, I thought. If the bird needed an explanation of honor, then it obviously was an unknown concept to her.

Hannah looked up into the two large yellow eyes of Latalizq. "By revealing our secrets—that we are invulnerable to physical destruction and have toxic skin—I have saved the life of your two young ones.

I said I would prove to you it was true, and so I have done, as you have seen in your failed destruction or injury of my body.

"Among my people, honor is a respect and reciprocation shown even to adversaries who have proven their mettle, or to anyone that has greatly favored you. And when a debt is due, even to an adversary, it is paid by those who are honorable.

"I have saved not only the lives of your babies but have saved you the endless sorrow you would have carried all the remaining days of your life if you had fed us to your young ones and they died after I warned you it would be so. You would have been the cause of death of your own children and never would have been able to forgive yourself for that failure."

Latalizq nodded her head in agreement. "I understand this concept. What is your name again?"

"I am Hannah," my wife said, smiling. "And even after all you have done to terrify, torment, and even try to kill us, we hold no grudge against you. We know that you simply did not fully understand who and what we are. We wish to part ways in peace.

"Knowing us as you now do, we have only one request. To show your honor for me saving the lives of your babies and from preventing you from having a lifetime of sorrow, please carry us through the air with your majestic wings and bring us back to the place where you discovered us, that we might return through the portal to our own land."

Latalizq did not hesitate. She strode to the entrance of the cavern, standing on the edge of the cliff, and looked back toward us. "Come. I will not carry you as prey, but pick you up gently with my beak and place you on my back. Hold on tight to my feathers and I will return you to the place you desire."

Hannah and I looked at each other and nodded in agreement as we walked beneath Latalizq. We wanted to smile in joy but held back, not wanting to do anything to sabotage the moment of our escape.

One at a time, Latalizq picked us up and placed us on her back. Once we assured her we were holding on tight, she leaped off the cliff and swooped down in a rapid, almost vertical descent along the cliff and the nearby waterfall.

The plunging descent was terrifying. As I gripped a handful of feathers with both hands and squeezed my spread legs together with all my might, I kept remembering how easily birds' feathers plucked out. I had visions of falling off into space clutching a handful of pulled-out feathers!

Just as we neared the verdant valley floor and it seemed as if she was going to crash into it, Latalizq arched upward and we soared up into the bright blue sky. Having somehow remained safely on the bird's back, in retrospect I can say that our trip back to the gateway was the most exhilarating thing I had ever experienced up to that point in my life.

Even after two millennia, the thrill of soaring flight atop the back of a giant bird is fresh and joyously memorable.

After landing just below a meadow of yellow flowers, Latalizq carefully removed us from her back with her beak and set us gently down upon the ground.

"Thank you, Latalizq," both Hannah and I said with great sincerity.

The giant bird gave a single nod in silent acknowledgment with her enormous head. "It is I who give thanks to you, Hannah and Lazarus. You have saved me and my children from an awful fate. And you have opened my consciousness to possibilities I had never considered. I hope I will remember to never call you bugs again. And I hope... I hope there will be an again."

This trip continued to be one big surprise after another. It seemed we were now on the verge of becoming friends with Latalizq. I never would have thought that even remotely possible five minutes earlier.

"Perhaps we can return again someday and learn more of each other in peace and as friends," I offered.

"I hope so," Latalizq said. "I truly do."

"If that day comes, bring a large red object with you and place it on the ground near this spot. Every day when I fly over the valley, I will look for your beacon. When I see it, I will come for you... as your friend."

Those were her last words in parting. With a mighty whoosh of her massive wings, she lifted off and quickly flew high into the sky, back toward her nest and her children.

Walking the rest of the way back up the small hill toward the portal, we paused while standing amidst the ground covering of beautiful, small, five-petaled yellow flowers with azure-blue centers. I gathered a few and inserted them into Hannah's hair. "A memory of our time in another world," I said as I adjusted her hair to hold the flowers.

"Do you think they will pass through the portal to our world?" Hannah asked.

"We will find out!" I chirped, as I began to feel a building excitement about our return.

It only took a few more minutes of walking for Hannah and me to get back to the portal. As we walked, I had to ask her about one tiny part of her rescue of us from what seemed like certain death. "You told Latalizq that our protective bubble would be toxic to her babies. I don't think that is true."

Hannah shrugged her shoulders. "I don't think it is either. Yeshua taught us that in defense of your life or the lives of your family and loved ones, you can use whatever means are necessary. If we are allowed to take a life in such situations, surely a little lie is insignificant."

"You are absolutely correct," I agreed. "I just wanted to be clear on why you did it. Brilliant, I should add, perfectly brilliant. I have never been so proud of you. You astounded me with your bravery and quick thinking. Thank you for being MY wife!"

We were holding hands walking up the hill. Hannah swung them back and forth a little more with a big smile on her face. "You have saved me in so many other situations, from true danger to the escape from tedious boredom. I am glad I could reciprocate a little bit.

"The very fact that we are a couple on this immortal journey is obviously of greater importance than we have given it credit for. Neither of us would have escaped with our lives if we had been alone. You used your dagger to help us escape the babies' gullets, and I used my wits to help us escape a second feeding and have the opportunity to come home. Together, each with our own skills, we succeeded where both would have failed alone."

"Elohim is wise to have created this template," I admitted.

"Yes, Elohim is wise," Hannah agreed.

As we passed the portal opening and entered the tunnel, I looked at Hannah, smiling and shaking my head in amazement as I thought about all that had occurred to us in a single day—perhaps even a few hours. "I don't think anyone will have a better story about their passage through the portal than we will," I said, laughing.

Hannah laughed back. "If we tell it, do you think anyone will believe us?"

"Probably not," I laughed as we exited the gateway back into the courtyard in Bethany.

Chapter 7
THAT'S NOT RIGHT

What a cacophony of chaos we came back to in the courtyard! There was such a din, and everyone was so caught up in their conversations that our presence seemed to be completely unnoticed.

As we looked about, it was obvious that we were the last couple to return. It was equally evident that everyone else must have had fairly interesting experiences, because they were all standing up, milling around in small groups, jabbering and gesticulating at one another with abandon. There was not even one person simply sitting down and listening or quietly reflecting.

Nor did they stay in one group. Even in the space of a minute, several flitted back and forth between multiple conversations, obviously anxious to not miss a word of the account of others' adventures. The one person who seemed to not be present was Miriam.

I looked over at Hannah a little sheepishly. "This is somewhat of a surprise," I said, pointing to the riotous conversations among our fellow guardians in the courtyard.

"I expected we would make a fairly grand entrance upon our return and be the center of attention as we shared our harrowing tale. It's a bit of a letdown to not even have one person notice that we are even here."

"Let us learn the lesson of humility from the circumstances, dear husband," Hannah suggested wisely. She reached over and held my hand, and together we walked toward the clustered groups.

It was astounding. Each and every one of our friends was so caught up in their conversations, nobody noticed our approach. Everyone remained completely oblivious to our presence as we moved away from the location of the portal and approached the groups milling in the courtyard. It was very weird.

Remembering my time as a ghost when I died after being bitten by an Aspis, I looked down at my hand holding Hannah's to assure myself that we hadn't somehow been rendered invisible.

"Lazarus!"

I looked up as I heard someone shout my name, almost surprised to suddenly be noticed. Valerius the Roman Centurion was beaming at me and quickly came up to pat me heartily on the back.

"Welcome back, Lazarus and Hannah!" he greeted in a booming voice, attracting everyone's attention.

"You are the last to arrive. Did you get lost?" he

inquired in jest, nudging me in the side with his elbow.

"Not exactly. We were delayed by circumstances," I spoke calmly, trying hard to restrain myself from shouting, We are late because we were eaten by monster baby birds as big as elephants!

"Nothing exciting then?" Valerius quipped in a tone of disappointment.

"All the rest of us had frightening trips! You probably got an easy one because you are Miriam's brother," he cajoled. "I thought I'd seen everything as a Centurion, but what we experienced left me quaking in my sandals."

"Trust me, Valerius. Whatever you saw paled in comparison to what we experienced," I assured him, certain in the truth of my assertion.

Valerius was about to reply when his wife called him over to return to the group conversation he had left to come greet us. She waved hello to us, and we waved back as Valerius walked away.

We wandered over to a different group where Salome and Elissa were speaking to Kudar-Iluna, Joshua, Gimiel, and Sanah. Everyone was paying such rapt attention to every word Salome said that once again nobody even noticed us standing next to them.

I cleared my throat to catch everyone's attention. "We're back!" I announced happily. Salome stopped speaking for a moment, and everyone glanced up at us. Almost in unison they all greeted us and then turned once more to listen to Salome.

"What is she talking about?" Hannah asked, leaning over and whispering in my ear.

"I assume she's talking about what she and Elissa experienced when they went through the portal. They must have had a very interesting adventure. Everyone is paying such close attention to every word she speaks."

"I want to hear too!" Hannah exclaimed. "Let's move closer."

We nudged our way into the circle of listeners between Sanah and Elissa, who was standing to her right. They glanced at us momentarily, but it was a bit disconcerting as they had very vacant looks on their faces. I assumed they were so enraptured listening to Salome's recounting, their focus so much upon her, that they barely registered us as more than a momentary distraction.

Salome was gesticulating quite a bit as she spoke, and we were finally close enough to clearly hear her words. "And when I was sixteen I needed to decide if I was going to wear the blue gown from Egypt or the white one accented with Tyrian purple from Lebanon."

"Oh, I hope you chose the Tyrian one," Elissa interjected gleefully.

Hannah and I looked at each other with eyebrows raised in incomprehension. Why in the world was Salome talking about clothes she wore when she was sixteen? We suppressed laughs. I even had to cover my mouth to keep quiet. It was such a ludicrous thing to be talking about that in a warped way it was funny.

I couldn't help myself. I just had to interject. "Salome," I said, waving my hand to get her attention. "Can I ask a quick question?"

"When I am finished you can talk," she replied curtly.

"I don't want to talk, Salome," I replied. "I just want to ask a little question."

She remained silent, neither giving me permission to interject nor forbidding me, so I continued with my question.

"Why are you talking about the clothes you wore when you were sixteen? We came late to this conversation, so I'm sure we missed some important connection at the beginning. Please tell us what bearing your clothes from years ago has to do with what you and Elissa experienced when you went through the portal."

Salome looked at me blankly for a moment, as if my simple question was too much to comprehend. Everyone else was looking at me with perturbed looks on their faces, apparently for having the audacity to interrupt Salome.

"Nothing," Salome said with finality.

"Nothing? Nothing what?" I asked, perplexed by her one-word answer.

Salome took a deep breath and exhaled it out with an audible puff of frustration. "Nothing. My clothes had nothing to do with our trip through the portal. If you will stop being rude, I will continue my story."

"Yes, yes, continue, continue," everyone encouraged in unison.

At that point I'm sure my mouth was gaping open a bit as I shook my head, trying to awaken a sense of understanding.

Before Salome could get started talking again I interjected one more time. "Why, and this is a big why, are you talking about clothes from when you were a teenager instead of what you and Elissa just experienced going through the portal?"

Salome seemed miffed in her reply. "It's plainly obvious, Lazarus. The choice of what I was going to wear for the big party my stepfather the king was sponsoring is a far more interesting story to me and everyone else here than the boring time on the other side of the portal."

"Really?" I asked incredulously.

"Yes, Lazarus. Really," she replied firmly.

This was all too much for me to wrap my poor head around. I was sure I felt a headache coming on. Hannah and I barely made it back to Bethany with our lives, while Salome and Elissa experienced boredom? What was the point of even sending them through the portal if they didn't experience anything interesting or different?

"Where's Miriam?" Hannah asked Salome.

"I have no idea," Salome replied, as if Miriam's

whereabouts really weren't an interest. And that, I took immediate mental note, was very odd coming from someone who loved Miriam dearly and had seldom been away from her side since the day they first met.

Salome glanced around the courtyard. "She is not here." Then, without missing a beat, she started talking about her clothes from bygone years again, with everyone leaning forward to catch her every word.

"There is something strange going on here," I whispered quietly to Hannah.

She nodded her head in agreement. "First, Valerius seemed to have a similarly frightful experience as we did. So much so he wasn't interested in hearing about our adventure but wanted to hurry back to his group to talk about his own."

Hannah pointed to the group listening to Salome. "Yet here, we have just the opposite; an audience of great people called to high and holy stewardships, listening in rapt attention to the most ridiculously mundane of subjects."

I looked around the courtyard again, watching as people were once more flitting from one group conversation to another. "Let's wander around and see what the other clusters are talking about."

Hannah and I held hands as we walked, weaving our way around the various groups. Everyone seemed to notice us as we came close, which was encouraging, but a little wave of a hand in greeting was the best we got acknowledging our presence, as they were all so riveted to the conversations they were listening to or participating in.

Bai and Ting were in a group with Nicodemus and his wife Avital and Daksha and his wife Vidya. Like Salome, whoever was speaking was very animated in their hand movements as they described their adventures. But the extent of the adventures with this group seemed to be limited to a comparison of the rocks on the three worlds they had visited.

Nicodemus asserted he had never seen a more beautiful gray rock. Bai, who now seemed to be speaking perfect Aramaic, insisted that the rocks on the world he and Ting visited certainly outshone any other rocks, as they came in wonderful dull hues of brown.

Daksha and Vidya were practically jumping up and down, exclaiming that on the world they went to there had been both gray and brown rocks! The fact that a walk down any road in Bethany would reveal plenty of rocks of both colors and many more seemed to not be pertinent in their intense conversation.

Walking over to the next group we found Gaweson the Nubian enthralling his audience of Fatima, Dion and Xenia with the exceptional invigorating qualities of the air they breathed on the world he and Fatima visited. While admittedly that was a subject a step up from talking about Salome's clothes or brown and gray rocks, I felt certain the clear air in Bethany would have been comparable. And I thought surely there must have been something more interesting on the world they visited than the invigorating quality of the air.

"Let's go listen in on the group of Valerius," I suggested to Hannah, nudging her in that direction. "At least he spoke earlier about them having frightful encounters on the world they visited. If even some of our compatriots are speaking in normal and expected ways, I will be somewhat mollified."

She nodded in agreement. "Before listening to Salome's conversation if you told me things were odd here, I would have thought you were just being a bit petulant because Valerius seemed to have had just as exciting an adventure as we did and hence was not that interested in hearing our account."

"There was probably that to some degree," I admitted. "I really was looking forward to sharing the amazing things that happened to us with everyone else and was somewhat let down that Valerius didn't seem interested in hearing about it."

"Perhaps he is finished now with his account," Hannah surmised, "and they will all be ready to hear what happened to us."

I nodded in silent agreement as we came up to the group Valerius was in, which included his wife Laelia, Aaron and Kiva, and Teoma and Rachael. "I tell you it was one of the most horrifying things

I have ever experienced," Valerius was exclaiming with a flourish. "I am a brave man; leader of a Roman Century of eighty soldiers. I have seen much of death and violence, but in that other world, the worms were so big, no fish could ever eat them."

Ah ha! At last someone with a real adventure! I felt so much better hearing Valerius describe an actual threat. Although I was dubious that worms could be much to worry about, even very big worms.

Hannah and I entered the circle of listeners so we could hear more.

"We were just sitting peacefully on the grass near the entrance to the portal," Laelia explained. "Everything had been blissful for the half hour or so we had been sitting there just enjoying the beauty of the world and the blessing of the warm sunshine."

"Then we saw the ground in front of us begin to move," Valerius interjected. "Suddenly a gigantic, pink pointy thing, like an enormous penis, poked up through the ground, wiggling about."

"I almost fainted from fright," Laelia exclaimed. "It was bigger than us, and that was just what was showing above the ground. Who knows how large the creature was below the surface!"

"Did it attack you and try to eat you?" Kira asked with wide eyes.

"Fortunately not," Valerius assured her. "And I suspect like the worms of our world, people were not on its menu. And shortly after it appeared above ground it ducked back under cover and we never saw it again."

"What was so frightful about that?" I blurted out before I realized I was even speaking.

Valerius gazed over at us. "Lazarus! I'm so happy you have come to hear of our adventures. I've already told this story several times, but I am happy to tell it again from the beginning!"

"No, no, that's alright Valerius, I understand the gist of your adventure. I just am not understanding what was so scary about a big worm that did not threaten you and disappeared back underground. When I spoke to you earlier you made it sound like you had a life-threatening adventure."

"And so we did!" Valerius insisted. "As soon as that worm went back below ground Laelia and I made haste to return through the portal. We had seen enough to know that is a world we never want to go back to again and certainly want to prevent anything from over there coming over here!"

"A worm? You are afraid of a worm?" I asked with some disdain. "A big worm would probably make a nice feast. What is there to be fearful of?"

He smiled contentedly. "Indeed Lazarus, you have grasped the problem exactly."

"I have?" I asked, confused by his reply.

"Of course," Valerius assured me. "The worm probably would make for a good meal for my entire Century of soldiers. And therein lies the crux of the fear. Do you understand now?"

I thought about it for a moment and had to shake my head negatively, trying not to feel stupid at the dullness of my perception. "I'm sorry, you lost me somewhere Valerius. The worm doesn't threaten you and you agree it would make a nice meal, so... you were afraid... why?"

"By Jupiter! It is plain you have never been a soldier Lazarus. A soldier always ascertains not just the threat before them, but what other possible threats might be lurking. I quickly surmised that if that giant worm would make a great feast for me and my men, there were likely hordes of native creatures of immense size upon that world to which that worm would be proportionally no bigger than a worm on our world is to the birds that eat them. It is of the unseen creatures such as those, ones that would obviously be too large to fight even with my eighty soldiers, that we fled back to the portal and to our world."

"Oh," I muttered astutely. "In fact that is exactly what happened to me and Hannah. And our nemesis was not some imagined beast. We were actually eaten just like worms, by giant birds!"

Valerius was looking at me intently as I spoke. "Fascinating," he acknowledged, "but let me tell you more about this worm we encountered. You cannot even imagine a worm as big as this one. Just the tip of its body was wider in girth than my own."

I turned my head slowly to look over at Hannah.

We both had our eyebrows raised in wary curiosity. Something was amiss. How many times had big, brave Roman Centurion Valerius repeated his lame story? Still holding hands we slowly backed away from Valerius' circle of admirers. No one seemed to notice that we were gone.

"Something is very strange here Hannah," I said warily.

"It is as if our friends have been possessed by devils," she added.

"It's more than that," I conjectured. "Don't you find it odd that everyone is here except Miriam; that we came in last and probably late, yet everyone is standing up and yakking away like chirping birds, as if they also just arrived and are excitedly sharing their adventures? But they are not adventures at all, unless one considers staring inanely at your navel an adventure.

"And other than Valerius, nobody seems to be paying any attention to us. No excitement at our safe arrival; no interest in what happened to us on the other side of the portal. I've seen many glance over at us, so they know we are here. But they do not seem to care. And there was a peculiar flash of heat as we came toward the center of the courtyard. Did you feel it?"

"I did feel it," Hannah acknowledged. "I really had no idea what to make of the sensation. It was so brief I just let it pass through my mind."

"Definitely something is amiss here," I mused.

"Maybe we should go back through the portal, then turn around and come right back here to the courtyard," Hannah suggested.

"Why would that do anything?" I wondered, unconvinced of the merits.

"I don't think it would," Hannah admitted, "but it might. And nothing appears to be being gained by remaining here. This is a great puzzle, but I'm unsure of the pieces and the big picture. Have our friends been bewitched or have we?"

"I don't know Hannah. Let's go into the house and see if we find anyone home. I'm not optimistic, as no one has yet come out, and we had sent them all away earlier so the meeting with Miriam could have privacy. But we should check the house and call out for Martha and the children. Perhaps they returned but were captured by brigands."

"Don't be ridiculous Lazarus!" Hannah scoffed. "Even if there is nobody at home, I doubt they have been captured by brigands!"

"That is because you have lived too sheltered of a life Hannah," I countered dismissively. "I have had many run-ins with bandits and one of the traits of the more successful ones is they are quite bold. They wouldn't hesitate to kidnap our family if they thought they had a reasonable chance of financial reward and limited risk to their lives."

"You think Miriam would allow such a thing while we were away on Elohim's mission?" Hannah huffed in disbelief.

"No... I don't suppose she would," I agreed. "But then again, Miriam is the one person that is not here."

Before Hannah could say anything more we arrived at the backdoor to our house. Cautiously I lifted the latch and opened the wooden door just in case there were any brigands inside. What I saw was far worse. I stopped dead in my tracks, stupefied by the scene before me.

"What do you see Lazarus?" Hannah whispered urgently. "Why are you not moving? Go inside so we can search for our family."

"I cannot," I answered, speaking very slowly as I continued to stare forward in shock and dismay.

"Why can you not?" Hannah asked in a hushed, irritated tone. "Just put one foot in front of the other."

When I didn't reply Hannah nudged me out of the way so she could come up and peer through the open doorway. Like me, she became frozen in place in horror at the scene she beheld.

"Now you understand why I could not go inside," I said quietly, hoping to soothe her shock.

"Yes... yes I do, dear husband," she spoke slowly. "For how does one enter that which does not exist?"

On the other side of the door there was nothing, just an endless blank white. It had no boundaries or borders, no beginning or end. There were no rooms, no people, no anything, just white. I reached out my hand. The moment it passed the threshold of the door it completely disappeared into the white. I moved my fingers against the others. I could feel them perfectly fine. But I could see neither them nor my arm at all.

Hannah called out, "Martha!" No answer returned from the whiteness.

One by one she called out the names of all of our children and of Miriam's and Yeshua. Once again the silence of the whiteness was deafening.

"I'm going to venture in," I said bravely. "Perhaps this is just like the densest fog that ever was. I remember the layout of our house perfectly. I can work my way along the walls and call out for Martha and the children as I pass from room to room."

Hannah nodded her head in agreement. "Do it."

Cautiously I reached a leg over the threshold and into the impenetrable whiteness. But as I stepped down to the floor, there wasn't one! I withdrew my leg back outside the threshold and reached inside the whiteness to feel an inner wall of the house. I was no longer surprised to discover it too was not there. How could there be an outer wall but not an inner wall on the other side of it? Surely there was strange and powerful magic at work here.

"There's no floor is there?" Hannah asked, already knowing the answer.

I shook my head negatively. "And no wall either."

I smacked the hard substantial stone wall next to the door. "Outside is solid. Inside is nonexistent.

I have no idea what this means Hannah. But you were right. Any answers are likely on the other world through the portal."

I waved my hand back toward the courtyard. "For this... none of this is real is it?"

Hannah shook her head negatively in acknowledgment of the truth. A tear ran down her slightly bowed head, then another and another. I cupped her chin in my hand and gently lifted her face to mine with a soft kiss on her warm tender lips, wiping away the tears on her cheeks with my other hand.

"It will be alright my love. Remember, the Elohim will ask nothing of us that they have not given us the power to accomplish."

"I know," she replied after exhaling a deep breath.

She looked over to our right where the entrance to our portal was just a few paces away. She held my hand and pulled me toward the portal. "Let's go find some answers."

DESTINY

Chapter 8
IN BIRD WE TRUST

As we turned to walk toward the portal I reached down and grabbed the mat for cleaning the soles of sandals at the entrance to the door of our house that didn't exist beyond the outer wall.

"What are you doing with that dirty thing?" Hannah scoffed.

"There's a very important reason I have picked it up," I assured her. "In fact, it is a vital item for our return to the other world."

Hannah let out a little chuckle. "To ensure we have a mat to wipe our feet on before we leave the portal?"

I held up my nose in pretend indignity. "When we parted ways with the big bird she said she was going to be our friend if we ever returned. She specifically told us to bring a red beacon to let her know we were back that she could see from the air. This mat will be that beacon."

Hannah looked at the dirty mat, then up at me with doubt written all over her face. "If Latalizq still remembers to be our friend, and I consider that a big 'if,' I seriously doubt that little, dingy, dirt-covered mat will be recognizable as a beacon. Nor do I see any red in it."

We continued talking as we entered the portal and began walking down the short tunnel. "It is red!" I protested. "Don't you remember, it was a gift from your Uncle Nathaniel for our tenth wedding anniversary. It's a nice woven rug from Tarsus."

I proceeded to hit it violently with my right hand while shaking it vigorously with my left which held it, to clean off some of the dirt to show Hannah that it really was mostly red underneath. Of course I failed to take into account that we were enclosed within a small tunnel. Coughing and sputtering from the dust storm I created, we sprinted the last distance out of the tunnel and back into the world unknown.

We were covered in a sprinkled layer of dirty dust. I could see by Hannah's pursed lips that she was biting down hard, obviously willing herself to not speak ill of me for my absentmindedness. I sheepishly reached over and used my hands to brush the dirt off of her clothes. As I was patting her back she grabbed her long black hair with both hands and bent over at the waist shaking her hair to remove the dust. The flowers I had put in her hair fell down onto the ground. But they had already begun to wilt so I just let them remain where they had fallen.

I placed the mat on the ground in an open spot

unobscured by any trees and walked back toward Hannah brushing the dirt off myself. "You see," I said, pointing toward the mat on the ground about ten paces away. "It is mostly red, once you get all the dirt off."

"So it is," Hannah said with a forgiving smile. "I just hope in future rug cleaning episodes you remember the object is to remove the dirt, not merely transfer it from the rug to us." And with that we both laughed heartily! I am so lucky to have such a wife!

We sat down on the grassy ground, enjoying the warm sunshine and the splendid view of the broad valley and distant waterfall to wait for Latalizq to hopefully see our red signal. We didn't have long to wait. We had barely begun to talk again about the strange situation back in Bethany when we looked up as we saw the expanse of Latalizq's wings spread wide, along with her tail as she swooped down from the sky and landed beside us.

"That was quick!" Latalizq snorted in my mind. Ouch, that was loud! "I have not even yet found a new meal for my babies to take the place of you two. Have you returned to tempt me to reconsider my decision to spare your lives?"

"No, no... no," I asserted, standing up with arms spread and palms forward to greet her in peace. "Remember, we would be indigestible," I reminded her.

"Relax Lazarus," Hannah advised. "Latalizq is

just kidding, aren't you?" she asked, standing up to come over and touch the bird on her massive beak.

Latalizq nodded her head in agreement. "Are all males so easy to fool on your world?" she inquired with a shake of her massive head.

"Sometimes, yes," Hannah answered, laughing. "It depends upon the subject."

"Speaking of fooling," I interjected, completely ignoring that the females had been making fun of me, "we have come back here to solve a mystery. We suspect some type of foolery is happening back on our world. Nothing was as it should have been when we returned. It was so confusing and abnormal that we could not even find a clue to the puzzle. So we have returned here, hoping with a thread of hope, to glean some answers because there are none back on our world."

Latalizq was immediately serious in her tone. "Tell me what is your mystery?"

So we told her every detail of the strange goings-on back in Bethany. About how odd all of our friends were acting and speaking. How my sister Miriam, the key figure in everything, was conspicuously absent. And most egregious, our house had an outside wall, but nothing but impenetrable white without substance inside!

Latalizq listened patiently without speaking as both Hannah and I explained the events in Bethany. When we concluded she surprised and gratified us with her first words. "The solution is obvious," she elucidated. "Either your sister Miriam, who you said has great powers, has created an illusion to test you, or someone or something else of equal ability has."

"It would not be Miriam," I said, shaking my head in denial. "She would not make the challenging situation of new worlds and dangers even more perilous by adding to the fire. She was just using the portals on the very first day of our training to gently introduce us to the strangeness of other worlds. After all, other than me and Miriam's companion Salome, none had ever experienced such bizarre realities."

Hannah was not convinced. "Then where was Miriam? Why was she the only one of our little secret society not present?"

"I don't know Hannah," I replied defensively. "But I know my sister. And I know she was not the cause of the confusion. She brings clarity and light, not bewilderment and darkness."

Hannah placed her hand on my arm and looked at me lovingly. "I was not speaking ill of your sister Lazarus. I know she is an angel of light. Nevertheless, what we saw was probably within her power to create. Please let us not discount that as a possibility until it is usurped by a more likely one. It may simply be a way she is testing us."

"All right," I agreed begrudgingly.

I looked up at Latalizq. "Is it possible that something from this world might have come through the portal with us and changed the reality of our home?"

"Anything is possible," Latalizq ventured. "However, I know of no intelligent creature or microbial malady that could account for what you described. Therefore, I am inclined to attribute it to your sister who you say wields unusual powers. She is the most likely answer."

I threw up my hands in frustration. "I am certain Miriam has nothing to do with this!"

"All right then!" Latalizq said abruptly. "I need to return to feed my babies. It seems I cannot really be of help to you."

With those parting words she spread her great wings and crouched down like a loaded spring to launch herself skyward with a mighty leap.

"Wait!" Hannah cried out, waving her right hand high in the air to catch the attention of the monster bird.

"If you know of no answer to our mystery, is there anyone else on this world that might have an insight that might help us?"

Latalizq folded her wings back close to her body and cocked her enormous head in thought. "There is a place that you might find answers or at least additional insight, but you may also lose your life if you venture there."

Hannah and I looked at each other to weigh the prospect. "Elohim will not let us perish so quickly before we have even begun to fulfill the stewardship they have given us," Hannah said with conviction.

I shrugged my shoulders and spread my arms a bit with my palms up, showing my innate skepticism. "I am not so certain of divine protection. My experience with the higher beings is they give us knowledge and purpose, but then let us fight through life and grow or shrink, live or perish on our own merits."

Hannah obviously disagreed with my lack of faith and was about to utter an objection, but I held up my finger to stop her and quickly added an addendum. "Nevertheless, I DO have faith in the protective energy shields that encase our bodies, for they proved their strength when Latalizq first captured us in her mighty talons to take us as food for her young ones."

Hannah had folded her arms and was tapping her pointer finger while looking at me in silence with a bit of a scowl on her pretty face. I took that as a positive sign that she was willing to listen further.

"Therefore, good wife, I completely agree that we should go wherever Latalizq recommends and feel fairly certain we will not perish. In any case, we have no options on the other side of the portal. We have no choice other than to look in this world to see if we can find a clue to the mystery, or even better, an answer!"

Latalizq had been listening to our conversation and interrupted before either Hannah or I could speak further. "I must be leaving. My babies are hungry. So I will tell you quickly where you need to go."

She lifted her left wing and pointed in the direction of the sun in the sky. "A morning's flight in that direction will bring you to a city of gold and crystal. In it you will find a people called the Nartese. They are bugs similar in appearance to you, but much smarter. That is the only place I can think of that you might find insight into your predicament. The Narts are an ancient race. Their city was already here before the egg of my first ancestor ever hatched. Their accumulated knowledge is vast."

"People who look like us?" I blurted incredulously. "How can that be? I assumed from what my sister told us that everything we encountered on other worlds would be very different from what we had ever seen or experienced on our Earth."

Latalizq looked down at me disdainfully. "I know nothing of your world or have any more answers to your ridiculous questions than you assumed I would."

"Please answer one question for me that I am sure you do know," Hannah asked sweetly. "If the Nartese are what you consider to be bugs like us, does that mean you eat them?"

Latalizq let out an incredibly loud squawk in reply. Both Hannah and I quickly slapped our hands over our ears to protect our hearing. I'm not sure if her squawk was in derision at Hannah's question or laughter. But either way, her question certainly provoked a surprising response.

"I would love to eat the little Narts and feed them to my young ones," Latalizq freely admitted. "But their land is protected by fearsome monsters. They are like a cruel mix-up of fat worms, serpents, and lizards. They have a head full of teeth, spiked and horned heads, muscular legs with sharp talons as powerful as mine, and strange-shaped wings that lift them high into the sky, despite the fact their wings appear too fragile to lift their heavy bodies off the ground.

"The flying worms would also likely make a very tasty meal indeed, but they can shoot a long stream of fire out of their mouth. Fire is our weakness. Our feathers burn. None of my kind would risk their life venturing too close to the demesne of the Narts.

"It is recorded in the annals of our history that in ancient times a flock of warriors of my kind, so vast the shadow of their numbers blotted out the sun, tried to attack the Narts. Few returned to tell the tale of their destruction. Before any could get close enough to the city to capture a Nart, they were attacked by the winged monstrosities that breathe fire. In a single breath, rotating their head around, they set a dozen of our mightiest warriors ablaze and they tumbled from the sky to their deaths.

Over one thousand warriors left to attack the city of the Nartese and capture a new food source. Less than one hundred returned alive."

"Then why did you try to feed us to your babies?" Hannah asked. "If the Nartese look like us, weren't you afraid we were them and that capturing us would bring retaliation?"

"I knew you were not Nartese the moment I spotted you," Latalizq explained. "There are many bugs on my world that look somewhat like you and resemble Narts in some ways, but you are not Nartese and neither are the other bugs."

"How can you tell?" I asked, wanting to know what could possibly distinguish one human from another, especially by a bird flying high up in the sky.

"Narts come to trade with us from time to time. They live almost exclusively within their walled city, which limits their available resources. Virtually everything they need or want, other than a small amount of locally grown crops, must come from places beyond their domain," Latalizq explained.

"There are multiple ways to distinguish Nartese from common bugs. Conspicuously, they wear very little clothing, mostly just jeweled adornments. The other bugs of your species on this world all like to cover up their hairless bodies the same as you do.

"But lack of clothing is not the definitive indicator of a Nartese. When they arrive to trade or whenever they venture away from their city, it is always atop their flying worms of terror. There is no defense against those despicable creatures; therefore, nobody threatens or bothers a Nartese, even when they travel alone and far from their city."

Though I wasn't convinced that the Nartese were as formidable as Latalizq made them out to be, she had swayed me enough that they might have knowledge of how to solve our puzzle in Bethany.

"How can we go to their city?" I asked, somewhat daunted by the distance of a 'morning's flight.' I was certain that in the time of a 'morning's flight' a giant bird like Latalizq could probably fly as far as we could walk in a month through the tangled jungle in the valley below.

Latalizq pointed again with the tip of her long extended wing. "Work your way down to the river at the bottom of the valley. Follow it downstream until you reach the city of the Nartese."

"Will there be other cities along the way?" Hannah wondered.

"There are many hovels of bugs along the river for all of its length," Latalizq replied.

"How will we know then when we are at the right city?" I asked in innocent ignorance.

Latalizq held her head down a bit and shook it back and forth. This seemed to be a universal body language for disappointment. "Because you can speak in your minds, I have given you more credit for intelligence than is obviously due," Latalizq mentally muttered forlornly.

"Did I not say that the land of the Nartese is guarded by fearsome, flying, fire-breathing serpents? And did I not say that they lived in a magnificent city of crystal and gold? Is it not plain that the word 'hovel,' which I used to describe the cities of bugs along the river, does not depict the city of the Nartese? When you see it, it will be like no other, and you will certainly know that you have arrived.

"If that is still too complicated for you to fathom, the city of the Nartese is at the mouth of the river where it empties into the ocean."

"Can you fly us there?" Hannah asked timidly, hoping for a positive answer.

Latalizq's reply was another earsplitting squawk. "And let my babies starve? Or be eaten by predators and not ever see my young ones again? What kind of mother would ask such a thing? Your species must have little love for their children."

Hannah suddenly was stifling tears. "I love my children with every fiber of my being," Hannah proclaimed. "I want so much to see them again and hold them in my arms. I would die for them, suffer torture, deprivation, or anything for their well-being. It is to see them again, more than anything else, that I asked what I did.

"I am sorry that I was thinking more of us and our children than you and yours, Latalizq. Of course we will walk down to the river and begin our journey. Thank you so much for all the information and wisdom you have shared with us. I hope we meet again."

With that, Hannah reached out for my hand and

pulled me down the hill toward the river before I could even say goodbye to Latalizq.

"Pause for a moment." We heard Latalizq call out to us in our minds. "I cannot take you to the city of the Nartese, but I know one who might. Let me call him and see if he will agree."

There was an uneasy silence for a few minutes. If Latalizq was communicating with another of her kind, we could not hear their conversation in our heads. But she must have been talking to him nonstop because we just stood there for several minutes in silence without her speaking again to us.

Then from the direction of the waterfall, we saw another giant bird flying toward us. In just a couple of minutes it was flapping its great wings and spreading its massive tail in a wide crescent to break its descent. The bird landed next to Latalizq and was slightly smaller in size than she was. His markings were dramatically different, with plumage that seemed to come in every color of the rainbow, but it looked as if he had just been in a fight because his feathers were sparse in several places and seemed to grow with some deformity in others.

"These are the bugs you said are not food but can speak in their minds like us?" the bird asked with obvious doubt.

Latalizq nodded her mighty head in acknowledgment and looked toward us. I took that as my cue. "Um, hello big, really colorful bird," I began hesitantly. "I am Lazarus," I said, pointing to my chest.

"And this is my wife and eternal companion Hannah," I introduced, putting an arm over her shoulder.

"Amazing!" exclaimed the male. "Truly a freak of nature. I never would have imagined bugs could talk!"

"Well, tell them your name," Latalizq prompted.

"You mean they can hear and speak in their minds?" the male asked. "Unbelievable. Truly unbelievable!"

After a few minutes of conversation, the male bird, whose name was Danarz, accepted that we were not the average bugs he was accustomed to eating, and we got down to the business at hand.

"I will take you to the land of the Nartese," Danarz offered, "but only in exchange for something most precious. If you do not return with it, I will kill you if I ever see you again."

"And enjoy eating you very much," he added.

I gulped in some trepidation. "And what would this valuable item be?" I asked, almost afraid to hear the answer.

Danarz was quick to provide illumination. "The flying worms of the Nartese are covered in scales that are impervious to their fire. The largest scale is in the center of their chest. I will bring you to the land of the Nartese in exchange for you returning with a large chest scale from a worm that I might thereafter use as a shield of protection from their fiery breath."

"But I would have to kill one to obtain a scale."

"Undoubtedly," Danarz agreed. "Obviously an impossible challenge for a bug."

With that dismissive comment, he prepared to take flight and leave us.

While I just stood there dumbfounded, ready to let him go because I could not fathom an adequate response, Hannah called out to him.

"We will do it!"

I looked over at my wife. Where had this tiger been hiding for the sixteen years we had been married? She put a raised finger to her lips, letting me know I needed to not speak. Good thing too, as I was just about to look over at her in disbelief and ask, We will?"Then why did you try to feed us to your babies?" Hannah asked. "If the Nartese look like us, weren't you afraid we were them and that capturing us would bring retaliation?"

"I knew you were not Nartese the moment I spotted you," Latalizq explained. "There are many bugs on my world that look somewhat like you and resemble Narts in some ways, but you are not Nartese and neither are the other bugs."

"How can you tell?" I asked, wanting to know what could possibly distinguish one human from another, especially by a bird flying high up in the sky.

"Narts come to trade with us from time to time. They live almost exclusively within their walled city, which limits their available resources. Virtually everything they need or want, other than a small amount of locally grown crops, must come from places beyond their domain," Latalizq explained.

"There are multiple ways to distinguish Nartese from common bugs. Conspicuously, they wear very little clothing, mostly just jeweled adornments. The other bugs of your species on this world all like to cover up their hairless bodies the same as you do.

"But lack of clothing is not the definitive indicator of a Nartese. When they arrive to trade or whenever they venture away from their city, it is always atop their flying worms of terror. There is no defense against those despicable creatures; therefore, nobody threatens or bothers a Nartese, even when they travel alone and far from their city."

Though I wasn't convinced that the Nartese were as formidable as Latalizq made them out to be, she had swayed me enough that they might have knowledge of how to solve our puzzle in Bethany.

"How can we go to their city?" I asked, somewhat daunted by the distance of a 'morning's flight.' I was certain that in the time of a 'morning's flight' a giant bird like Latalizq could probably fly as far as we could walk in a month through the tangled jungle in the valley below.

Latalizq pointed again with the tip of her long extended wing. "Work your way down to the river at the bottom of the valley. Follow it downstream until you reach the city of the Nartese."

"Will there be other cities along the way?" Hannah wondered.

"There are many hovels of bugs along the river for all of its length," Latalizq replied.

"How will we know then when we are at the right city?" I asked in innocent ignorance.

Latalizq held her head down a bit and shook it back and forth. This seemed to be a universal body language for disappointment. "Because you can speak in your minds, I have given you more credit for intelligence than is obviously due," Latalizq mentally muttered forlornly.

"Did I not say that the land of the Nartese is guarded by fearsome, flying, fire-breathing serpents? And did I not say that they lived in a magnificent city of crystal and gold? Is it not plain that the word 'hovel,' which I used to describe the cities of bugs along the river, does not depict the city of the Nartese? When you see it, it will be like no other, and you will certainly know that you have arrived.

"If that is still too complicated for you to fathom, the city of the Nartese is at the mouth of the river where it empties into the ocean."

"Can you fly us there?" Hannah asked timidly, hoping for a positive answer.

Latalizq's reply was another earsplitting squawk. "And let my babies starve? Or be eaten by predators and not ever see my young ones again? What kind of mother would ask such a thing? Your species must have little love for their children."

Hannah suddenly was stifling tears. "I love my children with every fiber of my being," Hannah proclaimed. "I want so much to see them again and hold them in my arms. I would die for them, suffer torture, deprivation, or anything for their well-being. It is to see them again, more than anything else, that I asked what I did.

"I am sorry that I was thinking more of us and our children than you and yours, Latalizq. Of course we will walk down to the river and begin our journey. Thank you so much for all the information and wisdom you have shared with us. I hope we meet again."

With that, Hannah reached out for my hand and pulled me down the hill toward the river before I could even say goodbye to Latalizq.

"Pause for a moment." We heard Latalizq call out to us in our minds. "I cannot take you to the city of the Nartese, but I know one who might. Let me call him and see if he will agree."

There was an uneasy silence for a few minutes. If Latalizq was communicating with another of her kind, we could not hear their conversation in our heads. But she must have been talking to him nonstop because we just stood there for several minutes in silence without her speaking again to us.

Then from the direction of the waterfall, we saw another giant bird flying toward us. In just a couple of minutes it was flapping its great wings and spreading its massive tail in a wide crescent to break its descent. The bird landed next to Latalizq and was slightly smaller in size than she was. His markings were dramatically different, with plumage that seemed to come in every color of the rainbow, but it looked as if he had just been in a fight because his feathers were sparse in several places and seemed to grow with some deformity in others.

"These are the bugs you said are not food but can speak in their minds like us?" the bird asked with obvious doubt.

Latalizq nodded her mighty head in acknowledgment and looked toward us. I took that as my cue. "Um, hello big, really colorful bird," I began hesitantly. "I am Lazarus," I said, pointing to my chest.

"And this is my wife and eternal companion Hannah," I introduced, putting an arm over her shoulder.

"Amazing!" exclaimed the male. "Truly a freak of nature. I never would have imagined bugs could talk!"

"Well, tell them your name," Latalizq prompted.

"You mean they can hear and speak in their minds?" the male asked. "Unbelievable. Truly unbelievable!"

After a few minutes of conversation, the male bird, whose name was Danarz, accepted that we were not the average bugs he was accustomed to eating, and we got down to the business at hand.

"I will take you to the land of the Nartese," Danarz offered, "but only in exchange for something most precious. If you do not return with it, I will kill you if I ever see you again."

"And enjoy eating you very much," he added.

I gulped in some trepidation. "And what would this valuable item be?" I asked, almost afraid to hear the answer.

Danarz was quick to provide illumination. "The flying worms of the Nartese are covered in scales that are impervious to their fire. The largest scale is in the center of their chest. I will bring you to the land of the Nartese in exchange for you returning with a large chest scale from a worm that I might thereafter use as a shield of protection from their fiery breath."

"But I would have to kill one to obtain a scale."

"Undoubtedly," Danarz agreed. "Obviously an impossible challenge for a bug."

With that dismissive comment, he prepared to take flight and leave us.

While I just stood there dumbfounded, ready to let him go because I could not fathom an adequate response, Hannah called out to him.

"We will do it!"

I looked over at my wife. Where had this tiger

been hiding for the sixteen years we had been married? She put a raised finger to her lips, letting me know I needed to not speak. Good thing too, as I was just about to look over at her in disbelief and ask, "*We will?*"

DESTINY

Chapter 9
PREDATOR OR PREY?

Danarz wanted to wait until dark. He said we would have the best chance to approach the land of the Nartese undetected under the cover of darkness. He was brave but did not foolishly want to risk detection by the guardians of the realm during the day. He flew away with Latalizq shortly after he arrived and promised to return before the sun set below the horizon.

True to his word, he came back about four hours later while the sun was still in the late afternoon. Hooked around one of his large toes was a tiny shield.

We walked over to him after he landed nearby, and he held up what appeared to be an entirely inadequate little toe shield.

"This is a worm scale I have latched to my toe with a sytanamee vine. The vine is fireproof and virtually indestructible once it has hardened into whatever shape it is formed into when it is green and freshly cut."

"You killed one of the flying worms?" I asked,

impressed by his prowess.

"I wish it were so," Danarz replied firmly, "but I merely spotted this scale lying on a rock in a clearing one day while flying over the valley. The creature must have lost it—who knows how? I knew what it was and fashioned this shield from it."

I looked at the little shield dubiously. It was about half the size of a Roman shield and looked a bit ridiculous on the tip of the bird's large toe. "Is it big enough to actually be of help, or is it just like a ring of ornamentation?" I asked with sincere interest.

Danarz let out one of those loud squawks that seemed to be either laughter or upset. I never could make that determination. "Of course it is for protection!" Danarz shouted loudly in my head.

"It has already saved my life. It was barely so, but here I still live today. That is why I want a bigger one."

"What happened?" I asked curiously, unsure if the bird would answer, but he seemed to relish telling the tale.

"One day I ventured too close to the land of the Nartese. I was simply exploring to gain a greater understanding of the lay of the land. So intent was I upon the ground below me that I momentarily lapsed in my observation of potential threats that might be approaching from the distance.

"Only at the last moment before my certain destruction, I sensed a presence bearing down toward me from above. I heard the blast of fire coming at me from the flying worm before I had a chance to flee in fast flight. All I could do was flip over on my back and hold up the shield I had fashioned, as pitiful as it seemed, against the wide stream of fire a mere breath away from engulfing and incinerating me.

"Upside down, I was plunging rapidly toward the ground. Though I knew I could die on impact, that maneuver also helped. As I fell straight down, I was also falling away from the stream of fire heading straight for me.

"I held up the shield in front of my face as the stream of fire rushed upon me. Though it is only a tiny worm scale, it almost entirely protected my face as I moved it rapidly about."

He looked down at his body in silence for a moment. "You have probably noticed my feathers are not as lustrous and beautiful as Latalizq's, nor any others of my kind. My chest was not spared from the fire. But because I was falling, it did not fully impact me.

"The worm was flying alone, just a perimeter sentinel. It takes them some minutes before they can rekindle their fire after they have expelled one. Before the creature could shoot another, I limped away in flight, almost passing out from the pain and the nauseating smell of my burned flesh and feathers.

"If you can somehow obtain a larger scale, I will

fashion a shield adequate in size to better protect me from the fiery fiends."

"Why not just stay away from the demesnes of the Nartese?" Hannah asked.

"That would seem to be the prudent choice," Danarz replied stoically. "However, there are unique qualities to that land that make it enticing to visit despite the dangers. And for me, I have no choice. I must continue to go back until I succeed at my most cherished goal or die in the attempt. I intend to succeed."

"You wish to kill a flying worm?" I asked.

Danarz shook his head vigorously, expanding his head feathers like a headdress. "If they leave me alone, I will do the same for them. No, I go for the healing spring that lies in a corner of the realm.

"Look at me," he said, gazing down at his own chest. "I am one of the most beautiful of my kind, or I was. As you can see, the scarred flesh of my chest is so damaged from the fire of the worm that my feathers no longer grow sleek and lustrous, and my bare skin is showing through in places where feathers no longer grow at all. In truth, among my kind I am now ugly. No female will mate with me.

"My only hope for a life of fulfillment is to bathe in the spring of healing waters. But sadly, the healing qualities of the waters are activated by the light of the sun. I have successfully snuck into the land of the Nartese at night on more than one occasion to bathe in the spring. But not even one feather was restored to its former glory."

"Perhaps it is just a myth," I suggested. "Maybe the spring does not really have the power to heal."

"Not so, Lazarus," Danarz refuted, calling me by name for the first time. "I know many creatures that have been healed in the daytime and many others that have tried to be healed at night, and all were unsuccessful. I had hoped it would be different for me, but it was not. The powers of the spring are only activated by sunlight."

Hannah came over and touched Danarz's mighty beak, and he allowed her. "If the flying serpents patrol the borders of the Nartesian land, even if you made it to the healing spring during the light of the sun, it would seem a hopeless effort. Surely you would once again be attacked by the worms."

"It is fairly certain," he agreed. "And I do not know how long I would need to be in the spring for the healing to be achieved. But I have to try, even if the chance of success is very small, because life as an outcast is barely worth living."

Hannah approached the massive bird closer to his face. I thought for a moment she was going to kiss it. But instead, she ran her fingers gently through the feathers near the rear of its enormous black beak, and once again Danarz allowed her to touch him in a loving way. His giant red eye on the side of his head nearest to where she was standing swiveled down to look at her, the coal-black pupil peering at her in intent silence.

It was unnerving to me. I didn't know if he was enjoying her attention or contemplating eating her. "Well, let's be off then," I urged telepathically loud in my mind to break his focus in case the bird was contemplating the latter choice.

Danarz stood up quickly, moving away from my wife, and ruffled his feathers as if shaking off a spell of kindness and compassion Hannah had been weaving upon him.

"Of course," he said gruffly. "If we depart now, we will be able to travel most of the distance in the day's remaining light."

He squatted down as low to the ground as he could go so we could climb up to his neck. I went up first, holding onto feathers like climbing a rope hand over hand, then reached down to help pull Hannah up.

We nestled deeply into his neck feathers. I held on tight to the feathers with both hands, and Hannah sat behind me, holding fast with her hands encircled around my waist. We both locked our legs around his massive neck as much as was possible. His neck, even below all the feathers, was as wide in girth as a camel.

In moments he sprang into the air. With mighty flaps of his long, broad wings, we were once again experiencing the exhilarating thrill of flying in a rush through the sky! Launching from the hillside near the entrance to the portal, he swooped down toward the bottom of the verdant valley. Soon we were skimming barely above the narrow, sinuous river, close enough that the tips of his wings often touched the water on their downward thrust.

"Why are we flying so low?" I asked out of curiosity, not concern.

"It is easier to avoid detection from any and all creatures if we skim above the river and follow its course," Danarz explained. "Unless there is an adversary directly above us, we will remain safe and unseen."

"You seem very smooth and proficient in your flying. Are you familiar with the route of the river?" I asked.

"I have flown this section many times," Danarz acknowledged. "Just around the next bend, you will see a settlement of bugs that look somewhat like you, but they are dirtier, hairier, and far stupider."

No sooner had he spoken than we came around the bend, and there was a small village of people. I saw about two dozen grass-thatched, circular huts and one larger building in the center of the huts. There were some women and children playing and working in the shallows near shore. Everyone seemed to be wearing crudely fashioned animal skins for clothing, mostly just like shapeless dark-brown bags loosely draping their bodies. A thin canoe with four men was just putting into shore as we came into their view.

In what seemed to be the exact same moment, everyone in the village noticed us, and screams of terror and alarm resounded from everywhere! The men in the canoe quickly stepped out onto the shore and were joined by at least a dozen others, all armed with long, sharp-tipped spears, which they quickly launched directly at us!

Instantly Danarz changed direction by almost ninety degrees with a single flap of his mighty wings, and we rapidly ascended almost straight up! Hannah and I held on for dear life to not fall off. After not much of an altitude gain, he leveled off and circled the village.

"We are safe at this height," he assured us. "Even the strongest bug arm cannot throw a spear very far straight up in the air."

We were tilted at a slight angle facing inward toward the village as he made his loop around.

"Those villagers seem very inhospitable," I observed. "Are all the inhabitants along the river so unfriendly?"

"All the ones my kind eat for food," he replied matter-of-factly.

I'm sure Hannah was feeling the same queasiness in her stomach, being reminded that for these giant birds we 'bugs' were usually just dinner.

"I am making you two famous," Danarz proclaimed. "You will be recorded forever in the mythologies of bugs."

"How so?" I asked stoically, still unsettled by his previous cold-hearted statement.

Danarz elaborated with a tinge of glee in his

words. "How will those dimwitted bugs ever explain or understand how you two bugs are riding on top of the creature that they are accustomed to seeing only as the nemesis that ends their lives? They will never be able to comprehend or explain it," he laughed in my mind at his own humor.

"If you wanted to stay here and live, you could easily become King and Queen of all the bugs!" he added with mirthful glee.

Neither Hannah nor I were moved to laugh at Danarz's humor, and we just remained silent and unresponsive for a few minutes.

As we flew away from the village and continued our journey down the river, Hannah challenged him about eating living creatures with families and children, such as those in the village we had just passed. He was sullen and almost angry in his response.

"What do you expect me to eat, rocks? It is perfectly normal for every higher life form that exists to consume lower life creatures for food. Unless you do eat rocks, surely it is no different upon your world.

"We eat bugs like you. They are tasty, easy to catch, and active enough breeders that we never seem to diminish their numbers.

"The bugs in turn eat the simpler creatures that live in the river and other lesser creatures they catch in the forest. Those creatures in turn eat smaller and simpler life forms as their food. It is the same up and down the chain of predator and prey. For every creature that is a predator of a lesser creature, it is in turn the prey of a greater one, until you reach the highest. I dare you to try and tell me it is different on the world you come from."

"For many people on our world, it is as you say," Hannah admitted sadly. "However, on our Earth nothing eats our kind unless someone is foolish enough to venture unprepared into the wilderness that is filled with large predators.

"I guess that means in most instances, we are the highest on the food chain. Many of our kind take unrighteous and wasteful advantage of that privilege. They slaughter and eat every lower creature that exists, it seems. Many consider it as their birthright, as if all the life in the world has been given to them by God to eat for food."

"Of course, it could be no other way," Danarz gloated. "Even on your strange alien world, the foundation of sustaining life is the same.

"While that is true for many, it is not true for all," Hannah objected. "There are many higher creatures that are strict vegetarians; they only eat grasses and plants. Among our kind it is the same. While most kill animals for food, some eat only vegetables, fruits, and grains. They live just as long lives as the carnivores. In most instances, they live lives of greater health as well.

"Lazarus and I are among a group of people known as Celestines. We eat all the foods of those who eat only from the plant kingdom, but also eat any renewable animal resource such as non-fertile eggs from birds, cheese made from the milk of goats and sheep, and honey from the bees for sweetening. Because of our diet, sickness and disease are almost unknown among us. The same cannot be said for the carnivores of our kind."

"Yes, yes, we have some of those dumb plant eaters on our world too," Danarz puttered. "They are easy prey for the vast majority that are carnivores. They make up for their frequent tasty demise by reproducing and multiplying in prodigious numbers. I dare say they would destroy the world with overcrowding if their numbers weren't regularly culled by the predators.

"But let me change the subject, as I am slightly confused. I thought you said your world was called 'Earth.' But now you have called it 'God.' Which one is it, or is it both?"

Hannah seemed startled by Danarz's question. "Surely you understand the concept of God, of beings greater than any of us, including you; beings who have been the creators of all that is, from our world to yours and every bit of life everywhere."

Danarz let out a loud, derisive squawk. "You are more primitive bugs than I realized. Only very simple-minded creatures that are as ignorant as they are powerless believe in such subservient concepts.

"I have studied the cultures of primitive societies

that have various beliefs in invisible higher beings, such as your God. Beings they call out to all of their lives with supplications for everything from improving their food to bringing them wealth, health, or protection from danger.

"I am convinced those simple-minded beliefs are one of the principal reasons those societies remain backward and retarded in their growth. Their dependency on supplications to higher beings that do not exist and therefore can never aid them in any of the manners they request prevents them from gaining a greater degree of self-sufficiency that would truly be a trait to advance their culture."

"Contrarily, look at any advanced civilization and almost universally they no longer hold primitive beliefs in invisible higher beings to whom their supplications will mystically be answered. Once a society throws off those simplistic notions, they begin to advance much more rapidly."

"We came to your world through the power of the higher beings we call Elohim," I defended. "It is through the portal of their creation that our worlds connect."

"It is a common practice of primitive cultures to ascribe things they cannot understand or explain to the power of their 'Gods,' " Danarz replied disdainfully. "I have no doubt that a little investigative research would reveal your conduit between worlds to simply be a natural phenomenon."

"Perhaps," I conceded, "but it would have been Elohim that created the natural phenomena in the first place. Beyond that, not long ago I died. I traveled in the afterlife to the higher realms and can personally attest to their reality, even more so as one of the Elohim brought me back to life, and here I am today flying through the air with you."

"Simple, simple-minded primitive bugs," Danarz muttered contemptuously. "Did you see your Gods when you went to your afterlife?"

"No, not then," I admitted reluctantly.

"But I have lived with one, my sister's husband Yeshua," I contended.

Danarz uttered one of his loud squawks. This time I had no doubt he was laughing. "You believe in your primitive notions so much that you do not even realize how ridiculous that statement sounds to one whose mind is not cluttered by inane thoughts."

I started to answer him, to make another point proving the reality of God, but he cut me off before I could begin. "Enough of this silliness about mythical Gods," he said scornfully. "Speak to me more about your warped thinking on food. That at least has enough humor to keep me jovial and enough intellectual content to keep me interested for a tiny bit more."

"I will gladly increase your understanding on food," Hannah offered. "But if the opportunity arises, we should speak more about God with you.

Once you understand some other points, I'm sure you will see things differently."

"That will not happen," Danarz asserted firmly.

"I will ask you one more question. If you answer it with any sanity, I might listen to your God ramblings further on our long flight back to my domains if you succeed in your quest, which will spare you from being my next meal. If you answer it as I am sure you will, then we shall never speak about this laughable subject again."

Talk about being put on the spot! I felt a great weight on my shoulders to answer Danarz's question correctly. "Ask your question, Danarz. I will give you a truthful answer I hope will inspire you beyond the limitations of your beliefs."

"Very well," Danarz agreed. "When you died and went to your higher realm, if you had seen your God, or gods, what would they look like? Would they look like you, or would they look like me and my kind?"

I felt defeat in the pit of my stomach. I already knew why Danarz had asked that particular question. I knew how I had to answer, and I knew how he would react. "The Elohim look like us. We are made in the image of our Father and Mother from the Celestine realms."

"End of discussion," Danarz bellowed. "You want me to believe in a God, a being higher and greater than me, that is a bug, something I eat for food? That is the funniest, most ludicrous thing

I have heard in a very long time!" He squawked loudly several times to emphasize his point.

"What about the Nartese?" Hannah challenged. "You said they look like us, but they live in a grand city with fierce flying worms that protect their realm. You even fear them when they come in solitary to trade with you. If they can be that great and powerful, perhaps there are others like us even greater that could be Gods and creators over all."

"You are mistaken in your assumption, missy bug. I have no fear of Narts and do not consider them superior to my kind in any way. They are an improvement in intellect and ability over the barbarian bugs that live primitively along the river, but without their flying worms for protection, they would just be a food source for us like any other bugs."

Danarz cocked his head back for a moment to look at us with a big red eye. "Trust me, I have seen every type of bug that exists. While you two are the first I have ever known of that can speak telepathically, something even the Narts cannot do, all of you are lower life forms."

Hannah held onto my arm and leaned sideways, trying to look back at Danarz as he flew. "Besides using a criterion of who eats who, why do you think your kind are a superior life form to our kind?"

Danarz bellowed out another of his derisive squawks. "We have been flying over the river for some time now, and you have seen hovel after hovel of what passes as the civilizations of bugs. Is that not evidence enough?"

Hannah shook her head, though I doubt Danarz could see her. "I'm sorry, it is not. The homes on the river are primitive, but at least they are homes built with enough ingenuity to construct walls and a roof. I mean no disrespect and am only trying to understand this strange world, but all we have seen of your kind is a nest in a cave on a cliff. It does not seem better by comparison."

In response, Danarz, without a word of warning, headed straight up and continued his arc until he was upside down. Hannah and I gripped his neck with all the strength of our legs. I held onto his feathers in a death grip as Hannah held tightly to my waist, both of us praying the feathers wouldn't pull out and plunge Hannah and me to our deaths.

Thankfully, the moment didn't last long as Danarz continued around with his arc into a complete loop, and we were soon once again flying level over the river. Both Hannah and I let out a big gasp of relief.

"That was for your ignorance and impudence!" Danarz snarled.

"The females nest alone high in caves for protection of their young from the giant serpents of the forests that would eat the eggs or the newly hatched young. The serpents cannot slither up the high cliffs, but they have stealthily penetrated even the most secure cities of our kind in the black of the moonless nights.

"Once their young fledge, the females return with their children to one of the several beautiful communities in the Mountains of Arceny, where most of us dwell. Our demesnes are not ugly angular monstrosities like the towers of the Narts. Our constructions blend with the natural surroundings in a harmonious synergy that is such a marvel to behold that words simply cannot do it justice.

"Perhaps someday, if you live beyond the next few, I will take you there. I'm sure it will be the highlight of your pitiful lives. The brilliance of our learned leaders and the artistry and beauty of our creations and domiciles are unsurpassed upon this world. You will understand at your very first amazed gaze why you are bugs and we are the greatest, most superior creations that have ever existed!

"But now end our talk and be more alert, for darkness has fallen while we have been conversing and we approach the boundary of the land of the Narts. We must be ever vigilant. The flying worms will be scanning the boundary even in the darkness for intruders. Once we have safely passed the perimeter, where most of the worms congregate, we will be at less risk of detection."

We were skimming across the surface of the river lit only by the reflection of the stars in the pale moonlight. Suddenly Danarz swooped upward and just as quickly dropped back down near the surface of the placid river.

"What was that all about?" I asked him.

"There is an invisible detection beam that crosses the river at that location," Danarz explained.

"I mark it in my mind by the Fridap Tree that grows along the river. That is not a common tree. It is most helpful for our travel at night, as the leaves are phosphorescent.

"When I see that tree day or night, I know to rise in altitude to avoid the Nart intruder detection system. If the beam is broken by travelers on the river or fliers like us that are staying low to avoid detection, the worms are alerted. I'm not sure how, but they arrive very quickly if the perimeter beam is breached."

"That is very fascinating," I marveled. "But I did not see a phosphorescent tree. Are you sure you had the correct location?"

"That's because you are a bug," Danarz retorted. "Bugs' eyes are so limited they cannot perceive the phosphorescence. Just another example of the inferiority of your kind."

As soon as we passed into the domain of the Nartese, Danarz left the river we had been traveling above for our entire trip and began flying low over the top of the verdant forest canopy. When I asked why, he explained, "If a worm were flying above us and we were on the river, they would see us easily as the moon cast our moving shadow upon the water. Flying low over the trees, we are much more camouflaged."

We flew in silence then for some time. I held on tight to Hannah's arms as I felt her body go limp with sleep. It was all I could do to not sleep as well. As it was dark and there really wasn't much I could see, I allowed myself to drift into a semi-sleep stupor to get a bit of rest, while still remaining conscious enough to continue holding onto Danarz.

After what seemed like just minutes of rest with my eyes closed, but actually was at least an hour, I was summoned back to full alertness by Danarz. "Look ahead. I have flown into a dark canyon just below the walls of the citadel. I will return to this location each night for the next seven nights to retrieve you if you have been successful in your quest.

"The Narts look almost exactly like you. You may be able to pass yourselves off as Narts while you seek to acquire the chest scale of a worm. But you do not know their language, and they are not telepathic. It is therefore imperative that you speak to no one, lest your ruse be immediately discovered."

I nodded my head in agreement. "That sounds like good advice, but from what you say we may need to leave in haste. If that should occur in the daytime, can you hear me telepathically if I call out to you for a pickup before nightfall?"

Danarz alighted silently onto the ground of the canyon. He lowered himself down so we could step off as he answered my query. "Except for the few that have very powerful minds, telepathy only works when those who are speaking to one another are at least within sight. Even then, if I was too distant to hear your yell with my ears, it would also be too far to hear your mental call. There are species that can use telepathy over vast distances, but mine is not one of them."

"That's troubling," I admitted, a bit worried. "But comforting to know there is at least something at which your species is not the most adept."

Danarz completely ignored my salient point. "You could build a large fire," he suggested. "Other than the fire-breathing worms who produce it from their bellies, the Narts do not build fires. They heat their domiciles and cook their food by some other means. If I see a large column of smoke, I will come to you at that spot if I feel I can do so without detection or risk to my own life."

"Very good," I agreed. "Hopefully we will be quick and safe at our task and see you tomorrow night with a worm scale in hand."

Danarz nodded his head once in acknowledgment and took a leap up in flight. "Tomorrow night then at this place and time," he said as he flew off.

We watched him fade into the blackness of the night as he swooped down low toward the mouth of the canyon. Hannah and I turned to look at one another for a brief moment and then turned together to look up the canyon toward the city of the Nartese.

"What is that strange glow toward the city?" Hannah asked.

We were looking up toward the rim of the canyon. The Nartese citadel was somewhere above, out of our sight. But in that direction, the entire area above the rim of the canyon was glowing in some strange, ethereal glow. It was something the likes of which I had never seen. My head cocked in curiosity and my mouth gaped a little open as I tried to fathom its nature and origin.

"I don't know what that peculiar light is," I answered, somewhat spellbound. "But lest we fall and injure ourselves trying to make our way up the canyon in the darkness, we best wait until daylight to solve the mystery."

"And I really need to sleep," Hannah added. She pulled me by the hand just a short distance to a flat area of ground covered with a layer of thick grass. She sat down and pulled me down with her. I lay on my side and cradled her in my arms as she snuggled up next to me, and we both quickly fell into a much-needed sleep. Whatever mysteries or dangers awaited us above the rim, they would probably still be there in the morning.

Chapter 10
LAND OF THE NARTESE

We awoke as the bright sun crested the horizon, infusing our bodies, cold from sleeping outside without cover, with much appreciated warmth.

My first thought was decidedly inauspicious. "I am really hungry."

Hannah laughed a little laugh and added, "Me too, but we should probably wait until we get to the city to try and find some food."

She looked around at the many nearby plants, including some with succulent-looking red berries. "None of these plants grow on our world. I have never seen their like even in the markets of Jerusalem, where exotic goods from far-off lands can be found."

She walked over and picked one of the berries and held it up so we could both examine it. "It looks like it should be edible, but I don't think we should risk eating it. Our protective body shields will not save us if we eat something that is poisonous."

I nodded my head in agreement, resigning myself to continued hunger. I pointed up the canyon. "Then let's make haste to get into the city and find something to eat!"

It took about an hour of careful scrambling on the steep slope to reach the top of the canyon. As we stepped up onto the flat plateau after cresting the canyon lip, we gazed up for our first close-up view of the city of the Nartese. We both just stood there for a minute or two, dumbfounded into awed silence at the city of the gods that our eyes beheld. In all seriousness, though I never saw the palaces of the Elohim when I died and briefly visited the Celestine realm, I doubted even the grandest palace on high could rival the wonder we saw before us. It made primitive, dingy Jerusalem look like the collected dung pile of camels by comparison.

The city was immense. It spread out as far as we could see in both directions, surrounded by a palisade the height of ten men that seemed to be made entirely of enormous clear quartz crystals tipped in amethyst scepters.

Every single part of the city was made of a crystalline substance of many hues, with chaotic veins and veinlets of what seemed to be pure gold running throughout! The sun was at our back and its light reflected in brilliant flashes off many parts of the city, both from the crystals and the gold, as we walked a little toward the palisade.

Scintillating towers of many heights extended skyward from behind the walls of the city, some standing straight up and others clustered together and protruding at varying angles. All seemed to be made of gigantic quartz crystals in brilliant colors.

The crystals, whether part of the perimeter wall or the towers beyond, were all translucent with thin, wispy clouds of white inside. Some had amethyst scepter tips like the palisade, others had tips and streaks the color of red raspberries or a light green or orange.

The most amazing aspect was that the walls and towers were clear enough that we could see people moving inside! Rooms and passageways to accommodate the people had been cut right into the gargantuan crystals! And there was gold literally everywhere! Enough gold in the walls and towers of this one city to make Rome seem like an insignificant pauper state.

Finally breaking the spell the gleaming city had cast upon us, I realized we had a problem. "There is no way into the city," I pointed out to Hannah. "The wall of crystals is too high for us to scale, and we would likely be detected if we tried. Beyond that, as far as we can see in either direction, there are no gates! How do the inhabitants get in and out of the city?"

We did not have to wait long pondering the question. Moments after I spoke, the answer came upon us. We were suddenly overcast by a large moving shadow. Looking up and over our shoulders, we saw one of the fearsome flying worms bearing down upon us.

I have never in all my long life felt so helpless. It was obvious that the monster would descend upon us in less than two frightened breaths. In that time we could not have run more than a few steps, and there was nowhere to run to; no place to hide, no way to escape, and no weapon to mount even the feeblest of defenses. I just hoped our invisible barrier of protection would shield us from the fiery breath of the monster. Miriam hadn't mentioned that as one of its abilities, so we could only hope it was up to the task. Fearing the worst, I cradled Hannah inside my arms as she laid her head upon my chest and held me tight around my waist.

I closed my eyes, waiting for the inevitable blast, but it never came. After a few more seconds, well beyond the time the monster should have already tried to toast us, I opened my eyes a peek to see what was going on. The flying monster was standing on two muscular hind legs upon the ground not six paces away from us. With its smaller forearms it seemed to nonchalantly be picking pieces of food out of its large, sharp-pointed teeth. Perhaps it had just recently eaten another interloper and wasn't interested in barbecuing us yet.

I spied a man just as he was climbing off the back of the beast. After he stepped onto the ground he turned and immediately walked over toward us. He didn't seem to be armed, and his manner wasn't threatening, but I suppose when you have a fire-breathing demon as your ally watching your back, you can be fairly cavalier.

Hannah must have blushed with her first glance at the Nartesian. He stood about half a head taller than me and looked more like a living sculpture of a Greek god than a man. He was as muscular as the strongest gladiator, his brawn bulging and rippling with every movement. His lightly tanned face was clean-shaven, square-jawed, blue-eyed and topped with a mane of glossy black hair freely falling to his broad shoulders. He wore some type of leather-like harness, studded with scintillating, inlaid jewels, forming an X shape diagonally across his chest. The tiniest of cloths, tied on with a string around his narrow waist, covered his loins. His bare feet were protected by a pair of Greek-style sandals with crisscrossing straps up the calves. Other than those barest of necessities, he was completely naked!

He stepped right up to us and proceeded to let loose with a stream of unintelligible gibberish. We answered him in our own gibberish, and it was quickly apparent that neither of us could understand the other. He took one step closer and reached out to touch Hannah. She quickly pulled her arm back away from his grasp.

The man looked back at the monster and gave it a hand signal. It responded by turning its head to the side and shooting out a long stream of fire into the air.

Message sent, message received. Hannah looked at me with resignation. I nodded my head in acquiescence, and she reluctantly stuck out her arm so the nearly naked man could touch her.

But it was not her body that he wanted to touch. As she stretched forth her arm, he reached out to feel the fabric of Hannah's garment where it terminated at her wrist.

Like all people raised as Hebrews, we used to dress according to the dictates of our religion. But through Yeshua we became Celestines, and he taught us that we should dress in our own colorful style with new cuts and fashion. This was something Hannah excelled at. Because we were a wealthy trading family, to delight my wife, I often returned from caravan trips with exotic fabrics and descriptions of unusual clothing I saw in far-off places. Hannah relished creating clothing from the fabrics and descriptions I brought back home.

On this day she was wearing a thin robe of finely combed sheep's wool, colored in wide, flowing ribbons of Tyrian purples and Egyptian blue dyes that draped her shoulders and covered her body like a loose dress from her neck down to her ankles.

The Nartesian reached out slowly to show he meant no harm and gently ran his hand over the sleeve of Hannah's outer garment. As he reached the hem by her wrist, the undergarment was just sticking out. The delicate white fabric was fine linen made from the fibers of the flax plant. He fingered this for some time and seemed quite amazed by it.

Abruptly he stood up and motioned for us

to mount his beast. With little recourse, we trepidatiously approached the behemoth. In size, its sinuous form was about twice as long as the giant birds we encountered, but far less bulky. However, it was much more fearsome and deadly in appearance. It was completely covered in scales like a fish, but the scales were like an armor plate, hard as rock and, from what Danarz had told us, impervious to fire. I saw the large pentagon-shaped scale in the center of its chest that Danarz had charged us to obtain, but I couldn't even imagine how that could occur.

The beast was obviously a supreme killer. It certainly didn't need fire to do its deadly deeds. As we clambered up upon its back by holding onto the edges of its thick, adamantine scales, I doubted there was any weapon in existence that could pierce that armor. Offensively, it had long, razor-edged talons on the toes of its short forelegs and smaller, but equally lethal-looking talons on the toes of its hind legs; talons that would shred a man into an unrecognizable puddle of flesh in seconds.

Its head seemed disproportionately large for its slender body and had small, sharp-pointed spikes protruding out at numerous places. Its mouth ran the entire length of the lower part of its head and was filled with glistening white, pointy teeth protruding everywhere. The smallest tooth was about the size of my fist and the largest about the size of two hands butting together at the fingertips.

If an invulnerable skin, razor talons, a spiked head, a mouth full of deadly canine-like teeth, and a breath of fire were not already far more capabilities than any one creature should possess, the monster also had a nasty set of horns atop its head with one curving inward on either side and a third longer one sticking straight out. I shook my head negatively in silent contemplation. Gaining the chest scale from one of these beasts would simply be impossible.

On top of the creature's neck there was a saddle attached with straps. Our captor indicated I should sit in front of the saddle and Hannah behind it. After we were in position, he climbed into the saddle. He made a double-clicking sound with his tongue on the roof of his mouth, which must have been a command to the beast because it immediately lifted us skyward.

It was an easy and gentle ride as our trip was very short, a minute or two at best. We simply flew over the palisade of giant crystals and landed in a large circular plaza within the walls of the city.

Our captor got up out of the saddle and disembarked from the back of the beast first, then beckoned for us to follow and helped Hannah down by holding her hand.

As we stood together on the ground, our backs still near to the winged monster, we had our first opportunity to take a good look around. Considering the breathtaking uniqueness of the crystal city, which seemed to be overflowing with gorgeous, colorful flowering plants from every structure, we should have been marveling at its wonder.

But we were too distracted by an even greater wonder than the architecture and flowers of the city of crystals. Seeing the perfection of human form in our captor, both in his physique, which was well displayed because of his near nakedness, and by the pure artistry of his masculine face, we both considered that he was likely the most eligible bachelor in the city. How wrong we were!

As we gazed around at the gathering crowd of curious onlookers, four things immediately stood out. First, there were no children, not even one of any age, nor any dogs, cats, or any other animals. Second, every person had flawless white skin like the people from the far north countries on our world. There was not one other race among them. Third, I could see no weapons of any kind; no swords, spears, slings, axes, nothing. Fourth, every single person we looked at, both male and female, was the epitome of human beauty and perfection.

Some had black hair, some had blonde, and others brown or red, but all had full, lustrous manes. The hair of most men fell freely to their shoulders, though some had various braids or styles of pulling back their hair. Every man was clean-shaven and had no body hair whatsoever, which made me conspicuously stand out with my full beard. Each Nartesian male was as muscular as our captor and just as scantily dressed or less. Some were entirely naked! Even the men that had little patches of material covering their loins just had bare derrieres on the back side.

If the men were living Adonises, the women were the Greek goddess Venus come to life. Their faces were as smooth and radiant as... well, like nothing I had ever seen in a woman before. So perfected in form, color, and luster that there is no woman from our world that could compare, not even my sister's beautiful companion Salome or Elissa the High Priestess of Tyre. Long wavy hair falling about midway down their backs framed their resplendent faces.

Like the men, the women were barely dressed or completely naked other than a great deal of jewelry. Many had ornate armbands on their upper arms, intricate earrings, jeweled bracelets of gold on their wrists, sparkling gemstone rings on many fingers, and numerous gold chains and pendants around their necks draping down to dangle between the perfection of their naked breasts. Some did have bejeweled, circular ornaments covering their nipples, and small patches of jeweled fabric covering the privates, but it had to be for adornment, as it certainly wasn't for modesty!

Our captor walked behind us and nudged us forward toward the center of what had become a circle of at least three hundred people, all looking like naked Greek gods and goddesses. A woman with long blonde hair stepped out from the crowd and approached us. Like all the women, she was the manifestation of every dream a man ever dreamed of a woman. She did seem just a bit taller than the other women, actually even taller than me by a bit. She was completely naked, including bare feet, except for a scintillating jewel-encrusted tiara on her head, some golden armbands, a tiny jeweled triangle barely covering her privates, and numerous jeweled toe and finger rings. Due to her superior size, tiara, and authoritative manner, I assumed she must be a high official or maybe even the queen if they had such things. I soon found my assumption was correct.

She stopped about three paces away from us and uttered some unintelligible words while pointing at us. Immediately four burly men came over to me and four women to Hannah, and with little we could do to stop them or even slow them down, they stripped us completely naked and forced us to our knees. Our remnants of clothes were thrown to the crowd, and they seemed to take great joy in ripping them into shreds. Only then did the lady approach us closer.

She came and stood close enough that I could feel the heat radiating from her naked body as she towered above me with her legs spread slightly and her hands on her hips. I was very grateful she had the little jeweled triangle covering her womanly region, as my face was exactly at that location when she stood in front of me. I made sure to only look up at her and never straight ahead.

She stepped over to Hannah and stood dominantly in front of her in the same manner. She reached down and grabbed Hannah by her chin and lifted her head to look directly at her.

Hannah was shivering, and it wasn't cold out. I reached over to grasp her hand to give her moral support, but the woman quickly kicked my hand away. She blurted out another unintelligible stream of words at Hannah, who of course could not respond.

She gave Hannah some gentle slaps on each cheek and ordered some attendants to come over. A man and a woman approached, each carrying a small box. The woman stood in front of Hannah and the man in front of me. The men and women who had just moments ago stripped us naked came up behind us. One stood on either side, tightly holding each arm near the shoulder, and the other two pushed down on our shoulders from above to prevent us from standing up.

The two people with the boxes standing in front of us opened them and, using a pair of long tweezers, withdrew a scorpion-like insect from the box. The tweezers were grasping the little devils by the center of their bodies, and they were furiously flicking their tails in attempts to sting the tweezers that held them.

One of the men standing behind me, pushing

down on my shoulders, reached out with one hand, firmly grasping my nose, while the other reached a hand and covered my eyes. I couldn't see or breathe and was sure they were going to throw the little stinging beastie on my naked body. Even worse, on Hannah's too! I struggled mightily to move. I tried to jerk my head side to side to dislodge the hands covering my eyes and clamping my nose shut, but the muscular Adonises were too strong. Starting to feel a bit of panic, I opened my mouth to gulp in a big breath of air. That was a mistake.

Immediately the scorpion-like creature was pushed into my mouth, and the hand that had been sealing my nose released it and reached down, pulling me up by my chin so I couldn't open my mouth. The agony inside my mouth was beyond words. The scorpion creature stung me over and over on my tongue, my cheeks, the roof of my mouth, and even far down my throat. Every point its stinger jabbed felt like someone had cut a small hole in my tongue or cheek and poured boiling tar into it. Remembering the day I had been bitten by the viper, that agony no longer seemed so bad by comparison.

The men released me and I flopped over prostrate on the ground, my body basically paralyzed from head to foot. Unfortunately, my eyes still worked, and I had to suffer the emotional trauma of seeing my beloved wife, lying naked on the ground before cruel strangers, enduring the same agony I was, and there was nothing at all I could do to come to her aid or give her solace.

All this time the cursed scorpion continued to sting me inside my mouth. After a few minutes, apparently completing its deadly deed, it crawled out on its own as my head lay sideways on the dirt courtyard ground and slid down the stream of drool I could feel slipping uncontrollably out of my wide-open mouth.

Several people—I was too disoriented from my pain to even notice if they were men or women—came and picked up my limp body. They carried me to an altar-like platform and laid me on my back, with my head leaning over to one side, drool continuing to drip out of my mouth.

After a few minutes I was still unable to move at all, but the pain in my mouth was beginning to subside slightly. It was with much consternation that I could see my beautiful, naked wife lifted off the ground by four burly men, one holding each leg and arm, and laid down on another altar next to mine. Thankfully, they let our heads lean toward each other so at least we could look into each other's eyes to silently pass our love.

From the limited, one-direction perspective of my unmoving head, I could see the throngs of people gathering closer to the altars, apparently to more keenly observe our final throes of death.

But rather than resign myself to die once again, I felt an inner peace remembering the faith of my dear wife that the Elohim, having just called us to a sacred mission to protect the Earth from threats such as the ones we now endured, would not let us die so easily.

And so it was. After a few minutes the paralysis left my body and the agony in my mouth disappeared. As my wife and I sat up on our own power and dangled our legs over the edge of the altars, I looked up at my captors intending to give them a scathing, gloating look proclaiming, *do your worst, you can't kill us!* However, I was quickly deflated when I saw no surprise on any of their faces, just an emotionless curiosity as they looked at us.

One of the lessons I have learned well in my two thousand years as a Guardian is nothing surprises me anymore. Even if it is something I have never seen, experienced, or considered, I expect to encounter the unexpected often. But I hadn't quite reached that point of understanding yet on that day so early in my life.

So I was completely surprised when the naked, voluptuous Amazonian director of our torture walked over to me and said with complete friendliness, "Hello Lazarus, I am Queen Leiaza. Welcome to Nartese City."

I was so shocked that she knew my name and was speaking to me in Aramaic, my native tongue, and was suddenly being so nice, that my mouth just dropped open and I couldn't speak. I watched in disbelief as she turned to Hannah, reached out for her hand, helped her off the altar, then gave her a full kiss on her lips.

"Welcome to your heaven," she told Hannah as she leaned forward and kissed her once more.

Still holding my wife's hand, she turned to me again. "You wonder how I know your name and can speak your language?"

I nodded my head in dazed agreement. "That, and why you are being so nice after trying to kill us, why you kissed my wife and are holding her hand, why nobody wears any clothes and are completely naked, as are we, and a host of other questions as well."

"All in good time, young man," she promised, which was a rather funny thing to say coming from her, as she was surely younger than me.

"For now, you and Hannah are our guests. We so seldom receive visitors that are also cultivated Alamars, that it is an occasion for a citywide banquet, which we shall hold tonight in the great hall. Until then, you are free to wander through the city in the public areas unaccompanied. You will find our citizens to be knowledgeable, personable, and more than happy to answer most of your questions."

I confess to being somewhat gobsmacked. Moments earlier I was sure that heartless fiends were trying to torture and kill us. Now the same people were treating us like honored guests. And that is not even throwing in the shock that they spoke Aramaic and the jewelry-adorned but otherwise naked queen seemed to be entirely too affectionate with my equally naked wife, who didn't seem to be objecting.

Looking at Hannah and the queen—they were still holding hands and conversing in little whispers I could not hear—I felt a pang of self-consciousness at our nakedness. It didn't bother me as much as it probably should have that we were naked and surrounded by other men and women that had on little more than jewelry and ornamentation. Their only clothes consisted of sparse fabric and leather-like material whose sole purpose wasn't modesty but merely as a platform to attach their numerous large gemstones, gold chains, and jewelry.

My ego was deflated simply because though we were in good shape, our naked bodies paled in comparison to any and every person in Nartese City. Both Hannah and I had a few pounds of excess fat. And like most every woman that has brought children into the world, Hannah's stomach had a little pooch. Plus, I was sure we were older than any other person in Nartese City.

Compared to the men I knew back on our world, I was strong and fit, more so than most others. In Nartese City I looked like the weak runt of the litter. Not only was every single man as tall or taller than me, but their fine-toned muscles rippled across their bodies. By comparison, I must have looked like an out-of-shape, muscleless scarecrow—a cloistered hermit who had lived his life never getting any physical exercise.

Without further ado, the queen turned and began to walk away, but she was still holding onto my wife's hand and leading her along.

Hannah looked back and waved to me reassuringly as she walked away with the queen. "It will be alright, Lazarus. Leiaza wants to give me a personal tour and take me to the Crystal Palace of Women to give me some adornments so I no longer need to be entirely naked. I'll see you soon at the banquet!"

Strange. After all we had just been through — the mental, emotional, and physical torment — my wife seemed far less affected than me.

After the queen departed with Hannah, the people loitering in the plaza soon dispersed as well, heading out into the city in every direction. I soon found myself standing all alone, naked, in the middle of a large circular plaza of a strange and wondrous city, still unsure of what had just happened.

I noticed the shreds of clothes they had ripped off of us were still lying scattered about on the plaza. I walked over and picked up the largest pieces, hoping to find some scraps I could wear to at least partially cover my nakedness. But it was a fruitless effort. Though I found a few shreds of sufficient size to cover my loins, they were too small by themselves to tie around my waist, and there were no remnants of cordage long enough to tie a loincloth in place.

I started to pick up a few scraps I could use as cordage, thinking I could tie them together until I had a piece big enough to encircle my waist and the loincloth, when I noticed a man approaching. It was our original captor.

"Greetings, Lazarus!" he boomed. "Everyone seems to have left you here alone. Quite rude. If you will have me, I will be happy to be your guide of our beautiful city, and get you some food and drink."

He looked down at the pitiful remnants of clothing I was holding in my hands. "If you feel more comfortable, I can also obtain something like I am wearing to cover your sexual organs."

I looked dubiously at the scant triangle of material that covered his loins. "Can I get one that covers my backside as well as my front side?"

He laughed a hearty laugh. "They don't come that way. But if you have enough time, you could probably sew a few together to achieve the stifling cover you desire, but I cannot imagine why you would want to do so.

"By the way, my name is Kzon. Are you hungry or thirsty?"

In fact, I was ravenous. I nodded my head. "Yes, I am, but can I first ask you some questions?"

"Most certainly!" Kzon replied, seeming to be

almost giddy at the prospect. "Provided I can ask you some questions in return."

"That's certainly fair," I agreed. I also realized that I would learn more about the Nartesians not only from my own questions but also from the questions Kzon asked me. I still had no trust in these people despite the apparent sudden friendliness they all currently exhibited. His questions would demonstrate what they didn't know about us and perhaps a weakness in them I might need to exploit to affect our escape if they didn't continue to be friendly hosts.

"My first question to you, Kzon, is how is it that you speak and understand Aramaic, while when we first met, you spoke gibberish which I understood not a word of, and when I replied, it seemed you had no understanding of my words either."

"Oh yes, I can see why that would seem to be a mystery," he acknowledged.

"When we first met, I did not understand you and could not speak your language. None of us could. That is why Queen Leiaza put the Scrax in your mouth. I know it must have hurt for a while and you probably thought we were killing you, but it was the only way to be able to communicate freely with you as we are now doing."

"How could putting a venomous creature inside my mouth, paralyzing me and bringing me near to death, possibly help you speak and understand Aramaic?" I exploded in anger and disbelief.

Kzon seemed hurt by my displeasure. "There are no people like you and your companion on this world. So I know you have somehow arrived here from another. I am fascinated by that and want to know everything about how you came to be here and what the world you came from is like."

We had begun to walk together off the plaza and toward some buildings that looked like a cluster of fat, green crystals protruding skyward. Kzon hung his head a bit as we walked, apparently contemplating what to say to me.

"I know your world must be very primitive if you do not even know what a Scrax is. We are aware of many worlds and the beings and creatures that live upon them. Though they are called differently or look somewhat different on other worlds, any place worth noting has their version of a Scrax.

"No world advances very far in its evolution until all the people of the same species can freely communicate regardless of their country or native language. That is why every culture, as they rise above the primordial soup, eventually develops a Scrax."

"You breed a poisonous insect to torment visitors to near death?" I shook my head in disbelief. "And somehow, if they don't die, it allows you to understand and suddenly speak their language? I must not have gotten enough sleep last night because that makes absolutely no sense to me."

"It is not from lack of sleep that your mind is in

a fog," Kzon said matter-of-factly. "As I deduced, you come from a very simple world."

I looked up in the sky at the living, breathing, flying furnaces circling above the city. "How is it that your people have tamed those ferocious beasts?"

"Sorry, my friend," Kzon said apologetically. "That is a secret of our people that I cannot answer. I could lie to you and make up a story, but I prefer not to."

Hmm. With his forthright answer, I didn't intend to press Kzon about this question any more. But anything that was a secret was something I should know, and I intended to be more diligent, looking elsewhere in my exploration of the city for an answer to that particular question.

We had come up to the green crystal building. There were no doors, just open passageways made by the crisscrossing crystals overhead. Inside it was very spacious. At least three dozen Nartesians were lounging on what appeared to be very plump, cushy couches. There were no chairs anywhere to be seen. The couches were arranged in circles, one person to a couch and six couches to a circle. In the center of each circle of couches there was a very large, short, round crystalline table laden with delicious-looking foods and goblets of drinks from which the various people were consuming with relish.

I noticed they were all gabbing in their unintelligible gibberish, so apparently the stings of the Scrax didn't work for me to understand their language like they were able to conveniently understand mine. Curious. I inquired of Kzon why he could understand and speak Aramaic but his language was still undecipherable to me.

"It is because the Scrax and Nartesians are linked and you are not," he explained.

"The Scrax is not a living creature as you surely imagined. It is a construct of ours made of liquefied crystal, metals and other substances that are undoubtedly unfathomable to you."

Unfathomable? How right he was! Not a living creature? I looked at him as if he was absolutely daft!

"I will try to simplify this so you can understand," he said patiently, like a school teacher to a first year student.

"The Scrax injects a fluid that rapidly passes from your mouth and tongue to your brain," he elaborated.

"Do you know what a brain is?" he asked in sincere innocence.

"I know you are referring to the thoughts that come from my head when you say that," I replied lamely feeling like an idiot. "And I have seen the inside of people's heads that have been bashed in by bandits and assume that gray mass of stuff is what you are calling a brain."

"Very good!" he exclaimed like a teacher whose star pupil just got a correct answer on the test.

I laugh today, two thousand years later, at my utter ignorance in those early days. Even though I did refer to the place where thoughts resided in terms of a brain, I really didn't understand exactly what it was or how it functioned back then.

Kzon began using hand motions to describe how the Scrax worked. "Inside the fluid that enters through your mouth and travels to your brain are tiny components, completely invisible to the naked eye, that send signals from your brain to ours once they have squirmed their way into the needed places in your mind.

"Different parts of your brain are for different purposes. The Scrax components lodge in the part of your brain that is for language. We have resonate connections in our brains. Once connected, every Nartesian shares that part of your brain and we are instantly fluent in any language you speak."

"And you knew my name as well?"

"Yes, that is a part of your language and used so frequently that it leaves a rut in your brain. Only your name would get used and heard that much to make such an impression."

Wow! I was overwhelmed with the depth of my ignorance and the limitations of my life experiences. In my only previous visit to another world, I had encountered little beings not much bigger than rats that were very intelligent and flew in the sky in shinny spheres. They had a pretty fancy city too. But they were telepathic with us, which by its nature is self-translating, thought to thought. But the Nartesians accomplished inter-language communication by means of some incomprehensible stinging insect device? How could that be possible?

Kzon introduced me to several men and women at the green crystal restaurant. They all had strange names and though they were friendly and welcoming we didn't linger to talk with them.

Kzon ordered some food and drink for us. Everything was strange in both appearance and often in texture, but it was some of the tastiest food and delicious drink that I had ever had the pleasure of consuming. I made a mental note to plan on returning to Nartese City in the future just for the food!

When I commented on the delight to my palate, Kzon laughed. "These are just little snacks, simple tidbits. Wait until the queen's banquet. There you will have such divine food and drink that you will think that here you have just been eating dirt and drinking mud!"

Even though Kzon promised to answer my questions, he seemed to put me off every time I made attempt to do so. Unless, the question was a simple one like, 'do you have many sunny days here?' Even in those cases his answers tended to be polite, but curt, 'yes' or 'no' being the most typical replies.

I was anxious to see more of Nartese City, but

Kzon insisted we stay for some time at the green crystal cafe so he could teach me to play Zontog, a game that was all the rage in Nartese City. Reluctantly I agreed, but quickly found to my delight and Kzon's displeasure that it was a game I was actually fairly good at. In a short time everyone in the cafe had gathered around to watch us play and most were cheering me on!

Zontog is a game between two players. It is played with very well-balanced daggers with six inch blades. Each player is given six daggers with sharp-tipped points of fine steel. The edges are slightly dulled so the blades can be handled without fear of cutting your hand.

Players stand against thick, circular wooden walls, only a little larger than the distance of your arms spread out. The walls are about ten paces apart. One player had to stand completely still in an exactly marked location while the other player throws their six daggers trying to embed the blades in the wooden wall on small targets that were adjusted to be as close to the target person's body as possible. One target under each arm pit, one just below the juncture of the crotch, one just beyond each hand and one just above the top of the head.

When they are done throwing all six blades, points were scored for proximity to the center of the six targets. If a thrower actually missed and stuck a blade in their opponent they would be disqualified and their opponent would win, if they lived.

The person being thrown at had their arms stretched out at about a forty-five degree angle with their hands gripping straps to help keep their arms immobile. Their legs were also spread at forty-five degrees and the tips of their feet inserted through small loops to keep their legs from moving.

However, the feet and hands were not bound and the person that was the target could easily move to avoid a misdirected flying dagger. Slight movement was allowed, but if either hand released its grip on the straps or a foot moved out of a loop, the person targeted would be disqualified and forfeit the match. The fact that they did so to prevent injury or perhaps even death did not seem to be relevant to the Nartesians.

On my world this would seem like a very foolish game. However, on this world the same laws of nature did not seem to apply, which I suppose made the game safer than it would have first appeared. When the daggers were thrown they flew through the air, flipping over and over in flight as daggers do. But that is where the resemblance to daggers I had known ended. In a manner incomprehensible to me, another thing to add to my increasingly long incomprehensible list, the daggers in Nartese City seemed to fly at less than half the speed the same dagger would fly when thrown on Earth. It still rapidly covered the ten paces separating the two opponents, but it was slow enough that you could move out of the way if you thought it was going to hit you.

Kzon threw at me first and he was very good. From my perspective out of my periphery vision, it seemed like he hit every target. The entire ordeal was stressful for me, especially so when he threw the last dagger. I am not an overly fearful man, but there is an irrational, anxiety-induced, teeth-gritting apprehension that rushes upon a man when someone is intentionally aiming a sharp dagger for their naked, fully exposed crotch! Hannah would not be pleased if I met her at the banquet missing some of my family jewels! Of course my protective body shield should have prevented such an injury, but I preferred to not put it to the test. However my worries were unfounded as Kzon put the dagger right on target. His final score was 21 points out of a possible 30.

I was actually quite experienced with daggers and had thrown them in practice at tree trunks innumerable times while encamped during caravan travels. The few times I actually needed to throw them in battles when brigands were attacking our caravan, they found the mark I was aiming for every time. And so it was with Kzon. Though this was my first game of Zontog I topped his score with a tally of 25 when it was my turn to throw at him.

Thinking the game was over I felt a rush of relaxation wash over me. But I let my guard down too soon. "You need to get back on the board," Kzon directed me.

I shook my hand and deferred. "I think I'll pass Kzon. One round is enough for me. Besides, I want to quit while I am ahead."

"You cannot," Kzon stated strongly. "That is against the rules. You must continue to meet every challenger until you are either defeated or there are no more challengers.

I looked around the room. There were at least three dozen men and women. "How long is this going to take?" I asked. "I don't want to be late for the banquet."

"Not to worry," Kzon assured me. "If we need to leave for the banquet, you can resume meeting your challengers afterward, but you had the luck of a first timer. I'm sure you will be out in the next round."

And so it began. The rounds did not actually take that long. I bested the next three challengers, two women and one man. My fourth challenger was a woman named Aslass. We both scored a perfect 30. I assumed an unbeatable tie would be the end of the game. Would you be surprised if I told you my assumption was incorrect?

"Congratulations Lazarus!" Kzon exclaimed as he came up and patted me heartily on the back. It is astounding! You are going to level two and this is the very first time you have played Zontog.

"And what is level two?" I asked in innocent curiosity.

It is the same rules as level one," Kzon explained.

"But the board you are attached to is actually a wheel. It will be turning around and around on level two while Aslass throws the daggers at you. In the unlikely event that you have another tie, you will go to level three and the wheel will spin faster.

I threw first at Aslass. I was so nervous that I might accidentally hit and injure her that I purposely missed the board completely with every throw. The daggers all stuck in the wall behind her.

"What are you doing?" A very agitated Kzon exclaimed. "You are purposefully missing. That is not allowed!"

"That's fine Kzon. I don't want to risk hitting your friend with a blade," I explained magnanimously. "By missing I am also conceding. I really do not wish to play this game anymore. So she wins and I would still like to see more of the city before the banquet. Can we go?"

"No we cannot go!" A bug-eyed Kzon protested. "We are in the middle of a game. Quitting by any means is not allowed in the rules unless you are too injured to continue. All of us have bets on the outcome of the match. You must play the next level for us to settle our bets."

"Are you sure about that?" I inquired innocently. "I did not see anyone placing bets or exchanging money with anyone else."

"Of course you did not!" Kzon said in a raised voice. "We have not used physical money since our ancient ancestor's ancestors were born. Bets are made with eye contact alone. Look around the room Lazarus. Do you see any happy faces peering at you? Everyone is upset with you for trying to sneak out of the game. However, considering you are a visiting guest we will give you a chance to redeem yourself."

Kzon went over to the wall and pulled out all of my daggers and brought them back and handed them to me. "Now throw again and this time be serious!"

I didn't know what else to do, so with nervous apprehension that this was not going to end well, I did as Kzon bid and threw the daggers once more at the spinning wheel holding Aslass. However, I still threw carefully to miss. I hit the wooden wheel; no errant throws into the wall behind. But I aimed as far from the helpless lady's body as possible. I silently hoped she would be as considerate when she was throwing at me. Such was not the case.

Aslass knew I had thrown wide. I could tell by her pursed lips and the angry scowl on her pretty face that she was incensed that I hadn't given my best effort. As if somehow I had demeaned her because I tried to protect her from injury. She was not so kind to me. Her first dagger was thrown under my left armpit. I couldn't see where it landed, but I felt the breeze when it slipped within a hair of my body and imbedded with a thud in the spinning wooden wheel.

Her next four throws were equally as close. If I

moved my body even slightly I could feel the cold knife blades stuck into the wood against my naked skin.

Her last throw of course was to the area I was most trepidatious about – the tiny space beneath the crotch of my spread legs where helplessly dangled my naked, completely exposed, family jewels. I almost decided to close my eyes but at the last minute decided to keep them open. I should have kept them closed. I could tell immediately by the trajectory of the blade flipping through the air that it was going to hit a little too high.

It's interesting how in moments of crisis your mind speeds up and it seems like time slows down. Though it took not more than a second for the spinning dagger to cover the ten paces separating me from Aslass, that short time was enough for me to look up and see by the grimacing faces of some of the male onlookers that they too knew the dagger was going to geld me. I also had time to consider that my protective body shield should protect me, but doing so would reveal one of my secrets I didn't want to reveal to the Nartesians.

At the last microsecond of dagger flight, I let go of the strap I was holding with my right hand and swept aside the half-speed spinning dagger. It fell to the floor to my left with a metallic clang.

Looking up at the ashen faces of everyone, you would have thought I had just assassinated the queen. Each and every person had a dumbfounded look of disbelief written all over their face.

"You cannot do that!" Someone in the crowd shouted. "It is against the rules!"

"How did he do that?" Another wondered with incredulity. "How can anyone move so fast as to intercept a dagger in flight?"

I had a bit of a wry smile at that comment. I had moved fast, but the blade was also traveling slow. It was curious. Perhaps what to me seemed be an avoidable half speed flight, was an unavoidable rapid speed to the Nartesians. Either that, or despite their Adonis and Venus-like appearances of bodily perfection, they had so many bulky muscles it didn't allow them to move as quickly my sinewy form.

One of the men came over and grabbed my hand that had slapped away the dagger and held it up. "Look at this. He does not even have a scratch on his hand. How can that be? I would have expected the dagger to have completely pierced his hand and still be stuck in it. Instead it's laying over there on the floor."

Now several people came over close to me. One person after another rudely grabbed my hand and pulled it nearer to them to examine. An Amazonian-like lady came over. She was half a head taller than me, ornately covered on many parts of her body with gold chains, jewels and gold lattices. The areolas of her generous, uprightly projecting breasts, which I tried without full success to ignore, were covered with golden cones tipped by a large ruby-like gemstone. The people closest to me backed away to give her egress and I assumed she was someone of at least slight importance.

Kzon who was standing behind me leaned forward and whispered in my ear. "Now you've done it. You have drawn the attention of the queen's sister Ireven. It was nice knowing you Lazarus."

Ireven was standing directly in front of me now. Almost no space separated us. The golden cones tipping her breasts were touching my own naked, hairy chest and I could feel the radiating heat of her body against mine.

"I think you have been deceiving us stranger," she accused in a slow deliberate voice. "Why can you move faster than a man should be able to move? Or perhaps it just seemed so to us and there is a greater secret you are hiding that was the real reason you were able to deflect the dagger from its path without any injury to your hand."

I laughed a nervous little laugh and tried to explain. "Please don't make more of this than it actually was," I pleaded.

"The dagger did not have sharpened edges. The only dangerous part was the tip. I feared for my most personal body parts and reflexively, without thinking swatted the dagger away with my hand. I was just very lucky that I hit it on its side and did not take the point through my hand. Nothing more than that. I'm sorry I ruined your game and wagering," I offered contritely.

Ireven whipped a dagger out of a jeweled scabbard held by a thick golden chain encircling her shapely, hourglass waist. She held the shiny blade right up near my face. "I do not believe you."

She reached over to a woman standing beside her and grabbed the end of her long hair. Holding it in front of her she sliced it off at the base of her fist closed around it and let it fall to the floor. "Unlike the throwing daggers, this one does have razor sharp edges as you can see."

She took a step back, then reached out and grabbed my wrist holding my arm out toward her. "I am going to shave off the forest of short hairs you have growing on your arm. I am suspicious that there is more to your body than being able to make exceptionally rapid hand movements. You don't mind losing a little hair to prove me wrong do you?" she asked with a malicious cunning belying her pure beauty.

"If you must," I replied with a foreboding feeling rising inside of me. What would they do when they found my protective body shield did not allow the dagger to cut my hair?

"Although I am rather fond of my arm hair and would prefer you just accepted that it was sheer luck and that I am not fast or special in any way," I added with little hope of changing her mind.

And I didn't. Starting just below my elbow she held the extremely sharp edge against my skin and slowly ran it across my arm until she reached my wrist. I was the most startled person in the room to see a neat pile of my arm hair scraped right off. My protective shield wasn't working! By the stars, any of those dagger throws could actually have injured me if they had missed their marks!

Ireven looked at me with a curious scowl. "Perhaps you were telling the truth."

With those words I let out a slow exhale of relief. Who would have thought that a defective body shield would actually be something that helped me?

"Perhaps not," she quickly added with renewed determination.

She directed four men to hold me by my arms and legs. She came close to me again with a very menacing look distorting the beauty of her face and held the tip of her dagger against my exposed family jewels.

"Happily, I must be the bearer of bad news. You and your companion will be given the honor of being allowed to remain in Nartese City; but it will be as slaves."

She tapped on my jewels with the flat edge of her dagger. "Male slaves have no use for these dangly parts. As you spoiled our game, I am going to take yours now to give myself some solace for my disappointment at an inconclusive game of Zontog."

I felt the pressure of the sharp edge of her blade

pushing against my testicles. I cringed as I felt a sawing motion. But then, to my utter relief, I felt no pain and realized that my sporadically effective body shield must have thankfully decided to work again. My relief was short-lived.

"As I suspected!" Ireven yelled triumphantly. "This creature is more than he appears. My blade cut his hair, but to a true wound his body is as impervious as a rock."

Before I could object or try to come up with a plausible explanation, she pulled her hand holding the sharp-pointed dagger far back, then plunged it with great force into my stomach. Or at least that is what she tried to do. The protective body shield was like a second skin and it was completely invulnerable to the needle point of the dagger. She had jammed it with so much force into my shield that the tip of the blade actually broke.

"To the tower with this one!" Ireven spat vehemently as she whipped her hand, pointing her finger at me. Two very big, muscular men immediately grabbed me by my arms to restrain me.

"I can walk on my own power," I assured them. "And where would I escape to?" I asked, pointing out the obvious.

Ireven glared at me. "I prefer male slaves and condemned prisoners to be dragged." And so I was, all the while wondering which was my fate—slave or condemned?

Every time I tried to walk on my own two feet, braced by the two burly men on either side of me, one of them would whop me upside the head with their giant paw of a hand, practically making me see stars. The first time he quietly reprimanded me, "Ireven said to drag you. Just go along for the ride and don't upset her anymore. She has a wicked temper."

Yes, I noticed she has a bit of a tyrant in her, I murmured philosophically to myself.

Thankfully, we did not have far to walk, or in my case be dragged. The entire crowd at the green crystal café followed us outside to the center of the spacious plaza. A man in the crowd had a whistle on a chain about his neck. He blew three long bursts, then two short ones. In less than thirty seconds one of the fearsome giant lizards appeared and landed in the plaza in front of us. I call them lizards as that was their appearance to me, more than a worm. But their bodies radiated warmth, which told me that despite their appearance and my own description, they were not members of the reptile family.

One of the men holding me pushed me roughly toward the fire-breathing demon. "Mount!" he ordered.

Not having any other options, I did as he bid and climbed up the side of the kneeling lizard by holding onto the edges of its massive scales as I had done previously. I sat in front of the saddle and my captor clambered up and sat in it behind me.

As soon as he was settled the slithering beast spread its wings and we became airborne after a single downward stroke.

Not far distant, toward the very heart of the city, there was a tall tower rising high above all others. As we continued to gain altitude and fly toward the spire, it became obvious that was our destination.

There was a wide, flat pentagon-shaped platform extending off to the side about one hundred feet below the tip of the glistening spire, which was brilliantly reflecting the rays of the sun. The flying beast sat us gently down upon the platform and both my escort and I climbed down.

My captor grabbed me by my arm and pulled me over to the side of the platform, leaning me precariously over the edge. For a moment I thought he was going to throw me off the precipice. Far, far below I could see the city and the large square we had just left, which now looked very small. The drop straight down had to be at least two thousand feet!

"This tower is only an observation platform," he explained gruffly. "The shaft is solid. There is no passageway to the ground and no way up to the top except the way we came, by the flight of a Nagasa."

He pointed to a narrow open passageway leading into the confines of the tower. "There is a small room through that passage. You should go there to stay out of the wind, which can be quite strong at this altitude."

"What about my wife? What is happening to her? And what is going to happen to me?" I inquired, hoping to know my fate that I might plan a way to circumvent it.

"I know nothing about your female companion," he replied with the same gruffness. "The queen has taken her to be her property. What happens to her now is not for me to know, but it will probably be more pleasurable than what is going to happen to you."

"What is going to happen to me?" I asked again, hoping for some glimmer of information to understand the depth of my plight.

"The queen will decide that as well," he replied brusquely. "The last outsider that was not enslaved and was instead taken to this tower, and as my memory serves, the six before them, all were slow roasted by a Nagasa. When they could no longer scream in agony but were still alive, they were given to the Nagasa to eat, one limb at a time, as a snack."

"Your flying beasts eat people!" I asked with apprehensive incredulity.

He looked at me in amazement. "How can you even ask such a stupid question? What do you think those large, pointy sharp teeth are for, eating berries? That is why all the villages nearby on the river are abandoned. The Nagasas ate all of the people. They are needing to go further and further afield to find primitives to eat and it is getting quite time-consuming in their day. So we certainly appreciate when visitors like you are considerate enough to bring a meal to them."

He laughed heartily at his own warped wit. "Although you are very scrawny. You are not going to appease their appetite very much.

"It's actually too upsetting to my sensitive stomach to watch them eat," he admitted with enough relish that I knew he was just rubbing in my fate.

"They like their meat really warm, with the blood still squirting out the veins. That is why they eat one limb at a time. Immediately after they bite off a leg or an arm, they breathe fire on the stub to cauterize the wound so the victim will remain alive and not bleed to death."

Laughing at his own morbid sense of humor, he left me with that unpleasant thought. Mounting his beast and still chuckling but without another word, he flew off the tower. I peeked over the edge of the platform and watched as the Nagasa made wide, slow circles as it descended back down toward the milling crowd below.

My gaze lingered at the long spread wings and the graceful, undulating body of the Nagasa in flight. I reflected that it was too bad they were such terrible monsters. If you could ignore their unpleasant aspects for a moment and just take in the grandeur essence of their raw power, they were quite majestic, even awe-inspiring beasts.

Chapter 11
TOY

I spent a windy night alone in the small tower room huddling in a corner on the floor as far away as possible from the open entryway to avoid the bite of the fierce, howling wind on my naked body. I was so worried, wondering what was happening to my wife Hannah, that I didn't sleep much that night.

Early the next morning, shortly after the sun had crested the horizon and kissed the day, Hannah's fate became known to me. I had roused myself from my fitful, cold slumber and was stretching awake as I looked down on the gleaming city below. I noticed a Nagasa rising up from the depths and was hoping it was coming to remove me from the lonely pinnacle. Instead, as the beast came closer, I could see that Hannah was sitting on the neck of the Nagasa in front of the saddle where sat my own erstwhile captor.

I backed off to the side to give the Nagasa room to land on the small tower platform and rushed to embrace my wife after she climbed down with little assistance. The fact that we were both entirely naked as our bodies met no longer seemed to be an issue in my mind. After so much time being in a similar state as everyone else in the city, I no longer cared about hiding my nudity, and it no longer seemed shameful.

Without a word of greeting, the Nagasa and his master abruptly lifted into the air and banked down and to the right, leaving us alone on the high tower. As I took a step back from Hannah, I realized there was something extremely different about her. She looked as young, vibrant, and bounteous as any of the peerless women of the city! She was perfectly slim, and her belly was as flat as the day before she ever bore a child. Her hair was more lustrous than I ever imagined it could be; more so than even the days of her youth. Her breasts seemed to have doubled in size and were defying gravity!

"What happened to you?" I exclaimed in disbelieving wonder. "You are beautiful and alluring beyond measure. How did you ever get this way in one day?"

Hannah didn't answer. She just smiled at me in a most beguiling manner. I stared at her, spellbound that this vision of beauty was my wife! I forgot all about the precariousness of our situation as my eyes and all my thoughts were occupied in an unexpected bliss.

"I am glad my transformation pleases you, Lazarus," Hannah said softly as she continued to hold both my hands with our arms outstretched toward one another. "But I would have thought your first question would have been why I am here and why you are, and what is to be our fate."

"Uh, yeah, um, you're right, that should have been my question," I agreed, trying with little success to divert my thoughts to something other than my highly desirable wife. "Do you know the answers?" I asked, surprised.

"Let me tell you what has happened to me," Hannah proffered. "By my account you will learn the answers to all of your questions, including how I have become the epitome of your manly fantasies."

I nodded my head in agreement. Taking Hannah by the hand, I led her into the small tower room so we could be out of the wind, which not only was chilly on our naked bodies but howled enough that it was also difficult to hear what the other person was saying, even though they were standing right next to you.

Hannah took a deep breath and slowly exhaled as she began her tale. "At first, going with Queen Leiaza after I left you seemed like a dream come true. She was so sweet to me. I was certain everything was going to work out wonderfully for you and me among the very hospitable Nartesians.

"We went to the Crystal Palace. It is an amazing place. The entire building is made of a translucent, crystalline substance. Some parts are clear as water, and other sections are in many soft, pastel colors.

There were also opaque sections. There is not one sharp angle in any part of the building. Every edge of a surface is curved in shape. As Leiaza explained, the building was purposefully designed that way to emulate the sensuous curves of women.

"As I'm sure you too have ascertained, women are in authority in this city. The Crystal Palace is their special sanctuary where only women are allowed entry. In fact, the queen told me if a man ever had the audacity to cross the threshold of the golden gates, the penalty would be his life.

"The very first place I was brought to was a spacious, luxurious circular room. It had what seemed to be, at first glance, a large cushioned altar in the center. At the base of the walls around the entire room was a continuous bench with plump, red cushions. In parts, it was just narrow enough to sit upon. But there were sections where it was wide enough for two or more people to lay upon.

"When we entered the room, there were at least a dozen beautiful women inside. Some were sitting together, some standing in conversation with one another, and to my shock, there was one couple and another threesome in passionate embraces laying on the larger sections of the circular bench."

My eyes widened a bit at that last tidbit. But I didn't say anything, and Hannah continued to share her experience.

"The queen asked me to lay down on my back on the altar. I was a little nervous, but she assured me everything would be fine and I would be most pleased with my time on the altar.

"She called over to the women, and several came over until I was surrounded on all sides. Once they were in position, they began to gently touch me and massage me everywhere on my naked body.

"It was very pleasurable physically, but morally uncomfortable to have many fairly naked women, all of whom were complete strangers to me, touching and massaging me.

"When all those hands first touched me, I tried to get up. 'What are you doing?' I protested with some upset. 'I do not wish to be touched like this.'"

Queen Leiaza, who was standing directly behind me, put her hands on my shoulders and gently but firmly pushed me back down onto the altar. "Be not concerned, Hannah," she reassured me. "We are only going to give you pleasure. In the process, we are going to reshape your body so you will be perfect, like us."

"Looking at all of their exquisite naked bodies leaning over me, I lay back down, resigned to endure their ministrations but certain I would never look anything like their perfection of womanly form."

"But you do!" I exclaimed, still marveling at Hannah's beauty and, and... other physical attributes.

"Ssh," Hannah whispered, holding her extended index finger up to her sensuous lips. "Let me continue the story."

"Yes, yes," I encouraged. "Please continue."

"They massaged me for at least two hours, maybe three. It was not always the same women. Sometimes others in the room would come over and take the place of one who had been with me for a while.

"At first I was quite tense, having so many strangers touching me. But after a bit, with continued reassurances from Leiaza, I relaxed. I began to lose my inhibitions and just enjoy the marvelous sensations their ministrations were creating in every part of my body."

"Every part?" I asked hesitantly, afraid of what she might be implying.

"Yes, Lazarus," she answered calmly, looking me steadily in my eyes as she did. "There was no part of my body they did not touch. Even my most intimate parts. In my mind I silently objected. But I became in a semi-awake state. My body was limply immobilized and would not obey the commands from my dulled mind to move.

"After a time, what they were doing to me felt so good, I did not want to move. Wave after wave of radiating pleasure overcame me, and each wave was more intense than the previous.

"When at last they were done with their ministrations, I was pleasantly exhausted and as content as I have ever been. My mind was empty of thoughts of you, or our children, or our mission, or our situation. I just lay upon the altar so totally relaxed and satiated. I could not move to get up, and my mind was in such an empty state that it was literally devoid of a thought.

"Leiaza dismissed all of the women, and they soon departed the room. She came over to me, and as I looked upon her beautiful face and shapely form, the only thought I had was that she was the most beautiful, desirable woman that had ever existed. That was a thought I never would have imagined myself having before I was in that room alone with Leiaza.

"She put her hand gently on my forehead and leaned down to kiss me deeply on my lips, and I kissed her back.

"She gently stroked my forehead and the edge of my hair as I gazed up rapturously into her deep blue eyes. 'Rest now, Hannah. Remain here on the altar as long as you wish. When you are ready to leave, just push the small green button on the wall by the entry portal, and I will soon come to gather you for the pre-banquet festivities.'"

"She kissed me once more, quite passionately, then departed the room, leaving me alone. I lay upon the altar for several minutes, maybe as long as half an hour. Time did not seem very relevant.

"For a while all I could think about was Leiaza. I am ashamed to admit that I desired her, Lazarus, like a woman desires a man. I know Yeshua has told us this is a perfectly natural urge, but it is not one I had ever experienced before.

"After a time, my mind cleared, and I once again had thoughts of you, and our children, and our great purpose in life. As I approached the portal to push the green button, there were mirrors on either side. I saw my reflection and thought at first I was somehow looking at someone else! But after a moment, I realized it really was me.

"Somehow, with just their hands massaging me, they had morphed my body into the form of a goddess, even as Leiaza had promised they would. It seemed impossible. It still does. But here I am standing before you, very worried about what they might do to us, while another part of me, the part that is probably too vain, is grateful and amazed at the perfection of womanhood I have become."

"Me too!" I quipped. "To… both parts," I stuttered, "both our precarious situation and the admiration of your beauty," I elaborated.

My moment of bliss of soaking in the vision of loveliness that was my wife vanished when I was jolted back to the moment at hand and remembered that though Hannah might have been perfect, our situation was far from it. Reluctantly, I had to stay focused.

"What more do you know about our fate?" I asked with all the gravity I could muster.

"Patience, Lazarus, you will know all that I know by the end of my story."

"Then please continue," I encouraged.

"After I pushed the green button, there was no

sign or sound, but shortly afterward Leiaza came and opened the doors. She embraced me very affectionately and once again gave me a lingering kiss on the lips. I realize now that she was exerting some type of control and manipulation of my thoughts, but at the time it did not seem odd at all to me that a woman would be kissing me or that I would be kissing her back.

"She led me by the hand through a vast, opulent palace. All the rooms were made of crystal or a crystalline substance in beautiful hues and colors. They were luxuriously apportioned with ornate furniture, heavy with gold, rich, colorful fabrics, and amazing art from paintings to sculptures. I cannot even imagine that the Celestine Kingdom of Elohim could be more grand than the palaces of Nartese City.

"We came into a wing with such grand architecture and so extravagantly apportioned that all I had seen to that point paled into mundane drabness by comparison. We had entered the queen's private quarters.

"The strangest part was that the entire trip through the enormous palace complex, from the altar room to the entrance of the queen's chambers, there were no guards and very few other people."

"I don't find that peculiar," I countered. "As far as we've learned, the Nartesians have no enemies on this world. It seems all other creatures are wary and even afraid of them. So they really have no need for soldiers or guards. They seem to only protect their borders and mostly use the Nagasa for that purpose.

"I don't think it is from fear of attack that they guard the border so diligently. They simply seem to be a very insular and private community and do not want visitors."

"The entire population traipsing about mostly naked might also have something to do with it," I added.

"What I do find odd, besides the fact that they all look like Greek gods and goddesses, and now so do you... is that this city seems to be their only place of habitation. Where do they even get their food from?

"When we flew into the city on the back of the Nagasa I did not see even one cultivated field of crops. Yet their food is sumptuous and overflowing in abundance. If they hardly trade with others and don't grow their own food, where does it all come from?"

Hannah held her palms up and wide with questioning uncertainty. "We have seen so little of this world, perhaps there are more communities of Nartesians in other places that grow their crops and raise their food, and it is with these that they engage in trade."

"Perhaps," I nodded my head and stroked my chin in contemplation. "But let me not interrupt you. What happened in the queen's chamber?"

Hannah took in another deep breath and let it slowly exhale out. I knew from years of living with her that it was a sign she was going to talk about something she was uncomfortable discussing.

"Before I begin..." Hannah said hesitantly. "Please know that I was not myself. I cannot explain why, but I simply could not resist Leiaza and did not even have a thought at first to resist, physically or mentally."

She looked perfectly fine to me, even more than perfect, uninjured in any way. I looked at her with a bit of wide-eyed curiosity, trying to fathom what she would reveal.

"The queen took me to her bedchamber..." Hannah began in faltering explanation.

"She led me to her bed and the two of us lay down together upon it. In moments we were in a passionate, intertwined embrace, pushing all parts of our bodies together as closely as we could."

Hannah hung her head in sadness. "I am ashamed to say I had no thought of you, Lazarus. But I lusted after Leiaza with a passion I had never before felt, even for you, dear husband."

I came up and embraced Hannah, and she laid her head on my shoulder, trying to stifle the tears welling in her eyes that I could feel falling on my bare skin and running down my chest.

"It's all right, Hannah. You did nothing wrong. You have nothing to be ashamed of or to apologize for. We are on a world with strange people and even stranger customs. For all you know the queen may have drugged you to take advantage of your innocence.

"It really doesn't matter to me, what you did or what the cause. I love you with all of my heart and I know you love me the same, and nothing you or anybody else ever does will ever change or diminish my love and loyalty to you."

I had thought my words were very appropriate and would have been comforting, but they just made Hannah cry even more.

"Thank you, Lazarus," she said feebly between sobs. "But it would have been better if you had not reminded me of the word 'trust.' For I broke your trust in my unabashed affections for Leiaza."

I held Hannah with a hand on the side of each of her shoulders and looked into her watery eyes with a small smile on my face, hoping to cheer her up. "Don't talk nonsense, beloved. I don't care if you have affections for another woman, any more than Yeshua minded that Miriam and Salome were and still are inseparable."

"Within the sacred bonds of marriage," Hannah reminded me.

She took another deep breath and her tears ended. "The story is almost over, so let me finish it." I nodded affirmatively for her to continue.

"I was enthusiastically ready to begin making love to another woman and she to me, when we were unpleasantly interrupted by a loud knock on the tall, thick double wooden doors that were the entry to the bedchamber."

"'Scazod!' Leiaza screamed in anger.

"She was very wroth, and I feared for the life of whoever had the idiocy to knock on her door and interrupt our passion.

"Leiaza grabbed onto a handle of each of the doors and violently ripped them open. 'Today is your day to die!' she yelled as the doors opened, before she even saw who it was that had such temerity.

"Fortunately for the imprudent intruder it was her sister Ireven. I'm sure if it had been anyone else they would not have survived the encounter with Leiaza. But when she saw it was her sister her wrath abated a tiny bit.

"'What?' she yelled in exasperated annoyance.

"'The person in your bed is not some innocent wayfarer as you might have imagined,' her sister pointed out.

"'I did not imagine she was,' Leiaza countered. 'And I don't care. DO NOT interrupt me in my bedchamber again, EVER!'

"The queen swung her arms back, preparing to slam the doors in her sister's face. But Ireven held up her hand. 'Stop! You must hear what I have to say. You may be in danger, sister. For no other reason would I dare to knock on the door of your bedchamber.'

"'There is nothing and no one upon this world

that is a danger to me,' Leiaza spat out at her sister.

"'That has always been true,' Ireven agreed. 'But the one constant in the universe is change.'

"She looked over at me sitting up on Leiaza's bed. 'I have already sent her companion to the tower. I suspect she has similar abilities and what their source is remains unknown. Nothing has ever been able to hurt you, Leiaza. But as long as the full capabilities of our visitors remain a mystery, we can no longer say with certainty that it is still true.'

"'What abilities?' Leiaza asked dismissively.

"She looked over at me a moment then back at her sister. 'Her mind is weak and easily influenced. Her body has little strength even after the improvements of our crystal sisters. I have touched her mind deeply and her knowledge is on a very primitive level. How could she possibly be a threat to me or any of us?'

"Ireven walked into the room and over to the bed. She ordered me to stand up and I did because Leiaza did not object. Ireven withdrew a dagger without a tip from a sheath on her waist belt. She held it up for her sister to see. 'This is what happened to my dagger when I tried to stab her companion.'

"'She probably has the same abilities.'

Ireven looked to her sister. 'Do I have your permission to test my theory? I promise I will not hurt her... much,' she asked with a cruel smile and a sinister glint in her eyes as she looked over at me. Leiaza nodded her head in silent agreement.

"Ireven stuck the tip of the broken dagger against my bare stomach and began to push. I felt the pressure, but no pain, even when she began pushing with great force. As she pulled the dagger back she purposefully raked the jagged broken edge over my stomach."

"'You see!' Ireven exclaimed triumphantly. 'She is not hurt and the dagger cannot even scratch her skin!'

"'Most curious,' Leiaza admitted. 'But nothing to be afraid of,' she said dismissively, to her sister's obvious disappointment. 'To the gentle touch her body is soft and supple and that is all that I care about at the moment.'

"'But I am curious as to what led up to you trying to stab the male and discover his secret. Did I not say to treat him as a guest?' Leiaza asked.

"'And so he was being treated by everyone,' Ireven defended. 'But he was caught cheating at a game of Zontog.'

"Leiaza nodded her head in understanding. 'Certainly cheating at our national wagering sport would be an acceptable reason for immediate punishment. But how did he break the point of your dagger?'

"'Incredibly, like the female, it could not penetrate his bare skin. The blade broke as if it had encountered a piece of solid adamine crystal when I stabbed him.'

"Leiaza looked at her sister dubiously. 'Are you

saying they are invulnerable?'

"'To daggers anyway,' Ireven affirmed. 'Perhaps not to other implements and means. Send your toy to the tower with her companion and tomorrow we can play a game of "Let's See" and test them with various things from projectiles to poison and see if they are affected or killed by one. Just imagine how high the betting will go and how much we can win as we experiment with their vulnerabilities.'

"A wicked smile lit up Leiaza's face. 'Yes. We will do as you suggest, sister. I will look forward to winning many wagers. But I will send her to the tower tomorrow. Tonight, as you have said, she is my toy.'

"Ireven's eyebrows shot up and she licked her lips. 'Can I play too?'

"Leiaza gave her sister a gentle smack on her bare derriere. 'Perhaps later after I am satiated. But out with you now. Leave us alone.'

"Ireven gave a slight bow of her head, then withdrew from the room. Leiaza closed the door behind her, bolted it, then looked at me with a glint in her eye such as I had not seen before; like a predator looking at the prey she is about to pounce upon.

"'So you have been hiding things from me, my pet,' Leiaza said, approaching me. 'Naughty, naughty. But knowing you have mystery about you will just make tonight more enjoyable. Now get up on the bed,' she commanded me.

"But I had come to my senses during this short turmoil while Leiaza had been focused on listening to her sister. More importantly my mind was no longer in a fog. I knew who I was and I was determined not to jeopardize all I held precious. 'I will not comply,' I spoke firmly to Leiaza.

'I cannot be your lover. I am a happily, devoted married woman and I have no desire for anyone, a man or a woman, other than my husband Lazarus.'

"Leiaza walked over to me. She did not embrace me but her face was a breath away from mine. The tips of her bountiful breasts rubbed the tips of mine and I could feel the heat of her body from my toes to my head.

"'Of course you will obey me,' Leiaza said. 'With your simple thoughts you really have no choice. Your archaic feelings for your "husband" are quaint, but silly. Nartesians put away such ridiculous provincial attachments long ago. You'll find if you broaden your relationship horizon your life can be immensely more enjoyable and fulfilling.'

"I tried to take a step back from Leiaza but my legs were already pushed up tight against the bed. I only succeeded in losing my balance and falling back onto the bed, the very place Leiaza had commanded me to go.

"Leiaza crawled up on the bed with me and kneeling, straddled my body at the waist. She looked down on me with a most contented smile.

"I felt my mind going into the daze again, as if

it was not all there. Once again I felt a passionate stirring throughout my body and an overwhelming desire to please and pleasure her. With my fading resistance and reason, I knew that she was somehow controlling both my mind and my passion, but I had no idea how to stop her. Silently, I desperately called out telepathically for help to Miriam and to Yeshua. But no help came.

"With the last vestige of my own will I asked Leiaza, 'How would you know?'

"She gave me a curious look with a perplexed smile. 'How would I know what, my pet?'

"I struggled to resist the building passion and desire so I could get out the last true thought of my own. 'If you have never experienced the contentment and joy of dedicating your affection and your body to the one person you love above all others, how would you know if perhaps that was not the more enjoyable and fulfilling choice?'

"Leiaza had no answer to my probing question. She hesitated a moment as if contemplating a reply, but instead brought the subject back to her entertainment for the night.

"'Enough philosophical meandering, my pet. Your mind is simply not up to the task. But I am going to love playing with your new body and you are going to love it too. So let's postpone serious matters until tomorrow and let the games begin tonight. Shall we?'

"I could no longer resist her will. I no longer

wished to. I nodded my head in agreement, gave her a warm smile and an invitation with my eyes and she came to me in a passionate embrace with a deep, long kiss, running her hands over my body and giving me sensations I did not know I could have."

I took a deep breath and exhaled slowly, emotionally wounded by Hannah's account. I felt a turmoil of emotions all at once: sadness to know my wife had been most intimate with someone other than me, but also great love and empathy for her because of the ordeal she had no choice but to experience. And in honesty, no small degree of anger that despite her pleas, neither Miriam nor Yeshua had come to help her in her time of most desperate need, when she had specifically called out to them.

Hannah was looking at me with her beautiful brown doe eyes, waiting expectantly and hopefully for my reaction. I reached over and embraced her tightly and she me. I gently stroked her head and her soft cheeks. "I love you, Hannah. I love you more today than I ever have. Nothing in the world or on any world could ever change my love and admiration for you."

She smiled then, and lifting her head up, gave me a soft, warm kiss. "You are my world, Lazarus. Thank you for understanding."

"What else happened last night?" I asked. "Once Leiaza was 'satiated,' did you have to go to her sister as well as they had spoken about?"

Hannah shook her head in negation. "Leiaza was never satiated, Lazarus. And while I was in her power, neither was I. I did not sleep a wink at all and am truly exhausted now such as I have never been. Only once the sun rose did Leiaza reluctantly call for me to be taken here to the tower."

I sat down on the floor of the small room with my back against the wall and gently pulled Hannah down. I patted my lap and she lay on her back, resting her head on my thighs.

"Sleep, my precious Hannah. I don't know for how long. But let it be sweet and deep as you are embraced in the true love of the man who honors you above all other women, and always will."

Hannah smiled gently at me and closed her eyes. She was fast asleep within a minute. I closed my eyes and decided I should try to get some sleep as well. The future of this day promised to be a challenge, for which we would need all of our alertness, wits, and strength.

Chapter 12
ESCAPE

It took me longer to fall asleep than Hannah. So many thoughts were running through my mind. We had been gone so long I wondered if anyone was looking for us. I assumed not, although I could not fathom why, because I was sure Miriam could have found us at any moment she desired as an angel of the Elohim.

That brought me back to my anger. How could Miriam just abandon us, even when we never returned from what was supposed to be just a short sightseeing excursion to experience a different world? If we were so important in Elohim's master plan, why had we simply been abandoned to such torment before we could even begin fulfilling that which they had asked of us? And what of our beautiful children? How were they taking our absence? And what would happen to them if we never returned?

Foolish thoughts, I know. My faith was greater than to simply abandon all hope. However, I could not make the nagging negative thoughts go away.

I was finally beginning to drift off to sleep when I was jolted back awake by someone speaking to me telepathically. "Lazarus! Where are you? The night is very dark, and it would be an excellent time to retrieve you from the city undetected. Have you obtained my scale?"

I hung my head in disbelief. Not only was obtaining a Nagasa scale for the giant bird that had brought us to Nartese City impossible, it had not even been a thought in my mind for a single second since we landed in the plaza of the city.

"No, Danarz. There have been complications. I'm afraid we will not be able to obtain a Nagasa chest scale for you. They do not seem to drop off on their own, and we are actually prisoners at the moment with very uncertain fates. It seems the Nartesians are going to have a game in the morning of trying various means to kill us until one succeeds. Even if we could figure out a way to obtain a scale, I'm sure the occasion will not arise. I guess you should have eaten us when you had the opportunity."

"Are all of your kind such pessimists?" Danarz asked. "It is no wonder you are still so primitive. You must believe in a better future, or you will be condemned to the lesser one you accept. If you are alive, you have a chance. Do not succumb to mental hopelessness, or it will become your master from which there is no escape.

"And of course I would not really try to eat you.

Surely you knew I was jesting. Latalizq told me about your poison skins. Perhaps eating you would kill me, perhaps not. But it would likely give me indigestion, and I prefer meals that don't start wars in my stomach."

Danarz's dry humor and positive encouragement brought a reluctant smile to my face, but I knew I needed to explain our seriously precarious situation. "Do you recall that single spire in the city that towers above all others?"

"Yes," Danarz affirmed.

"You might as well return to your home in the beautiful city you spoke so fondly of, because we are imprisoned atop the spire and our fate does not look good. Within a few short hours we will be back on the ground among the Nartesians, who, it seems, will be taking great joy in our torture and eventual death."

"That does not sound too disadvantageous," Danarz answered nonchalantly. "As you may remember, I too can fly. I will simply fly up and bring you to safety. Then we can plot together to come up with a better plan to obtain the chest scale of a flying worm for me. I really do not wish to leave without one.

"Even more importantly, I must bathe in the Spring of Renewal until my feathers are restored to their former glory so I can compete for females."

I was surprised to know Danarz would so casually risk his life to try and rescue us, but I knew

I had to dissuade him from such a foolish action.

"I am grateful to know that you would attempt to bring us to safety," I expressed with sincerity. "But it would be for naught, and you would surely lose your life in the attempt.

"I cannot see them in the darkness of the night, but I hear the flapping sound of the wings of the flying worms continually circling near the tower, keeping a close guard upon us, which is kind of ludicrous, as there are no stairs between here and the ground and the flying worms are the only way to arrive or leave this place."

"Not to worry, Lazarus," Danarz assured me. "I will come for you. I will fly high above the spire and float straight down, barely moving my wings so there will be no sound for the worms to detect. Be prepared to escape at a moment's notice, as soon as I land upon the spire."

It would be a foolhardy endeavor, but if there was even the slimmest chance of success and Danarz was willing to risk it, I knew we had to take it. Our chances of life and liberty among the Nartesians seemed much less by comparison.

"We will be ready," I promised. "But even if you succeed in arriving here by stealth, there is little likelihood we will not be noticed trying to escape. As we have all witnessed, the worms can shoot fire a great distance, and there is more than one worm continuously circling this tower. After we unite with you, how will we escape the vicinity without getting toasted alive?"

"It is a problem, no doubt," Danarz admitted candidly. "But west of the city there is a long, narrow canyon filled with a dense forest. If we can get beneath the canopy of the trees, the cover and narrowness of the canyon will prevent an effective search for us."

"That sounds promising," I agreed. "If we can make it that far before being inflamed. If not, what is your alternative plan?"

"There is no alternative plan," Danarz replied gruffly. "Be ready!"

I waited with all my senses alert, expecting Danarz to arrive any moment, but he must have had more difficulty than he imagined trying to arrive undetected. Or perhaps he had been detected and was no longer among the living. I only came to that morbid thought because since we last spoke telepathically he had failed to answer several times when I called out to him.

After a time, despite my best efforts to stay awake, the weariness of my last hours began to overtake me, and I slipped into slumber. But once again, I was destined to get no rest. No sooner had I begun to dream very pleasant dreams of Hannah and me playing with our children in Bethany than I was rudely awakened by the clarion call of Danarz.

"Run now to the platform, I am almost upon it!"

Instantly, I was awake. With a rush of adrenaline coursing through my body, every sense was immediately heightened. I shook Hannah by her shoulders to awaken her. She was groggy and awoke too slowly. I realized I should have rousted her when Danarz first revealed his plan for our escape so she would have been more prepared to run.

"Hurry, star of my life. Awaken. Danarz has come to rescue us."

"What... Danarz... the vicious bird that eats people?" I pulled her up to her feet, supporting the weight of her still somewhat limp body, almost dragging her toward the portal to the platform.

"Yes, my star, that very bird," I replied, still halfway working to convince myself it was true.

As soon as we were on the platform, the cool, biting night wind assaulted our naked bodies, immediately helping both of us to be wide awake. Without thinking about it, we stopped speaking verbally and effortlessly slipped into telepathic conversation with one another so we would not alert the guardian Nagasa to our escape.

"Why would the bird want to rescue us?" Hannah asked, disbelieving. "We did not obtain the Nagasa scale he wanted. Why would he risk his life for us? You didn't tell him we had the scale to induce him to come, did you?"

"No, no," I assured her. "It was all his idea."

I shrugged my shoulders because I really had no answer as to why he would risk his life for us now. It did seem to be out of character from the savage bird we had known.

"I think perhaps he feels we might yet serve some useful role in obtaining a scale for him. He seems very determined not to leave this place without one. Or maybe he has a boring life and just wants to be around us for the excitement in ours," I quipped in a more light-hearted tone than I felt.

"Maybe a little bit of both," we heard Danarz respond to us in our minds. I had forgotten that among the unpracticed such as Hannah and me, there were no private mental conversations when you were in close proximity to others that had the gift.

"Look up, bugs, I am landing. Climb up quickly," Danarz urged.

There was no moon, and in the murky darkness of the night we could not clearly make out his massive shape as he alighted on the deck of the spire. But his dark form blotted out the light of the stars in the sky behind him, so we knew where to run toward.

Danarz squatted down as low as he could. I grabbed onto feathers with abandon and raced up onto his neck, then quickly reached down and helped Hannah up. Within ten seconds after the bird landed, we were airborne.

Rather than actively flying, where the soft sound of his flapping wings might alert the guardian Nagasa, as he had done in his vertical descent to the platform he merely leaped off the edge of the precipice and began a silent downward glide through the darkened night.

It was in those silent seconds, where for a brief moment nothing was immediately threatening us, that I came to a marvelous realization: Hannah and I had been freely conversing telepathically before Danarz even arrived on the platform of the spire, without the presence of any other telepathic person or creature to facilitate our abilities! If we were not in such a precarious situation, I probably would have been giddy at the realization!

"Me too!" Hannah quipped in my mind. "I can't wait for better circumstances to allow us the opportunity to explore this amazing gift!"

For a moment, I thought we were going to escape undetected. But it was not to be. I had no inkling that the Nagasa had even noticed our escape until the stygian darkness of the night was suddenly illuminated by a hot blast of red-orange Nagasa fire from directly behind us and two others from either side.

I was completely startled as the night sky burst into fiery light, and the heat of the flames so close behind singed my naked back. I felt as if my heart would burst in anxiety at our plight. And I am not too proud to say that with three angry Nagasa in fiery pursuit, I was as scared as I had ever been in my life up until that time.

Now that our escape had been discovered, stealth was no longer helpful. Danarz flapped his mighty wings vigorously, and it seemed for a time that with his robust strength we were pulling away from our pursuers. Then to our horror a fiery stream came down upon us from above. Danarz quickly made a steep dive to escape the unexpected appearance of a fourth Nagasa. But we were getting perilously close to the ground, and soon there would be no room for him to maneuver.

The large yellow sun had crested the horizon, and the morning sky was lighting up with a few thin red streaks painting the brilliant blue sky. With some powerful beats of his massive wings, Danarz gained altitude again, and looking back, the gap between us and our pursuers seemed to be increasing.

We flew directly toward the rising sun. Just as I was about to breathe a sigh of relief, thinking we might just escape, my momentary appreciation for the splendid panorama of the morning sky and erstwhile hope for escape vanished. A shadow blotted the light of the sun as a fifth Nagasa loomed straight ahead of us, already taking in a big breath of air as it prepared to blast us with the fire of death! Even if our shield skins managed to protect us from the fire, we would likely suffocate from the heated air. And poor Danarz, if he wasn't killed immediately from the fire enveloping him, he would still tumble helplessly to the ground, his already ragged feathers burned into useless ashes.

"We are not dead yet, bug!" I heard Danarz proclaim angrily. "Keep your pessimistic thoughts to yourself, else they affect me as negatively as they affect you."

We closed the distance between us and the Nagasa in front of us very rapidly. It took in a big inhale of breath and blew out another searing blast of fire straight at us, and we were well within its range. It seemed like immediate, inevitable destruction. Both Hannah and I screamed out for help in our minds to Miriam and Yeshua. And thankfully for the moment, we were miraculously saved. But it was not by either of them.

Our salvation came because of the amazing aerodynamic combat maneuvers executed by Danarz. Even as the blast of fire was speeding toward us a mere second from enveloping us, Danarz avoided it by diving steeply toward the ground and skimming rapidly over its surface so closely that the tops of the small trees on the hillside were whipping lightly across his underside.

I was sure he would use that small window to continue trying to escape to the refuge of the forested canyon he had spoken of. However, he had something far braver in mind. As soon as we passed beneath the Nagasa, Danarz banked up hard and to the right. For a second we were simultaneously sideways and nearly upside down, hanging as tightly as we could to not plummet to the ground. Moments later, Danarz was flying right above the Nagasa. This one was riderless, but looking at the four others rapidly approaching, I could see two of them had a Nartesian rider sitting in the saddle on their necks.

I couldn't fathom the strategy of Danarz. Moments ago, it seemed as if he had expertly outmaneuvered the Nagasa and opened a path to our escape. But rather than fleeing for the refuge of the canyon, he had turned about, and we were now headed right back toward all of our pursuers!

Rather than creating distance between us and the nearest Nagasa, he was soon flying right above it. Unexpectedly, he dropped down and grabbed the beast by its neck with his mighty talons. Nagasas are large, but their size is extended out in a long thin length. Danarz, however, was larger overall, and his more compact body gave him immense power in his wings and strength in his legs and feet.

The Nagasa flailed about viciously as it was held in Danarz's unrelenting grasp. It clawed him with its short forearms and ripped clouds of feathers out of the parts of his body it could reach, especially around his head. It whipped its long tail upward and slapped it down hard upon Danarz's back. We were hit several times by the massive tail and certainly would have been killed with the first blow if not for our protective skins. I heard Danarz telepathically cry out in pain with each vicious blow of the tail on his unprotected back. But he did not let go of his iron grip on the neck of the beast.

In moments the other four Nagasa were upon us, encircling us on the four points of the compass, preventing further escape. For a short time it seemed as if we were all suspended like flying ballet dancers in the air. I could feel Danarz tiring from trying to maintain altitude while carrying us and the weight of the Nagasa.

One of the Nartesians yelled out a command and the Nagasa he was riding let out a stream of fire toward us. There was no way to avoid it and I was certain the end had come, at least for Danarz and probably for us as well.

But Danarz lifted up the Nagasa he was holding by the neck and used its body to shield us from the fiery blast. As the fire enveloped the living shield Danarz was holding, he momentarily pulled his feathered wings in tight to his body to protect them from the streams of fire passing on all sides of us. This caused us to drop suddenly downward during the moment he had pulled in his wings, and much of the fiery blast passed above us without harm. The air around us was still very hot, and all of us were singed in places. But as Danarz would say, we still lived.

The brilliant action of Danarz seemed to enrage the Nartesian on the Nagasa that had shot the first stream of fire at us. He yelled some more commands, and immediately the other three Nagasas inhaled big breaths of air and from three different directions blasted their columns of fiery death upon us. Though nearly at the same time, there was enough delay from one blast to another that, with unbelievable speed for a bird that was carrying weight and basically just hovering in place, Danarz quickly turned from one direction to another and once again used the body of the Nagasa he was tightly gripping to shield us from the hottest part of the flames while also avoiding some of the blasts by plummeting rapidly downward as soon as he pulled in his wings.

The Nagasa he was holding was not so fortunate. Though I thought their scales made them impervious to fire, which is why Danarz wanted one as a shield so badly, it was apparently not true. For the Nagasa now hung lifelessly in Danarz's grasp, killed by the fire of its fellow beasts. Danarz let go of it and it plummeted down to the ground where it hit with a thud and did not move.

"What are you doing?" I cried out in startled dismay. "Using the beast as a shield was working. Now what are we going to do?"

"Now we flee," Danarz answered as he quickly turned and flew toward the canyon that had been our original destination. I looked back and was surprised to see the Nagasa only following us in a leisurely pursuit.

Danarz must have heard my thoughts of bafflement because he explained as we flew onward, "It takes a great deal of energy for the worms to blow a full stream of fire as these did. It will take at least a few minutes for them to recharge the furnace in their bellies before they can expel it at us again. They must also fly slow to conserve their energy to build their fire more quickly. They can follow us at a distance, but we will be safely hidden within the sanctuary of the canyon forest before they will be able to threaten us again."

Chapter 13
HANNAH

While it was still daylight we remained very still, hidden deep within the towering forest. Movement, even very slight, is one of the easiest things for a predator to detect.

Well concealed beneath the canopy of the thick forest with its towering trees that spread out with wide, heavily leafed branches, we could peek up through the small spaces between leaves, watching the Nagasa flying overhead searching for us in vain. We were completely camouflaged beneath the branches of the protecting trees.

When Danarz first flew into the forest he continued to amaze me with the dexterity of his flying ability. Flying at breakneck speed, there were many, many times when we had to pass between two trees with barely enough space for his body to fit through, let alone his gigantic wings! But at the very last second, he would pull his wings in tightly to his body and pass through the close-spaced trunks by sheer momentum without losing any of his rapid speed. Immediately past the tree trunks, his mighty wings quickly spread out again and we continued our race through the forest as if we had never even encountered an obstacle.

At one point we came upon a spacious inset in a forty-five-degree angled overhanging cliff. Taking refuge underneath it rendered us completely invisible from the Nagasas seeking to find us from above. Here we remained until darkness fell and Danarz felt we could move once more through the forest without detection as long as we continued to remain silent and exercise caution.

I for one was most anxious to be as far away from the land of the Nartesians as possible. But of course, Danarz had other ideas.

"First, we are going back to that dead worm and I am going to get the chest scale I came here for."

I was exasperated that Danarz would even consider wasting time returning to the Nagasa.

"That's crazy!" I exclaimed loudly in my mind. "As you saw, the protection of the Nagasa scales from fire is a myth. The flames of its fellow beasts doomed that one to death."

"And..." I added with some mental emphasis, "it is very likely the Nartesians did not leave the body, but retrieved it; if for no other reason than to thwart creatures like you from trying to obtain scales from the dead Nagasa."

"You are probably correct on both accounts," Danarz agreed. "Nevertheless we are going back to that spot. And if the worm is still there I will have my scale. It may not be impervious to fire when three other worms are simultaneously blasting it, but it will work enough to make me safer when traveling in their demesnes than without it."

So despite my better judgment and contrary wishes, we flew on, returning to the point where we had just recently escaped death. Once again, it was a very dark night, but Danarz flew unerringly to the spot where the dead Nagasa still lay in a crumpled heap at the spot it had fallen.

"Grrr," Danarz growled in upset when he saw the Nagasa. "The beast is lying on its belly. We will need to flip it over onto its back so I can pry the center scale off of its chest. I knew there was a good reason I saved the two of you, as this is not a task I could easily do by myself."

I think Danarz was just trying to make us feel as if we were not excess baggage, because I was certain that a bird of his stature and strength would have no problem flipping over the corpse of the Nagasa by himself.

Danarz approached its head and grabbed onto its neck with one foot. He directed me to the center of the body and told Hannah to go grab onto the tail.

"Alright now, on my count of three flip the beast to its back. Ready? One, two, three, flip!"

With our combined effort, the Nagasa flipped over easily. It was actually not as heavy as I had expected it to be. As we turned it onto its back a big breath of air escaped its body. I thought it must have just been the last remnants of the air still in its lungs when it hit the ground being expunged out. But then it opened its big green eye, blinking it a few times as if rousing from a deep sleep, and looked right at me!

I nervously took a few steps back, rapidly moving both hands in backward motions to signal Hannah and Danarz to move away. "Hey, this beast is still alive," I called out a loud warning in my mind.

Even as I spoke the Nagasa stirred some more and tried weakly to regain its feet. Danarz acted quickly. As he had in the air, he leaped upon the Nagasa's neck and grabbed it tightly in a death grip of both feet. The beast was still too weak to resist and barely moved. Although I wasn't sure even with Danarz's powerful grip if he could exert enough pressure to crush the beast's neck through its armored scales.

In many ways it was a sad scene, one beautiful creature killing another. A brief thought flashed through my mind as I considered how one creature taking the life of another, either for food or in war, seemed to be such a prevalent trait of not just man, but even the creatures I had met on other worlds. Why did such pervasive violence need to be part of the worlds we all lived on? I know that the Elohim are all wise, but this did not seem like a good plan of life to me.

"No matter how hard I squeeze I cannot collapse

this worm's neck because of its armor!" Danarz yelled out in telepathic anger.

He looked over at Hannah and me standing beside each other about ten paces away from the gruesome scene.

"You two, go fetch some rocks big enough to plug the nostrils of the worm. It may take longer, but we can slowly suffocate it by blocking its ability to breathe."

"No! I will not help you kill this beast!" Hannah proclaimed to my surprise.

Danarz looked at Hannah with incomprehension. "This is the very beast that not long ago was trying to kill you, foolish bug. If he regains his strength he will undoubtedly try again and call back his friends. But more so than that, I saved your lives at great risk of my own. This is a small thing that I ask in return."

He looked at me. "Lazarus bug. If your female is too weak to do this simple and logical action, you can do it by yourself. Do so now."

I looked at Hannah and she shook her head indicating I should not aid in the death of the Nagasa. "But Danarz is right, Hannah." I tried to explain to her with logic.

"As much as we may detest the necessity of killing it, the Nagasa is our enemy, one that did try to kill us and will certainly do so again if we let it live."

Hannah continued to strongly shake her head

negatively. "I do not feel that way, Lazarus. There is something about this Nagasa that I cannot explain. Despite its attack on us, I feel a kinship to it, like I do to you or our children. In my heart, killing it would be like killing one of you. I cannot do it, or let you do it. If I had a way to stop Danarz I wouldn't let him do it either."

Hearing our conversation Danarz was not happy. "I am done with you bugs. It is a lot of trouble, but I will kill this worm myself, take his scale, and then because of your ungrateful impudence, I will leave you here to your fate!"

With just a couple of flaps of his expansive wings Danarz flew a short distance to some nearby loose rocks. Retaining his grip on the Nagasa's neck with one foot, he reached over with his other and grabbed a rock he ascertained to be the correct size and stuffed it into one of the Nagasa's nostrils. The beast started to feebly thrash about in his grasp trying to escape what it realized was going to be certain death.

Hannah ran over and stood right next to the two immense beasts. I quickly followed to stand beside her. "Stop! Do not kill this Nagasa!" she cried out loud in anger.

Danarz completely ignored her and continued searching for another suitable-sized rock. He found it and stuck it into the Nagasa's other nostril hole. After he was satisfied the holes were well plugged, he used his free foot to grab the snout of the Nagasa and gripped it tightly closed so it could not breathe through its mouth either.

"Stop!" Hannah began screaming out loud like a wild woman. "Stop! Stop!"

Danarz looked at her with cold, implacable red eyes and did not respond or heed her pleas.

I didn't really know what to do. Of course, I supported my wife, but I didn't have a thought as to how that could translate into tangible action that would make any difference. So I just stood there somewhat befuddled.

Hannah picked up some fist-size stones and threw them at Danarz. Her aim was quite good and she hit him with one on his beak and another just under his eye.

Danarz, however, barely noticed. "If I could feel your little pebbles I would be irritated and might have to drop you in a lake or some other suitable grave, but what you are doing is so ludicrous it is humorous, so I will let you live. It is almost over anyway. I can feel the beast's breathing becoming very labored."

Hannah slumped her shoulders and walked back over to me in defeat. I put my arm over her shoulder and held her close to me.

"You tried, my star. Your intent was noble, but against a bird of that size and strength, we are little more than what he calls us - 'bugs.' "

"My babies," a faint voice rang in my head.

Hannah looked at me quizzically. "Did you hear

that?"

I nodded my head in acknowledgment.

"Please save my babies." The ethereal voice floated again through our minds.

"That is the Nagasa!" Hannah shouted aloud in somewhat of an emotional frenzy. "It is not a male, but a female!"

She looked up at Danarz still holding tightly to his prize. "Did you hear that bird? This is a mother with children. Do not take her from them."

Danarz looked at her disdainfully. "Are all the people on your primitive world so stupid? If I kill this one and because of her death some babies die too, they never grow up to be threats. That is a good thing, not bad!"

"NO!" Hannah screamed aloud. "You must let this mother go!"

"Will you be quiet, bug?" Danarz said with upset. "Your screaming with a loud voice is going to alert the other worms to our presence."

He called out to me. "Bug Lazarus, if you value your own lives, silence the female."

But Hannah had other ideas. "I will not be silenced. I don't even care anymore if the other Nagasa come. If that will stop you from killing this one, then let them come!"

Once again Danarz did not answer, but just continued to crush and suffocate the Nagasa.

Hannah went over to the bird and beat with her two fists on one of his massive yellow legs at the bottom where there were no feathers. I went over to pull her away because I don't think he noticed her feeble effort any more than he did the rocks she threw at him. But Hannah pushed me away.

Now instead of hitting Danarz she grabbed onto one of his big toes just above a giant talon with both of her hands and tried to pull it open to make him release his grasp on the neck of the Nagasa. "Let go of her!" Hannah screamed in building fury. "Let go of her! Let go of her! Let go of her!"

Suddenly to everyone's enormous surprise, Danarz was ripped free of the Nagasa by some invisible force and hurtled backward several paces. He landed on his feet and ruffled his feathers, shaking his head trying to understand what had just happened.

I looked at my wife with both awe and pride. I had no doubt what I had just witnessed. Like Miriam and Salome before her and many other women among the Children of Light, in her anger and passionate desire to free the Nagasa, she had called up the greater Celestine Light from within her essence and manifested its power with a might that could never be achieved by her frail physical body.

Hannah seemed oblivious to what she had just done. She ignored both me and Danarz. Instead, she quickly stepped over to the head of the Nagasa. She reached in its nostrils and pulled out the stones blocking its breathing. Then, as if she was cuddling her favorite dog, she knelt down next to the head full of large, angular sharp teeth and sharp protruding spines.

"It will be all right, mother. It will be all right." She reached out her hand and ran it softly over the cheek of the Nagasa. "Everything will be all right."

Chapter 14
LASSOON

I looked over at my wife still gently petting the ferocious face of the Nagasa with unabashed affection and decided to leave her alone with her new monster friend for a few minutes. Even if the Nagasa remembered that it was tasked with killing us and managed to muster enough strength to chomp on Hannah, her shield skin should protect her long enough for me and Danarz to rescue her.

Danarz was scanning the sky and crouching low as if he was worried about being attacked from above. I sauntered over to him and joined him looking at the sky.

"What are you looking for?" I asked nonchalantly, even though I already knew the answer, and knew it was not one that Danarz was going to like.

"How can you ask such a stupid question?" he spat out with disrespect. "I was just attacked by an unseen assailant, one whose strength was great enough to pry my fiercely locked grasp from the worm and hurl me through the air. This is a formidable enemy such as I have never before encountered. We need to be very wary of a creature that can attack in such powerful ways with invisibility."

"Well, about that," I began, choosing my words carefully. I scratched the nape of my neck with my index finger as I contemplated how to diplomatically reveal this to Danarz without offending him into anger. "This will probably be a bit difficult for you to grasp..."

Danarz glanced down at me with an intimidating, inscrutable look. "Yes..."

"Um, you will not find your assailant by looking up in the sky," I began.

Immediately Danarz looked alertly in one direction after another at ground level. "You saw the assailant attack from the ground behind me?"

"Um... no."

Danarz shook his head in frustration. "Speak directly, bug Lazarus. While you are dancing around the subject, the enemy may even now be preparing to attack again."

"Actually, there are probably no worries on that account," I assured him. "At least if you don't try to kill the Nagasa anymore."

Danarz stood up and took in a big breath of air. "Of course I am going to return to my task and kill the Nagasa. I will not leave here without the scale I came for, and that has nothing to do with defending ourselves against this powerful unseen assailant."

He looked over toward Hannah and the Nagasa

with an angry scowl creasing his eyes. "Move your companion away from the worm so I can resume the kill. I will deal with her impudence later for removing the stones I was using to suffocate it."

"That's probably not a good course of action," I advised. He did not reply but looked down at me silently with an angry scowl.

I let out a big breath of air with a little trepidation as I revealed the truth about his unseen attacker. "Well, you see, the assailant that attacked you, the one you are so worried about... that ugh... that was actually my wife Hannah."

Danarz let out a telepathic squawk of mirth. "Your company is agreeable if for no other reason than the humor I get from the ridiculous things you bugs say and do. The female bug could no more pry away my littlest talon, let alone tear away my grasp and hurl me through the air, than you could lift up that mountain to the south and cast it away into the sea."

"Actually, I have been told on good authority that casting mountains into the sea is within the realm of possibility," I retorted reflectively with a chuckle.

Danarz ignored my comments and took a couple of steps threateningly back toward Hannah and the Nagasa to finish what he had begun. I hurriedly stepped in front of him.

"Wait!" I cried, holding up both hands in front of me. "I am not jesting when I speak of this.

Among my people, not my race, but only among the Children of Light in my community, there are some women who manifest potent powers stemming from their thoughts and emotions. Their abilities have nothing to do with their small stature or frailty of their bodies. Some train for many years to bring forth their gifts. Others begin to show their power spontaneously only in a moment of distress, danger, or passion.

"This is what has just occurred with Hannah. Even now, I'm sure she feels the power and connection to the light stirring within her. You would be very unwise to threaten her or the Nagasa again."

Danarz stopped and looked at me skeptically. "I have never heard of invisible powers that can exert a physical effect. I suspect you are trying to deceive me. But being the prudent and intelligent being that I am, I will do a small test of your words."

Danarz walked over to the tail end of the Nagasa, grabbed its tail in his beak, and gave it a violent enough shake that it lifted it up slightly and pulled it away from Hannah.

Surprisingly, for a creature that seemed minutes ago as close as one could be to death without crossing the threshold, the Nagasa leapt up. It turned to face Danarz, jerking its tail from his beak. Hannah, who had been shunt off to the side by the Nagasa's quick movement, quietly stepped in front of it with her back against its chest, and together they faced Danarz.

Hannah looked at Danarz with love, not anger or hate. "Great and noble bird, you have put your life in danger many times in the last day for us when you could have left us for dead and never looked back. For that, we are so grateful. I plead with you now to give us consideration once more and spare this equally noble creature a fate it does not deserve."

Danarz shook his head slightly in disagreement. "I think you are deluded, bug Hannah. I am sure I will kill this despicable creature anyway despite your pleas. However, in my curiosity, I will listen to a few more of your words; but be quick. It is already a marvel that we have not been discovered as we squabble here. Our good fortune will not last if we remain much longer."

Hannah bowed her head slightly in appreciative acknowledgment. She turned slightly, reaching up with her right hand, and began gently stroking the Nagasa. "What Lazarus told you is true. I felt the power flowing through me when you were thrown away from my friend. Her name, by the way, is Lassoon."

Danarz snorted derisively. "I suppose even villainous creatures such as this must have names."

"She is not a villain," Hannah said in defense. "Her attack on us was not done of her own choice but by compulsion by the Nartesians."

"And you know this little tidbit how?" Danarz

asked skeptically.

Hannah explained. "From the moment I came to her, Lassoon and I have been in earnest conversation. It has only been a few minutes, but already I know that she is an unwilling slave and she fears for her babies more than for her life. A life that, were it not for her children, she would gladly submit to you killing her to end her misery of tortured servitude."

"Are you making this up as you speak?" Danarz asked sarcastically, rejecting Hannah's explanation. "The facts belie your words. First, I have never seen you speaking to this creature. And if you were, it being just a worm, it could not reply back to you. Nor would you understand its language even if it did. It is doubtful if such a rudimentary creature even has a language.

"Second, the worms are far more powerful than the Nartesians and most of them fly around freely on their own. They could leave these lands at any time if they chose to, but they remain and allow the Nartesians to ride and direct them. That would indicate they are merely stupid but loyal pets.

"So you have not convinced me of anything. Move aside now so I can kill the worm quick, and I may yet take you and your companion away from this loathsome land."

Lassoon took in a big breath, the kind of breath the Nagasa take just before they are going to shoot a stream of fire out of their mouth. As she was facing us, both Danarz and I moved backward as rapidly as we could. I looked at my wife. "Hannah! Don't let the Nagasa breathe fire on us!"

But it was too late. Before Hannah could intercede or we could get out of harm's way, the Nagasa exhaled. Though I counted on my shield skin to protect me, I still instinctively held my forearm up in front of my face for feeble insurance. But it was unnecessary. I was expecting to be engulfed in a massive blast of fire. Instead, just a tiny trickle came out of her mouth and barely made it a couple of paces before it dissipated. She obviously had not recovered enough yet to build much of a fire in her belly. Her head slumped momentarily in obvious disappointment at her failure.

Danarz took the Nagasa's attack as a signal to renew his own assault. With a mighty flap of his wings he lifted off the ground and rose up above the Nagasa, preparing to once again drop down and grasp its neck in a death grip.

Just as he began to descend, Hannah held both of her hands up high with the palms facing the bird. He didn't get thrown back by her action as he had previously, but it was as if he was encountering an invisible wall in the sky and he could descend no further. In frustration, he settled back down to the ground near me.

"Perhaps the bug does have some unfathomable power," Danarz conceded to his own surprise.

Hannah lowered her hands and shrugged her

shoulders. "I did not want to hurt you, Danarz. Honestly, I don't even know if I could. This has never happened to me before. It is something I never expected, and I am ignorant of the capacities and boundaries of my abilities.

"But you must stop your blood lust for Lassoon. She is not the vile creature you think she is. As I have been with her so briefly, there is almost as much that I do not know as you. Perhaps we should let her explain herself, and then we can all learn the reality and the truth together."

"How can a worm 'explain themselves'?" Danarz asked mockingly. "Is it going to draw pictures in the dirt with one of its claws?"

"No, I will speak to you in your mind as you are accustomed." We were shocked to hear an unfamiliar voice reply.

Danarz looked at the Nagasa in abject disbelief. "You can speak telepathically?"

"Of course. I am glad to see it is not beyond your capabilities," Lassoon replied with a bit of condescension.

Danarz shook his head rapidly back and forth trying to grasp realities that were beyond his system of belief. "Bugs that can talk telepathically, worms that talk telepathically, bugs that have invisible powers, nobody is going to believe this when I return home. I am not sure I do either. Maybe this is all just an elaborate, very real-feeling nightmare."

Lassoon took a few halting steps toward Danarz.

He looked at her cautiously, very wary of her intentions.

"I understand you want to kill me to pry my center chest scale off."

"That has been my intention," Danarz acknowledged.

"And now?" Lassoon asked.

"I am ambiguous," Danarz admitted. "I still want a chest scale off of one of you creatures, but perhaps it does not need to be yours."

"You can have mine," Lassoon offered.

We all looked at her quizzically, without comprehending her last statement.

She extended and held up one of the long claws from her right foreleg. "There is nothing you could do to obtain one of my scales," Lassoon explained.

"If I had died, my body would have instantly vanished. It is the way of my kind. If I am alive, there is no tool in existence strong enough to pry off one of my scales.

"But to demonstrate to you that I would rather be your friend than your enemy, I will give you that which you seek."

Lassoon took her extended claw and, using the tip, she inscribed a line all about the perimeter of the large five-sided scale at the center of her chest. We could hear a high-pitched, grating cutting sound as she drew the line around the scale. Once she had completely circumvented the perimeter of the scale, she reached with her claws from both of her forelegs around its edges and slowly pried it right off of her underlying skin. Silently she handed it to Danarz, still dripping red blood.

"Only the claw of a Nagasa can cut or pierce our armored scales. This is the only way you could ever obtain one."

Danarz was at a loss for words. He was holding the scale in one of his claws and simply staring at Lassoon.

Hannah looked up at her friend. "What about you? Will you grow another scale to replace the one you removed?"

"No," Lassoon replied sadly. "Once a Nagasa is a full-grown adult, the scales are not replaced if they are damaged or, in rare cases, torn off. Only another Nagasa can pierce our armor, so damaged scales are not a problem we usually face."

"Then you are vulnerable now on this scaleless spot?" Danarz asked.

Lassoon nodded her head affirmatively. "You can kill me easily now if you desire, as can anyone else. The center scale protected my heart. A simple spear thrown to that vulnerable location will kill me quickly. If another Nagasa ever breathes fire on me and it hits my bare skin where the scale was, it will burn me as easily as it would burn you.

Danarz extended the scale he was holding back to Lassoon. "Take it back. I do not want it at such a price."

Lassoon demurred. "It is a gift, Danarz. Please

use it as you have wished. In any case, it would be pointless to return it as it cannot be reattached to my body."

Chapter 15
REVELATIONS

Lassoon's gift to Danarz of the armored scale that protected her heart was a very touching act of generosity and humbling to all of us. Such a sacrifice not only for one she did not even know, but for one who until moments before had been resolute in his desire to kill her. I have been in the presence of mighty kings and pharaohs, even Yeshua the Lord of Light, but never have I experienced a greater essence of simple nobility than at that moment with Lassoon.

"Thank you for your sacrifice," Danarz acknowledged quietly.

"In honesty, I gave it to you in selfishness," Lassoon explained. "I did not want you as an enemy seeking my death. I must return soon to my babies if they are to live. I thought perhaps if I gave you that which you sought you would no longer seek my life and I would be able to quickly leave and return to my children before it is too late.

"Even in my weakened state you would find it very difficult to kill me. And for no end because it would still be impossible for you to obtain a scale from my body. Now you have that which you desired and I hope I can bid you goodbye and we can part in peace."

"Of course," Danarz agreed.

Lassoon pointed back toward the canyon we had been hiding in. "If you enter the canyon and follow it to its end, it will come out into the land of the Glitorees after about a half day's flight. They are not friends of your kind, but neither are they your enemies. If you do not threaten them, I believe they will let you pass through their territory unchallenged. From the border of their demesnes you may safely return to your own."

With those parting words Lassoon spread her translucent wings to take flight.

"Wait!" Hannah called out. "I want to help you. I do not wish to say goodbye like this."

Lassoon turned her long neck and looked at my wife. "I cannot delay, Hannah. When I was called by the Nartesians to come attack you I had to leave my eggs unprotected and unfortified in the nest. I only lay eggs on the eleventh year, so their viability is extremely important to me. The eggs remain warm because of where they are placed, but a mother must return at least once a day for a short time to share energy with her young ones. That is how a bond is created that forms the children in the mental and emotional template of their mother. Without that link, as adults they will likely go rogue and be destroyed by the Nartesians. I do not want that fate for my children. Goodbye, Hannah.

"You must flee now to the canyon as I told you. Danarz was correct. You are still being searched for. Even now, I can feel many Nagasa flying towards us. They know you are here and they are not far away. Please go, even as I must."

"Let us come with you," Hannah pleaded. "You asked us to save your babies. Let me help you do so."

"No," Lassoon replied firmly. "I asked that when I thought I was going to die. If you accompanied me now it would make the situation worse for both of us.

"I have great joy in the connection we made in our hearts, Hannah, and I will always remember you, the first being of another species that ever showed me kindness. But sentiment cannot overrule good sense. It will be safer for both of us now to part ways."

Lassoon spread her wings to depart in flight again. I could see the sadness on Hannah's face and feel it in her aura. A crazy thought popped into my head that I normally would have tapped right back down lest everyone think me a fool. But compassion for Hannah's stressed emotions made me blurt it out.

"Why did you not die and disappear?" I shouted out to Lassoon.

Once again she aborted her flight, folded her

wings back against her body and looked at me. "Disappearing is not one of my abilities, else I would do it right now."

She scowled at me. "Why do you make frivolous conversation when every moment we remain here puts all of us in graver danger?"

My thought process was percolating and expanding. I began to realize this might really be an important point. "You said that when your kind die, they just disappear. How is that even possible? Beyond that, you did die, or so it certainly seemed. However, you did not vanish."

"That is true," Danarz interjected. "I was holding you and using you for a shield. I felt you die in my grip and I dropped you to the ground after your body expired and became a dead weight. You even let out a last gasp of air as many do in the moment they perish."

Lassoon looked at us in silence. "In truth, I too thought I died while in your grasp when my body was engulfed by the killing fires of the other Nagasa. I even remember thinking that this was my last breath of life. I recall my final thought being of great sadness that without me, my babies too would die in the egg or grow up rogue and be killed by the Nartesians. Then I awoke and saw Lazarus. That was most unexpected, but not cause to remain here at our peril."

"Then let us come with you!" Hannah pleaded enthusiastically.

Before Lassoon could answer, likely once more in the negative, Danarz raised an alarm. "It is too late. Look to the east. A veritable armada of Nagasa approach in the not too distant sky."

Looking eastward, ominously, there were many, many flying black dots heading directly toward us.

"If I do not help you, your fate of death is certain," Lassoon revealed candidly. "But if I do help you, your chance of escape is still but slight. While the likelihood of my slow and agonizing death as a traitor becomes far more likely."

"You think too much, worm!" Danarz bellowed. "Take the female and I will take the male and let us just go!"

"As you say," Lassoon agreed.

Hannah and I hurriedly mounted the necks of our two friends and within seconds we were flying at a blinding speed toward the refuge of the forested canyon, thankfully outdistancing the approaching horde of Nagasas.

Once under the protective canopy of the forest cover we remained silent in our thoughts for some minutes before I had to ask a nagging question.

"Lassoon, I am grateful for the cover of the forest. But why do none of the Nagasa search for us in here? If you can fly in here so easily, why do none of them? They were close enough that they must have seen us flee into this canyon. When we were hiding here earlier I caught occasional glimpses of them flying high up in the sky above.

If the Nartesians want us so badly why do they not pursue us into the forest?"

"An astute question," Lassoon complimented. "I am not entirely certain of the answer. But it has something to do with the boundaries of the city. We Nagasa have a symbiotic relationship with the Nartesians. We provide them security of their realm against all intruders. They in turn provide us an assurance of life as long as we obey them when they call or command and we stay within the boundaries of their realm.

"Some of us are still killed each moon in the arena games where they force us to fight one another to the death. But that is a small number and is reserved as a punishment for rogue or disobedient Nagasas. As long as we strictly obey the Nartesians our lives are spared and we are allowed to live as we please among our own kind when we are not on duty in service to the Nartesians.

"This forest is past the boundaries of the Nartesian city. We may venture anywhere on this world if we have a Nartesian rider. But on our own we are forbidden to travel beyond the boundaries of the realm.

"Still, there are always some of our kind that try to escape, hoping to somehow be free of the Nartesians. Even if death is the result, for many that is a happier choice than continued slavery.

"This forested canyon has been a mystery from time immemorial. In any other direction, if a Nagasa departs the realm on their own, we can watch them disintegrate into dust as they fly off into the distance beyond the boundary. But because of the thick foliage obscuring our view we do not know the fate of those that transit the forest canyon.

"On the other hand, neither do we ever see or hear from them again. It is thought that they meet their end as they traverse through the canyon. But we cannot be certain as none of us have ever seen their demise."

"Perhaps they have finally found freedom," I suggested. "Once tasted why would they ever return to the bitterness of slavery?"

"I wish it were so," Lassoon lamented. "But as I said, we travel widely in company with a Nartesian rider. If there were escaped Nagasa in other parts of the world we would sense their presence when we traveled to the lands we visit.

"No, I am afraid for some inexplicable reason they all perished."

"Maybe there is a bigger, meaner monster in the forest that eats flying worms," Danarz suggested.

I thought Danarz was just making an insensitive comment, but Lassoon's answer left me apprehensively looking all around. "Maybe," she replied in simple sincerity.

"Yet, there are a few of us in recent times that have ventured into the Cursed Forest and returned to tell the tale. I am one. I explore the forest regularly. I am still trepidatious and do not travel deep into its depths. But each time I go further and return unscathed. One day, I will fly all the way to the land of the Glitorees and be free of the Nartesians forever."

"Why do you obey and serve the Nartesians?" Hannah wondered. "They are like ants to you. You are practically invulnerable with your armor. And your fire could kill a score of them with one breath."

"That has happened in the past," Lassoon admitted. "There have been times when one of our males has taken such umbrage at the cruelness of the Nartesians that they killed some of them with a blast of fire. But in retaliation the Nartesians slaughtered two score of our kind."

"How?" Hannah asked in disbelief. "How could a puny little Nartesian kill even one of you? They do not even have any weapons I saw except small daggers. I thought the Nagasa were the only weapon they needed."

"It is true," Lassoon agreed. "Though they do have some weapons larger than a dagger, we are their primary weapons of destruction. It is only so because we fear our fate if we do not obey their dictates.

"Left to our own, Nagasa are peaceful. We would not seek to harm others that were not being disruptive to our peace and serenity. Even then, we are just. We would only mete out the barest punishment necessary to make an antagonist reconsider their poor choices. Only in the direst of circumstances would we take a life.

"But for the Nartesians we are killing machines and weapons of intimidation to all other beings upon our world."

"How do they kill you?" Danarz asked gruffly. "I know you probably will not tell me, for fear I will use the secret against your kind, but I had to ask."

"I will tell you," Lassoon answered to our surprise. "Because knowing what I know will not help you kill a Nagasa. The simple reason is, I do not know.

"Punishment is common. The only mass retaliation I have seen in my lifetime was when fifty-two Nagasa were executed. That was three hundred and forty-three cycles ago."

"You are that old!" Hannah interrupted in surprise.

"You are not?" Lassoon replied with equal surprise.

"Our people pass from life of old age before their hundredth birthday," Hannah explained, "most before their fiftieth."

"That is sad," Lassoon answered with compassion. "So little time to learn anything.

"I knew you were from a part of the world I had never visited before because I have never seen your kind. You look like Nartesians but your mind is very different. Is your land terribly toxic that your people die so young?"

"I do not know," Hannah replied. "I understand there used to be more years in a life. What happened to make it less is a mystery."

"They are not from this world," Danarz interjected. "They came through a passageway that connects our world to theirs."

"That is most fascinating," Lassoon mused. "And it explains much. If we survive, perhaps you can take me and my children to your world that we might be free of the Nartesians."

"It would not be better for you and would probably be worse," I admitted remorsefully. "Our world is also a cruel, warring and enslaving place. You would have less peace than you have here. People would either wish to kill you because you are so powerful, or desire to enslave you to kill for them just like the Nartesians do."

Before I could add more to my thought Danarz interrupted. "Which returns us to my question. How do the Narts kill your kind?"

"Like Hannah's mystery of a short life, how the Nartesians kill us is a great mystery," Lassoon explained. "If we knew the answer to that perhaps we would no longer be slaves.

"Whenever a Nagasa offends or injures a Nartesian there are severe repercussions within a day. Sometimes it is body-wracking pain that comes without a source being discerned. But often it is death, even for slight offenses.

"The Nartesians have a power, when they wish to

use it, that compels us to obey them. A few of us can resist the compulsion, but not many. Oftentimes, those thought to be rogue are compelled to fight to the death with other Nagasas in the arena. Other times they simply become piles of ash when there are none to see."

Danarz squawked derisively. "How could fireproof, virtually indestructible creatures be suddenly turned to ash? I think you are making up a story."

"I am not," Lassoon assured him. "How the death is accomplished has been unfathomable to us since before the memories of our most ancient ones. And they have lived for more than one thousand cycles.

"Be it day or night, while they sleep, in ways that are completely undetectable, the Nartesians choose and execute their victims. All that remains for other Nagasas to discover is a pile of ash where the body had lain for its last sleep. Some are killed in battles to the death with other Nagasas in the arena, but most die mysteriously while they sleep at night."

We flew on for several minutes after that in silence as everyone thought upon the magnitude of what Lassoon had just revealed. A race of beings that could compel the obedience of the mighty Nagasa, or turn them into a pile of ash without even being detected in their nefarious attack, was a formidable adversary indeed. And these were the people chasing us. Yikes!

DESTINY

Chapter 16
QUEEN OF EVIL

We had been flying for at least an hour through the forest following a thin river that snaked through the lowest level of the verdant valley floor. Without warning Lassoon suddenly diverted about ninety degrees to the left and began a steep ascent up the face of a tall mountain whose lofty peak was hidden somewhere in a mass of thick gray clouds above.

As we passed into the foggy, gray mist of the clouds, the air became suddenly cooler and the visibility virtually non-existent. It was an uncomfortable, dark dampness such as I had never experienced, and I found myself involuntarily shuddering with an ominous foreboding.

Over the many years that have passed since that day, I have learned to pay attention when I get those sudden feelings of impending menace. But I was still just learning to use my gifts and listen to my higher self. Even if I had been more self-aware at the time, I probably would have ignored the feeling, as the entire last couple of days had been an ever-cascading cavalcade of nerve-wracking, life-threatening perils. I was becoming numb to the danger-induced anxiety. I still felt it, but it was so continuous that I just began to ignore it.

My unaccountable worries were soon forgotten as we continued to ascend and passed through the carpet-like layer of clouds and back into the brilliant sunshine. Lassoon led us on a course to the south side of the mountain peak, and near its summit she flew into an opening to a cavern. Danarz and I came in right behind her. Inside the cavern it was actually quite hot and there was a noxious smell of decayed sulfur in the air. These were indications that we were likely inside the bowels of a dormant volcano.

Once again I felt anxiety rising and radiating out through the frayed nerves in my body as I remembered an unpleasantly similar situation with Latalizq in a cavern on a cliff, wanting to feed me and Hannah to her babies. But I was relieved as our eyes adjusted to the dim light to see there were no ravenously hungry Nagasa babies wanting to devour us in this cave.

Instead, there were five clusters of large eggs about twice the size of my head laying in depressions in the rock. They had an amazing array of colors. Some had a sky-blue background with brilliant red spots. Others had an orange background with green splotches. Still others were white with small black dots, and there were other variations as well. There were five separate locations of eggs. One held only two eggs, most held three, and one held five. There were sixteen eggs in total.

Lassoon moved over to the clutch with five eggs and curled her sinuous body around them. She made a purring sound very similar to a happy cat. "All is well. You see, you did not need to follow me here. There is nothing you can do to assist me. It is my energy my babies need, and it is what they are now receiving.

"Make haste and go your way in peace. Continue on through the canyon to the land of the Glitorees and your freedom. Hopefully someday soon my children and I will follow you."

Hannah walked over to Lassoon and softly touched her face. "I will miss you and hope we will see each other again."

Lassoon gently nuzzled the edge of her upper lip against Hannah's cheek. "As do I, Hannah. To know you more, a being of both kindness and power, would be an honor."

Anxious as I was to leave this dreaded land, I am also by nature an intensely curious person. It would nag me endlessly if we parted without having all my questions answered, so, with some reluctance, mostly out of fear of retribution, I interrupted the mutual admiration society being formed by my wife and Lassoon.

"Whose eggs are all the rest? Surely they are not all yours?"

Lassoon looked at me with her big green eyes.

"Each clutch belongs to another female Nagasa. Many Nagasa have tried to enter the Cursed Forest over many, many cycles. But only we five have ever returned alive. Somehow, over successive generations, we have mutated in some mysterious way that gives us immunity, at least to some degree, to the unknown toxin in the forest canyon that has killed all other Nagasa from time immemorial.

"Interestingly, we are all on the same eleventh cycle fertility apex, while most of the other females fall on one of the other eleven.

"Because all of our eggs would be laid during the same time period and we were all of the sisterhood immune to the toxin of the Cursed Forest, we explored our sanctuary away from the Nartesians until we found this cavern high atop the mountain.

"Here we laid our eggs and hope that the children born here will carry our immunity and also be free."

"You are not free," Danarz exclaimed contrarily. "I think you delude yourself.

"You abandoned your eggs and came to confront us and kill us when the Narts ordered you to do so."

"It could be no other way," Lassoon explained contritely. "If we do not wish the Nartesians to know of our immunity, both to the forest toxin and to the compulsion to obey them that all other Nagasa cannot resist, we must usually respond when they beckon and execute their orders as they command."

"Then what is the purpose?" Danarz asked sarcastically. "Whether you are compelled or willingly do their bidding to hide your secret, in the end you are still obeying their commands. A being that is capable of resisting but chooses not to has no advantage over a being who cannot resist."

"I cannot always resist their compulsion," Lassoon confessed. "The closer we are to Nartese City, the more irresistible the compulsion becomes to obey the commands of the Nartesians.

"In this forest, canyon, and mountain we are truly free. I can still hear the commands of the Nartesians in the distant recesses of my mind when they beckon. But I can resist the urge to obey their commands when I am far from Nartese City. And sometimes, when I think I will not be missed, I do resist and do not heed the call."

"What about your mate?" Hannah asked with concern. "If you flee this land for freedom with your children, what will happen to him?"

Lassoon cocked her head and looked at Hannah curiously as if trying to understand her question. Then she glanced over at Danarz, and he perceived she was wondering if he could shed any light on Hannah's question.

"They are a very odd species," Danarz explained. "As difficult as it is to comprehend, these two, and apparently all the others on their world, remain for life with the same mate."

Lassoon withdrew her head back sharply in

disbelief. "You mean couples bond for a lifetime and all of their children are created by the union of the same male and female?"

"That is my understanding," Danarz acknowledged, shaking his head in bewilderment.

Lassoon stared blankly at the wall of the cavern for a moment, trying to make sense of what to her seemed nonsensical. "Why would they choose to limit the pool of diversity in such a severe manner? It would seem ultimately to be suicidal to their species."

She looked over at the other four clutches of eggs. "You see there is a mix of colors in the eggs and even within the individual clutches. This reflects the contributions of multiple males, each with their own unique physical characteristics. This ensures genetic diversity within our species and produces the strongest and most capable offspring."

Lassoon looked at Hannah skeptically. "Is it true? Are you and Lazarus committed to remain with each other for your entire lives? You limit yourself to sexual relations and children only with him?"

"Yes," Hannah affirmed, "and beyond. There is great joy and fulfillment in a life shared together. Even with our visit to your world, we have survived only because we have each contributed individual skills that blended very harmoniously as a result of our many years of companionship, of living together and of knowing every aspect, every strength, and every weakness of the other.

"Without speaking or communicating I know when it would be best for him to use his skills and abilities in a challenge, and he instinctively knows when it would be best for me to use mine. We are stronger and more capable by far together than either of us would be alone."

"But what of your children?" Lassoon lamented. "If all of your offspring have the same sire and they follow that pattern with mates when they are adults, your species must inevitably become very defective both physically and mentally because of the lack of diversity."

As the discussion progressed and I recalled everything I had seen and heard about on this world, I thought I might have an answer that would make sense. But first I needed to ask a question.

"Lassoon, how many Nagasa are there altogether?"

"That is an easy question," she quipped, "as I know them all. As of this time, there are exactly four hundred adults."

"That seems too small of a number," Hannah commented, a bit perplexed. "If you have five eggs and lay a clutch every eleven years, and your species lives for hundreds of years, there should be an uncountable number of Nagasa by now."

"So it would seem," Lassoon agreed, "but despite our capacity and potential for longevity, we have a high mortality and few make it into old age."

"I thought your kind was virtually indestructible," Danarz commented.

"Except in fights among ourselves or mysterious execution by the Nartesians," Lassoon pointed out. "As you saw when I removed the scale from my body that I gave to you, our claws can cut through our armor as easily as your beak could snap a branch of a tree."

"And as I mentioned, one of the greatest pastimes of the Nartesians is to compel us to battle against one another. They have a big arena in Nartese City. Every hundred days they hold a tournament; a spectacle of fights between Nagasas. Fights that are most often to the death.

"I am sure one of the reasons we are forced to kill each other is to control our numbers. There are less than three thousand Nartesians. Even though they compel us and force us to do their bidding, I believe there is a limit to how many of us they can control at any moment.

"If our population was allowed to increase, I am certain we would all soon be free of those despicable beings. But the fights to the death in tournaments and mysterious vanishing that sometimes occur ensure that for every birth of a child, there will come an offsetting death of an adult. Hence our population seldom varies from four hundred adults."

"That is so sad," Hannah said sympathetically.

I just couldn't grasp the crux of what Lassoon

was saying. "How can the Nartesians possibly exert such absolute control over you even from a distance?" I asked.

"It is a mystery," Lassoon admitted ruefully. "We hear their commands telepathically, and despite what we desire otherwise, we cannot resist doing as they wish. Even if they command us to kill one another, we must obey. It is a terrible agony to be unable to resist an action that breaks your heart even while you do it. Even as mine is breaking now."

We all looked at Lassoon with incomprehension. "Why is your heart breaking now?" Hannah asked. "You are free here, far from the Nartesians. You are with your children and we who are your friends. Certainly your past has been traumatic and tragic, but I believe the future will be much better for you."

"Well then, you would believe wrong." We all turned with adrenaline-rushing anxiety to look at the source of the stern voice behind us. Standing with her arms on her hips and her legs spread in a dominating stance was Leiaza, queen of the Nartesians!

Looking past her out the portal, I could see many Nagasa flapping their beautiful translucent wings as they held position in the air facing the cavern entrance. Each of them had a Nartesian warrior riding in the saddle astride its neck.

"I am sorry, Hannah," Lassoon said with deep sadness and regret. "My ability to resist the Nartesians is only effective when I am a great distance from them. When they are this close and there are so many, I must obey, no matter how greatly I do not want to."

"The Nagasa speaks the truth," Queen Leiaza confirmed, "and to a lesser degree, but still effective enough, it is the same truth for all of you."

She stepped into the cavern and walked over to Hannah. My wife did not move. Nor did I or Danarz. It was as if we had lost our will to react.

Leiaza gently grasped my wife's delicate chin. "I have missed you, my pet. You ran away before we could finish our play."

She slowly dropped her hand, spread out her fingers, and slid it down over my wife's naked breasts, then across her flat stomach until her arm was fully extended and her hand came to rest on my wife's most private area.

In my mind I knew Hannah wanted desperately to resist, even as I kept ordering myself to move and attack the queen to defend my wife. But I did not move despite my fervent intentions, nor did Hannah despite the intrusive sexual caresses of the queen, shamelessly done in front of me and everyone else watching.

"Hannah, dear pet, it is time for you to be collared." Leiaza held up a thin leather-like strap that had been hanging from her waist belt. "Put this on your neck," she commanded.

Hannah reached out without objection and, grasping the strap on either end with her two hands, she wrapped it around her neck and snapped the two ends together in what appeared to be a very permanent lock.

More Nartesians had entered into the cavern. Leiaza gave a hand signal and another woman came forward with a length of thin, small chain and gave it to the queen. She reached up and attached it to a small D-shaped ring on the collar. Holding the other end of the chain, she led Hannah back toward the cavern entrance.

As they passed out of the cave, she commanded the Nartesian warriors, "Collar and chain the bird and the other one and bring them back to Nartese City."

As two burly men approached me, with one carrying a collar similar to the one Hannah was wearing, my mind was screaming out for me to fight, to resist, but my body would not obey the commands of my mind. Instead, I just stood there like a mindless idiot and let the men put a collar around my neck, then meekly followed the one holding the chain attached to my collar as we walked out of the cavern.

There was a Nagasa hovering in front of the cave, facing away from it. The end of its long tail was laid out on the floor at the edge of the cavern. We merely stepped up on the tail and walked down it onto the Nagasa's body, continuing until we reached the saddle at the beast's neck. I obediently sat in front of the saddle as I felt compelled, and my guard sat in the saddle behind me.

Looking to my right I could see Hannah with the queen on another Nagasa. But unlike me, she was sitting in the same saddle with the queen. Her naked back was pressed tightly against the queen, who had both of her arms wrapped around Hannah, holding her tight in very familiar sexual ways.

They had a bit more trouble with Danarz. Apparently, he wasn't as weak-minded as Hannah and me and resisted mightily having a collar put around his thick neck. Though I could not see exactly what was occurring, ferocious noises reverberated from within the cavern. A cloud of dust and feathers was soon billowing out of the entrance, and then a Nartesian went flying out, in a way Nartesians cannot fly, and bounced hard and dead far below on the ground. He was followed by a second Nartesian being expelled from the cave in the same manner and with the same fatal results.

Queen Leiaza was showing some anger at the situation and ordered four more warriors into the cave. After a few more minutes of battle, they at last emerged, looking much worse from the experience, with Danarz collared and chained like me and Hannah. He seemed dazed and lethargic. I wondered if they had drugged him or if he was just exhausted from the fight. He was held by long chains attached to his collar and going in opposite directions to warriors on either side sitting astride Nagasas. A third chain was attached to one of his legs.

Poor Danarz was barely flapping his wings enough to stay aloft. The Nartesians were so cruel I had no doubt that if he stopped flying, they would simply continue onward to Nartese City with him hanging like a dead weight by his neck from the chains suspended from the flying Nagasas.

The queen now spoke aloud to Lassoon, who was hovering just to the right of the queen's Nagasa. "Expel the highest fury of your fire into the cavern. I want you to be the one that burns your babies alive and those of the other rebellious Nagasas, that it may be forever seared into your tiny brain that you must NEVER disobey a Nartesian!"

"Please do not ask me to do this terrible deed," Lassoon begged in a forlorn, pitiful plea. "I cannot kill my babies."

"Whether it is you or another, it shall be done." The queen sneered with cruel contempt. "But I much prefer it to be you. The thrill of watching a hapless mother kill her own offspring is just too delicious to describe. I can't wait. And neither can you, because I was not asking you. I was commanding you."

With her head hung low Lassoon obeyed the queen and flew over to the entrance of the cavern.

"No! Don't do it, Lassoon!" Hannah pleaded in a loud scream. "Resist!" Hannah was struggling and thrashing about trying to free herself from the grasp of the queen both physically and mentally.

It only seemed to give Leiaza pleasure. She pulled the chain tight and grasped Hannah firmly about her waist. A wicked smile lit up her face and it was obvious every aspect of what was transpiring was a joy to her.

I am not usually very sensitive to the energy auras of others, but so great was the heartbreak and sorrow of Lassoon that I palpably felt her pain heavily in my own heart. With great reluctance Lassoon slowly inhaled a big breath of air to stoke the fire in her belly. Then, with a mighty rush, she bellowed out an immense horizontal column of orange fire.

"No!" Hannah screamed at the top of her lungs as if it was her own children being burned to ashes. "No! No! No!"

Her enraged protestations, despite their heartfelt vigor, were as useless as Lassoon's feeble resistance to the queen's command. The fire Lassoon breathed into the cavern was so enormous and consuming that a good portion of it blew back out of the entrance after hitting the back wall of the cave.

Then there was silence. The morbid silence of death and hopelessness. I seriously wondered if I would ever see my own children again.

As I was wallowing in my own sense of defeat, a voice of hope came to me. "We still live," Danarz proclaimed strongly in my mind. "We still live. And while we do, there may yet be a tomorrow."

I looked over at him and smiled weakly in

acknowledgment.

"Perhaps it would be a good time to pray to your gods," Danarz suggested. "Maybe it will make you feel better."

As we flew off in a mighty cavalcade toward Nartese City—we the three prisoners, the tragically compliant Lassoon, and at least a hundred other Nagasas and Nartesians—I reflected with renewed hope upon Danarz's words of encouragement. I realized that since our visit to this world, my pleas for higher assistance had been disappointingly fruitless. But my faith was not dimmed. How could it be any other way for a man that had been brought back from the dead five days after he had died? Danarz was correct. It was time to call upon my gods, but not just to make myself feel better.

"Elohim, hear my words..."

Chapter 17
ROAST

As we were approaching Nartese City a fleeting thought that had been nagging me came to the fore. I looked over at Danarz and was happy to see he had thrown off his lethargy and was once again fiercely awake and alert. I called out to him in my mind.

"Danarz, how is it that the queen was speaking telepathically? I thought you said the Nartesians lacked that ability."

Before Danarz could answer the voice of my faux friend Kzon spoke contemptuously in my head.

"Of course we can speak telepathically. It is a very rudimentary skill. We merely hide that reality from the lower denizens so we can have advantage over them. It is amazing the secrets you can learn when the others think you cannot understand their method of communication. For instance, everyone knew about your plans and actions to escape Nartese City. We allowed you to escape."

That was shocking to learn. "Why? If it was all a charade, what was the point?"

I couldn't see Kzon among the many flying Nagasas with riders, but his words were stinging. "Think Lazarus. I know your brain is tiny and barely functioning but if you try very hard, really push yourself, I'm sure you can recall the greatest passion of the Nartese, considering you have already had first-hand experience with it."

"Oh," I nodded in understanding to myself as I remembered how everything had begun to unravel on our visit to Nartese City. "Your silly game of Zontog? All of this is about a stupid game with a dagger?" I thought with outraged exasperation.

Kzon seemed very disappointed with my answer. "Lazarus, your lack of deduction is lame-brained in the extreme. Your pathetic void of intelligence just made me lose a wager."

"Good!" I spat out in thought. "But I have reconsidered my answer anyway. Given everything I have seen and heard about since I have had the unfortunate experience of visiting your city, I have no doubt that the greatest passion of Nartesians is to try to outdo one another in cruelty!"

"Ouch, that hurts," Kzon protested. "I was never cruel to you, just the opposite. It is not my fault that you were discovered to be in the city under false pretenses, hiding your unique defensive abilities. If you had not been revealed to be deceptive, and if the queen had not decided to take your companion as a personal sexual plaything, I am sure we would have just enslaved you.

"And as an additional unwarranted insult, you have just made me lose another wager. I was certain that given a second opportunity to state our passion, it would be so obvious that even a being of your limited mental capabilities would be able to elucidate it."

"It is fairly obvious Lazarus," Danarz interjected in a bored tone. "The ogre has been giving you enough hints that his wagers would not even count as fair in my land."

"Alright! I'm an idiot," I agreed facetiously. "Just tell me what it is so we can be done with this ridiculous conversation that has no bearing whatsoever upon the fate we are flying to. Then maybe we may have time to start asking some questions that might actually prove helpful."

"Astounding ignorance," Kzon blurted in disbelief. "If everyone on your world is as dimwitted as you, I think we need to begin regular forays there to capture slaves. We have been using the river people but since we don't give them much to eat and there's not much to forage in the city, they die off faster than we can replenish them. And the birds also eat many, so they are very hard to come by these days.

"Plus, as I'm sure you've noticed, we are a very sensual people and we like sex - a lot! Those river people are so ugly that even with our best efforts to spruce them up it is still necessary to cover their heads with a sack when you want to use them for pleasure."

"Now, if everyone where you come from looks like you and your companion...well that's a nice step up in appearance. And you are stronger too, so you will last longer before you die of starvation."

I was horrified by the callous thoughts Kzon was thinking aloud. Hannah and I had been ordained to be Earth Guardians to keep threats like the Nartesians away from our Earth. Instead our presence here was leading them right to it!

"Hopefully you have a big population," Kzon continued to muse. "It would be nice if it didn't matter how many slaves died off because there was a ready supply to replenish them."

Looking ahead, I could see we were rapidly approaching the high walls of Nartese City. After all this useless and frightening conversation I still had no idea what the greatest passion of the Nartesians was and really didn't care. I did have my own questions I would have loved to have had answers to from Kzon, but then there was no more time.

And it was absolutely maddening that, knowing that everyone was telepathic, I couldn't even have a thought to myself!

No sooner had I expressed my continuing ignorance about the inconsequential subject that Kzon, who had obviously been listening to my private thoughts, interrupted.

"In fact, you are erroneous in your thoughts.

Asking you to be aware of our greatest passion, is a subject of the utmost consequence to you, which is why I brought it up in the first place. I was trying to help you be prepared for what will surely come next Lazarus."

Seeing I was still unresponsively ignorant of what he was hinting at, Kzon finally answered the question as we flew over the walls and headed for the large open-air arena where Lassoon had said the Nagasa were forced to fight to the death.

"We are all gambling addicts," he confessed. "There is hardly an action a Nartesian can do without someone wanting to place a contrary wager. We will wager for big events like the Nagasa battles and for something as trivial as who the next person to enter the room will be. No wager is too insignificant."

"Why are you telling us all of this?" Danarz asked. "It seems your queen would be less than pleased to know you are revealing secrets that might someday be used against you, such as the reality that you have telepathic abilities."

"Not to worry," Kzon assured us. "There are no secrets from the queen. I have no doubt she has been listening to our entire conversation. I could freely reveal all that I did because carcasses tell no tales, and very shortly that is what you all will be, at least the two of you. That is why we are going to the arena.

"Your female will have a different fate because

of the queen's interest. As long as she provides the queen with sexual pleasure throughout the day and night, I am sure she will have a long life.

"Surely the queen will feed her well and let her sleep often enough to maintain her health. And the special ministrations of the sisterhood of the crystals will be able to keep her looking almost as good as us for quite some time.

"I hope that is some condolence to you Lazarus," he said with obvious sincerity, "to know that your companion will live and be well cared for."

His sincere concern for my feelings notwithstanding, I was fuming with upset at the situation and the fate Kzon had outlined for me and Danarz and an even worse one for my beloved Hannah. Despite his candid concern for my feelings, I gritted my teeth in anger and frustration and remained stoically silent in response.

Moments later we alighted on the dirt floor of the expansive arena. It was far larger in size than would seem necessary for the small population of Nartesians. The arena was made from cut stone. It was circular in shape and had a high wooden wall all around the infield, followed by about thirty tiers of bench seating. There was one very large ornate booth on the lowest row closest to the arena floor, which I assumed was for the queen and her retinue.

One peculiar aspect compared to Roman arenas I had seen was the floor of the arena was very small in relation to the overall size of the structure. In diameter it was less than one hundred feet.

I was led off the Nagasa and my chain was fastened to a stout wooden post in the center of the arena. They were more cautious with Danarz. Despite the collar around his neck and being held by three strong chains, he was fighting to be free.

As soon as he saw the Nartesian detach the end of one of the chains to his neck collar from the saddle on the Nagasa, Danarz grabbed the chain with his one unchained foot and jerked it so hard the Nartesian went flying and landed on his face on the soft ground of the arena with a dull thud. To his credit he still held on to the end of the chain with both hands and his arms extended fully above his prostrate head as he lay on his belly on the ground.

Before Danarz could escape or even do any real damage, I was surprised to see a large, heavily weighted net drop down on top of him, effectively immobilizing him. I looked all around trying to figure out where it had come from and was completely mystified. I saw a number of Nagasa with Nartesian riders flying low above the arena so I assumed one of them had dropped it when my attention had been focused on Danarz on the ground. I could see the logic of using it, as Danarz was so big, strong and in an understandably foul mood that little else would have been able to subdue him, short of killing him.

They didn't keep him netted for long. Besides the stake I was attached to, there were several others in the arena, as well as some large iron rings around the perimeter embedded in the thick wooden walls. A fourth chain was put around the ankle of Danarz's one free leg. The two chains coming from his neck were affixed to heavy posts the thickness of a man's body on either side of him. The two chains locked around the ankles of his legs were attached to two other posts spread out behind him. Once he was firmly held fast the net was removed.

During the next ten minutes or so the arena began to fill up with Nartesians, or at least fill up as much as their small populace could, which was only about a third of the seats. The sky on the other hand was thick with flying Nagasas. They were actually quite beautiful as they gracefully flew around each other, like living currents of air.

About five minutes after the arena started being populated, Queen Leiaza entered the large box seating area with about a dozen other ladies, including Hannah who was still collared and led by a chain held by the queen.

My wife was also the only entirely naked woman in the group. All the others were wearing elaborate ornamentation and jewelry, including wide gold wristbands, jewel-encrusted loin coverings, and shallow, ornate gold cones covering the areolae of their breasts.

All of the women also wore various designs of golden, bejeweled headdresses. The queen's was the largest and most elaborate. It had an exceptionally large red ruby cut in an oval shape and set in the center of the crown above her head. The golden, flat, curved projections sweeping upward on the top and sides of the headdress were reminiscent of the natural form of the heads of the Nagasas.

I was happy to see that Hannah was no longer meekly acquiescing to the queen. Since her horrified screams when Lassoon shot her fiery breath into the cavern roasting her own eggs, Hannah seemed to have regained her spunk and an ability to resist the mental control of Leiaza. Even now as the queen sat on her throne at the center of the box, Hannah was jerking on the chain trying to pull it out of the queen's hand and resisting being forced by two other women to sit at the queen's feet. Finally, she was subdued, but only after the two women pushing her down remained by her side holding and restraining her.

The queen stood up and walked gracefully over to the edge of the arena. She jerked the chain wrapped around Hannah's neck and pulled her to the parapet overlooking the arena floor. The two women guards accompanied her and continued to hold Hannah by her arms as she stood beside Leiaza.

The queen reached up and stroked Hannah's long hair. Hannah thrashed her head back and forth trying to avoid the queen's touch, but to no avail. "I hope you will enjoy this my pet. This is an auspicious day - the end of your old life and the beginning of a much more pleasurable and fulfilling one.

"I was sure you would want to bet on your traveling companion so I have opened an account for you at the wagering office. For now, you are only allowed to make wagers with me and whoever loses must pay the other in orgasms.

"I am hoping you have great confidence in the prowess of your companion and will wager for him accordingly. I, of course, will need to take the opposite position and wager for the bird."

The queen came up to Hannah and put her face very close to my wife's. I thought she was going to kiss her as she gently stroked the bottom of Hannah's chin with her index finger. "Don't worry pet, whichever of the brutes kills the other, regardless of our wagers, we both will be winners," she cooed.

I'm sure Hannah's reaction was not what the queen expected from the woman she had grown accustomed to obediently acquiescing to her dominance. Hannah spit a big glop of goo right in the queen's face! Even from the arena floor I could see the runny blotch of spit dripping from Leiaza's eyes and down her cheeks. There was a collective gasp of disbelief from many Nartesians once they saw or realized what had happened.

"Aaaag!" Leiaza screamed in anger. "You will pay with your life for that, you little cur!" She let go of the chain she had been holding that was affixed to the collar around Hannah's neck. Grabbing hold of Hannah's long hair with both her hands she jerked her out of the grasp of the two Nartesian women that were restraining her.

Hannah was bent over as the queen controlled her by her hair. Leiaza violently jerked Hannah's head back and forth a few times. Suddenly she pulled her forward and threw her over the parapet. Hannah flew through the air, arms and legs all askew, and landed with a dull thud on the dirt floor of the arena.

I wanted to run over to her to protect her and comfort her, but instead was left to grit my teeth and struggle in powerless, impotent frustration constrained by my bonds.

Quickly after she fell into the arena, two burly, muscular men entered from a hidden door along the perimeter wall. They walked over and, reaching down, grasped Hannah by each of her arms and lifted her up. She was still stunned from her fall over the parapet and the men needed to support her as they dragged her mostly limp body over toward me and Danarz.

They locked an iron ring around one of Hannah's ankles. The chain was about thirty feet long and secured into one of the thick wooden posts.

After a minute or so, Hannah revived and stumbled over to embrace me. I held her close and tightly. Just being united with her and feeling the warmth of her body against mine invigorated me with hope and happiness.

She leaned her head against my chest and clasped me around my waist. "My precious Lazarus. I am so happy to be with you again."

"And I you," I said, kissing her forehead, "but I fear you are now going to suffer my fate. And at the moment it doesn't look very promising." I smiled a bit, trying to lighten the somber mood.

She kissed me passionately on my lips and held my eyes steadfastly. "I would far more prefer to share your fate, my love, than watch you suffer it alone."

Before I could reply, Leiaza's shrill voice resounded throughout the arena. "Uninvited interlopers. I am going to give you the opportunity to win your freedom. It is more than any of you deserve, but the wagering public demands it."

As she was speaking, several men came out and changed my bonding chain from my neck to one of my ankles and added a longer length so it was about thirty feet, like Hannah's. They also pulled us apart and to opposite sides of the arena with Danarz situated between us.

Throwing a net over Danarz again, they put a new chain around each of his ankles, also about thirty feet in length, then removed the chains from his neck and his previous ankle chains. After they scurried away, he was able to reach back with his beak and throw the net off and over to the side. The three of us now stood facing Leiaza, who was just out of reach of our thirty-foot chains.

Leiaza smiled in wicked glee as she announced our fate. "The three of you will have the opportunity to win your freedom by fighting the others to the death. If any of you live after the other two are dead, we will heal you of your wounds and set you free to return to your land.

"To aid you, the bird may use the net he has thrown to the side, as well as his own sharp talons, fearsome strength, and mighty beak, not to mention the power of his wings, which will surely stun the others into unconsciousness or even death if they allow themselves to be struck by one.

"My traitorous pet, being the physically weakest of the three, shall be given the most potent weapon." A man came out of the hidden door to the arena carrying a satchel and a weapon of some kind. He put the heavy satchel around Hannah's neck and handed her the weapon. It was similar to a crossbow of the Middle Ages on Earth. But the cross arm was not straight. It curved down sharply at the front and then back up where a person gripped it. And instead of a string to notch an arrow, it had a flat piece of leather like a sling.

Leiaza looked at Hannah. "Reach inside the satchel, ungrateful wench, and you will find some sharp-pointed, lead projectiles. The weapon you have been given will automatically recock itself whenever you hold it straight down toward the ground. Merely reach in your bag and withdraw another projectile. Place it at the apex of the elastic V, aim, and pull the trigger. It will allow you to attack your opponents from a distance."

Hannah reached in the bag and followed the directions of the queen. Once her weapon was fully loaded, she quickly pointed it at Leiaza. "You mean like this," she uttered with vehemence as she pulled the trigger. The lead projectile flew through the air so fast it was barely visible. But it never hit the queen. Instead, it impacted some type of invisible shielding above the arena wall and dropped harmlessly to the ground.

"Yes, exactly like that," Leiaza said approvingly, showing no concern whatsoever that she had just been attacked. "However, you will find it much more to your benefit if you point it at one of your two opponents."

The same man returned and handed me a long, sharply pointed pike that was at least twice as long as I was tall. He also gave me a pointed iron spike about the length of my forearm that had a stout iron handle with a comfortable grip.

Leiaza addressed me, "You have been given two weapons. One will give you somewhat of a reach to impale the bird, and the iron spike can be used to pierce the ungrateful, heartless wench.

"Take three deep breaths to plan your strategy and let the games begin!" she exclaimed enthusiastically.

I threw both of the weapons I had been given

down on the ground and looked over at Hannah. "I will never harm a hair of your beautiful head."

Before Hannah could respond, the queen interjected. "A very unwise choice, scrawny one. Together you and the wench might defeat the bird and at least one of you return to the precious children you seem to have such affections for, but if you are defenseless, I am sure he will make gruesomely quick work of both of you."

Sadly, Leiaza was speaking words of truth. With great reluctance, I reached down and picked up my weapons again. I looked over at Danarz. He had proved to be much more of a friend than the selfish, gruff bravado he projected. "I am sorry, Danarz. I am grateful for everything you have done to aid us on our quest and do not choose to have it end like this. But I must defend my wife, even to the death."

Danarz chortled one of his dismissive squawks. "Very noble of you, Lazarus, but unnecessary."

He reached over to his side, grabbed onto the net with his beak, and flicked it in front of him.

"I have no intention of fighting either you or Hannah. Even if I killed you both, which I surely would easily do if we engaged in combat, I have no expectation of freedom. These people, led by their wicked queen, are duplicitous in the extreme. If they promise one thing, it is sure that the opposite will occur.

"Fighting each other would simply fulfill their need for a novel wagering situation and feed their bloodlust. I kill for food and in self-defense, but I do not fight or kill for my own or others' entertainment. That is a trait of barbarians.

"Until I had the unfortunate opportunity to come here and meet these despicable creatures, I had thought more highly of them. Now I know the river rats are more evolved than they are."

"Then let us vow to not fight," Hannah urged. "We can deprive them of their pleasure, deny them their precious wagering opportunity, and keep our own dignity."

"Ha, ha, ha!" Leiaza laughed loudly. She was soon joined by nearly everyone in the stadium. Being at the bottom of the circular structure, the sounds of their combined laughter were very loud. In fact, it was inhumanly loud for their numbers, as if they were somehow amplifying their voices. Hannah and I both put our hands over our ears to mute the sound.

"Foolish idiots you are!" the queen screeched. "Your stupidity does not save your lives. If none of you will fight the others, you merely have changed the method of your execution, not the outcome. And now, I assure you, your end shall be much more prolonged and agonizing. And there will be even more wagering to see how long you will last, who will die first, who will be second, and who will be able to hold out the longest."

The queen gave a little jiggle of excitement. "Oooh, I can't wait for the torture. It is going to be so exquisite!"

She spread her arms wide. "Hear me, citizens of Nartese City. As our uninvited guests have chosen to not give us the pleasure of seeing them battle each other to the death, we will instead let them cook as slowly as possible by the fire of the Nagasas. We will take a short intermission in the festivities to allow all of you to place your bets.

"The roasting shall begin within fifteen minutes, so don't be late!" she added gleefully.

Most of the Nartesians in the stands stood up and began milling about like a bunch of excited ants and chattering like monkeys to find others to place wagers with. Hannah and I walked back toward each other, dragging our ankle chains behind us. We met next to Danarz, who was positioned between us. I gave him a respectful nod of my head.

"Thank you for not fighting us. It was something I dreaded, and I feel foolish for not realizing there would be another way, as you have suggested."

Danarz ruffled his wings a bit. "I don't believe my suggestion will be doing us any favors. The queen seems very determined to win wagers by seeing us perish, one way or the other."

"But at least we die on our terms, not theirs—as friends, not enemies," I said resolutely.

"Or maybe we will not die at all," Hannah said wishfully.

I looked at her with my head cocked a bit with curiosity and waited for her to elaborate.

"We must not forget who we are, Lazarus," she chided gently. "We have been called to a great mission. Elohim would not have sent us to a place where we would perish before our destiny has even begun. The fire of the Nagasas will not hurt us. Our protective skins will protect us. We may even be able to shield Danarz somewhat."

I was proud of my wife for her bravery and optimism, even though I knew the latter was founded in the naivety of someone who hasn't faced many situations of death from a determined adversary.

"Our shield skins may protect us for a short time," I acknowledged. "The Nartesians are probably counting on that and factoring it into their wagering.

"I do not mean to throw cold water on your idea, but we need to be realistic. Even if our skins protected us from the fire of a Nagasa, would it protect us from the fire of two Nagasas, or three?

"And even if the skins did protect our bodies, we still need to breathe. Our lungs will not survive breathing in super-heated air any more than they would survive breathing in water, causing us to drown.

"And realistically, we are too small in size to be effective shields for Danarz, and his feathers will go up in flames as quickly as dry kindling wood the very moment the first fire touches them."

Danarz cocked his head and stared intently at

Hannah. "Is your companion always so optimistic?" he asked sarcastically.

Hannah suppressed a little laugh with a tight-lipped smile. "Usually he's not so bad."

I had to smile, realizing that despite the gravity of our situation, they were lightening the mood, even if it was at my expense.

"In any case, I was not done with my suggestions," Hannah added impishly.

I bowed a bit and swept my arm dramatically across my body. "By all means, my love, please continue."

"We can pray," Hannah said with simple sincerity. "Perhaps the Elohim do not know our true situation."

I held up my hands in a bit of frustration. "I did so in great earnestness as we flew here from the mountain of Lassoon's cave. Sadly, we have already tried praying, Hannah, multiple times. Nothing has come of it. For whatever reason, the Elohim do not answer, and we are on our own."

"They do not answer or come to your aid because they do not exist," Danarz interjected. "May we please stick to considering tactics that involve reality?"

"You err in ignorance, my friend," I said cautiously, not wanting to stir up his ire. "I assure you my sister is real and can do things the like of which none of us can imagine.

"And in truth, I died from the bite of a deadly

poisonous serpent. My body lay in the grave five days and was resurrected back to life by Yeshua, the Lord of Light.

"This was not something I dreamed or imagined. As Hannah can verify, this actually happened to me. And while my body slept in the grave, my spirit rose to a place of peace and wonder. The Elohim are real. Of that I am most certain."

My testimony had no effect on Danarz. He shook his enormous head dismissively. "If it makes you feel more confident and less pessimistic in our situation, please implore your mythical gods as you wish, but do not involve me with such nonsense."

And so we did. People were already sitting down again in the arena. Hannah and I only had time for a quick prayer as we held hands and faced each other under the watchful presence of Danarz looming above us. Praying for both of us, I implored, "Elohim, thank you for giving us this exceptional opportunity to see new worlds and grow and expand from our experiences, but it seems those experiences are about to be permanently cut short unless you would be kind enough to intervene. If there is a way we can escape our predicament by the power of our own thoughts, strength, and Celestine gifts, let it be so. But if there is more here than we can bear on our own..."

I never got to finish my prayer. A large, fearsome Nagasa suddenly alighted right in front of us, perching on the rim of the lower arena wall. Two others came down on either side and also stood on the wall. And of course, a fourth one landed on the edge of the wall behind us.

The first Nagasa lifted up its head in surprise, then scooted off to the side a bit, clearing the view for Leiaza to be looking right at us from her box seat. I suppose she must have just telepathically told the Nagasa to move away from her line of sight. The queen addressed us personally in a most pompous, condescending tone of voice.

"Lazarus and Hannah: do not dwell upon your inevitable destruction. Please remember the good times you have had visiting us and the kind hospitality and pleasures we showed you before your traitorous hidden agendas were revealed."

"In consideration for the good times, please think about the happiness you will give to all of the spectators and the profits to those who place the best bets. We are all counting on your strength and fortitude. Please try to last as long as possible before expiring."

Despite myself and our predicament, I had to chuckle. That was the most ridiculous, self-serving, audacious speech I had ever heard!

I looked at Hannah and Danarz. "What is our plan?"

Hannah just looked at me blankly. She was a very intelligent, talented woman, but battle strategy was not her forte.

I looked up at Danarz. "What say you?"

"I say I am stumped," he replied stoically. "If we were free of these chains, we could take a fight to the flying worms that they would never forget. But immobilized by chains and attacked by streams of flames from adversaries beyond our reach, I do not see anything we can do offensively or defensively. I think we will just have to improvise after we see how they attack us."

I hefted the long pike I had been given as a weapon. Danarz knew immediately what I was thinking. "It will not work. The Nagasa's armor would not be pierced by that puny weapon. I could strangle them if I could get my talons around their neck. But even then, my talons would not pierce their armor, and I'm not sure I could actually succeed in killing one by strangulation.

"We cannot just do nothing!" Hannah exclaimed in frustration.

"That is exactly what you will do!" We heard the queen's irritatingly shrill voice proclaim.

"I thought about letting you have some type of defense so we could be entertained by a battle, but that would be letting you die too noble of a death, fighting for your lives. And we can see much more interesting conflicts to the death among the Nagasa.

"No, you are worthless. A clod of dirt is more valuable. This will not be a fight for your survival. You will not survive. I don't wish to hurt your feelings, but the truth is this is an execution. It will just be a nice slow one for entertainment and profiting purposes. I'm sure you understand, don't you?"

I took in a big breath of air to shout an angry reply, but the queen continued speaking aloud far louder than a voice should be able to speak, cutting off my words.

"The man and the woman will die first, but very, very slowly and painfully. The bird will be spared until the end. His feathers will catch on fire so easily that we will be unable to prolong his death once he is ignited. So he will just have to watch the other two suffer while he contemplates his own looming demise."

Leiaza clapped her hands together loudly above her head. "Let the roasting begin!"

Several more riderless Nagasas dropped down from the sky and settled onto the parapet wall until we were completely surrounded by Nagasas packed shoulder to shoulder around the perimeter wall. The only gap was a space left for the queen's box so she would have an unimpeded view of our destruction.

A net was once again dropped on top of Danarz. A half dozen men, each one far larger and more muscular than me, came out into the arena. They roughly grabbed me and Hannah, and despite both of our vigorous attempts to prevent them, they tied us back to back with a thick post between us in a way that we were perpendicular to the queen and she could easily see both of us.

The Nartesians departed back through the hidden door through which they had entered, and the queen stood up at the edge of the parapet.

"ROAST!" she screamed. "But cook them very slowly," she added in a perfectly sane voice. "The louder they scream, the greater will be your reward. The faster they die, the longer will be your punishment. Now ROAST!"

Chapter 18
UNBEARABLE

At the queen's command, all the Nagasas that were perched on the arena parapet in a hundred-and-eighty-degree arc started shooting their hot flames at us. Those behind us refrained and held their fire, obeying the queen's command to not torch Danarz, who was standing behind us, until the end because he would burn too quickly.

Initially, the heat of the flames was not too bad. Our protective skins prevented our real skin from burning, and the air wasn't so hot that our lungs were hurt breathing it. If this was all it was going to be, a small part of me entertained the notion that we just might survive.

But the queen had other ideas. As we didn't appear to be uncomfortably warm, she commanded the Nagasas to jump down to the arena floor so they would be closer to us and to alternate their fire breaths so that only every third Nagasa was breathing fire at any time. This ensured that there would always be fairly constant streams of fire as one Nagasa expelled his breath of fire and another began as the first ended and needed to catch his breath to rekindle the fire.

However, even with that technique, it wasn't long before all of the Nagasas had depleted their fire and could blow no more. Rather than give us a respite, Leiaza ordered the diminished Nagasas to depart from the arena and commanded fresh, new replacements that had been flying in the sky above to come down and take their place. All too soon, we were once again enduring the roasting fires of the Nagasas. Only now they were closer and fresher, and the fire was certainly hotter.

Because the Nagasas were closer, their fire coming from multiple directions at once enveloped us more completely. The air quickly became superheated, and breathing soon became difficult. Hannah was gasping and obviously having even more trouble than me, and I was struggling for every breath. My instinct to breathe in life-sustaining air was offset by the pain I knew was coming as my lungs burned with every intake.

"Use your Celestine gifts!" I yelled out to Hannah in my mind. I dared not do it vocally, as my open mouth would have allowed in even more superheated, lung-shriveling air.

Hannah shook her head in frustration, looking at the ground, and cried out to me telepathically. "I cannot. I do not know how."

"Just think what you want to happen," I counseled. "Start with some kind of bubble over us to protect us from the fire and heated air."

"I am trying, Lazarus," she called out forlornly in her mind while desperately trying to stifle her sobs to limit her breathing. "Nothing is happening."

I hung my own head in total frustration. For all three of us to be unable to do anything at all to help ourselves made me just want to scream out in anger and frustration. Even in that, I was maddeningly stymied, as I couldn't risk breathing in any more of the heated air than necessary.

Seeing us begin to falter, the Nartesians in the stands were going riotously crazy in their enthusiasm for our demise. They were screaming and shaking their fists, some imploring us to hold out longer and others to just give up and die. I assumed each was calling for the desired outcome that would win them their wagers.

I don't know if it was due to the heat or just incompetent tying of our bonds, but our chains loosened enough that Hannah and I were able to wiggle closer to each other. Despite the peril of our situation, I felt a small comfort in my heart when I was able to reach out and hold her hand. It seemed like such an insignificant thing, but up until that moment, I had never felt such overpowering love for Hannah as when we shared our fate, hand in hand, before the deathly flames of the Nagasas in the arena of Nartese City, on a world unknown.

Without warning or command from Leiaza, a Nagasa suddenly descended upon us from above.

My first thought was if it started breathing fire upon our heads, we were surely doomed. But to our joyous relief, this Nagasa was not an enemy, but as true a friend as any I have ever known. It was Lassoon.

She landed behind us, stretched her translucent wings out wide, then brought them together and overlapping, wrapping us in a fire-protective cocoon.

Her traitorous act of shielding us incensed Leiaza almost beyond comprehension. She began yelling and screaming commands at the other Nagasas. Although I couldn't see her through Lassoon's wings and the streams of fire being blasted at us, I winced at her shrill voice and was certain she was so worked up she must be foaming at the mouth like a rabid dog.

Four Nagasas with riders descended from above and hovered just over our heads. Lassoon shot short blasts of fire at each of them, trying to keep them at bay while conserving her fire so she could continue to fight.

But her gallant effort to aid us was soon for naught. The warriors riding the Nagasas each held a large, tube-like weapon. Simultaneously, they all used the weapon to shoot snaking lines of chains at Lassoon. All four wrapped tightly in several loops around her neck. The other Nagasas then lifted skyward, and Lassoon was pulled up underneath them, dangling by the noose of chains encircling her neck.

Lassoon flapped her elegant, long wings fruitlessly. There was no escape from her strangling bonds.

For a moment, we had a respite from our burning. The Nagasas scorching us stopped to witness the scene of death taking place above our heads. As Lassoon struggled mightily, the four Nagasas pulled the chains about her neck taut as they each sought to pull away in four perpendicular directions. It was obvious the Nartesians intended to choke Lassoon to death despite her armor.

"Wait!" Leiaza called out. The Nagasas strangling Lassoon let up a bit on the tightness of her chains.

"This despicable Nagasa is missing her center chest scale. Yet another sign of her renegade, delusional intent. Do not strangle her. Bring her down to the arena. Secure her with chains, spreading her precious wings so she has no protection for her exposed chest. Let her die like the others by the blast of fire from my loyal Nagasas burning through her foolishly unprotected chest until the flames incinerate her traitorous heart!"

As the queen ordered, so it was done. Hannah and I were moved to separate posts, and Lassoon was positioned to the side of Hannah, who was on my left and in the very center of the arena. Danarz was still chained directly behind Hannah.

Lassoon's wings were spread out wide. One of the other Nagasas used its armor-piercing talon to cut a hole in the thin, translucent part of her wings just below the first joint from the wing tip. A strong chain was run through the hole and around the wing bone, then affixed with some type of lock. Her feet were not chained, as there was hardly any movement she could make with her wings, immobilized as they were.

Queen Leiaza mounted a small platform that had been moved to the edge of her box overlooking the arena, which gave her the closest possible view of our fates. As she stood up on the pedestal, a large number of Nagasas descended from above and alighted on the top of the wooden wall around the floor of the arena. Once again, in an overly loud voice, Leiaza made an announcement.

"Citizens of Nartese City. You see twenty-one Nagasa ringing the entire perimeter of the arena. Twenty-one more wait to immediately take their place once they have expended their fire, and another twenty-one await their turn as the third wave of executioners.

"All four of the condemned shall be roasted together. But of course, how long each will last before becoming burning torches of flesh and giving up their last breath is the question of wagering importance. Place your bets and enjoy the spectacle. I personally am betting that the girl will scream the loudest."

Leiaza looked directly at Hannah. "Do not disappoint me any further, slime woman. Be sure to scream very loud!" she spat with vindictive malice, bursting into an insane cackle of laughter.

The Nagasas began to inhale and exhale as they built up their internal fires in preparation for our "roasting."

I called out telepathically to my fellow condemned prisoners. "Can you all hear me in your minds?"

"Yes," everyone affirmed.

"By every means of our own, our situation seems hopeless."

"We still live," Danarz reminded me.

"But to no avail," I countered. "We are completely immobilized and have no means to either attack our adversaries or defend ourselves from their attacks. We must seek the help of a greater power than our own."

"I hope you are not referring to your mythical gods," Danarz said with sadness tinging his voice in my head. "I do not wish our last moments to be in disagreement over your primitive beliefs."

I hung my head in disappointment that he would not even consider what would seem to be the only option left to us. He sensed my letdown and tried awkwardly to patch the rift.

"Do as you wish. Perhaps I will follow suit and invoke the rocks on the ground to fly up and knock the queen in the head. Inconveniently, the rocks have never heeded my wishes in the past, so I cannot put much faith they will in the present.

"But you go ahead and beseech the gods of your world, and perhaps I will talk to the rocks of mine, and something good may yet come of it. I am sure it will not make anything worse for us," he said, trying to cheer me up.

"I will pray with you, Lazarus," Hannah assured me.

"What about you, Lassoon?" my wife asked. "Will you let us include you in a prayer to Elohim for our salvation?"

"I do not understand your meaning or intent, Hannah," she responded with some confusion. "Like Danarz, I cannot see what can be accomplished by beseeching nothingness. If it makes you feel better, you may include me.

"But in truth, after having been forced to kill my own children and being unable to protect you, I no longer wish to live, and death is welcomed."

"No! Do not think like that!" Hannah pleaded.

"It is not what I think. It is how I feel," Lassoon elaborated sadly.

Before anyone could say anything more or I had a chance to say the prayer I desperately wanted to say, from every point around the circular arena, the Nagasas began to blow their deadly streams of fire at us. Though they had been cautioned by Leiaza to "roast us slowly," it immediately felt like we were inside an unbearably hot oven.

For at least a minute or more, we all endured in silence, much to the disappointment of the

Nartesians, I'm sure. Our protective skins were thankfully protecting Hannah and me so far. But toward the end of that short time, I heard a whooshing sound behind me and knew that Danarz's feathers had succumbed to the unrelenting fire and burst into flames. If I had been wearing clothes, they would have been burning off my body as surely as the feathers on poor Danarz were being incinerated.

"Scream!" Leiaza insisted with her overly loud voice at us. "Scream, lest I lose a wager!"

But rather than have cause to scream from the burning pain, we were given a momentary reprieve when the Nagasas all ran out of fire. It was only enough for a few quick breaths of relatively cooler air and for Danarz to tamp out his burning feathers with his denuded wings.

The first group of twenty-one fire-expended Nagasas opened their beautiful wings and took off in groups of two and three and were quickly replaced by the second wave of twenty-one that descended down from above and took their place perching on the arena wall.

"Get down into the arena!" Leiaza ordered. "Get close enough that your fire is sufficiently hot to make them scream in despair! I really must hear them scream to have satisfaction," she prattled.

The Nagasas obeyed and all hopped down to the arena floor, putting them less than ten paces away from us at most.

This time, despite my shield skin, I felt the searing pain of the relentless fire as the Nagasas breathed out their flaming orange streams of death. My body wasn't burning, but I was hurting—a lot! I needed to take big gulps of life-giving air, but I could not do it, lest I breathe in the superheated air and torch my vulnerable lungs.

Once again, I heard Danarz's remaining feathers burst into flames behind me. And far to my left, I heard Lassoon finally utter a heart-rending sound of agony as her unprotected chest was penetrated by the focused fire from the other Nagasas.

Then I heard the greatest anguish to my heart. My precious Hannah called out to me in telepathic torment. "Lazarus! I cannot breathe. The air is too hot. Ieeeee!" she cried aloud.

She thrashed about wildly and screamed aloud in drawn-out anguish, "I am burning inside!"

As terrible as the fire felt and my lungs burned, the pain I felt in my heart to hear my beloved screaming in agony within sight of me, and to be completely powerless to help her or comfort her—this was a far greater pain than any my body endured.

Just when I thought it was the end, when we would all surely perish, the second group of Nagasas ran out of fire. Once again, we were granted a blessed reprieve of about a minute as the second group flew away and the third wave of Nagasa executioners descended to take their place.

Before the Nagasas could begin their final deadly task, Leiaza told them to hold. She left her box and entered the arena from the hidden door along the perimeter wall. As I was nearest, she walked over and stood right in front of me, so close to my face I could feel her fetid breath on my skin as she spoke.

"Your protective shielding is impressive. I would have expected your skin to be blistered and melting off your body by now."

She reached up and ran her hand over the top of my head. "I see your shield does not protect the top of your head very well, as all your hair has burned off."

What! I didn't want to believe it. But I could feel Leiaza rubbing my bald pate with her hand.

I looked over at Hannah. She was slumped in her chains, barely standing up. And she too was completely bald! I knew then that it was true and we had already both lost our hair to the fire.

Leiaza walked behind me. I looked over my shoulder and saw her standing just out of reach of Danarz. I also could not help but notice that he no longer had a single feather anywhere on his body. They had all been incinerated.

"Nagasas, hear me! Do not burn this bird to a crisp. Roast him slowly and tenderly so we can enjoy his carcass for a feast after the execution."

She then walked over and stood in front of Hannah. "My poor little pet. You could have had such a good life. You have no one to blame except yourself for your misery."

Leiaza reached up and cupped Hannah's chin in her hand. "You could have been the pampered slave of the most powerful being in the world. In your last moments of life, I hope you grieve over the needless stupidity of your loss."

Leiaza tried to give Hannah a quick kiss in parting on the lips. But as their lips touched, she suddenly drew back with an exclamation of pain. Despite our dire situation, I had to crack a smile as I realized Hannah had bitten her on her lip when the queen tried to kiss her.

Leiaza swung her arm back and hit Hannah with a vicious open-handed slap on the side of her face. "You little piece of dirt! That will be the last rebellious act of your pitifully worthless life!"

The queen strode away, fuming in anger from Hannah, and went over to Lassoon. Of the four of us, she still seemed the least affected by the fiery assault we had been enduring.

"There is something very peculiar about you, Nagasa. I cannot place exactly what it is. Who is your master or mistress?"

Lassoon did not respond to the queen's query.

Leiaza looked up and around at the Nartesians in the arena seating. "Who is the master or mistress of this rebellious Nagasa?"

A man with curly blonde hair quickly stood up five rows up and off to the right. "I claim that ungrateful, disobedient brute," the man exclaimed in disgust.

"Come here!" the queen demanded. The man with the curly hair quickly made his way down to the arena floor. He approached the queen timidly, with obvious trepidation.

"How is it that this creature tried to defend the interlopers? You must have had something to do with it!"

The man was now obviously fearful because he was literally trembling. "I assure you, Leiaza, I had nothing to do with this creature's behavior. She has always been obedient to my every command."

The queen's face lit up with a wicked smile. "So you admit that you prompted her to protect these miscreants?"

"No, no, no, my highness. I was abhorred when I saw her drop from the sky and envelop the condemned with her protective wings."

"Then why did you allow her to do it?" Leiaza asked menacingly.

"I did not!" the trembling man said, protesting his innocence. "I was commanding her to depart the arena from the first moment she entered it, but she would not obey my commands."

The queen called out in her loud voice. "This fool claims his Nagasa did not obey his commands, even while he was sitting right here in the arena looking at her."

The entire crowd laughed uproariously at the queen's comment.

Leiaza spoke again to the man in a very threatening tone. "You realize, of course, that what you are saying is impossible?"

The poor man was shaking like a leaf in the wind now as he silently nodded his head in agreement.

"I know now that I have been punishing the Nagasa when it is really you who should be punished, isn't it?"

The man vigorously shook his head, denying the queen's assumption. Leiaza faced him with her hands on her hips and spat her words at him with vehemence.

"I should tear your lying heart out of your body and feed it to the river rats, but that would end our fun with your Nagasa too soon.

"Considering your own lies and treachery, you will need to share her fate. Go stand in front of her and remain there until you are consumed by the fire! And make sure your Nagasa stays there as well!"

The doomed fellow was shaking so violently he could hardly stand. In fact, he fell down to his knees and began feverishly kissing Leiaza's sandal-clad feet. "Please, my most powerful, omnipotent queen, please..." he pleaded. "It is not my fault. Perhaps I am just not well. I beg you to have mercy. Please send me to a physician, not to the fire."

While he was pleading for his life, the crowd was taking up a chant, yelling in a frenzy of excitement, "To the fire! To the fire!" I had always thought the

Romans were a bloodthirsty lot with their frequent scourgings and crucifixions, often for petty crimes and offenses, but they seemed almost forbearing in comparison to the maniacal Nartesians and their insane queen. To my astonishment, the curly-haired man went docilely to his fate and stood in front of Lassoon to await his death by fire, as he had been commanded by the queen.

Leiaza returned to her box, raised one of her arms high, and called out to the Nagasas. "Hear me, all you creatures of fire and sky. I have honored you by letting you be the executioners for the worthless rabble below. When my arm falls, you are to begin your final fires of death and destruction upon the unworthy miscreants and continue until they are ash, save the bird. Create a dome of flames which consumes all within.

"However, those of you on the backside, spare the bird your hottest fires. Remember, he is to be part of our feast during the festivities after the execution."

She was quiet for a moment, still holding her hand high while dozens of Nagasas fluttered above awaiting her signal. Without warning, her hand fell in a quick descent. I took a big gulp of fresh air, realizing it would be my last before the fiery onslaught. Then it began: scalding hot flames from every direction. The Nagasas literally fulfilled Leiaza's instructions, as there was soon nothing but a wall of fire everywhere I looked: in front of us, on both sides of us, completely enveloping the sky above us, and even flowing like a flaming carpet along the ground of the arena and lapping at our feet.

It would be more dramatic if I could tell you how we all were in tortured torment by the final fiery assault, but such was not the case. Something far more wonderful and unforgettable occurred that made us oblivious to the heat and the pain.

As the blast of incandescence enveloped us and the fiery tongues of flame licked at and encircled our bodies, there was suddenly a profound connection between all of us who were condemned to die. It was far more than a mental, telepathic connection. For that moment in time, all of us — me, Hannah, Danarz, Lassoon, and even the Nartesian who was named Froyglo — were connected as one. We were not five individuals, but one magnificent common mind and heart. There were no secret thoughts, no hidden emotions or agendas. We were one.

And in that oneness there was a peace and serenity, a disconnect from the horror of our situation. It was as if we were not even there. Though I could hear Leiaza screaming in excitement and the roar of the crowd as they watched our demise, they seemed only like faint echoes in a distant canyon.

In that moment of oneness, we discovered a shocking secret about Froyglo and Lassoon — one that at that juncture I had neither the time nor mental capacity to understand.

And then it was over, but not in the way any of us expected, least of all Leiaza. Amidst the dome of fatal fire, there was suddenly a brilliant white light that filled the space of our fiery furnace and rapidly expanded outward in a wave of thundering concussions.

Unable to bear the intensity of the white luminescence, I closed my eyes for protection. The thunder that shook the very ground we stood upon like an earthquake was followed by a deafening silence. The maniacal screams of Leiaza were no more. The riotous cacophony of the crowd was replaced at first by silence, then by the faintest of disquieted murmurings.

I took in a big gulp of fresh, beautiful, cool air and opened my eyes to an unbelievable, wondrous sight. In front of me, hovering in the air about my height above the arena ground and facing the box of Queen Leiaza, was my sister Miriam.

She had a scintillating, white, ethereal glow emanating from all parts of her body. Seeing that, I realized it really wasn't my sister Miriam at all, not anymore. In her majesty and the fullness of her power, I knew what the Nartesians were about to discover: that they were in the presence of the Angel of the Covenant! And to use a modern euphemism, I expected there was soon going to be hell to pay.

Chapter 19
ANGEL OF THE COVENANT

My first intentional gaze was over to my wife Hannah. I saw her chains and slave collar lying limp on the ground and realized mine were as well. We stepped away from the cluttered pile of enslaving links at our feet and rushed with big smiles of joy into each other's embrace.

For a moment we just held each other very tightly as if we were trying to merge our bodies as one. To be embraced in the warmth of her love was a piece of heaven amidst what had been our hell.

Hannah rubbed her hand over the top of my bald head. "I like you better with hair," she said with a mischievous smile.

I rubbed my palm over the top of her equally bald pate. "You seem to be missing a few hairs yourself, my love," I noted with a wry smile.

I held her gaze, so happy to be holding her and looking into her eyes once more. With the outside of my fingertips I softly caressed her cheek. "I love you with or without your beautiful locks. But if I have a vote, I hope you will grow back your lovely tresses."

Hannah nodded in agreement. "That and finding some clothes to wear and holding our children once more in my arms are absolute certainties."

"Oh, I don't know, I've kind of become accustomed to nakedness," I jested nonchalantly.

Considering our nakedness, I looked down to once again admire my wife's perfect female form and was surprised to discover that her old, still beautiful, but less voluptuous body had returned. She looked down and noticed it too and seemed just a bit disappointed.

We both turned questioningly towards Miriam to clarify our confusion and that's when we saw Leiaza. At least I assumed it was Leiaza as she was in the queen's box seating and was wearing the queen's headdress. But the body beneath it was not the epitome of womanly perfection I had grown accustomed to seeing. In her place was a very old and extremely shriveled woman whose withered teats hung down to her waist. A quick glance at the other Nartesians in the queen's box and continuing up into the grandstands revealed that every single Nartesian had been transformed into an aged, withered old person, tottering around humped over and enfeebled.

Lassoon came over to us and put her face near ours. Warm air bathed us when she exhaled her breath.

"What has happened?" Lassoon asked,

perplexed. "Why are the Nartesians old? And where did all of the Nagasas go?"

So much had happened so quickly it hadn't even yet registered in my awareness that all the Nagasas that had been hurling streams of deadly fire at us were gone. There was not a single one in the arena area other than Lassoon.

Looking skyward I counted four others high up, but no more anywhere!

Danarz loomed over us. His body was denuded of feathers and scorched black and bleeding in many places. But his spirit was not broken. "You see," he asserted confidently. "As long as we still live, there is hope."

He looked over at Miriam and our eyes all followed his gaze. "It would seem that the glowing creature's sudden appearance has caused drastic, inexplicable changes to everything, by a power I cannot even fathom.

"But what is it? It just hovers in place without feet on the ground or wings to keep it aloft."

"That," I said with both humility and pride, "is a who. Once upon a time, a time that seems far longer ago than it was, she was my sister Miriam. Now she is an angel of Elohim; one known for her temper. If the Nartesians are not yet afraid, they probably should begin being so."

Danarz cocked his monstrous, featherless head as he tried to fathom the meaning of my words. "Elohim? The mythical god you called upon?"

"You best reconsider that opinion," I advised Danarz. "As you can see, Miriam, who is an emissary of Elohim, is not a figment of my imagination. Nor is our salvation from death, for which we can be thankful for her intervention. And as you have observed, she wields an unfathomable power beyond mere mortals like you and me."

Neither Danarz nor Lassoon seemed inclined to accept my explanation for the recent fortuitous turn of events. But from the blank looks on their faces they couldn't think of an alternative either.

The four of us approached Miriam from behind. We didn't have far to go and she sensed our presence the moment we began to move toward her.

"Hello Lazarus and Hannah," she spoke without turning back to look at us. "'Tis amazing the quandaries you can get yourselves into in such a short time on a simple observation trip."

"Yes," I agreed facetiously. "We have never ceased to amaze ourselves at our propensity for attracting challenges."

"And 'short' seems to be a very relative term," Hannah added. "To us it seems as if we have been here a fatiguing amount of time.

"But we are sooo happy to see you, Miriam. How are our children?"

"They are fine," Miriam assured her. "Your time away has just seemed like another normal day to them."

"Just a day?" I asked, incredulous.

"Yes, Lazarus," she confirmed. "Just a day, actually even less than a day to their perception."

Danarz stuck his bald head forward so he could look at Miriam from the front. "Are you really Lazarus' sister?"

"Yes," Miriam assured him.

"Have you been the cause of our freedom and the transformation of the Nartesians into doddering ancients, who now seem so dimwitted they just stay in their seats staring at us stupidly?"

"Yes again, to both," Miriam acknowledged. "At least to some degree. I did not make the Nartesians look as they now do; I merely removed their facade so you now see them as they really are in appearance. I have also cast a temporary mind-numbing spell upon them so they will remain docile until I decide their fate."

"Their facade?" Hannah asked with brimming curiosity.

Miriam turned around so she could face all of us. "Yes, their facade, Hannah. It may be difficult for you and Lazarus to fully grasp, but the Nartesians are masters of illusion.

They are an Alamar race, the same as you, but they are the final small remnant of a very ancient people that once had cities far across the lands of this world. Their existence here predates the arrival of the very first Alamars on your Earth by many tens of millennia.

Over many generations they learned some of

the secrets of longevity that stem from diet and behavior. Generations later, they mastered an enormous expansion of certain abilities. Together, this knowledge and these abilities have allowed their bodies to continue to live for thousands of years.

"Thousands!" I stammered, astounded. "That is older than Methuselah, who at 969 years was supposed to be the oldest man ever!"

Miriam smiled slightly as she replied. "On your Earth, he may have been among the oldest, but on this Earth, these people would consider Methuselah not even middle-aged."

All of us seemed too shocked to reply, so Miriam continued with her explanation.

"In the earlier generations, despite their best efforts to extend their lives, most of the Nartesians died before they reached 500 years. Centuries before they died they were already looking gray-haired, wrinkled, and decrepit in appearance as you see them look now.

"They had accomplished as much life extension as could be gained by eating the optimum foods, by drinking the life-enhancing teas, and by keeping their bodies physically active.

Some of the brightest of the oldest among them discovered additional hidden secrets of longevity beyond food, drink, and physical activity. Chief among these was the importance of daily sexual activity.

"This presented a large problem. Though it would serve the younger Nartesians well, it was a secret discovered by oldsters, who looked as old as they were. Even if they could muster the urge and capability themselves, no one would care to have sexual relations with their elderly form, not even their own husbands or wives.

"At first they tried to make themselves more physically attractive with makeup, cosmetics, and jewelry to appeal to younger generations, but it was understandably met with little success.

"One of the advantages of living even for hundreds of years is the vast amount of knowledge that is acquired and abilities that are mastered. A tremendous breakthrough was accomplished about twenty thousand years ago. Some among the oldsters mastered the skill of living illusion.

"I am not referring to the simple illusions of magicians or temple priests, which make the viewer think they are seeing something that is really not there. The ancient Nartesians mastered Celestine-level illusion, which transcends mirage and becomes real substance in their own bodies, and in the case of created creatures, also includes self-guided sentience and full physical function within themselves.

"Thus began a rapid, evolutionary expansion among a select few that mastered this rare skill. Those that succeeded acquired the ability to live for over a thousand years and some far beyond that.

"Using the power of their mind, they fashioned and formed a younger and completely beautiful image of themselves with a perfect and desirable male or female body that had tangible substance and form. Once created, the form was self-sustaining with minimal maintenance.

"They were also able to use the power of their minds to literally become the masters of their bodies. They still continued to eat the best foods and follow other foundational principles of health, but the strength of their minds allowed them to almost completely stop and even reverse the natural deterioration of their bodies with age. Because of this, even without the facade created with their mental illusions, a two-hundred-year-old Nartesian still looked like they were just entering the youthful side of middle age.

"At first, this was only a handful of people. Most Nartesians failed to master the skill of complete illusion. Though the secrets of ultimate longevity soon became widely known, the results were still unattainable to them in their wrinkled old bodies."

"Ick!" Hannah suddenly blurted out in disgust. "Ick! Ick! Ick! It is bad enough that in my idiot zombie state I kissed and had intimate relations with Leiaza."

She pointed up into the box at the queen still sitting passively in her chair looking at us, seemingly without a care in the world. "But now you are telling me that it is the lips of that wicked, shriveled prune up there that touched mine? And... and... touched other parts of me! Iccck!" she hissed through gritted teeth, squinting her eyes tightly closed as if trying to make the memories go away.

Miriam nodded her head affirmatively. "You will need to learn to cope with such atrocities and affronts to your customs and moral values if you are to succeed as Earth Guardians. I am sure Leiaza will not be the only one you will encounter that will test your resolve and the foundation of your faith, morality, and goals.

"As you have learned in this short visit to just a single world, the creations of Elohim in the vast numberless worlds of existence are immensely varied and radically different in every aspect, compared to the limited life and diversity you have known on the world you call home."

Lassoon, who had been listening silently, quietly interjected a question. "What about me and my kind? Nagasas never stray far from the Nartesians. Those that have wandered or explored beyond the realm never return."

She looked skyward at the only four Nagasas besides her remaining. "And now it seems my entire species except for me and four others have disappeared. Are you the cause of this?"

Lassoon took in a big breath of air, the kind of massive intake Nagasa take in as they stoke their internal furnace and prepare to breathe fire. She looked with anger upon Miriam. "Did you kill my kindred?"

I was afraid of what might happen next. But Miriam must have put a little spell on Lassoon because she smiled a gentle smile at her and you could see Lassoon visibly relax.

Miriam came down to the ground and took a few steps over to Lassoon. She gently stroked her just above the top of her nose as Lassoon bent down her head. "You are very intelligent, Lassoon, and I think you already know the answer to your questions."

"You know my name?" Lassoon asked with surprise.

"Yes, and much more than your name. I know you are special and you have perceived that truth as well, haven't you?"

Lassoon nodded her head in agreement. "Wild thoughts are in my head. They make no sense. But I know something is peculiar. I know that I am somehow different than most of my kindred."

She hesitated a moment, contemplating putting her thoughts into words. "I sense that my kindred are destroyed, but not quite dead, is that right?"

Miriam shook her head, affirming that the other Nagasa were not dead.

"But they are not alive either, are they?" Lassoon asked forlornly.

She was silent for a moment, then nuzzled the tip of her nose against Miriam's upraised palm. "First I lose my babies. Now I have lost all of my kind save four others. Life is not worth living," she spoke softly in our minds with sad dejection, resigned to a fate she obviously did not feel she could bear.

She brought her large head down so she could look directly into Miriam's eyes. "You have done all of this, haven't you? The aging of the Nartesians, the destruction of the Nagasa. All of this to save Hannah and Lazarus?

"I am sure you had reasons you felt were just. And I am happy to see the Nartesians reduced to being powerless. But the loss of all my kind hurts me. It hurts me very deeply. What good is my freedom if it came at the cost of the loss of all of my kindred?

"Seeing all that you have wrought in an instant is inconceivable. But the evidence is undeniably before our eyes, making it as indisputable as it is incomprehensible.

"In acknowledgment of your power, most mighty friend of Hannah and Lazarus, I beseech you to please use it on me. I plead for you to end my life as you have my kindred. I have nothing left to live for. Wherever you sent my kindred, send me there too."

Hannah hurried over to Lassoon and embraced her as much as her arms would allow, around Lassoon's long neck. "Please don't say you want to die, Lassoon. Stay with me. I will love you as much as I love my own children and my husband Lazarus."

"You are sweet, Hannah," Lassoon said, nudging her face affectionately with the tip of her nose. "But even with your love and attention, I would die of loneliness without my own kind in a community to associate with regularly. My kind thrives on living with extended family all around, but languishes without it."

She looked skyward at the four other Nagasas still circling high above, then looked at Miriam. "Do you know if any of the survivors above are male?"

Miriam shook her head negatively. "Like you, they are all females. They are the other egg layers of your nesting cave on the mountain."

Lassoon had a look of ultimate dejection writ upon her scaly face. "It is the final blow. Eleven years to wait between fertility and young ones is a long time. But to know there will never again be little ones, never again the opportunity to be a mother..."

Miriam touched Lassoon gently on the side of her head. "Describe to me how you would have your world be, if you could have it exactly as you would want it to be."

Lassoon let out a long sigh. "Your effort to cheer me up will not succeed. I still want to die and now would be my chosen time. That is the world I would create, one where I am no longer in it to suffer."

"Lassoon," Miriam spoke gently. "Don't let your grief overwhelm your perceptions. You know there is more here than it would seem. I trust you. I trust your experiences and your knowledge of the interrelations between species on this world. If you could make it better... better for you and your kin, better for Danarz and his kin, better for the people of the river and even better for the Nartesians, how would your world be?"

Reluctantly Lassoon answered Miriam. "Speaking of this only makes me sadder. It makes me feel my loss more deeply and expands my frustrations more greatly. Of what practical use is wishful contemplation of something that can never be?"

Lassoon let out a whooshing breath of frustration as she looked at Miriam. "If I answer your question will you end my life afterward in return?"

Miriam nodded her head affirmatively. "Yes, if that is what you wish after you hear my reply."

"Very well," Lassoon exhaled with slow resignation. "I would begin by having all of my Nagasa kindred alive and around me once more. I would have never done the foul, unforgivable deed of burning my own babies to death. I would see all the Nagasas free from the mental enslavement of the Nartesians.

"Of the Nartesians, I do not care what happens to them. Of Danarz and his kin, I would see the Nagasas living in peace with them as long as they live in peace with us. Of all the rest of life upon my world, I do not know them well enough to say. Let them go their way in peace and we will go ours."

She looked blankly at Miriam. "Now may I die?"

"You have not yet heard my reply; that was our bargain," Miriam asserted.

"I already know what you will say," Lassoon assured her, "so you have no need to speak it. My babies are dead and that cannot change.

"I don't know what you did to my kindred but I realize that somehow their existence was tied to the youthful appearance of the Nartesians. That is why we were slaves, and that is why when you changed the Nartesians into old people the link to my kindred that sustained their existence was broken. For whatever reason they no longer could be here without the Nartesians also being here in the fullness of their form. Whether they have perished or simply vanished to another realm of existence I know not. If you can send me to them wherever they are, do it."

Lassoon placed one of her sharp talons against her tender exposed flesh where she was missing her large chest scale. "If you cannot send me to them, then end my life, or else I will end it myself."

"You promised to wait until after my reply," Miriam pointed out.

"Get to it then," Lassoon grumbled as she dropped her sharp-pointed talon away from her chest with some exasperation.

"Perhaps I should give you the best news first," Miriam began. "Your babies live, Lassoon. They never perished. In fact, they have already hatched because of their trauma and even now await the return of their mother to guide them into life."

This was astounding news! I expected Lassoon to brighten like the noonday sun with joy. But she looked up expressing only the faintest interest. "I assure you it is not possible," Lassoon said with great sadness. If her kind could shed tears, I was sure she would be crying then.

"I blasted them with my full fire in a confined space. Not even an adult Nagasa would have been able to survive that concentration of heat.

"Nor can I give any credence to you, a peculiar being that just appeared moments ago, would be able to know the details of an event that occurred before your arrival, at which you were not present."

Miriam smiled. I'd seen that coy smile before when she realized she was about to reveal something that would greatly surprise others listening. And so it was on this day.

"I know you were hatched under the light of a full moon. I know that your mother was Relabask and her mother was Dilthz. I know you have planned to escape the Nartesians or die trying by continuing out of the canyon until you are beyond their realm. And, I know the fate of your babies."

Lassoon just stared at Miriam for a long, silent moment, impacted by her revelations. "They live? With certainty they live? But how? Did you protect them?" she asked with mounting excitement and joy.

"Hannah protected them," Miriam said, pointing at my wife.

"I wish it were so," Hannah replied wistfully, "but I was a helpless, bound prisoner. I screamed out trying to awaken Lassoon from the spell that was upon her mind, but it was to no avail. I failed."

Miriam had a big smile on her face now. "You did not fail, Hannah. In that moment of heart-rending anguish your Celestine gifts came forth in great power.

"It has always been in you and still has far to go to mature, but in that moment of greatest need, when there was no other way for you to change the situation, your greater gifts of light came forth to protect Lassoon's eggs when you screamed out NO! three times. Three is the number of the Elohim. It is a magical number for the manifestation of the power of light."

"But how did screaming 'NO' three times protect the eggs? It doesn't seem to connect," Hannah asked, confused.

Miriam was only too happy to provide us all with the explanation. "At that brief moment of greatest need and most dire of circumstances, all of the energy centers of your body were untied and rapidly expanding. The power of your heart center was the master of all.

"When you cried out 'NO' three times, you unleashed and called in the far greater powers of the Elohim from beyond this world. That amplified your own abilities for a few seconds. But that is all the time that was necessary.

"Because you knew what you wanted to protect, you didn't need to know how to accomplish it. Your will to protect it was enough to make it so.

"No sooner had the last 'NO' left your lips than an impenetrable barrier of energy surrounded Lassoon's eggs. During the few moments of the barrier's existence, nothing short of the power of the Elohim directly would have been able to penetrate it."

"I did not know I could do something like that," Hannah said, holding up her palms and looking at them in a daze of wonder.

I was happy for Hannah, of course, but I had to suppress a little envy. It seemed that other than Yeshua, it was almost exclusively the women in Celestine Light who easily gained all of the notable powers and abilities. And we really couldn't count Yeshua, as he was already an Elohim. I knew I could manifest amazing gifts as well. It just seemed that all of us men had to work so much harder at it.

After she had a few minutes to consider all she had seen and heard, Lassoon began to give credence to Miriam's words. She looked at Miriam somewhat in a daze, as if still trying to take in all that she had learned.

From her excited movements it was obvious Lassoon was anxious to depart and get back to her children. She bid us goodbye and prepared to take flight back to the nesting cave on the mountain. But first, she nudged Hannah gently with her nose. "I will see you again, Hannah?"

Hannah reached up and touched Lassoon on her cheek, but she didn't know how to answer. "I hope it is so, Lassoon, but my path in the future is unknown to me. I have committed to a lifetime of stewardship and service. I know not where it shall take me or if I will even be able to return to this world again."

Lassoon slumped her head a bit, obviously saddened by Hannah's reply. Hannah looked pretty dejected as well at the possibility that she would never again see her new friend.

Miriam stepped toward them and put a hand on each of their faces. "Ladies of light, before you become too sad, you should know that destiny will not let you part so easily. I assure you that you will see each other again. I'm sure you have many shared adventures still awaiting you. You have only just begun your journey together."

"Destiny?" Hannah asked with some confusion.

Miriam nodded. "When the path you walk upon in life and the path another walks have a very high likelihood to intersect as you both strive to fulfill your individual goals and ambitions, destiny coalesces to make it so. As it is and will be with you and Lassoon."

The faces of both Hannah and Lassoon

brightened with Miriam's words. But I was not so thrilled. With Miriam's announcement of Hannah and Lassoon's shared destiny, I found I was a little jealous that my wife was going to have a fire-breathing, nearly invulnerable monster for a friend. However, I convinced myself that I was actually simply upset upon the principle.

"I thought freedom of choice was a foundation of the light," I interjected. "It sounds to me like this 'destiny' is taking that away and substituting inevitability regardless of one's own preferences."

Miriam looked at me, seeming to be a bit perturbed by my ignorance. "Nothing is inevitable, Lazarus. Each of you creates your ultimate path by the choices that you make, both big and small. Destiny is merely the most likely manifestation of your hopes, dreams, and desires as they intersect with those of others on a grand scale in your life.

"Destiny can bring enemies together in a battle of good and evil, or allies together for the same confrontation.

"Through circuitous routes that would at first seem to have no connection, destiny can eventually unite the talents of multiple individuals to create a magnificence together that would have been impossible for any of them alone.

"At any point you can walk away. You can say, 'I do not want this,' and try to choose a different course. It is possible, but not easy. The pull of destiny is like a lodestone to iron. The closer you get to it, the more irresistible it becomes."

Lassoon spread her wings and flapped them a few times in preparation for flight. It created quite a breeze. "Then I trust we shall meet again, Hannah," she told my wife with confidence. "It is something I look forward to. I will need a distraction to keep me out of the depths of despair at the loss of most of my kindred."

Before she could take off, Miriam held up her hand and asked her to wait. "Your kindred can return, Lassoon, and I will leave it to you to decide if it is to be so."

That was a shocking statement that quickly made Lassoon fold her wings back close to her body and rivet her attention on Miriam. "How?" was all she asked.

Miriam smiled and began to elaborate. "As you have perceived, Lassoon, your kindred are joined to the Nartesians, but it is not a union. The Nagasas are literally creations of the Nartesians. And with the exception of your eggs and those of the other females of the mountain cave, all the young born to Nagasas were no more truly alive than the Nagasas themselves. They were merely new constructs of the Nartesians.

"The Nartesians could create and animate your kind, could make them self-willed and self-reliant. But they could not give them the spark of true life that would allow the Nagasas to freely reproduce, for that is only within the realm of Elohim."

Lassoon seemed confused. "But my babies, I thought they were real."

Miriam held up her hand. "Be at peace, Lassoon. Wait a moment longer and I will explain how your children are a very real exception."

Lassoon nodded her head and Miriam continued with her broader explanation of the events. "When I arrived, I put a stupefying spell upon every single Nartesian. It temporarily created a mindless population. Without the great power of their minds, they no longer had the mental power required to maintain the substantive illusions of their bodies of perfection. They degenerated into their true form—the withered, decrepit, old ones you still see sitting placidly in the arena.

"When their minds were taken away, so too was their ability to maintain the façade of reality that allowed your kindred, the Nagasas, to have self-directed, self-aware existence and what appeared to every sense of an observer's perception to be physical substance. I did nothing directly to the Nagasas. They simply ceased to exist when their creators no longer were capable of maintaining the mental power to sustain the illusion."

Danarz let out a loud squawk of disbelief. "How could it be possible that illusions, mirages, pretend creatures, could shoot real, blazing hot fire that has killed many of my kind?"

"There are many levels and layers to illusion," Miriam began, answering Danarz.

"Those that you speak of, mirages and pretend creatures, are the simplest forms. They have no substance and can do no harm if you know them for what they are.

"But the creations of the Nartesians are an order of magnitude thousands of times greater than simple illusions. They draw upon the essence of the air, the earth, the water, herbs, grasses, and woods to morph their own bodies into perfection and create creatures, buildings, objects, and even delicious food items that are perceived as real in every sense, from touch to taste to satiated satisfaction. But it is the stupendous power of their minds that holds all of their illusions together.

"To your perception and all other beings that interact with them, the bodies of the Nagasas are as solid and self-functioning as the bodies of any other creature birthed in normal ways. The fire they breathe burns because, like the Nagasas themselves, the fire coalesces real and tangible elements from the surrounding environment to manifest and project true substance.

"Once the Nagasas were projected and animated by the Nartesians, they lived as conscious, fully alive creatures capable of independent emotions, thoughts, and actions.

"It was an admirably complex and monumental achievement to create a creature as magnificent as a Nagasa. Each Nagasa that was birthed into life was the culmination of long, dedicated efforts by one or more Nartesians. But until the advent of Lassoon and her four friends, the births were ultimately nothing more than pretend life. As they grew into adults and later mated, it was not from the union of two Nagasas that eggs were laid and babies born, though that was their perception, but from the mind of the Nartesians.

"So challenging was the task to maintain the mental link required to allow the Nagasas to continue to exist that even the Queen, the most powerful Nartesian of all, was incapable of creating and maintaining a link to more than a few Nagasas at a time. She could command many, and they obeyed her out of habit. But she could compel only those few she was powerfully connected to because she had personally fashioned them from the essence of the elements and animated them by the power of her mind."

"The link to the minds of a Nartesian became the single requirement to the continued existence of the Nagasas and the seed of their destruction. Though Nagasas were self-willed most of the time, they still needed to retain an energy bond to the mind of the Nartesian that created them. They continued to exist only because of that sometimes tenuous mental link.

"When the link was broken, as it was when I arrived, or when a Nagasa wandered out of the realm and beyond the mental connection of the Nartesian, they ceased to exist. They dissolved into the essence of the elements from which they were created.

"It is by that same link, from the mind of the Nartesian creator to the mind of their Nagasa, that the Nagasas were compelled to obey any dictate of their creator or otherwise powerful Nartesian such as the queen."

Miriam looked up at Lassoon. "Even a command to kill their own children was one they could not deny."

"It is by these same mental techniques of coalescing real matter and manifesting true substance that Hannah's body was transformed into perfection in a matter of hours by the Nartesian women. The queen's mental link to Hannah maintained the substance illusion, allowing it to remain coalesced. Without that mental connection, her body reverted to its normal appearance, just as the Nagasas vanished into oblivion once the minds of the Nartesians connected to them were dulled."

I was incredulous at Miriam's explanation of the abilities of the Nartesians. "They sound as powerful as the Elohim. Like the Elohim, they are able to create life as they will it to be so."

Miriam wagged her finger at me. "No, no, Lazarus. They are far from the boundless abilities of the Elohim. Compared to you they may be god-like, but compared to the Elohim they are merely children that have advanced further than most.

"Consider that I am only a humble servant of the

Elohim. They have given me but a tiny portion of their power, enabling me to fulfill my stewardship as the Angel of the Covenant. Yet even that small endowment easily subdued the entire race of Nartesians, took away their veneer, and neutralized their abilities.

"Truly, Lazarus, if you are going to be a successful Earth Guardian, you need to gain some perspective."

Miriam turned back to Lassoon. "If I remove the spell I have placed upon the Nartesians, their minds will once again be free to create the Nagasas. As they are previously manifested creatures, their template is already formed. Restoring the Nagasas to the fullness of their glory should happen fairly quickly, if the Nartesians agree to do it.

"However, removing the spell will also restore the Nartesians to their perfected illusion state with the full powers of their minds available for mischief. That will likely occur, as I doubt they will come back in a very good mood. They may not be amenable to bringing back the Nagasas as anything more than the weapons and entertainment that they had used them for previously."

Lassoon was taken aback by Miriam's answer. I think she was expecting something different.

"But you are all-powerful," Lassoon objected. "You turned the entire race of Nartesians into old ones in an instant. Surely you can command them to do anything you wish, and they will have no choice but to obey."

The corner of Miriam's lips turned up in a slight smile as she contemplated her answer to Lassoon.

"What I am capable of doing is often constrained by what I should not do. One of the foundations of everything I live for is that each sentient being must be given the opportunity to freely make their own choices in life, for the better or the worse, without dictatorial decrees of compulsion by anyone, especially not by someone more powerful.

"Those that are compelled become slothful. The spark of enthusiasm dies, and they cease to grow and expand their potential.

"One of the primary reasons any of us experience life in a physical body is to enable us to grow and expand our boundaries and possibilities in ways that are unique to a physical existence. That opportunity must not be abridged or taken away, even from the Nartesians."

I had been keeping quiet for a while, not desiring to appear as ignorant as I was. But unbelievably, nobody had yet asked a question that seemed to me should have been at the top of the list of inquiries of Miriam. Finally, her reply to Lassoon provided me with an opening. I could contain myself no longer and blurted it out.

"Speaking of physical bodies, if the Nagasas are all illusions connected to the Nartesians, why is Lassoon still here? Why did she, or the other four circling up in the sky, not disappear when all the others did?"

Miriam smiled a big smile, and happiness radiated from her face.

"Lassoon and the other four expanded their boundaries. The Nartesians that projected them as illusions were among the most highly skilled. Their attention to detail and nuances was unsurpassed.

"At some point Lassoon and her friends made a leap from the substance of illusion to life untethered to the Nartesian that created them. They had every evidence, from their appearance to their thoughts and feelings, that they were real. There was not even an iota of doubt within them.

"Over time their minds and emotions expanded so greatly that an illusion, even one as masterful as the Nartesians created, could no longer contain them.

"The spark of life that comes from Elohim permeates all of creation, every world, every space. It is always present, ready to ignite true life whenever it is ready to burst forth.

"Thus it was with Lassoon and her four kindred."

Miriam's explanation did not elicit much response from either me or Hannah. Between her exploits and those of Yeshua, we had grown accustomed to miracles and unexpected outcomes.

On the other hand, Danarz and Lassoon were both speechless. They just stared with wide eyes at Miriam, unable to grasp the enormity of what she explained.

After a few moments of awkward silence, Danarz put the matter to rest. "I suppose all life has to begin somewhere. I accept that Lassoon is a real monster.

"As I walk home during the next long days, featherless and without flight because the imaginary fire from the illusionary monsters burned them all off, I will contemplate greatly how to explain all of that to my kindred."

Despite the seriousness of our situation, Danarz's dry humor brought a smile to everyone's lips.

"I am glad I am real," Lassoon affirmed. "It gives me hope that more of my kind will make the transition completely into life, but for that to happen they must first be restored to the fullness of their illusionary glory."

Lassoon looked intently at Miriam. "If it will bring back the Nagasas, release the Nartesians from your enchantment. If they are anything less than agreeable, they will discover how frail their beautiful bodies really are when they can no longer control the mind of this former slave."

"As you wish," Miriam nodded in agreement at Lassoon's desire. She turned and faced the queen's box and the majority of the Nartesians still sitting placidly in the arena. She raised and crossed her arms in front of her and uttered the words releasing the Nartesians from their stupor and restoring them to their illusionary beauty as she drew her arms to her sides. "Kadaz! Frodka! Habalish!"

The transformation of the Nartesians from doddering old people to ravishing beauties and ridiculously muscular men was startling, dramatic, and nearly instantaneous. And they must have been fully aware of everything that had been taking place while they had been subdued in old, mentally weak bodies, because the queen was instantly angry. She looked at Miriam with eyes burning with hatred. Given her illusion abilities, I was expecting steam to start rising out of her ears any moment.

"You! You!" Leiaza screamed as she jabbed her index finger in the air at Miriam. I wasn't sure if she had returned with a defective, limited vocabulary, or was just so upset she couldn't think of any other words at the moment.

"You dared to interfere with MY mind!" she yelled loudly, throwing her hands toward the ground, causing it to erupt in a little geyser of dirt.

Leiaza took a step forward and leaped over the rampart of the arena. She landed on her feet facing Miriam about four paces away. In the blink of an eye she materialized a large spear in her hand with a wicked-looking, four-bladed, barbed metal point.

Without another word, Leiaza stepped one foot forward and threw the spear with all of her might right toward Miriam. My sister just stood still, her hands clasped together and held low in front of her. She was as calm as a warm summer's morning, while I was in wide-eyed horror seeing the spear of doom streaking toward her heart. But before it found its mark, it disintegrated into dust.

This only seemed to further incense Leiaza. She screamed in fury. "Palace guards to my side, war spears ready!"

Immediately, at least two dozen burly warriors leapt over the rampart to join the queen facing Miriam. Each was armed with an even larger, more menacing spear than Leiaza's. The queen ordered them to form a half circle facing Miriam. She pointed at my sister.

"We are faced with a foe whose powers of the mind are as great as ours, but she is one and we are many. One spear she can turn to dust before it pierces her heart. I'm certain she will not fare as well with many. Kill her! Now!"

At her command, all of the warriors launched their spears simultaneously. Miriam continued to stand in one place with her hands folded together down low. While the queen had been ranting, Miriam even looked up at the sky and around the arena for a moment as if she was bored by the whole affair.

Much to Leiaza's angry surprise, the dozens of spears all flying together through the air toward Miriam met the same fate as the queen's. Before they had traveled half the short distance, they all became little glints of dirt and rained harmlessly to the ground.

The queen pointedly jabbed her finger in Miriam's direction. "You have talents, vile one, but they will not avail you much longer. Everyone has a weakness. You cannot be strong in all areas of the mind. I promise you I will find your weakness shortly. Enjoy your final breaths of life. There shall not be many more!"

Very athletically, Leiaza took a running leap and in one bound was over the parapet and back in her royal box. She ordered the palace guards to also return to the arena.

She spoke with loud vehemence to all the Nartesians in the arena, and I assumed telepathically as well to ensure they all heard her.

"Citizens of Nartese City. The newly arrived clothed one in the arena is a grave threat to our way of life. She has powerful mental abilities. You have already seen what chaos she has wrought; how she upended your carefully groomed lives in an instant.

"From the very moment of her arrival, she has attacked us and declared herself our enemy with no regard for our lives or way of life. We must kill her now before she wreaks more havoc.

"To ensure our power is greater than hers, we must be united as one in our intent. Focus now on this despicable wench. Look upon her standing idly in the arena, taunting us by her disdain, daring us to attack her.

"Let us show this misguided miscreant the power of the united mental capabilities of all Nartesians, a power against which nothing in the universe can stand."

Leiaza's voice rose to a crescendo as she screamed like a maniac. "Everyone, re-manifest your Nagasas. Command them to roast her. Make her die! Make it slow! Make it painful! Envelop her in a dome of fire from which there can be no escape. Let her and those she tries to protect burn in the same fire that will not go out until they are all ashes!"

Miriam still seemed somewhat disinterested in Leiaza's rant. But having had considerably more experience with the crazy queen, I was feeling quite a bit of insecurity and trepidation.

Suddenly, in an instant, all of the Nagasas popped back into existence. As they took in big breaths of air to charge up their internal furnaces, all of us huddled as close as we could behind Miriam.

And then it began. It was far more intense than what we had previously experienced. There was so much fire coming from every conceivable direction that all we could see was an impenetrable wall of flame wherever we looked. It was impossible to see through the barrier of fire at any point.

When the fire first began, I cringed, remembering our recent ordeal with the Nagasas. But I soon realized this time there was no pain, no heat, and no gasping to breathe through super-heated air. Though we were completely enveloped in fire, it was as if we were merely outside on a pleasantly warm summer day.

Miriam asked us to all face each other in a circle and just start having a normal conversation. "The

Nagasas will expend their fire after a short while," she noted. "At this point the Nartesians cannot see us at all, just like we cannot see them through the walls of fire. They imagine we are being consumed by it.

"When the fires die down, they will discover we are unharmed by all of their combined might and effort. And so unconcerned by their attempts to kill us, that we are engaging in casual conversation with one another. I'm hoping it will cause them to pause and reconsider their course of action. Perhaps, given the evidence of their inability to harm us and our total disregard for their efforts, the Nartesians and their queen will be open to reasonable discussions and courses of action that are more harmonious for all concerned."

"I think you are overly optimistic," I commented knowingly. "The queen has been accustomed to getting whatever she wants, from whomever she desires, for a very long time. She is ruthless, conniving, and has no regard for anyone else unless they are obeying and pleasing her. I do not think she will give up her efforts toward our destruction, and particularly yours, so easily."

Lest Miriam think the queen was her only challenge, I thought it best to add a bit more enlightenment to the situation. "Most of the Nartesians seem to think along similar lines as Leiaza, that everything else that lives in the world or is conjured by illusion only exists to serve them and give them pleasure. You may thwart their efforts to destroy you, but I do not think you will make any headway changing their desire to do so."

"We shall see," Miriam replied calmly, "we shall see."

Danarz squawked, indicating his desire to be noticed by Miriam. "Speaking of conjuring. Your mental abilities are impressive. But your timing is very bad. You may have noticed I am completely denuded of feathers. A bird that cannot fly is not much of a bird.

"While I appreciate your arrival and the fortuitous turn of events, and marvel at your power to nullify the illusions of the Nartesians, I am left to wonder why you did not arrive just a few moments earlier, before all my feathers were burned off by the pretend fire of the imaginary Nagasas."

Miriam smiled slightly at Danarz's serious question wrapped in dry humor. "I was hoping all of you would work matters out on your own and not need my intervention.

"And I was busy. As of yet, I cannot be in two places at once. I watch over many others besides Lazarus and Hannah. Some of them were in more dire straits, requiring my more immediate attention."

Considering all we had been through, that seemed hard to believe. "Seriously?" I exclaimed with more than a hint of disbelief in my voice. "Some of the other Guardians had greater challenges on their simple observation excursions than we have had?"

Before Miriam could answer, the walls of fire began to quickly diminish as the fires of the Nagasas were expended for the moment.

As the Nartesians in the arena came back into view, Miriam quickly reiterated our instructions. "Ignore the Nartesians. Continue to talk with one another as if there has been no fire or anything whatsoever to bother us. That should help many of them realize there is something here beyond their ken."

She looked up at Lassoon. "I will be needing your fire in a few moments, Lassoon. Please be ready when I call upon you." Lassoon nodded her head slightly in assent.

Miriam turned to face the queen and the bulk of the Nartesians in the arena. I looked up for a moment and saw they were all staring at us in abject disbelief and utter silence. The reality of our unscathed survival against their combined might was so incomprehensible to them that it left them speechless.

Miriam spoke directly to the queen. "Leiaza, and all the rest of you gathered here. I have not come to fight you or to compel you, as you have compelled others. I do hope my arrival and your inability to harm me in the least has given you a new perspective on your reality and will warrant changes in your attitudes and behaviors. But that is for you to decide, not me.

"However, the killing must stop, and the torture and destruction of the Nagasas for your entertainment. You are such an advanced people. I know you are better than this cruelty you have exhibited."

I looked up at the queen and her face was contorted with rage. Miriam's words of peace and harmony seemed to be having the opposite effect on Leiaza.

"You dare to come here, an unknown stranger, and dictate to us! You flatter yourself if you think you have defeated us. We will not change our way of life or stop our attacks upon you until we find your weakness and end your life!"

To emphasize her point, the queen manifested some kind of energy bola. It had several short ropes joined together at a central point in her hand. At the end of each rope was some type of scintillating, electric green energy sphere about the size of a fist.

Leiaza swirled this around her head a few times, then threw it at Miriam. The tendrils of rope wrapped taut around her body like the many-armed tentacles of an octopus, and the energy spheres stuck to her body at several points and began to glow.

The queen stepped forward and stood triumphantly at the edge of the rampart with both hands on her hips, gloating at Miriam. "I see you have met your match with the Balls of Qazot. This is my most special weapon, the one I save only for my most worthy and formidable foes. I am honoring you by using it for your death.

"You notice how the orbs glow? They are absorbing your essence. There is nothing you can do to stop it. Once the Qazot balls have attached to your body, they merge with it; they become part of it as they consume you. Your very life force is being sucked out of your body. It will not be as painful or slow as I would have liked, but in a few moments, all of your life force will be inside those orbs.

"After you are no more than a lifeless husk, I will eat the Qazot balls for my evening meal and gain your life force. All of your power will be mine!

"Oh, I cannot wait! Hurry up and die. Let your last thoughts be how ridiculous you were to think that an inferior being like you could defeat me!"

Miriam merely smiled back placidly at Leiaza in return. Knowing her past overwhelming reaction to threats, I was expecting something monumental in scope. But apparently she was under some sort of constraint as the Angel of the Covenant and just stood there without reacting, calmly letting her essence be absorbed by the glowing Qazot balls.

After a few minutes, the glow from the Qazot balls became blindingly intense. Without warning, the orbs suddenly released their attachment to Miriam, and the constricting ropes rapidly unwound from her body. There was an audible group gasp from the onlooking Nartesians as they realized that she was not dead and was no longer bound within the grasp of the Qazot bola.

Rather than fall to the ground after the bola was no longer on Miriam's body, it rose up in the air above her head and began swirling rapidly around. The balls were still glowing a brilliant green, but they became a blur of green light as they whirled through the air. A loud whistling sound also began to emanate from the twirling mass.

Suddenly, there was a blinding burst of green light as all of the bola balls exploded simultaneously with a deafening, reverberating concussion of sound.

As the sound quieted and the dust settled, Miriam still stood placidly where she had always been, completely unharmed and unscathed. She looked up at Leiaza, who was staring down at her with shocked disbelief.

"I'm afraid your Qazot bola has become extinct," Miriam spoke calmly.

She brushed the settled dust off each of her forearms with her opposite hand. "I must say, the unique energy was rather refreshing.

"But if you are done playing your games, I would like to have a serious discussion with you and the other Nartesians."

Leiaza's reaction to Miriam's more than generous entreaty was to throw a temper tantrum. She stomped rapidly up and down, screamed in frustration through gritted teeth, and pounded her clenched fists deliriously up and down in the empty air.

"You will die! You will die! I have decreed it!"

Miriam held up her hand. "Stop your rantings. I would have hoped that by now your extreme intelligence would have perceived that a different reality has asserted itself from the one you are accustomed to. But I can see you will need a bit more evidence."

Without turning to look back, Miriam motioned with her hand for Lassoon to step forward. Lassoon immediately complied. Even though the Nagasa was standing on the ground of the arena, her large size brought her head above Leiaza, who was still standing in her box above the arena rampart.

Miriam reached out and put her hand on Lassoon as she spoke to Leiaza.

"I am needed elsewhere and have no more time to dawdle with your obstinance and pettiness. It is not my place to judge or punish you or your people. But I strongly suggest you begin to treat all other creatures and sentient beings with respect, beginning with the Nagasas, lest the punishment you deserve for your wickedness comes to you before you have had time to repent and mend the errors of your ways."

Despite everything she had witnessed with Miriam, Leiaza remained defiant and undeterred. She laughed at Miriam. "I reign supreme. I am the only judge and the sole executioner. Do not dictate to me!"

Leiaza pointed at Lassoon while continuing to deride Miriam. "Though you have admirable survival skills, you are foolishly ignorant if you think a Nagasa is any threat to me.

"As I'm sure you have ascertained, the Nagasas are constructs of our brilliant minds. They are merely a thought with form, but no more of a threat to those of us who are their creators than a thought without form."

Miriam levitated up in the air until she was beside the formidable spiked head of Lassoon and above the head of Leiaza, still standing in the box slightly below, which forced Leiaza to look up at Miriam.

But Miriam did not look at Leiaza. Instead, she looked up into the arena and addressed all of the Nartesians. "I have not come to hurt you, but to help you. You are a great people, who have built marvels and wonders from your cities to yourselves. There is so much good you could do in your world.

"Instead, you selfishly sequester yourselves in a walled city and squander your wonderfully long lives on meaningless entertainment, addictive gambling, sex without love, and cruelty to lesser beings that robs you of the essence of your soul; something you will sorely wish you still had when your long physical life finally comes to an end and you enter the reality of the eternal life that continues on.

"Fortuitously, you can still redeem yourselves. You can still become better than you have been and seek to use your great knowledge and abilities to benefit others instead of hurting them, to respect them instead of enslaving them.

"This will not be a sacrifice for you. It will enhance your lives, both now and in the eternity to come.

"And it all begins with the Nagasas. Many of them, like this one who is named Lassoon, have changed in a very important way you are unaware of. For a long time Lassoon and others have only obeyed your commands so you would not realize that they could disregard your dictates if they desired."

Miriam's comment elicited a loud round of laughter from all the Nartesians. Queen Leiaza was laughing the hardest. Or perhaps we just heard her the most because she was closest. In any case, it was an obnoxious, disrespectful laugh.

"For such a powerful being you are very simple-minded," Leiaza insulted Miriam. "For our amusement, I will demonstrate to you the fallacy of your words."

She snapped her fingers and yelled out loudly. "Is the wretch that constructed this Nagasa still alive and in the arena?" From somewhere in a row far away, near the edge of the crowd of spectators, a voice replied that he was still living.

Leiaza snapped at him. "If you want that to

continue to be the case for a while longer, get down here immediately!"

His obedience to the queen's dictate was impressively rapid. Once he was standing trepidatiously beside her, Leiaza pointed at Lassoon. "Command your Nagasa to envelop that ignorant woman in a ball of fire."

Instead of obeying the queen, the poor man was looking down at his feet and fumbling for words. "Well...um...you see, my queen...it is as this woman has said. My Nagasa no longer obeys me. In fact, she just ignores me."

Leiaza pushed him out of the box with a violent shove. "Obviously your own mental capacity has been affected by recent events. It has nothing to do with the Nagasa, but only with your own defective abilities."

"I really must be going," Miriam interjected, "but I cannot leave while this situation is still unsettled. Perhaps a demonstration might persuade you to change your misguided ways."

Miriam looked at Lassoon but spoke loud enough for many Nartesians to hear. "If it pleases you, I would appreciate it if you could give the queen a taste of the fiery fate she condemns so many others to. Don't kill her, but sufficient to make a point."

Lassoon nodded her massive head and inhaled a big breath, stoking her fire. This made the queen burst out in another fit of maniacal laughter as she pointed at Lassoon and Miriam. "You idiot! I retract my former statement attributing any intelligence to you. Nartesians are impervious to the fire of Nagasas. The beasts are merely constructs of our minds. We know them intimately for what they are, rendering them harmless to us."

The queen stood right at the edge of the rampart with legs spread and a hand on each hip in a posture of supreme confidence. "This will be fun. Excellent entertainment before we resume finding a way to kill you," she spat at Miriam.

"Do your worst, Nagasa," she challenged Lassoon. "I will try not to laugh too hard."

Obliging the queen, Lassoon breathed out a wide stream of fire for just a few seconds. The queen never had time to laugh again. When the flames subsided, she was revealed to everyone blackened, charred, and with her luxurious hair still burning.

Her ornate headdress had slipped down her forehead as her burned-off hair no longer supported it. The little bit of cloth she had been wearing had caught on fire, and she was furiously patting out the flames.

The many pieces of metal jewelry the queen was wearing, from necklaces and pendants to large scrolling armbands, had turned red hot and were burning her flesh. It was actually smoking where metal met flesh.

In seconds the pain became unbearable, and Leiaza ripped everything off her body as quickly as possible and patted the fire out on her head with her hands. In moments she stood naked before everyone, without a stitch of clothing or ornamentation. She still retained the illusion of her perfected female form, but the very real burning pains left her voluptuous body visibly blackened and charred with ugly red welts and blisters wherever hot metal had been in contact with her skin.

"Oh, how I love this," I heard Danarz squawk. "What she has done to me has now been done to her. I love it! Sweet justice."

Leiaza was dumbfounded and almost speechless. Almost, but not quite. "How...how can I be affected... by the illusion fire of a Nagasa?"

Miriam descended down into Leiaza's box and stood non-threateningly beside her. She spoke to her both audibly and telepathically so all Nartesians could hear her words.

"It was not an illusion fire. The fire that burned your body and could have taken your life if it had continued was as real as the fire burning through a dry forest after a lightning storm."

"But how...how is that possible?" Leiaza mourned.

"The fire is real because the Nagasa is real," Miriam explained at last.

"Into the form that you and your fellow Nartesians conceived in your minds, the limitless power of Elohim has breathed the spark of true life.

Hereafter these Nagasas will live, reproduce, and die as intelligent, self-directed, sentient beings.

"For now, some are still the substance of illusion. And others, a number you will never know, are fully alive. You would be wise not to cross them or abuse them or their kind anymore. As you can see from this short demonstration, they would make very, very formidable adversaries, thanks to your excellent design.

"They have had a long relationship with you, and those that are still the substance of your mental abilities will continue to require your devotion if they are to exist. If Nartesians begin treating them with respect and not as slaves or even servants, I suspect a mutually beneficial relationship can emerge."

"I wish to speak!" someone from the audience yelled. Looking up, I saw a young muscular man making his way down to the queen's box. He arrived and introduced himself as Geclahn.

"Stranger who turns our world upside down," he began. "There is a big problem with Nagasas having real life."

Miriam nodded, indicating he should continue, which he did with worry in his voice. "As you have noted, they are fearsome monsters. We created them that way to be sentinels for our realm. Under our strict control, they have been incapable of venturing beyond our realm without a Nartesian to accompany them, so they are not a danger to the other creatures of the world, which would pretty much be defenseless against their blasting fire and impenetrable armored skin.

"Our games, which you deride as cruel, are the way we control the population of the Nagasa. For every egg that is laid and baby hatched, an adult has to die. If they are allowed to exist as free, truly living beings, they will reproduce in unchecked numbers and will soon become the unchallenged masters not just of the Nartesians but of the entire world!

"You hope for reconciliation and harmony. You ask the Nartesians to maintain the illusion of the Nagasas who have not yet found life. Don't you see, you are asking us to sustain the existence of creatures we now realize will eventually become either our masters or our doom.

"We will not do it! Go back to wherever you came from and leave us alone!"

Geclahn turned his back on Miriam without waiting for her to respond and stormed back to his seat in anger.

"What say you?" Miriam asked telepathically to Lassoon. "Can you reply to the Nartesians on behalf of the Nagasas?"

Lassoon nodded her head in assent. She spoke loudly and confidently in all of our minds. "Nartesians. You are right to fear my kind. You know better than anyone else what we are capable of, and how just a few of us could make the tiny race of Nartesians extinct within days if we wished.

"I'll admit that the thought is tempting as repayment for the cruel misery and death you have inflicted upon us without end. But we are also wise. We appreciate the marvels that you made us to be and are grateful for your mental abilities that allow some of our number to continue to exist.

"Having been slaves, we do not desire that fate for anyone else, not even you Nartesians.

"It is reasonable to assume that given our life and our freedom, many of us will leave this area and venture to and settle in other parts of our world.

"It is also reasonable to assume that given our new status as potential foes, you very intelligent Nartesians will come up with ways to protect yourselves from us, both offensively and defensively.

"Yet, because we will be dispersed across the world and no longer confined to a small realm, we will not fear being wiped out by your machinations.

"The same tactic might be wise for you to adopt for similar security. Re-inhabit some of your long-abandoned cities in other lands. You have been a slowly dying race for thousands of years. It is not too late to reverse that trend.

"Ultimately, it is not our nature, as you well know as our creators, to be domineering or offensively aggressive. We will defend ourselves to the death if we are attacked or provoked, but if you respect us and leave us to develop our community and society as we wish, then we will certainly do the same for you.

"It will be hard for some of our kind to forgive or forget the many injustices and indignities you have wrought upon us, or the heart-rending separation of friends when you forced Nagasas to fight to the death in this arena.

"But I believe if you prove yourselves to be changed for the better, respectful and kind instead of cruel, then you will not likely find any of us as your enemies and will more likely find some willing to be your friends."

That was quite a speech, and it seemed to have an effect on the Nartesians, even the charred queen. They were much more subdued in their voices and objections and seemed ready to listen more than dictate.

Miriam rose up in the air once more so everyone could see her. "In the land that we come from, there is an old saying you would do well to adopt if you would like to become a people with even greater possibilities than you already possess. It is said a bit differently by different cultures, but is a universally accepted truth however it is worded. This foundational truth is simply to treat others as you would desire to be treated by them.

"This simple but powerful truth can be further distilled down to a single word: respect. Respect the beliefs, culture, and habits that others choose for themselves, no matter how different they may be from the ones you choose for yourself. Do as you wish, as long as it harms no one. And if it does, then do it not. That is the essence of this golden guide for harmonious living. It is my parting thought and prayer for you."

Miriam turned her back on the Nartesians. They seemed to have accepted the change in their lives and world. Even the burned queen sat back passively in her charred throne and just watched us non-threateningly. She seemed to still be in shock that she had actually been burned by a Nagasa that would not obey commands and had shot out a real jet of fire upon her.

Miriam looked at our beat-up, threadbare group. "Lazarus and Hannah, it is time to return home. You will need to travel to the portal. I will depart now in ways that only I can and will leave some clothes for you just inside the gateway for you when you return."

Hannah put her hand up to cover her mouth that opened in surprise. "My goodness, I have been naked in front of so many people for so long I entirely forgot that I even was!"

I looked at her desirable womanly form with admiration, even without the Nartesian enhancements, and was flooded with happiness that she was my wife. Not because of her sexuality, which had been all but forgotten when it was commonplace everywhere you looked in Nartese City, but because noticing it again reminded me of her intelligence, ingenuity, diplomacy, cheerful, positive personality, and the many other wonderful abilities and traits she possessed. I was a lucky man!

"I too had forgotten I was naked," I admitted. "Though we are both now perfectly comfortable in such a state, even among crowds of strangers, I doubt we would be well received in our naked boldness among the people of Bethany or even among our fellow Guardians."

"I'm quite sure you are correct," Hannah agreed. "Yet, I am very grateful our personal horizons have expanded during our visit to this incredible world that is so different in a vast number of ways than our own."

Miriam looked to Lassoon. "Could you and some of the other living Nagasas allow Lazarus, Hannah, and even mighty Danarz to ride upon you that they may return to the portal with haste and Danarz to his demises?

"I know it is much to ask, especially for Danarz, whose kind has been adversaries of yours. But without your assistance and lacking his ability to fly, he may not ever make it back to his land alive. And Hannah and Lazarus are needed, even now, back on our world."

Lassoon swayed her long neck back and forth a few times as she nervously contemplated an answer. But it was needless worry on her part. Very quickly after Miriam's request, we saw three Nagasas descending from high above. They landed in the arena and introduced themselves as Udlund,

Kestan, and Lilloju.

Lassoon seemed surprised at their arrival. But Kestan explained. "We overheard Miriam's request. This is a small service to help repay a great one that your friends have done for our kind."

Miriam smiled in gratitude, then asked Udlund a surprising question. "Did you bring the item I requested?"

Udlund nodded and reached back under her left wing and withdrew a large Nagasa scale. "I found it upon the ground where you said it would be."

It was the one Lassoon had carved out of her chest to give to Danarz for a shield. She gave it to Miriam, who walked over and presented it to Danarz. "You don't want to return home without one of the objects of your amazingly dedicated quest."

Danarz took a step back from Miriam and squawked loudly in protest. "I do not want it. I am ashamed I ever wanted it."

"Then you do not mind if I return it to Lassoon?"

"Of course not," Danarz affirmed. "But sadly it will do her no good. She already told us she cannot reattach it, and another will not grow back to take its place. I have injured her for life, and I am truly sorry," he said, hanging his head down.

"You never know," Miriam gently teased. "I've heard that miracles can occur with those who live their life in the light."

She walked over to Lassoon and held up the

scale. "Good lady, I believe this belongs to you."

Lassoon took the scale from Miriam. "Thank you, kind one, but it is as Danarz said. This scale is a part of me from the past that cannot be reunited with the present. You may take it back with you as a keepsake memory from our world if you like."

"Can I first see how it would appear on you if it were in its rightful place?" Miriam asked innocently.

Lassoon looked over at her Nagasa friends. I suppose she was trying to fathom the eccentric requests of the strange woman from another world. But given all that Miriam had done for her and her kind, she humored her and held the scale up to the empty place on her chest and inserted it tightly.

"This is where the scale belongs," Lassoon explained.

She stood up just a little straighter and the scale fell out. She caught it in her right foreclaw as it tumbled through the air before it hit the ground. "But as you can see, it is no longer welcome in its former home."

"I beg you to let me see it in its place one more time," Miriam entreated.

Lassoon sighed and once more slowly put the scale in place on her chest and held it there with both of her claws so it would not fall out.

Miriam came up to it and put both of her hands upon it. "Perhaps you just need to move it into its perfect place," she said, pushing on the scale. The scale suddenly illuminated in a bright white flash of light. If you blinked your eyes, you would have missed it.

Both Miriam and Lassoon took a step back from one another. Miriam had a very big smile on her face. Lassoon was feeling her scale with both of her claws. She lifted her head and shot a joyous stream of fire straight up into the air. "My scale is back! It is a part of me again!"

She looked at Miriam. "You are a miracle worker?"

"Sometimes it has been known to happen," Miriam nodded in happy acknowledgment.

"Can you help Danarz too?" Lassoon asked quietly. "Can you restore the fullness of his feathers so he can fly majestic and free again?"

"I could," Miriam confirmed.

"No you cannot!" Danarz objected loudly to everyone's surprise.

Everyone looked at Danarz in confusion at his unexpected outburst. He quickly explained, "Restoring my feathers would have been a good thing had the alternative been to make my way back home on foot through the jungles and lands of those who would love to see me dead.

"But my feathers will grow back before we have made another circuit around the sun, and someday soon I hope to return here and make them perfect by bathing in the Spring of Restoration, which was one of my original goals. However, returning home denuded as I am is a once-in-a-lifetime opportunity I cannot ignore."

Danarz looked at Miriam and bowed his head slightly in acknowledgment of her abilities. "Restore my wing feathers if you will, so I can stand on the unflapping inner wings of two Nagasa and add my lifting power to that of their active outer wings, allowing the three of us to fly as one. They have been our fiercest enemy. Can you imagine the spectacle I will make returning while standing on top of two Nagasas?

"It will be a sight never even imagined. The fact that I am charred, bloodied and denuded of feathers will be meritorious, an indisputable sign that I have battled with the Nagasas and now triumphantly return home atop their backs. Every female that lives will want to mate with me. I will be in paradise!"

"But that is not exactly how it happened," Hannah pointed out.

"Well, I will not say that it was," Danarz said in slightly miffed justification. "And do not forget that I did battle with multiple Nagasas, expertly I might add.

"But they are my friends now. I did not conquer them. And I will explain that to my kin. I will do my part to make a reconciliation between our kind and their kind possible."

"That is good," Miriam agreed happily. "Let us all now depart, each our way."

At Miriam's urging, the four Nagasas squatted down as low as they could. Hannah climbed atop her bonded friend Lassoon. After seeking their permission, I scampered up to the neck of Lilloju, and Danarz gingerly stepped up onto the backs of Udlund and Kestan and spread his legs very wide so he had one foot on the back of each Nagasa.

All of the Nagasas lifted up into the air and hovered for a moment as we waved goodbye to Miriam standing on the ground below us.

There were two nagging questions I needed to ask before we left her. "What was happening when we returned the first time and found our home in Bethany and our fellow Guardians to be askew as if only parts of them were there?"

Miriam smiled. "I imagine that was somewhat disconcerting."

"So it was you?" Hannah asked, "Just as Latalizq surmised?"

Miriam shook her head. "It was not me, Hannah. It was a shared hallucination between you and Lazarus. You never left this land. As you walked toward the portal, you passed through a patch of bright yellow flowers with blue centers. Lazarus picked a few and put them in your hair."

"I remember," Hannah said happily. "They were very pretty flowers and I was touched in my heart that Lazarus thought to adorn me with them."

"They also emitted a potent perfume of hallucination," Miriam explained. "Just a few whiffs inhaled put both of you into a slumber and joined your minds in a shared hallucination. It did not end until Latalizq arrived and you walked away from the patch of flowers. Her kind are unaffected by the hallucinogenic effects of the flowers, and her piercing telepathic thoughts awakened you from your stupor."

"But Latalizq returned because she saw the red mat I brought back through the portal from Bethany," I protested.

Miriam shook her head. "No, Latalizq returned because she saw you were still there where she left you. She assumed you had either never departed or had darted into the portal and had inexplicably come right back out. The red rug was just part of your imagination, Lazarus."

"But I was coated with dust when Lazarus began shaking the rug inside the gateway," Hannah pointed out.

"Only in the recesses of your joint imaginations," Miriam explained.

"But you would be well served to remember that flower," she added. "You can concoct some potent potions with it that you will find useful in the future in many of your challenges as Guardians."

Well, hearing these revelations about the flowers of hallucination just made my final question yet to ask all the more pertinent.

"You said some of the other Guardians had even greater challenges than we have experienced. You were joking, right?"

Miriam shook her head in denial. "You and Hannah had it easy on this world. Some of the others had it easier. But others much worse. I'm afraid the experiences of some, as mild as they were compared to what is yet to come, were still so traumatic that they will no longer be numbered among us.

"Return home, brother, and you can hear the details of the exploits of others, share your own, and prepare for your next challenge.

"But along the way, remember to be thankful, even grateful, for the many friends you have made here. Others were not so fortunate."

I shook my head doubtfully, still trying to grasp how anyone could have had more challenges than those we had endured, but Miriam confirmed it.

"It is true," Miriam replied with sincerity. "As you have all learned, being Guardians of the Earth is not a gift, it is a task. You will need to earn your immortality every day, in ways that will challenge you beyond your knowledge, abilities, courage, morals, beliefs, and faith. But that is a greater blessing than you can imagine, as you will discover."

~ To be continued in book 3 of the
Secret Earth series! ~

DESTINY

I'd love to hear from you!

Thank you for reading Destiny. If Lazarus's account resonated with you, a short review would mean a lot. Your words help other readers discover this story and encourage me to keep bringing the series to life.

Here's How You Can Leave a Review:

1. Scan the QR code on this page to go directly to my review page.

2. Or, visit your Amazon Orders page, find this book, and click, "Write a Product Review."

By reading Destiny, you join the witness of this account and help keep its Light alive.
With heartfelt thanks and deepest gratitude.

Esoteric Mystery School

For enlightening explorations into the psychic, paranormal, and magickal, visit my YouTube channel, **Esoteric Mystery School with Embrosewyn Tazkuvel.**

Discover in-depth videos on **Positive Energy Vortexes, Angels, Crystals, Energy Work, Ghosts, Channelings, Words of Power, Magick, Past Lives, Spiritual Protection**, and more.

Whether you're beginning your journey or expanding your mastery, the Esoteric Mystery School offers clear guidance, powerful techniques, and uplifting wisdom to help you connect with the unseen energies around and within you.

Scan the QR code below to visit my YouTube channel, subscribe, and join a growing community of seekers walking the path of magick, mystery, and light.

Embrosewyn Personal Services

If your spirit is stirring and you feel called to journey deeper, visit **Embrosewyn.com**. Every offering is designed to help you awaken, align, and expand the light within.

Through **personal consultations**, we can explore your path—developing psychic and magickal abilities or navigating life's challenges in love, career, and personal growth.

Insight Card Readings reveal the hidden energies shaping your life and show what empowers or blocks your fulfillment.

Your **Soul Name** unlocks your unique gifts and awakens your highest self.

Discovering your **Guardian Angel's name** opens a sacred bond with the divine being who has guided you since before birth.

Scan the QR code below to visit **Embrosewyn. com**, learn more, and step into the radiant unfolding of your own majesty and light.

EMBROSEWYN.COM

www.ingramcontent.com/pod-product-compliance
Lightning Source LLC
Chambersburg PA
CBHW070306040726
47501CB00018B/229